THE PROMISE

THE PROMISE

EYE OF PANDORA PUBLISHING
139 Randolph Circle
Troy, VA 22974

Dedicated to Lily, Caitlin, and David.

THE PROMISE
Table of Contents

Chapter		Page

The Promise waits,
As the keeper searches blindly,
In stars to seek the signs.
The promise waits,
To illumine the ending,
Of worlds with gift divine.
The promise is,
At the point undivided,
Where it is that all points meet.
The promise was,
In the heart of the Old One,
The children's gift beneath the feet.
And the promise reached on and on
and into the ever,
For it lay beyond all fragments of time.
And the promise reached deeper and deeper into the
matter,
In all bits of earth to find.
Through all veils of heaven passed the
Word of Creation's mind.
Speaking in tongues of man and beast,
The promise came to bind.
It lies hidden in what can not be broken,
For it is and was forever free.
Unseen, the promise does remain,
In that which comes to be.

THE PROMISE
PROLOGUE

The time before the fall had been filled with magic. Dusty scrolls whispered to any with eyes to see and ears to hear of that fragile substance which was once the nourishing current of everyday life. Ancient scribes filled ancient text with tales of undines and mer-folk who lived beneath the seas. Legends flowed with accounts of fairies and sprites that had once graced the forests and fields. It was said that during those years the people had taught their children that all life was but a fragment of a larger life. Speaking often of freedom and beauty they caught glimpses of a glory deep within them and emulated those ideals throughout the days of their lives. Under the rule of the first Kings and Queens the people planted strong crops and none were hungry. They learned to channel the nourishing waters which flowed from the great mountains of the Apennines down to the green-gray sea. It was then that the first city, the city of Tessera, grew from small farms and villages and a new culture began to flourish. Grand ideas were discussed in great Halls of Learning and beautiful temples were built to celebrate the seasons.

The Queens and Kings commissioned extensive libraries to be maintained as the history of the city unfolded and these details were recorded by a line of scribes known as the Eratosthenians. Their duties were passed down through birth lines just as the crown of the royals or the staff of a priestess. Hidden deep in buried rooms their ageless words moved under diligent pens but the scribes were few in number and slowly the line faded away. As the centuries passed, only a few of the castle folk knew that the Eratosthenians had been more than legend.

And while the Eratosthenians wrote of the unfolding of time, the desires of the people swelled. Eventually the love of things began to supplant the nobler ideals of freedom and responsibility and the people used their magic for the smallest of wants. The most powerful of the realm employed their magical gifts in the manipulation of commerce and created trade routes far from their craggy shores. Powerful magnates and their duffers now came to the castle steps, hoping to whisper council into the ears of the reigning Queens and Kings. The farming and fishing was no longer enough. The people delved into the mountains to mine for the substances they found there. Metals formed the bars upon which all trade was based and these ballots were considered great treasures. It was through this love of metal and the lust for power that fighting became commonplace and the countryside was no longer safe to travel. The corruption continued to spread and it was not long before violence moved unchecked over the nations. Men no longer outfitted their fishing boats with nets and poles but instead filled their ships with horrific weapons of war and it was not long before the act of many small battles gave way to a bloody crusade. Not only did the people take up arms but they used their precious gift of magic to slaughter their brothers and sisters. The blood flowed upon the soil and poured into the salty waters until the once generous Sisters, the Earth and the Sea, shook in fury at the crimes they witnessed. When they had seen enough of the carnage they purged themselves of the human corruption. Death and devastation lie across the land and the survivors mourned their fate.

The Sister Earth and Sister Sea did not heed the people as they cried out for mercy. They felt no pity for the Land Walkers and turned to them a deaf ear. For one thousand years, the Sisters taunted them with drought and ice; deluge and heat; wind and disease. But time did faithfully pass and at length the Watchers of the Airs sent forth their messengers to speak to the Earth and Sea on the peoples behalf. With these councils their hearts softened and it was decided that the two Sisters would again bestow upon them the abundant gifts born of their bodies.

There was much to put right in the damaged world and the people rejoiced at the opportunity to correct their errors. It was quickly determined that the misuse of magic had been too great and the folk of Tessera could not be trusted with its power. The Watchers of Air chose to amend their loss by providing them with a servant. It was the Wizard Malthrom who was chosen to serve as the bridge between the earth and sky. Entrusted with The Promise, Malthrom sang life into the cryptic words. The Sister Earth and Sister Sea stood as his side as the dark tower rose above the ruin. The Wizard purged the people of their lust for metal and faith, hope, and charity became the foundation of the Kingdom.

A new King and Queen were set upon the throne and the House of Tessera came to be. The Sister Earth gave forth her bounty and the Sister Sea flowed with abundant food and soon it became common that mothers would live through the birthing of babes and those children would grow to have children of their own. The number of people increased and, what had been destroyed by war was remade. Houses, workplaces, temples, and towers were built over the old streets and as they worked the people uncovered the ancient vaults of Eratosthenians. When they looked upon the strange and beautiful creations of the ancient folk their desires grew strong and the Guardians of Tessera were soon aware that the people were sorely tempted once more. With grave concerns, Queens and Kings watched the want of metal burn again in the hearts of the people and, against their ardent advice, men were sent once more to work the mines. No longer allowed the gifts of magic, the workers were confined to the use of their hands and minds to fulfill their desires. Nonetheless, they learned much from the old libraries and as a result many remarkable goods again filled the marketplace.

Barons and the merchants cluttered the castle stairs. Cartels were formed to represent each guild. The love of things began to surpass the nobler pursuits and the guilds came to control all means of exchange. They wrote books controlling the ways of commerce and these texts were placed alongside the ancient words of the Eratosthenians. Filled with the virtues of power and ways of wealth, these new doctrines were intentionally intertwined with the old wisdom. Page upon page could be found dedicated to the passing of wealth from one generation to the next, the governing of trade, and the fulfillment of contracts. These men came to be known as the Haarshiam. They despised the sovereignty upon which the House of Tessera was founded and sought ways to usurp its power. Their influence carved a deep niche within the society and as the Haarshiam grew wealthy the common folk could barely survive. Ruler after ruler stood under the shadow of the Tower of Malthrom as this subtle change surrounded them. The Kings and

Queens found their ability to nurture, strangled and they lost the capacity to care for all the people. But time remained faithful and as the stars cycled through the heavens the eyes of the Watchers again turned to look upon the children of Tessera.

THE PROMISE

CHAPTER ONE
THE RIDER

The sea caught his cloak in a fistful of icy foam. Its coldness took him by surprise. He kicked at the shells and stones feeling the water seep through his woolen stockings as he hurried along his way. A crescent beach lay under the shadows of the black cliffs, its gray sand dull against the rocky walls. Above him, a wall of stone reflected a brilliant red sky as the setting sun stretched a golden thread of light across the water. The chimes of the tower sounded and Tristus lifted his eyes to look toward home. Built of the same black stone that formed the cliffs, the soaring monolith stood upon the highest point of the sheer walls, pointing its straight finger toward the heavens. Tristus could see the pale lights as they flicked though the narrow windows. The Priestesses of Tessera had once more tolled the evening bells and were now descending the spiraling stairs. The lamps they carried moved slowly past the thin casements. The immense city spread black under the tower's awesome shadow. Two thousand years had past since the wizard, Malthrom, had revealed the Promise. The illusive enigma was recited in the rhythmic chants of the priestesses as they descended the long stairs leading back to the earth. The words echoed in his thoughts.

The promise waits,
As the keeper searches blindly,
In stars to seek the signs.
The promise waits,
To illumine the ending,
Of worlds with gift divine.
The promise is,
At the point undivided,
Where it is that all points meet.
The promise was,
In the heart of the Old One,
The children's gift beneath the feet.

And the promise reached on and on and into the ever,
For it lay beyond all fragments of time.
And the promise reached deeper and deeper into the matter,
In all bits of earth to find.
Through all veils of heaven passed the
Word of Creation's mind.
Speaking in tongues of man and beast,
The promise came to bind.
It lies hidden in what can not be broken,
For it is and was forever free.
Unseen, the promise does remain,
In that which comes to be.

      As the centuries had past, new interpretations formed around the words and those renderings were written and re-written, time and time again. Through the passing of the generations the simple words of The Promise lost their inner life. Tangled with greed and bent by deceit the prophecy had been slowly tainted. To Tristus, what was hidden, had become as tasteless as dry leaves and, what remained unseen, held no nourishment for a seeking heart.

      Tristus was the first-born son of the twenty-third Queen of the House of Tessera and upon his brow he bore the Mark of the Star Bearer. This sign of stars had been foretold by the Eratosthenians, the ancient librarians of Tessera, and against this misfortune he held no power. He found within himself no faith in this star-crossed circumstance and no reason to cling to its nebulous rhymes. Years ago, he disregarded the dry lectures of his tutors as hopeless noise. Seeing their books and facts as fables, used to placate the ignorant or sway the willing, and the city of Tessera seethed with both. The Mark of the Star Bearer lay scattered across his forehead to extend downward to reach behind his right ear and, because of it, there were many folk within his kingdom who idolized him and saw him as a savior but there were also the others; powerful men of status and wealth who saw him as nothing more than a strangling nuisance, and ever-present threat to their worldly affairs. This uncomfortable position of awe and contempt was woven into every public appearance and courtly duty. Their mark had not only branded his skin with their unworldly stigma but burned into the mind, leaving him filled with unsettled questions for now the crimson stains had come to mean nothing but anguish.

The red sky blazed above as he made his way back to the castle. The disturbing portent troubled him for the sky had burned scarlet the night of his birth as well. On that evening, all of Tessera had stood under the crimson sky wondering uneasily of the fiery omen above them. When the sound of his first cry broke the airs of earth all in the birthing chamber were filled by a strange presence. Some of the midwives whispered concerns over the odd babe while others muttered curses about the foreign-born King, as the young prince was placed in his mother's arms. Though his skin was fair, his eyes appeared colorless and his hair was black as pitch and when the babe looked into her face, the overshadowing presence pressed deeply into the chamber. The force moved through the airs, but not as a thing present to the ears, it was more akin to an unnamed burden, like a gnawing thought imprisoned within the under-mind. Reaching soundlessly through the castle walls, the force pressed into the streets until all below were struck by a sudden sense of dread. A thick mist began to fill the room as the gloom spread through the cobblestone streets of Tessera, the blinding fog coming upon them as swiftly as a sea storm. Confusion filled the nursery as the midwives rushed into the unworldly cloud trying to find the mother and the new born babe. Their cries echoed through the halls and the young King and his guards ran to see what trouble had come. Frightened and confused, they struggled in the fog but the mist was endless and not one of them could find their way out. In the streets below, low clouds had moved in from the dark sea. The earth began to groan and the ground trembled as fear spilled into the stifling night. Calling out in terror the cries of the people reached the ears of the wizard in his tower. Hearing their plea Malthrom set the bells ringing and when the strange fog lifted, two new stars burned bright in the skies over Tessera.

In the Queen's chamber the mid-wife hurried to the birthing bed finding the palms of the newborn's hands bleeding and the young Queen struggling for breath. The King knelt by his wife to comfort her and as he pushed the damp hair away from his new son's brow the Mark of Stars was revealed. Upon seeing the crimson brand the Priestesses of the Tower rushed to the vaults of the Eratosthenians to better understand the significance of the sign.

The twin lights still lingered in the new morning sky as Elder Priestess went before the crowd. She told the people the Mark of Stars heralded of the coming of the New Magic and uttered once more the words of the ancient promise. A great shout burst forth from the innocents but her words fell like stones among elite. The decree brought them no comfort for change was seen not as something to be welcomed but something to be controlled. It was not long before quarrels broke out between the various factions and clandestine violence began to surge through the dark.

Tristus' unworldly presence did not fade as he grew. The babe rarely cried and slept little. His peculiar calm gave him an unnerving quality. It was whispered the young prince listened to a world that no others could hear and all too often the strange fog would return to surround the nursery. Panic would arise and the nurses would search madly for the babe until again the strange cloud would vanish. Bruised and silent, they would find him in his cradle and there seemed no way to save the boy from the cyclic battles with misty realm.

A troubled year had past in the House of Tessera when the Queen gave birth to her second son. The royal couple named the child, Arcus. His flaxen hair and blue eyes were not unusual in the realm and soon it became apparent that this boy was quite opposite from his brother, in not only appearance, but temperament as well. As he grew, the common people let go of their concerns about ancient prophecies and their thoughts of doom faded, for Arcus bore a magical gift they could more easily understand. His unexplained powers allowed him gentle insights into both man and beasts. Even as a young child, the fair boy could calm the wildest ponies or summon the furthest hawk using only his mind and hands. It was not long before he became the favorite son of the people and they accepted him in a way they could never grant his elder brother.

It was three years more before the Queen bore to the

Kingdom, a little daughter. The child had ivory skin and hair of woodland red. Though she was beautiful, the girl was frail and the wise women of the city spent long days tending her. Burning with fever and visions of unseen worlds, the little princess would call out in languages that none could understand and when she would return from those dreams she would be weak to leave her bed. The people of Tessera again shook their heads in disapproval for the gifts of the princess held the same sort of disconcerting qualities as her elder brother. The Queen and her husband worried for their daughter and as her condition worsened they began to search for a cure. Ships were commissioned to seek for a remedy for the child and after a time, the King would lead the quests to those foreign lands. He would return from his journeys with plants and procedures, scents and abolitions, but none seemed to help the princess.

Gossiping words hissed in the marketplace. The Haarshaim took the opportunity to further their interests by pushing the wedge of discontent deeper into the people. Plots of removing the Queen from power were whispered behind the closed doors of every guild and soon bickering erupted among the powerful as each one fought to usurp her position.

The time of trouble continued and the wasting of the little princess increased with every reoccurring vision. One day, word came of a place where the sea changed from green to blue. The sailors told the Queen and King of a generous people who dwelled there and knew the virtues of all living things that grew upon their islands. Here it was thought a cure for the princess would be surely found.

Tristus recalled the icy wind upon his face as his father's ship turned to face the southern sea. It was the last time he would see him. The people changed little after his father's disappearance. Their ill tidings still whispered in the streets and the days reeked of sameness. His heart ached as he watched the Queen work alone with the burden of circumstance. Feeling the sting of criticism the Queen often turned to the ancient texts, hoping to find the answers to help her rule, as she shouldered the burdens of the people. She raised her children according to the only values she knew well; those set down by doctrine.

After the disappearance of his father, the Queen found

her eldest son must be forced to listen to the daily extrapolations of the castle scholars. Having always read well between the lines of the books Tristus began to speak his mind. This did not please his tutors and they sought bitterly to restrain his ideas. Surrounded with facts and fictions Tristus sat at their elbows and considered many things. He saw plainly the words of the Promise had been strangled of any original intent and the founding virtues of the House of Tessera were more often used as a facade for activities of the Haarshaim than for the good of its citizens.

Tristus had learned well the stepping stones of one event to the next, memorizing the records of people and places, dates and events, which filled volume upon volume of heavy text. It was through these lessons he realized the many ways history and tradition mingled and he came to understand why the people drew their customs from the archaic writings. But among the endless drone of his lecturers there was one parable which served to capture his interest. These were the myths of what lie at the edge of the world, a place where all things, trapped in time and clay could not venture.

It was said that long, long ago, the seamen of Tessera explored the far Northern Seas were the mountains grew perilously high. League after league, they voyaged finding only black cliffs bordering increasingly hostile shores. The waters grew frigid as they passed by range after range of ice covered mountains and frozen seas. Dropping their nets into the inhospitable sea they found strange creatures lived beneath the chilly waves. Discovering they were good to eat they traded these unusual animals for the goods of other lands. But just gathering uncommon food did not interest the more intrepid seamen so further and further under the northern stars they pressed. Here the air grew thin and, while most could not endure the lack of breath, a stout few did continue on until they came to the place where all things ended. A goliath barrier pushed upward from the frozen waters; its cloud-like veil blocking any view what lay beyond. A Wall of Mist now abruptly marked the edge of earth and sea. It was the realm where all that was solid and earthy could go no further.

Legend held that the mist rose higher than the airs of

earth and passed downward through the green waters to a depth that knew no end. The place stirred within them a great awe for its source, nor its purpose, had never been revealed. In the libraries of Tessera many books were written concerning the origin and function of the Wall of Mist but for all the scribbled pages it remained misunderstood and what could not be understood came to be dreaded.

Fear bred in the minds of the people and stories sprung from the mouths of sea-wives of a place where doomed souls eternally drowned in the frenzied sea. The tales described the unfortunates unceasingly struggling in frozen waters, choking upon the airless fog, remaining forever in the painful moment just before a unconsummated death. These legends served to fill the minds of children with nightmares and those children passed those tales to their own children. Tristus loved to read these accounts and often dreamed of this place at the edge of the world. What lay beyond it would become the food of his thoughts for days on end. He longed to look upon the massive barrier which split the fabric of the world and spent his days brooding upon what mystery lie beyond the Wall.

The Queen worried over her son's dark notions for she held strong to the ideals upon which the Kingdom was founded. She believed that Malthrom, watchful and quiescent, still reflected upon them from the peak of the soaring tower and she clung to the thought that, when the proper time came, the Wizard would materialize once again and set all things right within the Kingdom.

Tristus disagreed with her simple convictions. The belch of oppression filled the streets and the poor suffered dearly under the pressures of the Guilds. But more than these old wrongs, Tristus perceived new a menace swelling in the streets of Tessera and he felt its shadow closing in upon him as the days passed by.

"Every act holds its consequence and one action builds upon the next. Only in ourselves can we know what is right or wrong." he would reply to his mothers misgivings. He held no faith in her ancient myths and those differing perceptions lingered in the castle halls as tensions grew between the boy-Prince and the Queen-mother.

Young Tristus became more outspoken against the lessons of doctrine as time passed and the Queen watched helplessly as his attention waned.

"The old wisdom is hidden in the past." she would say to him and Tristus would catch glimpses of her true nature. Immersed in the people of Tessera, she knew too well of their troubles and joys, prejudice and sufferings, and all the while the shadow of the Dark Tower stood over them holding a life of its own. The Queen struggled with the choices before her and finally made the only decision she deemed wise. She would let her son choose his path even if it meant he might be gone from her forever. And so it was that the Twenty-third Queen of Tessera set her eldest son free from the bonds of his royal birth and Tristus laid down his books and went to search for the answers that plagued him.

"He seems aimless." she thought, watching though the window which looked over the beach.

Tristus knew well of her worry for even within himself he found it difficult to understand his need to search the strip of land that touched the water. He recalled his mother's sigh of resignation the evening of his sixteenth birthday. The next day she dismissed the tutors and he found himself free; free but helpless. Free from the tutors he had long endured but helpless against the tide of his own destiny. The pull of the sea drew him. Day after day he traveled, sometimes on foot, sometimes by sea, but always alone. It was in these secluded journeys, he had first come to know the comfort which came from contact with the larger life. The isolation settled him. He could think freely, undisturbed by the demands of the court, his tutors, and most of all the watchful eye of the Queen. He heard the churning of the waters as it spoke in a language, old and unchangeable, and soon the constant voices Tristus grew to understand. He sensed the intention of the watery life. The shifting of the waves and the rhythm of the tides drew him into an unknown world. The days of solitude changed him and he found he could focus his mind simultaneously upon the work of the sails and the mood of the sea. He searched for the missing piece of a great riddle as he wandered the shore line and he wished to someday travel to the Wall of Mist which lay at the edge of the world. He knew it was this Wall that pulled his wandering heart away from his home. But the way was long and, he was yet too young to make such a perilous journey, so each evening he would return home to the House of Tessera struggling to put together the puzzle he did not yet understand.

The days came and went and the Queen saw to her duties, ever vigilant of her son as he left in the early dawn to wander the water's edge. Three years had passed and every evening found the young Prince wandering home to a late supper. His fathomless eyes faded ever deeper into black as he listened to a silent call the others did not hear.

Darkness at his heels, Tristus hurried down the beach holding his head low in the strong evening wind. The ocean waters were fast changing from gray to black as an autumn storm brewed in the thick air. Tristus picked up his pace. Still he was far from the stairs that climbed to the high garden overlooking the sea. Large drops of heavy rain pocked the sand and he pulled his cloak around him looking up to check his distance home. It was then he saw the rider.

"Impossible." he thought for the beach he walked was wholly obscured by the black cliffs and only by foot could the sands beneath be reached. A single, thin stair had been carved centuries before and wound dangerously down the sheer clefts of stone. No pony could maneuver the worn path but still, the strange rider was there. The horse approached steadily as Tristus waited and when the beast was pulled to a stop he realized the rider was a woman. She was wrapped in a dark cloak, embroidered with knotted designs of silver thread. The moon was just rising above the water's edge and the gray fingers of the brewing storm clutched the orb's soft glow. The ivory hairs of the roan horse flickered in the changing light. The skies flashed but no sound followed. The stranger bent her face towards him and he could smell her dark hair. The scent filled his mind. The world faded as she held his gaze and then she spoke. The tremble of the coming storm touched each word and those sounds twisted as they took shape until each word became a burning wheel of fire and the wheels turning one within the other. He felt her hand reach out to touch the stars upon his brow. A white bolt of light burst through him and he fell to the ground. Cold swells of water washed about knees. Looking up he tried desperately to focus himself. "Where is she?" he thought crawling from the wet sands. Frantically he searched the empty beach but only the stony cliffs and darkening night remained. In the airs above, the stain of the red twilight faintly streaked the sky and the moon rested peacefully over the horizon. She was gone. But all was not the same as before for the stars upon his face burned as if they were seared by a fresh brand. His mind rushed with questions. Was this vision a lunacy brought on by the full of the moon? Had he allowed his thoughts to wander too far, unwittingly inviting the beginning of madness? Or was this woman simply a delusion of one whom had spent too much time in solitude? Heat pulsed through him as he stumbled toward home. Looking down upon the sand he watched as the cold waves wiped away the deep prints of the roan horse. The woman who had touched the Mark of Stars had been no madman's dream.

CHAPTER TWO
THE DOOR REVEALED

The morning sun touched his face and the heat from the Mark of Stars pulsed through his head. A thin curtain swelled out into the room and the fresh breeze brought with it the smell of the sea. His hands ached as he reached for a pitcher. He wet a washing cloth and pressed it against his burning forehead noticing the angry tears along his palm. An old nurse was at the hearth tending the fire. A bucket of smoldering ash rested near her feet and smoke curled around the edges of the metal lid as the old woman carefully swept the stone. She turned as she heard him stir. The fire behind her leaped into flame.

"Lord, you are awake. I shall call the others."

"No ma'am. No." he said hurriedly. "I should be on my way."

The sky outside was already a soft blue and he was accustomed to being far down the beach by this time of morning but the brand upon his face pulled at his skin and he hesitated at the edge of his bed. His usual habit no longer made sense.

"I need to speak to Arcus before I go." he said to the nurse. "Do you know where he is?"

"My Lord, your mother is worried about you." answered the old woman. "I am to call her when you wake."

Tristus felt a twinge of discomfort at the thought of the Queen.

"I need to speak to my brother." he repeated.

The old woman bowed her head, "Master Arcus is in the stables."

"Thank you." he muttered, feeling strained. He pulled on his trousers and noticed the scent of the White Blossom hanging on his skin. Looking around the room for his cloak, he tried to remember how he had gotten to bed the night before. He shook the disquieting thought away and left the chamber with his boots untied, hurrying to the back hallway. Quickly he tread the narrow stairs that wound through the castle walls, knowing he would not meet his mother along the little used exit. The stairwell turned along the back wall descending several floors before reaching the door which led outside. Tristus rested against the threshold watching his hands bleed as he laced his boots. He pulled down the stiff latch and he shoved the old door. His stomach lurched as it suddenly gave way to the misty courtyard. Carefully he closed it behind him, checking twice to be sure that the latch had caught. The passage led through the kitchen garden. Chamomile and thyme grew in thick patches between the pavers and spiky shrubs of lavender stretched out from the gray wall. He picked a handful of comfrey as he passed by and after crushing the leaves in his palm he pressed them against the burning mark. The day was already warm and the sun glowed white upon the morning dew along the short lane that led to the stables. The barns lay against the western side of the castle and were tightly flanked to the north by a thick forest that climbed along the steep hills of the Apennines.

"Where is he?" mumbled Tristus as he reached the gates. Walking into the large barn the smell of horses filled the walls and the dusty air glittered in the scattered light.

"Arcus." he called. His sound was impatient and from a far corner he heard the creak of hinges. Tristus turned down the center aisle to find his brother standing there, holding a bucket of grain in each hand. A pair of young cats followed behind him, pouncing on the small crumbs that fell to the ground. The horses were nickering impatiently and the elder cat walked stealthily upon a beam above his head.

"We were to be called when you woke." Arcus replied, looking up.

"I need to talk with you."

"I am glad. It has been far too long." he replied watchfully. "What happened to you last night?" he pressed, his clear blue eyes probing his brother's thoughts.

Tristus felt suddenly sick. He backed against the wall as the memory of the night before flooded into his mind.

The long stairs leading from the beach were worn from decades of wind and brine, the crumbling stones and the inky dark had made his climb home difficult. Lichens clung to the edges of the slippery steps and gnarled trees rooted their fingers into the bony rock, their tenacious branches providing Tristus a hold. Arduously he made his way as the sea groaned behind him. Thick fog soon blotted out the moon. Tristus bent closer to the ground and slipping on the damp stairs he scrambled his way upward. A pelting rain began to press from every direction and he huddled against the narrow ledge. The wind began to scream and baleful voices called out his name. Swift gullies of black water began to flow around him and he bowed his head to shield himself from the rain. Grasping the slippery stones he felt the shades pass over him as they moved swiftly toward the city. Anxiously he continued up the steep stairs, a jutting rock, a twisted root, a friendly branch, delivering him to the next step. Brushing aside his dread he felt his way until finally his fingers fumbled over the doorway which led to the castle garden. He pressed upon it with all of his force, expecting it to be swollen by the rains, but to his surprise the gate gave way suddenly and he found himself stumbling forward.

Blackness swallowed the world he knew. There was no castle, no tower, no gardens, no grounds, only a vast emptiness that loomed before him. Losing his footing, he clung to the garden gate struggling for air as images of destruction flashed into his mind. In sharp flashes of light, he saw his city burning and the storming seas seemed filled with blood. The screams of men and the wails of women filled the airs as long shadow swallowed up the land. But soon the unworldly emptiness consumed even these things and an intense pressure squeezed his body. After an endless time in the terrible dark he wondered of himself. "Where is the rest of me?" he thought, "Where is my body?" He struggled with the idea until all sensation diffused into the black.

The recollection stunned him. In a staggered, slow motion he watched Arcus turn to face him. Thankful for the coolness of the barn he steadied himself allowing his brother to touch his thoughts. The picture of the evening's events formed in a jumbled sequence within Arcus' mind and finally his brother spoke.

"We found you upon your bed, drenched to the skin and streaked with blood. You were alone but your chamber window stood open and you were ranting like a drunkard. The nurses gave you something to help you sleep and after you quieted, I went with the guards to search the castle grounds." and he paused looking into his brothers black eyes. "When we returned to the ocean gate we found it had been destroyed. Splinters were scattered in every direction and its pieces were strewn across the northern lawn. Grass and turf was dug from all around its threshold." he shook his head and added, "but we could find no footprints leading away."

The air had grown heavy in the barn as Arcus ended the tale. Concern stirred in him as he watched his brother tremble with cold. He called to the stable boy. The boy answered quickly and they heard him moving along the back wall. The young red-head had been working in the high lofts and bits of straw fell through the spaces in the planking as he made his way toward them.

"Coming Arcus." he called out as his wiry frame jumped lightly from the ladder.

"Clade, would finish feeding the horses? I shall return to help shortly but I must go with my brother for a bit.

"Yes sir." answered the boy politely and taking the grain buckets he went to the horses whistling happily. The cats scurried after him.

"Tristus, I will tell you what else happened last night." said Arcus as they left the shadows of the warm barn and entered the sunny day. "A storm squall pressed us fiercely. Mother rushed up from her study for the wind carried more upon its shoulders than just the evening rain. Shades were whispering out our names and a strange dark moved through the streets. We went to Aleryn and found her lying upon the floor of her chamber, rambling in a feverish fit. The Priestesses were called to her room, they chanted and lit the lamps of protection as guards were placed at every door and we watched the beach from her window, awaiting your return. Soon after the squall passed the dark presence seemed to disappear and Aleryn came back to herself. But the night had grown old and you had not returned so we sent out a search party.

As Arcus told him the tale of the night before Tristus could easily see his mother at the window of his little sister's room. She sat there often, looking out to the horizon holding her thoughts tightly to herself. It was hard for him to cause her such uncertainty but once more his reflections were interrupted by the sound of Arcus' voice.

"Tristus, we had searched the grounds and you were nowhere to be found. It was a maid who discovered you in your chamber. But that door had been guarded for hours and it was the place we would have never thought to look. When we came to see for ourselves, we did not understand. There was no mud, no trail of debris, and no sign of forced entry but you were covered in filth. You lie there with your hands torn, possessed of the same fit that had consumed our sister just hours before and I will tell you brother, it was as if an unworldly wind spirited you there. Mother sent for the High-Priestess, for your wet clothes smelled strongly of the White Blossom, but no one of that order claimed to have been with you last night."

Tristus then remembered the mysterious woman from the beach. A jolt of electricity raced through his head and, at that same instant, a black gull screamed harshly. It swept low in the sky above them. Tristus noticed the shadow the bird cast was momentarily disfigured. A strange wind rushed by his ear and it carried with it an impression.

"I am being pulled away from here brother." he spoke glancing up at Arcus' face. "I cannot ignore it. The sea calls me to her.

"I understand Tristus and I will not deny what has always been so." was the soft reply.

Tristus could not tell if it was fear or relief that stirred within him as he looked down at his injured hands. He hoped for better insights but he could see nothing more.

CHAPTER 3
THE SEEKER RESPONDS

The chimers climbed the stairs. They were thirteen in number and each carried a small oil lamp. The Priestesses of Malthrom tolled the bells which rang at the beginning and end of each day. As Tristus slept in fitful dreams and the young princess lay quiet in a pink fever their pure tones sounded once more over Tessera. Arcus walked along the damp path on his way to the horses. He had not been to his bed at all as he listened to them ring. The robes of the priestesses rustled faintly against the black stone. The climb was a long one. The dark tower rose ten thousand steps and the chimers made the trek twice each day. Their songs changed with the stars and today, the bells sang mournfully.

The priestesses had prepared the morning sacraments. The temple halls were filled with offerings and the Queen waited at the alter. She bent her knee as the bells rang sadly over the kingdom. Through the flames, Malthrom watched the chimers come and go but the priestesses performed their duties unaware of his presence. The Queen felt a pain run through her breast recalling her son, pale and incoherent, upon his bed.

"What magic comes to taunt us." she thought. "and why does it steal what is best?"

She took a breath to stop the seething of her thoughts. She cared for the folk of Tessera but there were so many; needing all things. The want and ugliness crushed in upon her.

"I am jaded." she scolded herself softly. "I do not know what to do." she sighed then and rubbed her face. "What kingdom shall I leave to my far-eyed son?"

Resting her head upon her knee she looked into the candlelight and she saw Malthrom's reflection within the flame. They watched one another through the waves of heat. Silence hung between them and the restless Promise vibrated in the air. Malthroms' eyes were upon the Kingdom. She offered no petition for herself and she offered none for the people. Quietly she watched the flames, seeing the tides rise and the ocean churn. A choice was at hand. She wished she were a wiser woman as she turned to go.

Blowing out the candles she rose from the bench and a sound like the rustling of robes moved down the hall. She opened the chamber door but saw no one was there so she brushed the memory away and went to find her children.

The voices of her two sons echoed down the hall. "Such an odd match." she mused looking through the door to see the two brothers by Aleryn's bed.

"When will you bring the yearlings home Arcus?" Aleryn asked, sitting up and looking considerably better. "The first moon of autumn passed over last night. It is the customary time."

"Yes it is, little one."

"My legs are getting too long for my old pony and I have the name picked out for the red filly." Aleryn smiled. "I will soon be fifteen. This is the year of my coming of age, in case you have forgotten."

"That I could not forget." Arcus smiled back.

"The Festival of Light is soon upon us so I could begin to train her immediately upon your return," continued the princess with cheerful confidence. "I could go to the stables this morning and make the preparations for her arrival."

"Today", interrupted the Queen, "what do you think your nurses shall say?"

"Good morning mother," smiled the princess, "I should think my nurses shall say how glad they are I am feeling so much better and how the fresh air will do me good."

"Aye, that is what they could say," answered the queen, "but only if it is the truth."

Aleryn smiled again, "but it is the truth mother."

Relief washed over her when she saw that, indeed, the girl was improved. The Queen then turned to study her other child. Tristus sat upon Aleryn's bed, holding her thin hand in his own.

"We shall eat our breakfast here; at the table by the window." said the Queen motioning to the maid. The servant nodded and left the room and for a few moments they were alone. Aleryn was happy in the presence of her two brothers and rose from her bed to admire the sea. Tristus followed and together they gazed from the window to marvel at the enormous city. The whorled stairs wound in twisting spirals up the hills toward the castle grounds. In the clear morning, drying leaves and the rich scent of the harvest hung in the air. Above the towers and trees, black sea birds cried out harshly as smoke from the foundries pushed through thin clouds and swallowed the flock as they made their way south but to the north, the great Apennines stood strong, austere and bare, as stone sentinels against the cold wind.

The mountains gave to Tessera, not only gold and silver, but a pale metal of unusual strength and flexibility. When prepared in the proper way the amalgam was as beautiful as it was useful. The refined product was Atricault and at night Tessera glowed with warm lights set with its fine filaments. The lamps were considered a great wonder and the Winter Festival of Light brought many visitors to the city to trade, barter and buy. The northern mines produced the raw materials to make the glowing orbs and the lamps were sold at high prices. But even for their worth and beauty, the House of Tessera kept a close check on the mining activities and all expansion was monitored carefully. The mines were always a source of contention between the Queen and the Haarshiam for the love of the sea gave the true life to the city and fishing was still the primary enterprise of Tessera. Tristus and Aleryn watched as a boat moved close to shore and occasionally, small snatches of the fisherman's song made their way through the open window. It was an old song. Aleryn recognized it and began to sing softy, filling in the spaces left by the drifting wind.

> Aye, upon the gray and green,
> The sea, the song, the shore,
> Aye, it was a bonnie lass
> That I shall kiss no more.
> I left her waiting on the stones,
> Where the earth does meet the sea,
> I left her waiting on the shore
> Does she still wait for me?
> For now the tide has carried me,
> Within its deepest green.

The sea, the song, the shore, the kiss,
Is but the fairest dream.

Her voice was comforting though it stirred each heart
that the knowledge that good-byes were drawing near.

"Tristus. Please, may I see your hands?" asked the
Queen.

Tristus held his hands out with his palms upward for her
to examine. She took them gently and brushed her finger across
their centers. His palms were cut and marred with splinters. She
recalled the image of Malthrom's face in the candles light.

"What caused these marks?" she asked.

"I fear it was my doing, mother" he answered but the
maid returned, carrying the trays of food and his explanation was
cut short.

It was the first breakfast they shared since Tristus had
began his daily treks to the sea, almost three years before.
Breads, fruit, sweet spreads, and cheese made up the simple
meal. They sat down at the small table by the window and, for a
little while there was no talk of prophecies, nor any mention of
visions, it was just an ordinary meal shared among a small
family. Tristus poured the final drops of the spiced wine from
the clay pitcher and as a knock came upon the door. The nurses
had arrived to take the princess to the baths.

Beneath the palace walls, a labyrinth of tunnels crawled
under its vast foundations. Storerooms and wine cellars,
libraries and apothecaries, were spread through an underground
maze, and there were places where the heat of the earth's center
rose up through stony vents. The steam was used to heat the
city and large scented baths had been built throughout the city
for both healing and comfort. The princess went with her nurses
with a minimum of complaints as they had promised her a trip to
stable if she remained well. When she had gone the Queen's
eyes turned toward her two sons.

"What happened upon the beach last night?" she asked
him.

It tired Tristus to speak of such things with his mother.
She carried the mantle of the kingdom upon her and that mantle
was always out for him to receive. It never suited him and yet its

responsibility loomed. Confusion pressed him but he cast it off and calmly told retold the story of his return to the castle.

The Queen listened intently and when she heard the account of the events at the garden door she understood. In the early dawn, she too had seen the shattered gate and the sense of her son's uncertain destiny troubled her. She looked into his dark eyes and asked. "What is it that you wish to do, Tristus?"

"I have no wishes mother." he answered solemnly. "I have nothing but a sense of duty that seeks resolution."

And as he spoke, Aleryn appeared at the door. Her gray eyes had grown pale and her form shimmered as she spoke.

"A choice is before you, Tristus. It is the same choice which lies before us all." she said reaching for his hand as she glanced nervously over her shoulder. "Through one door lies hope and possibilities. The other door opens to the darkness of the beginning." and taking a painful breath she spoke clearly. "And there is more brother. There is Tessera. She will not wait for you Tristus. Our world is the creature that veils the unseen. Without beginning and without end it exists. But alas, we live not in that place of eternity, but instead we live these lives in realms of regeneration and reflection. Things will change swiftly now. All around us shadows cast silhouettes which are not their own. I have seen them. And they have grown. The world is twisting, Tristus, twisting out of shape."

Tristus watched his little sister speak. Her body had become translucent and the scent of the White Blossom permeated the room.

"In the deep heart of the castle a voice is calling." she continued. "It is a voice with two sharp edges and between each parting sound, we walk in the valley of light and dark, casting shadows in all directions. The shades are watching, Tristus. They are close now. Close enough to see the weakness writhing within us. Close enough to call our dying name. In passing over we will fight them, these shadows of ourselves." then her body wavered like a liquid hanging in air. "The time has come to choose our way. We shall choose or time will choose for us and scatter us as grains of sand." she said studying his face with her clear eyes, her face shining with a light older than sea. "Unless we remember." and her voice trailed off as she cast her eyes to the floor. "Unless we can remember."

The Queen led the princess to the bed. "This wasting that consumes her," she thought angrily. "and its root lies outside these castle walls. This root lies in the heart of our people." The notion blared within her.

"Mother, the shadows of castle are no longer its own." said Aleryn catching the discomfort of the Queens thoughts. "I see them as they watch from dark corners. The specters were there when we entered the baths. The fabric is torn now, mother. The fabric is torn and yet; and yet the weaver spins on."

"She is not as young as her years," thought Tristus and looking into her pale eyes, he understood a small part of the vision she brought.

"The dark is ancient thing, little sister." he replied remembering the void, "Older than the tower that stands over us, older than any scribbled legend, older even than the wizard that will not answer our calls. It is the light that veils the unformed dark and we walk in that valley between the two opposites." he said, pausing to look down at his injured hands.

"Long has shadow desired to reign over Tessera. But the fates whisper still and I too have heard them call. It is from the edge of the world they beckon me and that is where I must go. Beyond the Mist little sister, there will lie the answers we seek."

Aleryn smiled at her brother touching the brand of stars upon his brow. "I am not ill today mother," she said sensing every thought within the room. She stood straight and, looking toward the tower of the unseen wizard, she said. "Tristus must prepare for his journey." Her words marked the end of times.

CHAPTER FOUR
THE WATCHER

Malthrom materialized within the obsidian walls at the same instant the last chimer stepped from the tower stairs. From the narrow casements he could see Tristus and his brother walking through the lanes that led back to the stables. The people of Tessera had begun the morning routine. Dust rose from the winding highway as travelers approached the gates of the city to start another day of trading. Through the cobbled lanes, mothers made their way to the market with their children following behind them, carrying baskets and playing games. The fishermen had set sail hours before and now their fishwives sat upon short stools mending nets upon the docks. Young men rolled barrels of ale through the alleys and the smell of bread and brine hung in the air. The voices of the people and sounds of the stock blended in comfortable mediocrity but even as the city hummed with activity there were few left in Tessera with easy smiles and light hearts.

Malthrom stepped back from the tower windows allowing his mind to reach through the years. He recalled how carefully he had been prepared for his duties by the Watchers of Air. He knew they looked upon him now, moving with the restless rhythms of the earth and seeing all that occurred under the black tower. The Watchers understood the evolving wisdom of the Ancient's Promise. It was from their high place they listened and with that subtle force they shaped the substance of the world below.

He remembered the years spent upon the burning ground. The focus of will had to be impeccable and the training for the moment was relentless. But as each step proved to be more difficult than the one before it, Malthrom's resolve never waned. Eons came and went as he toiled to perfect his motives. His part was crucial for he had chosen to turn the direction of Great Wheel, the very Heart of Fire that held every bit of matter and every spark of life the Sisters turned over and over again within their generous bodies. If he were successful to this end, the chains of fear could be loosened and the kingdom's long years of error might be undone, so he struggled on through loss and failure for the outcome of his battle was never certain as his greatest enemy always proved to be himself.

In the beginning it was fear that defeated him. So he tried once more only to fail yet again, this time from a sense of pride. But still the Ancient provided him with other opportunities and as the eons passed he eventually overcame the flaws of arrogance only to yet again find failure, this time in expectation. And his time of struggle wore on until the day arrived when he stood alone upon the battlefield looking into the silent sun. The elders had deemed him ready.

He could still touch the moment when the sky opened. The striking split had revealed to him more than the past and future; more than a turning point in the history; more than the twisting of fate, for in that instant he had glimpsed the fleeting natures of all realities. It was the moment in a lifetime that comes but once.

So it was the change came to Tessera and as the sign was given the dark tower pushed upward striving to reach the Upper Airs. Malthrom had played his part and the evidence of his victory now stood before all the people. Since that time the Wizard had hid himself in the obscurity of the dark walls of his tower and there he remained vigilant. Years past and as his name lingered in the threads of myth, the remnants of the first magic faded. It was only the most innocent of children who could catch a glimpse of the fairy folk and over the centuries the talkative river nymphs grew silent and the sacred trees slept in and out of season. He watched as the beautiful dreams of the people withered with each passing Queen-mother and he saw the darkness grow and spread. Malthrom recognized for all his triumphs his purity was yet flawed and it was his own imperfections which played a role in the ugly circumstance that lie in the street. Malthrom knew he had carried error back into the world and all he could do was wait. He would wait until the winds of change stirred and the distant stars moved in their oblique paths. He realized the people of Tessera could not understand the harmonies of these far-away suns. They strove to maintain their old ways, seeking the sense of comfort that could not be satisfied. Nonetheless, the starry force remained relentless. Intently it desired to awaken, and it forced a great tension between realms of earth and sea. It was by this action that the Star Bearer came to be. The Mark he bore was the sign the Ancient's Magic could be carried again into bodies of babes. The Watchers of the Air now looked upon Tessera with a keen interest. They understood the outcome was still uncertain and knew the conflict between the earth and sky would not lessen but intensify. Many of the townsfolk feared the change the newly evolved carried within them. Violent shadows began to pass more frequently through the city, infecting the weaker and causing the dull eye of the crowd to turn against the struggling souls. Wicked things now encouraged their grim desires and the people hid their actions from the Queen-Mother.

Malthrom saw these acts from the tower. He perceived the shadows as they grew strong, generating their force from the people of Tessera. He knew their unseen actions stirred within the Queen a keen sense of dread. Two thousand years had past and the Wheel of Fire turned to a new time. Rippling across the restless waves of the heavens the flawless magic brought with it the hope of freedom.

The Wizard focused his mind upon the Queen as she knelt in morning meditation. He saw the slight crack of light which escaped from the door behind her. Beyond that door, another pair of eyes observed her distress as the Queen struggled with her duties. The voyeur wore the robe of a priestess. Malthrom recognized her face. "The will is free." he reminded himself as the woman gathered her gown and hurried down the hall. "Free to choose."

Malthrom then turned to behold Tessera. He focused upon the dirty corners of the great city, watching as malicious intentions waved through the air. A shadowy wraith reached out its hand; a child cried out in fear; his mother struck him, an old man smiled in approval, and Malthrom saw the mischief go unchecked. He was tired. His heart longed for home but he would not ask the Ancient for relief. He was waiting for something whose time had not yet come. Once more he would hold vigil in the tower through the long day. Like the Queen, he knew his duty and as the two brothers entered the stables he focused his hope across the kingdom.

CHAPTER FIVE
THE HAARSHIAM

Clade had finished feeding the horses. He was shifting the hay bales in the upper lofts to make room for the winter store when he heard them come. The golden shafts of the oat straw floated through the air and the boards shook as he hurried to meet them.

"Lord Arcus! There was someone to see you." he exclaimed. "He wished to purchase yearlings for his stable."

Arcus frowned. The harvest moon had shed its light upon them just the night before. It was time to make the customary journey to the northern fields in preparation for the Winter Festival. Many people would travel to Tessera to celebrate the turn of the season and tradition demanded that the royal horses be brought down from the canyons for the yearly charitable auction. The beasts held great status in the eyes of the people and notice would be made of any delay. The timing of Tristus' departure increased the pressure he felt within him. The need for haste crawled under his skin.

"We shall leave early tomorrow Clade." he answered him as he hurried from the loft. "Can you prepare the gear? We will go together."

"Oh yes, Master Arcus! I surely will." he said jumping from the ladder and heading straight away to the saddle room.

Tristus smiled. Clade had just turned thirteen and had worked in the stable for almost seven winters. His mother and father had once been in the service of the Queen. Years ago they were been sent on an errand to the west-field farms and were never heard from again. His mother had taken the boy on as a charge after their strange disappearance. Tristus watched the kittens scramble behind him.

Arcus turned to face his brother, speaking softly so they would not be overheard. "It has been centuries since any have dared to venture to the Wall of Mists and only a few tales remain of those who returned. Truly, you can not know how far you must travel or how long you will be gone. It is a perilous journey."

"Do not fear for me Arcus. The hand of fate was set

before I entered this world. My mind can not be darkened by such notions."

"Aye, but times are dark," he answered "for even under the light of the day living shadows thrive."

"Yes," he sighed, "but my concerns lie more with you than with myself."

"We will do what we must. Mother is strong and Aleryn holds the gift of sight. I shall see to the mundane affairs of the Kingdom."

"It is easy not to worry for one's self. It only becomes difficult in regard for those you love." replied Tristus and the sound of his voice was met by a friendly nicker. Tristus looked down the dusty aisle and a large gray stallion tossed his head. Tristus smiled as he went to greet the horse. "Phaedras, you are a handsome fellow." he said rubbing the velvety nose.

"Several of the yearlings we shall fetch from the canyon are of him." said Arcus, "One is the red filly that Aleryn has her eye set upon."

Tristus opened the stall and the stallion stepped into the walkway, swinging his white mane and tail. Arcus put a halter around him and led him to the center aisle. Tristus brushed out his coat enjoying the smell of the warm horse as Phaedras nudged at his pockets rooting for treats.

"He remembers how you spoiled him." Arcus laughed.

"I have missed his company." said Tristus stroking the silky coat.

The young sun burned strong outside the wide doors until a pair of shadows dimmed its light. The brothers looked up to see two men. Even though the day had grown quite warm, one still wore a long coat. He was thin and rested his weight upon a walking stick. Beside him stood a much taller man, and as they entered the barns, the brothers could see by his dress he was Haarshaim. His riding breeches were fashioned of dark leather and his cape was a rich tapestry mottled with greens and blues. The white under-wrap lightly touched his flaccid chin and it silk lengths lay smooth beneath a fine black vest. His upper arm was bare but for pair of golden snakes twisting around it. Their amber eyes were inset with the atricault amalgam and upon a heavy gold chain, a matching amulet hung from his thin neck.

His hair was sparse but carefully curled. On his left hand, he wore a long leather glove which reached above the elbow and the slight fingers of the other hand seemed pallid against his garish rings.

His voice was shrill when he spoke. "Good day my Lords. I am Berdias and this is my man Hyand. It is unusual, and most fortunate, to see you both looking so well." he said gazing upon Tristus coolly. "I have business today," he continued abruptly, "as I wish to purchase yearlings for my stable. My man was here earlier and he spoke to your boy," and he looked around for Clade, the veins in his neck protruding, "but the boy could not tell him what he needed to know. I thought it prudent to come myself."

"Good sir," said Arcus. "it is customary for the Queen to select the horses for the royal stables before the others are offered at public auction.

"Of course. Of course, dear prince." he said smoothly, "That is why I am come. It is commonly known that most folk of Tessera can not afford such fine animals, particularly at such fine prices," he added raising an eyebrow, "We of the Guilds would like to suggest making the auction an invitation affair. I wanted to take that up with you Arcus. The commoners so crowd the market. It makes business difficult. I believe that such a new arrangement would prove advantageous to us all."

"The yearlings shall be auctioned on the final night of the Festival, just as they have always been sir. All interested people, be they commoner or Haarshiam, shall have their opportunity at that time. But now you must excuse me," he continued politely, "I have horses to attend."

"Of course Lord," said the man, his smile spreading thin across his face. "but I beg of you to consider my idea. I shall be back for your answer later." and turning sharply away from Arcus he addressed his brother, "I have not seen you in a great while Prince. Your journeys take you away from us so often." he smiled flatly as his eyelids lowered, "but the storm last night was enough to keep any sensible man away from the beaches."

"I have errands in the castle today." Tristus answered.

"Of course. Yes, of course you do. And your sister how is she?"

"Quite well." Tristus answered calmly.

"Hmmm, I had heard she was ill again last evening. You know we have so many common acquaintances. Be sure that you wish her my best."

"Of course."

"Then let me be off your majesties. There are many errands to attend too. I know you are busy, just as I. This year's festival shall be truly fantastic. We of the Guilds have a fascinating surprise in store for all. But that is a secret I must keep for now." he said giving the brothers a disturbing wink. "I will be in touch with you soon about the ponies Lord Arcus. Just sleep on the idea. I am sure you will see its wisdom." The man swung about letting the heavy cape flow around him. Hyand leaned hard upon his cane following his master through the door, his crippled leg dragging the dirt.

The brothers watched them go.

"He barely contains his disdain." said Tristus looking at the mark that Hyand had left upon the dirt floor of the barn.

"Their influence grows greater each year." said Arcus softly, "and still, they come to the castle each day, begging for the rights to dig deeper into the mountains even as the clouds of stench spew from the foundries. Of late they have refined the amalgam so its energy is enough to power a machine which glides in the air. I have seen it, rising and falling like giant dragonflies in the fields to the west. The people are in awe of them."

"Awe and fear are much alike. It is the people who suffer most by their hands." Tristus shook his head. "Sometimes I wonder if the Haarshiam might ever fear the poor."

Arcus shrugged. "I believe it is the poor that fear the Guilds. There are whispers in the market that the slave trade is growing. I listen to the talk but have no real proof of it and none have come forward to tell a sure tale."

"How is it that you come by these things, Arcus?"

"It is an advantage not to be the succeeding king. I have more freedom to come and go as I please. The people tell me of their concerns, but rumors are not enough to move against the Haarshiam, and proof of wrong-doing is hard to find."

"Aye, but it may be more than rumor." answered Tristus, "I have seen ships leaving the bay prepared for many weeks of travel and I have often wondered what cargo they seek from the southern seas. The folk of those realms do not mimic our ways. They have no need of our ballots, or of our flying machines."

"There is other news stirring as well Tristus, and this from more gentle sources. The street children tell Clade stories of little ones born with odd powers. "

"Powers? What sort of powers?"

"I have heard mention of firewalkers, scriers, and shape changers and they say that if the young one's powers are found out, instead of being brought to the castle to have these gifts recognized, they are taken from their families and what becomes of them afterward, no one is sure."

"But if these children bear the old gifts, that my brother, that is the stuff of prophecy."

"Aye Tristus, the stuff of prophecy foretold an age ago. They called them the Tahmurath."

"Yes, the Tahmurath." replied Tristus, shaking his head in wonder. "And who would dare to take them away from the families that brought them into this world. These children could hold the hope of us all."

Arcus smiled, "Perhaps you are not as cynical as you would have us believe. Change is on us all. Things will not remain as they have been.

"Change is necessary. There is much mischief behind the closed doors. There is much that needs to be found out and their secretiveness is disturbing. Indeed I wonder what surprise Berdias speaks of." said Tristus, grimly.

"Take heart, brother." smiled Arcus. "There are higher forces at play."

Tristus stopped grooming the horse and rested against his strong flank. "And I wish to understand the nature of that force, Arcus. There is not a moment that passes that I do not desire it. My errand can not wait another day." he said quietly running his hand down the horse's front leg and picking up the foot he looked at the bottom of the hoof. It was clean and healthy.

"I shall be back soon, Phaedras." he said scratching his

graceful neck. They walked the stallion back to his stall and Tristus threw him an extra measure of hay. Phaedras whinnied after them as they left out the side entrance on their way back to the castle. Just outside the sliding door, the bent Hyand was leaning against a water barrel.

"What are you doing here?" questioned Tristus with guarded surprise.

Nervous and flustered, Hyand sputtered, "I . . . I was coming back to fetch a stone. It was a. . . a ruby which fell from masters ring."

"It seems more likely you eavesdrop." said Tristus.

"No Prince. No! I do not!" he cried as a wrenched expression flattened upon his face, "Do not delay me please! I must not dawdle. He is impatient, very impatient. I am only retracing our steps. I must search for the stone. Excuse me now. Excuse me please." he muttered and the crippled man scuttled away.

"His steps are not difficult to trace." said Tristus looking after the mark of his ragged gait. "He was listening to us from this doorway. What do you think he heard?"

"We were not speaking of our plans directly but it is hard to say." answered Arcus. "To spy upon us appears to be the real reason for their unusual visit. You must leave today Tristus, in as much secrecy as we can manage."

"Yes," he answered, staring grimly at the mark Hyand had left behind. "Our time is running short."

CHAPTER SIX
A VEIL TO DIVIDE THE WORLD

Tristus stood upon the crest of the cliff, looking down at the narrow stair that led to the beach below. The perfect break in the garden wall was a clear reminder of the night before. Tessera appeared calm in the sweeping light of the broad sun. The sprawling city was layered against the valleys and hills. Foot-bridges and stairways, rooftops and towers, were tied together by winding cobbled streets. The mood of the people spread like a thick blanket over the land and it seemed as if the kingdom had moved into an ordinary afternoon. He leaned down to kiss his young sister and though she seemed but frail bone, it was only Aleryn who was not troubled about his departure.

"You will return Tristus." she said touching the stars upon his face. "The true destiny of the Mark is at hand." Her words trembled as he softly kissed her hand.

Arcus embraced him for a long moment and Tristus knew his troubled mind. "Do not fear for me, brother. The fates will see me home." he whispered and Arcus affirmed his words with steady blue eyes.

Then he bowed to the Queen. She accepted his courtesy with a nod of her head and from around her neck she loosened the clasp of her necklace. The amber stone caught a flash of the afternoon light. "Keep this with you." she said placing it around him. "With it I shall know if you are in need." He kissed her cheek and thanked her.

His boat waited upon the beach below. Arcus had seen to its outfitting and the small vessel was ready for many weeks of travel. Tristus carried a walking staff and around him hung a climbing belt, equipped with large clasps, hooks and strong slender ropes. Beneath the folds of his gray cloak were tucked flat packets of travelers bread and dried fruit.

All was prepared. He touched their hands in gentle farewell as he passed through the broken threshold of the cliff wall. "So different the world seems in the light." he thought as he reached the shore. His destination was the Inlet of Narcis and he hoped to reach it before the night fell. Tristus had discovered the grottoes long before and he had returned often to explore. Over the years, Tristus had stored many necessities of travel there. Water sprung freely from its cliffs and hidden behind those sparkling falls was a web of caves. The caves would provide him protection no matter what the unpredictable evening might hold in store.

He waved his arms toward the cliffs and the small figures gestured back. Quickly he set the sails and turning the vessel to the north he finally set of upon his long journey.

A cloud dimmed the light of the sun as his kin looked after the diminishing ship. In its shadow Aleryn perceived the shades stirring restlessly in the streets of Tessera. She closed her eyes and watched the dark phantoms move into the fabric of the world.

They had decided to keep appearances as they were, pretending that nothing had changed as Tristus slipped away to the Wall of Mist. Arcus would make the yearly trip to the canyon of Opherus and bring the yearlings back for auction and, each evening, they would act as if the prince had returned home. There would be no difficulty in spreading the rumor that his strange behavior had become stranger still. The trusted nurses would whisper that the Prince now barely slept and chose to speak to no one. They would say his daily journeys were ending ever-later into the night and beginning long before the dawn. They would tell the other staff the Queen sought to keep this secret close and to never speak of what they had heard, knowing well that soon the townsfolk would be murmuring the intended rumor around every table.

The cliffs extended far up the northern coast line. By their best reckonings, the ancient maps revealed that a thousand leagues lay ahead before the sea gave way to the Wall of Mists. Tristus felt the distance pass quickly and as the afternoon grew late all signs of city life were gone. In the clear waters he could see a school of fish racing beneath the belly of his boat. Their yellow eyes bulged from the sockets as they followed him through the shifting waves. The wind was brisk and he checked his progress often against the landmarks upon the shoreline. He made good speed to the Inlet of Narcis and as he turned his boat into the hidden moor. The ebbing tides had left the beach scattered with shining pools and drawing nearer he could see the crabs scuttling about the jellied parts of stinging cnidarians. Busy shells burrowed in the path of each rescinding wave and the seabirds wandered about the gnarled heaps of seaweed. The quiet of the cliffs gave him a renewed sense of calm and he drew in a deep breath. The answers he sought would push him forward.

Pulling his boat to edge of the stone walls he anchored it within a sheltered hollow. He brought down the sails and covered the vessel with a gray tarp. When he was satisfied that it was hid from view he took up his pack and went to the caves. Upon the open beach he began to gather seaweed from the pools. Curious fish came to nibble the edges of the tender plants as he washed away the sand. Shaking the water from the leaves he decided to wait to catch his meat until he reached the falls. He folded the salty greens and stored them in a pouch under his cloak.

The settling sky was layered in sheets of lavender light as he climbed to the caves behind Narcis Falls. A cascading thread of water had cut through the rock to creep between the ledges and finally to flow along the grainy shore to the sea. A rocky outcropping barred the path to the lower pool and Tristus climbed over the barricade to make his way to a stand of the trees that hid the caves. Gathering bits of bracken along the way, his arms overflowed by the time he slipped behind the falls. He carried his kindling to the back of the dry cave and set it down. A minor split in the rocks above provided the perfect draft for a cooking fire and he lit a small blaze. The yellow glow danced against the jagged walls. He found several flat stones and placed them to heat in the fire. He fed the flames until they burned happily. When he was satisfied he returned to the base of the falls, hoping to catch his meal before all light was lost. The pool beneath brimmed with fish. From his pocket he removed a net mesh and neatly he attached it to a freshly cut bough. Bending the slender limb into a circle the work for his dinner was quick.

Squatting near the stream, he cleaned the catch and when he had finished, he wrapped the fish in the seaweed. The sky had become a broad streak of gray by the time he returned to his fire. Placing his dinner on the hot stones, he ate sparingly of the travelers bread and sipped from his flask as he waited for the fish to roast through. The warmth of the cooking fire took away the night chill and he stared into the growing flames. The fiery sylphs stretched their golden arms to hiss about the salty wood. Soon a blue glow seared the stone and the fish above began to sizzle. Carefully he turned the packets with the blade of his knife until the leaf wrappings were drawn away and the steaming flesh fell about in tender white flakes. He pulled a small packet of seasoning from his belt and sprinkled a pinch upon his meal. He ate slowly for the fish burned his mouth. When he had finished, he filled his water skin from the falls which served as his doorway. Outside stirred the rumblings of another evening storm and he washed his face and hands looking over the rolling clouds that climbed across the waves. He left the cave to gather more wood just as large spattering drops began to fall upon the upper cover of leaves. It was not long before he had collected enough fuel and when the blaze was well stoked he left once more, this time to gather sea grass to make a palette for his bed. Walking under the obscured light of the moon, the sky above was streaked with fingers of mist. A chill wind blew from the north and a small break formed in the clouds and Tristus could see a small constellation burning in the settling night. He hummed the rhyme he knew from his childhood.

> In night, the heavens watch the world.
> Their eyes the starry lights.
> In dreams, a wish of little hands.
> May bring the earth delight.
> In hope, the heart's song whispers fair.
> To castles made of clay.
> In evening's slumber, all is well.
> To birth another day.

Just as he finished the song, the clouds closed the small window to the sky and the flashes of lighting and rolls on thunder moved onto the shore. The rain now pushed its way through the yellow leaves as Tristus slipped behind the falls. The fire had settled into an even burn as he prepared his bed against the low wall of the cave. The memory of the night before returned and he heard the woman whispering his name, pulling him into a netherworld he did not yet understand. He held her in his mind as he fell into sleep.

The morning dripped with rain and the gray sky offered little cheer. There was no need to linger so he quickly prepared a light breakfast of bread and fish. He wrapped his cloak about him and walked to his boat. Over the cries of the jeering black gulls, he could hear the sound of a ship's horn through the fog. The fisherman of Tessera were out early upon the rolling sea. Climbing on the stones he looked over the waves. The wetness did not hinder him for his thoughts were elsewhere and the voice of the woman still rang in his mind.

Releasing the vessel from its moorings he took up his oars and skillfully guided the craft through the unsettled water. In the distance he would sometimes pass near another ship but none were aware that it was the Prince of Tessera who traveled alone under the cloudy day. The coming of morning barely lit the sky but the lack of sun served him for his eyes did not grow weary and his skin did not burn. He docked his boat early in the afternoon. His hands were sore as the work of the sails had served to break open the cuts upon his palms. He reckoned he had traveled thirty leagues as he searched for a protected place to anchor the boat and soon he found a spot along some reeds huddled close to the black cliffs. Low trees grew among the rushes and Tristus walked along the tufts of bracken to make his way to the shore. The wind grew colder and the clouds began to fracture apart in the skies above. Despite his small discomforts he found the blue airs a welcome sight. He was in a place that he had never been before and he was anxious to explore it. He went until he reached a natural pier which curved under a steep overhang. Blue swallows from the cliff above dived down to greet him. Calling out to one another, they swung through in the air in wide circles, only to return in a moment to complain again at his intrusion. Tristus walked along the edge of the bird's stony sanctuary. The damp boulders ran like a twisted backbone along the foot of the summit and he stretched and leaped from one stone to the next.

A fleet of fishing boats moved along the horizon. The northwest wind sent the ships skimming swiftly over the ruffled water. The waves that spread from their helms soon came to splash along the ridge where he stood. Reaching up with foamy hands, the froth struck his boots and he crouched to look under the stones. Beneath the surface the rocks were thick with bony shellfish and he lingered for a moment to watch the feathery mouths open greedily as the tide rushed by them. The birds upon the slope above him complained. Clinging from their muddy nests they fussed at his intrusion. He looked up to see that bush of a parthenberry hung upon a shallow ledge of soil. The cluster of blue fruit was ripe and he reached up and took a handful. A swallow, clutching a cleat in the wall, cocked his head and called out his displeasure. Looking up, Tristus apologized to the creature as he stuffed the berries in his cloak. On the cliff above him the crown of a great tree swayed in the wind. One long, branch reached far over the precipice and sitting upon it he could see that another larger bird watched his progress. Tristus stared back at the creature and after a moment, the bird cried out and moved deeper into the trees. Tristus wondered of it as he walked up the shore looking for a place to camp. Soon he came upon an alcove cut in the base of the rock. The angle provided good protection from the wind and the roof above was a large pine. He built a fire and made himself comfortable. The green needles smelled clean. He slept curled in his cloak under the arms of the tree.

Morning glared from behind the clouds as shafts of sun broke through the mist warming the clammy shore. He rose from his open bed, unlacing his boots and brushing the damp sand from his feet, before crawling out upon the stone pier to sit amongst the waves. Softly the water tossed upon the rocks as Tristus cleared the chatter from his mind and began to listen. Intentionally, he reached his thoughts beyond the waves to move through the beams of sun. In his minds eye he passed over the churning sea until the stirring of the deep waved though him and he was surrounded with the motion of the watery realms. Beneath the ocean the larger life carried him, moving him into endless patterns until finally he touched a great school of fish. The pressure cradled his body as the salty elixirs rushed through him. Shifting columns of light swelled and faded as the safety brought by the group carried him along his way. The freedom of their singular motion was focused with hungry intention and as they swam through the darkness and light. But then something stirred him from the watery place and he remembered himself. Glancing about he saw the world, he was accustomed to, dull and plain, all around him. He picked up his pack and staff. It was time to move on and he returned to his boat to set out once more upon the open sea.

The wind shifted that day to turn a bitter cold. The harsh bite of the airs cracked apart his damaged hands. He smeared the tears with a oil which Arcus had stowed in his supplies and wrapped them in a soft cloth. As he worked the sails he thought of home. Touching the amber stone which hung from his neck he whispered that all was well. The mountains loomed behind the black cliffs. Dauntingly high, the Apennines rose and fell in steep, vertical drops. Miles above the sea their peaks gleamed in the cold light. A radiant mist rested within the valleys of the sharp walls and the bright clouds gave the impression that glorious beings lay hid in unreachable places. It seemed to Tristus that the splendor of the fog was intended to keep secret the faces of any who watched.

Toward afternoon, he came to a sharp crag which reached a long arm far out into the waters. The extending rock protruded further still to form a thin bridge of stone creating a peculiar link from land to sea. The peculiar overhang was connected to the beach by many lesser bridges and the fingers of curving stone looked like a spidery web stretching above the waters. For a time he watched the waves as they crashed against the barrier cliffs until he realized among the network of arches there lie quieter pools of water. Carefully maneuvering the boat through the feet of the stone relics, he set his anchor in a protected hollow under one of the smaller bridges. He jumped from his boat and walked along the ledges. Loosening his climbing tools he tied his belt outside his cloak. He tightened the band and secured his other gear so it would not interfere with his arms as he climbed. Flinging his rope the hook caught an overhang on the first try. Pulling sharply to check the line, he began to climb the side of the rock face. Catching what handholds he could find he quickly reached the first overhang. He looked up to see that several lengths above a knotty tree had dug its roots into a thick rocky sill, so again he threw his line until the strong prongs grabbed tight and Tristus ascended the stone with a strange grace. The cliff face was damp and he took care that his feet did not slip. His muscles burned hot by the time he pulled himself over the top of the precipice and he found himself among a row of scrubby pines. Their trunks were perpetually bent from the relentless ocean winds. He looked down the deserted beach beneath him. Coves snaked endlessly along the shore and paler colors now streaked the faces of the steep cliffs. The rising slopes stood high beyond the flat bridge where he walked. Evergreens climbed the along the lower ground and a little further in the larger arms of oaks were spread wide apart. He walked along until he reached the next rocky face. Swiftly he scaled the summit to travel along the edge of the thick wood which grew upon the uppermost rim of the crag. A small herd of deer waited among the trees. They had no fear of his presence and they took a few steps toward him. Their velvet nostrils widened as they sought to recognize the man. A young buck walked forward, tossing his head to challenge the intruder and as the stag pawed the dirt Tristus stepped toward him and met his glance. The creature startled and kicked back upon the ground. Alarmed, the others turned tail and scattered into the bushes. The young stag raced back after them. Tristus smiled and continued to walk along the edge of the cliff.

The landscape soon changed and from his new vantage point he saw that the next bay was more sheltered. Its back wall was lying well away from the crashing surf and another large fall entered the inlet from the ridge. Herons stood among the thick growth of water reeds and beyond this, the sea oats gave way to another group of mangrove trees. Their bowed trunks rested along knotty roots and those thick salty beds formed islands leading to more permanent ground. Further in and higher up, the banded stone cliffs looked out to the sea. Large, jagged sills jutted from the fractured rock and a series of waterfalls cut their way through the mountain face.

For a moment he considered stopping to make camp at the top of the canyon and he shut his eyes to think. The sun burned red against his closed lids and he brought to mind his brother and the trip Arcus must take to bring the yearling horses

home to the castle. He recalled making the journey with his
father many years before.

It was the autumn of his ninth year when the three of
them had caught his horse, Phaedras. The gray colt had not
given his freedom easily and provided them with a glorious
chase.   His father had watched from the ridge as he and Arcus
ran up and down the length of the canyon. The thought of that
day made him glad.

Tristus had often found his father in his study. His long
desk would be littered with histories, philosophies or the words
of mystics and together they would sit and read. He recalled the
hours the man would spend answering his questions. It was
upon his father's knee that Tristus had received his true
education.   The King spoke often of the virtues of free people,
explaining how this form of rule was superior to dictatorship, but
telling him as well how the regard for free choice was fraught
with pitfalls. Tristus remembered his smile and it seemed that
eons had passed since he had last seen it as the memory
unravelled.   Feeling suddenly insignificant, he found himself
upon the ledge of the lonely cliff with the days light fading from
the afternoon sky.   A pair of young goats grazed along the
steppes leading away from the falls and Tristus knew it was time
to return to his boat. Looking around he considered what options
he had. He could return the way that he had come, retracing his
steps along the grassy bridge of stone, but the tide was receding
and he could see new twisting catwalks leading through the
pools.   If he could reach his ship by way of the beach beneath,
he might find a crab for his dinner.

He bent down to survey his path of descent. Furrowed
cracks spread out from the rocky edge and the way down did not
look too difficult. Looping his rope around the base of a
scraggly pine Tristus descended to the closest ledge. Propelling
himself over the cushioned edge he allowed his feet to bounce
lightly over a pile of stones. Reaching his first destination, he
kicked the loose rock to the ground and heard them spray along
the beach beneath him. Placing his rope around a bolder he
continued to the next outcropping and pulling the line toward
him he secured the rope once again. Sharp stones jutted among

the side and he judged his height carefully. This next jump would be more difficult. A tangle of birch clutched the ledge and he looped his line around them. He would have to swing far to right to reach the next hold he sought. Slowly he lowered himself over the edge and holding tight to the fractured stone as he cautiously made his way. The northern side was heavy with mist and Tristus crawled along the slippery wall slowly. A sharp gust of wind came up suddenly and without warning the roots of the trees above him lost their grip upon the rock. His heart caught a beat when the line jerked sharply and he found himself hanging precariously from the thin rope. Swinging himself lightly to the side he grasped the cliff and creeping like a spider he carefully inched along the ledge. Foot by foot, he seized what narrow holds he could find and with each motion the line above him slipped slightly. Holding his breath he grasped the wall and considered the choices he had. A drop to the ground would be painful and the outcropping he sought was still two lengths away. Clutching the rocks he crawled closer to the ledge and the line jerked again. He was still for a moment.

"Just a few more feet." he thought and drawing a steady breath he continued to move down the wall. Looking up at the tree he saw its wooly head now leaned far over the rocky edge. He prepared himself to push away but instead he found himself free falling. In an instant something hard jarred his back. He was upside down looking back at the cliff above and as he caught his breath he realized he was cradled between a tree and the stone. The branches of the tree had broken the impact of the fall. His lip was bleeding and his legs were tangled in its limbs. He twisted himself around and climbed down the pine, grateful for every sting of the sticky needles as he touched the welcome ground. Seeking out a pool, he rinsed the grit from his hands but the resin stuck fast, leaving brown stains upon his skin. His injuries would need little more care than a thorough cleaning but still Tristus felt foolish for making this unnecessary stop. This idle error could have ended all his plans. Brushing off his gear and retrieving his rope he wrapped his things neatly and stowed them under his cape.

The bay cut deeply into the mountain and close to the foot of the cliffs, a grove of pines struggled in a mealy strand of soil. Their branches were filled with birds. He could hear their chattering as he walked by them. Their ugly sounds came from deep in the thick green limbs and Tristus what did not see was that every small, dark eye was upon him. He climbed over a cluster of boulders to the beach below and his muscles complained. Carefully he surveyed the new cove in hopes of finding fresh water to clean his wounds and in the distance he saw a fall cascading from the cliffs. Walking stiffly he made his way toward it. A flock of black gulls descended upon the shore just ahead of him. As they settled upon the beach they began to pick the meat from the listless shells that bathed in the angled rays of the light. Their eyes gleamed as they watched him pass; the captured slugs twisting in their beaks. Shrill screes pierced through the noisy surf and the birds came toward him flapping their glossy wings. Their empty eyes were disturbing so he picked up a stone and threw it hard among the flock. They scattered, screaming at the indignity, only to spin back to the shore coming to rest a few yards ahead of him. Tristus threw another rock and once more the birds settled a little way before him. They walked and screeched in the shallow waters but with each stride the beasts drew nearer to him. From the trees more of the creatures descended to block his way and their fear diminished as their numbers increased. Closer they came, pressing around him, their vile noise becoming louder and louder. In the middle of the screaming blare, the boldest swooped down upon him and seconds later, dozens of the birds set upon him.   Wielding his staff he fought them, bringing several senseless to the ground. But again, the birds descended. Some grasped his arms, their sharp talons leaving bloody rents along his skin while others flew about his face; pulling his hair and pecking his skull. Their open mouths screeched in his face and he could taste their fishy breath. They slashed and scored him, leaving burning rips deep in his shoulders. Over his head he spun his staff, breaking the black neck of a beast that assailed his eyes. Flinging the limp body into the cloud of claws and beaks he struck out again and again until a bloody mat of the vicious creatures lay at his feet. Ferociously he returned their violent assaults and as his blows fell dark bodies began to stain the sand beneath him. Their numbers failed as his strikes hit true leaving many of the black birds forever still upon the sands. Caution slowly returned and the wounded took to the skies. The afternoon had become the twilight as the last remnants of the flock departed. Tristus stood alone. Streaked in red under the diminishing sun, his own blood mingled with the blood of the murderous beasts.

He sought shelter under the foot of the mountain. His deep scratches burned with fever as the poison began to spread through his veins. He struggled through the heavy sands to reach darker soil just beyond the beach. Hidden by the pines he crawled into the jagged inlet and to his surprise he came upon a sharp rift cut between the black stone. A thicket barred his way and as he looked upon it closely he saw that the rock parted at a angle. Taking out his knife he cut a path though the briary gate. He pushed his way through the thorns and followed an uneven trail downward through the gorge. The air grew warmer as he scrambled along the stony steps as they fell sharply into a deep, green world. The sound of water echoed in the dim light as he cut his way through a mass of shrubs to finally stand in a small clearing. Looking upward he saw the canopy of leaves reached up to the upper edge of the cliffs. The trees around him were strangely designed and used their rooted feet not to burrow but to balance atop of the rock floor. The piles of roots reached to his shoulders and he had to climb over them to make his way along. The stone valley was swollen with the captured warmth of the bright afternoon and Tristus followed the sound of water. The valley ran like a deep scar along the grain of the rock and he walked on, exploring the strange world. Following the voice of a fast running stream he soon set his burdens down next to a swirling pool of clear water. Vines, thick with bunches of sweet fruits, climbed from the pale branches and through the trapped warmth the aroma of the White Blossom lingered strong. He drank in the clean air and sipped the the cold water until he noticed another scent passing through the canyon. The smell was sharp and burned his eyes and he went to find its source. Pushing his way through a stand of young cedars the ground crackled beneath him and the odor grew more pronounced. A bubbling puddle of yellow water steamed between the trees. Tristus bent over the pool breathing the steam deep into his lungs and as it filled his head he found that the pain was eased. The warmth welcomed him. Sore and shivering, he cupped his hands and splashed the strange substance on his face. He felt the heated rush of water pushing up through the earth and he stripped off his clothing and entered the pool. The yellow water soothed the wounds as it seeped into the cuts. The soreness of the fall melted into the brew as the angry welts faded in the bitter warmth. He lay there a long time and when he finally rose from the healing waters he was hungry. Returning to the place where he had set down his pack Tristus started a small fire. Above the stream he rested, watching the reflections the shadows cast in the dark surface. Curious eyes stared the light he had made. He dropped crumbs of dry bread upon the water and waited. Soon a hungry mouth came to swallow the bait and he caught the fish with his net. He killed it cleanly. Placing the fish upon a stone to roast, he hung his damp clothes out among the trees to dry, then wrapping himself in his traveling cloak, he watched his dinner cook. He did not realize when he fell asleep.

He was surrounded by crimson light. Above him burned a broad red sun and waiting in its center a dark shadow loomed. In its hands a burning stone glowed and putrid smoke rose from the belly of each palm. The lips moved. The strange hum filled the smoky mist and growing fogs took on a life of their own. Moving from the shadow in all directions, threads of sound shaped the maleficent clouds. They laughed as their misty fingers pushed through the world stealing light from all they touched. Tristus saw an image of himself waiting in the distance and he realized his reflection was pinned against a large wall. Moving swiftly towards his body he entered the image of himself and pain rushed through each pore. The shadows brushed by him and he heard his voice shouting. He was calling out after them; commanding them to stop, but they laughed and they rushed onward to raze the land. The dark presence in the center of the red sun then it laid its eye upon him. The specter spoke his name and its sound surrounded him like a prison wall. He touched the bars that held him trapped and the floor dropped away. He began to fall and the master of the smothering voice began to shout above him. The red shadow leapt over his head and then all light was gone.

He was awake. His hair lay wet against his head and he was drenched in sweat. Trembling, he stood up and went to tend the fire. Placing more wood upon the blaze, the growing light pushed the night back into the trees. The glow of many eyes appeared and the night creatures watched as he worked to build the fire high. He stared back into the silent eyes and he warmed his flask near the blaze. They looked upon each other as the night sky faded into gray and dawn pushed into the canyon. Tristus opened his eyes to realize he had again fallen asleep where he sat, his wine flask still resting in his hand and his visitors gone away to their dens and burrows.

He renewed the flames of the evening before and returned to the yellow pool. Washing his torn skin and sipping small amounts of the bitter water he welcomed the warm healing that coursed through him. When he had finished his bath he noted that most of his pain had gone. Nibbling a bit of the traveling bread, he drank the last of his wine before eating the overdone fish from the night before. He doused the fire and went to fill his empty flask with the bitter water.

The sides of the canyon echoed with life. In the light of morning he could see the creatures were every color and their vast numbers filled the trees. He said a silent good-bye to the warm valley.

"If chance provides I will come this way again," he reflected as he turned away to climb the jagged stair. Pushing through the tangled gate Tristus returned to the sea.

The tide was low and walking was easy beneath the foot of the cliffs. Glorious was the land that glowed before him and even as he passed the point where he had been assailed the day before all was peaceful. The ocean had pulled away the bodies of the dead leaving the shore with no sign of the evil birds.

He climbed out on the rocks and set his boat upon the waters. Pulling up the sails, he noticed that most of the hurts were healed. His hands were free from their wounds and the stabs inflicted by the birds had lost their heat. Above him the blue sky was dotted with clouds and he counted the days since his departure. He reckoned more than fifty leagues that had passed beneath the bow of his small boat and his thoughts reached toward home. The faces of his sister and brother appeared to his mind and he reached for the stone that hung around his neck to realize that it was gone. He had not touched the amulet since before the attack on the beach.

"Mother will worry," he thought but as he did he knew the skills of telepathy, between his brother and sister, were still in place. He moved his mind towards them as he worked the sails. He wished for a word, a message, an indication of their well being, but such wistful comfort did not come. He was left only with the notion that his goal was still far ahead. Worried thoughts turned inside him and he picked up his pace. There were many miles ahead before he reached the misty wall and the strange behavior of the black gulls was not a thing to ignore. He knew the deserted shorelines held no sanctuary so he set out for deeper waters, resolving to travel by day and night. Over the next week he sailed much and slept little. The weather was fair as his vessel swept over the watery swells and Tristus pushed toward his goal.

CHAPTER SEVEN
THE VALLEY OF ORPHEUS

The breakfast hour had almost passed as Arcus and Clade guided their horses through the streets of Tessera. The tents of the vendors cluttered the square and colored banners waved in the morning breeze. Breads and fruits were displayed upon covered tables; and trinkets and tools hung under low awnings. The shoppers and fishwives bargained with the dealers who called out to those crowding the streets. Children pushed between the tents, jumping over their ropes and taunting one another as they ran down the cobbled lanes following Arcus and his young companion. The shop-workers stretched their necks to look from behind the narrow shutters hoping to catch a glimpse of the two as they passed. Guildsmen came to the doors of their buildings watching as they went with smug indifference. Sharp eyes followed their every step and whispers stirred behind them. Arcus smiled and nodded at the townsfolk ignoring the unsettling sounds of the street. Clade felt their words hissing behind them and drew closer to his older friend. They went until they reached the city's limit. The northern guard pushed down the latch and swung aside the wide gates they passed through side by side.

Leaving the crowded city behind them they moved at an easy pace down the dusty road. Clade soon forgot his nervousness and spoke to Arcus about the horses they were going to fetch. Arcus enjoyed the boy's company but as they talked he found his thoughts straying to his brother. Silently he reached his thoughts toward Tristus to find him as he sailed. Perceiving the rays of sun around him he could sense the steady pace he kept and he knew, that at least for now, Tristus was safe.

Many narrow fields lay alongside the road in clean ordered lanes. The farms of Tessera were laid upon tiers cut from the mountain sides and the tended ground rose like broad steps against the sharp faced hills. Corn and winter bean rustled in the upper fields as they climbed higher along the mountain road. Few farms lay under the northerly cliffs for the earth held too much of the black rock which made up the ledges. The

Valley of Orpheus lay beyond these scattered homesteads and the two travelers must take an ancient passage to reach their destination. When they passed the last farmstead, the fields next to them overflowed with seed. The purple clusters of beans were waiting and ready for the hands of the pickers. A milk maid stood at the side of the road. Recognizing them as they came near she ran ahead to the canyon trail wishing to be the one to open the gate which led into the mountain. The channel had been carved long ago and this passage was the only entrance to the northern hills. The land beyond remained pristine as the mountain sides were kept by the House of Tessera. The Valley of Orpheus was tucked in between them a days walk away. Here, the yearling horses were taken each spring to graze and wander freely in the safety of that green valley. Arcus reached into his pocket and gave the child a bit of silver for her courtesy. She curtsied smartly to them before skipping happily back to the barn.

Leaving all traces of the city behind, they entered the stone corridor and followed its steeply bending path. Exchanging small talk they walked for more than an hour before the land opened up ahead of them. Tall cedars stood like sentries against the sky and the shady ground was filled with ferns. Still moving upward, they soon reached an open spot along the hill. Among the steep fields and rocky places, they realized a group black seagulls followed them. The birds screamed and stared at them with hollow black eyes and Arcus found his thoughts drawn again to his brother. Picking up a rock he threw it hard and sending a mental command through the trees the birds scattered in the air. The two continued on, upward and further to the north, walking through the quiet glens. After several hours, they took a bit of food from their packs and drank the cold stream that ran alongside the path.

It was late-afternoon when they reached the gully that lead into the Valley of Opherus. A metal gate barred the entrance. An impression of the city of Tessera was woven into its graceful lines and the Tower of Malthrom formed the center of the design. Clade pushed the door open easily. Crumbling stones jutted from the vertical sides of the passageway. Carefully the boys and their ponies stepped over fallen rocks which littered the way and soon the little valley opened before them. The basin thrived between the slopes of the wooded hills and in the center of the valley a small lake glistened. The sun tossed its shadows on the rustling leaves and from this vantage point they could see the horses grazing on the yellowing grasses of the furthest meadow. Clade sprang lightly from his pony and began to prepare the ropes.

"Shall we try for them this afternoon?" he asked.

"If you are willing for the chase then so am I." Arcus answered smiling.

They gathered their gear and made a quick plan of approach. Circling quietly, they moved around the horses and waiting in the shadows they watched the group. In the field before them were two dozen yearlings. Many of the herd wore shades of chestnut and mahogany and sported stockings in both black and white. Several among the group glowed with ebony and only by the paths of their white blazes could one be distinguished from the other. Three of the troop were golden with ivory manes and tails but the fourth colt was a deeper shade of gold wearing instead, a thick black mane and tail. The red filly stood at the edge of the crowd of ponies. She flicked her tail at a fly that taunted her. The insect fell to the ground.

"That is the one Aleryn has spoken for," Arcus whispered as they made a careful plan. Clade stepped forward from his hiding place to neatly rope a bay filly. Arcus drove the other yearlings back from their meadow until they were trapped against the sides of the basin. Clade returned and in another moment had captured a black colt. The others pawed the ground, agitated by the sudden assailment. The red filly stood beside the golden colt. They tossed their heads and stamped their feet. Arcus kept the herd together and circling around them he blocked their way with his own horse. The group pawed and snorted, trapped against the large outcropping of rocks as he held them to their position. Clade tossed the rope again and as it settled around her she rose in the air. Clade pulled the rope taut and she kicked and reversed. The suddenness of the movement caught him off balance and he was pulled sharply to the ground, his face meeting the grass. Arcus let his rope fly and captured the filly's tossing head. Clade leaped up but the horse pulled him with her and backed against the rocks. The golden colt bolted and he ran through the lines, ripping the rope from Arcus' hands. The cords were hopelessly tangled as the two ponies gathered their legs beneath them. They ran trumpeting across the field with the ropes dangling dangerously around their feet.

"They will kill themselves." Clade exclaimed, a streak of blood running from his nose.

Arcus chuckled, "It was going a bit too easy." he said rubbing his rope burned hands.

"We must get her. She will break her legs with those ropes hanging from her. Come on, hurry!"

"Let them calm down first. We will do more damage by chasing them. We will see to this group and then we will follow." Arcus suggested, turning to the wild eyed ponies. Offering bits of raw vegetables from his pack he spoke to them softly as Clade watched the runaways enter a stand of trees.

"I will guide them to the hold." said Arcus gesturing just beyond the edge of the lake where the rude manger stood. Its edges were enclosed with rough timbers and poles served as its gate. The horses were beginning to settle as Arcus' gentle poise put them at ease.

"They will be all right." he said running his hands along the shoulder of a tall black colt. "I will take these now. You go along the edge of the bracken, Clade" said Arcus. "Climb up on that ridge. See if you can spot them."

The drying grass was fragrant beneath his leather boots. Just ahead a stream whispered over round stones. He watched a fat rabbit scuttle along the clay bank disappearing into one of the many burrows which marred the sides. Then Clade glimpsed the golden coat of the runaway. His fine head was bent over the stream and his sides heaved from the chase as he took a long drink. Clade remained still, hiding behind the trunk of a large oak. A familiar whistle reached his ears and the boy responded with a soft trill of his own. Cautiously he prepared his rope and again he heard Arcus' signal. Through the trees, he saw the flash of his deep green cape. Arcus was in position just to the right of the golden colt. He nodded to him and Clade rose from his hiding place. The pony's dark eyes widened as he turned to run but Arcus was there, the rope already settling over his neck. In an instant, Clade's rope was next to his masters and both spoke steadily to the captured horse. He calmed quickly and Arcus shook his head.

"It does seem a bit too easy, Clade." said Arcus.

"I had imagined more of a struggle from them all." Clade agreed

"Look." said Arcus, pointing to the ledge just beyond them. "She is there, standing in the sun. And look at that. How strange. The filly is free from her bonds."

"How could that be? Those ropes were well thrown." said Clade

Arcus did not answer but looked warily through the wood. The valley was small, leaving little room for hiding places and so as they lead the golden colt to the hold, keeping their eye out for anything unusual. After securing the pony with the others they searched the southern ridge for the runaway filly until finally they saw her walking calmly along the ledge. A scattering of rock skipped down the wall as she passed by.

"I wonder how she got rid of those ropes?" whispered Clade.

Arcus shook his head, "We must be careful here, my friend."

Just ahead of the filly, a thick outcropping of rocks jutted over the valley. She was nibbling a shrub, and paid no attention as the two separated to surround her. Clade whistled softly as they drew near and the filly lifted her head. She snorted when she saw him, unaware that Arcus was coming up from behind. Clade drew closer, humming a low tune and the pony watched, intent and still, noticing the apple which lay in his palm. He walked closer and she did not pull away. He felt her warm breath upon his fingers and the horse looked into his face, her brown eyes deciding. Then suddenly she stomped and turned about. In that instant she was running and in another, she was face to face with Arcus. She could not stop nor could she turn so the filly did the only thing left. She jumped. Arcus dropped to his knees as the hooves soared above his head. The filly landed pristinely upon the ledge behind him. She shook her head before she turned and ran down the path.

"Master Arcus, you were right!" exclaimed Clade.

"Ah yes lad. This one plays with us." he laughed as they scrabbled after the horse.

"That will take to long! This way." and he pointed to the ledge beneath them.

They started down and quickly found that narrow footholds had been carved into the face of the cliff and well placed finger grasps lined the way.

"Look at these grips," said Arcus. "someone made them."

"And look! Look down there." pointed Clade.

Beneath them was a peculiar opening in the rock and, except from this odd angle, the mouth of the cave would be hidden from view. Dropping down, they noticed a fire smoldered within a neatly dug pit. Crude utensils lay carelessly tossed upon the ground around it. Peering inside, they waited a moment until their eyes adjusted to the dim light. The interior of the cave was spacious with smaller alcoves notched along side. They were covered in animal skins and seemed to be used for sleeping. Water vessels hung against the walls and plants were left to dry along the edge. Roots, chestnuts, and wild onions lay piled in a far corner and beyond this a pale light fell and they saw another opening near the rear of the grotto.

"I wonder how many stay here?" said Arcus looking around.

"I wonder who they are?" answered Clade. "They seemed to have left in a hurry."

"Or maybe they did not have time to leave at all?" whispered Arcus, pointing towards a rumpled skin which lay in an alcove a few feet away. Clade eyes widened and silently he backed away to glance into the opening. Arcus moved to stand above the tousled palate and reaching down he pulled away the furs.

The child shrieked, her black eyes wild with fear as she leapt from the floor. Arcus grabbed her as she passed him but she twisted and writhed until he firmly surrounded her with his long arms.

"It is all right. We are not going to hurt you." he said, "It is all right, now. Please be still."

As she struggled, Clade noticed the beaded pattern worked into her skin. It wrapped all the way up her thin arm. Clade blinked to focus his eyes for it seemed the painting twisted of its own accord as she tried to free herself. She stopped her fight to look at him and a puzzled expression passed over her face. After a few more frustrated attempts she stopped her writhing and was still.

"Girl, we will not hurt you. Believe us. We are not your enemy." consoled Arcus but still the child was bright with fear. "Where are your parents?" he asked.

She looked away at the mention of her parents. Quiet tears streamed down her cheeks and she tossed her head so that her black hair fell over her face. Just then shouts and the sounds of feet came from outside. Arcus looked out to see a dozen children standing in the little clearing. They were dressed in rough cloth and their bronzed skin was stained with symbols. All of them held weapons and in an instant, swords, staves, and bows quickly circled the cave. The tallest took a step ahead of the others, his arrow ready. Looking defiantly into Arcus' eyes he aimed for his chest.

"Let her go." he said, his voice burning.

"We have not come to hurt you." said Arcus.

"Let her go." he demanded sternly. The blue eyes flashed as he looked into the faces of the strangers. His black hair was thick, with bits of the forest bracken hopelessly tangled within it. His brown chest rose and fell with even breaths. The painted designs upon him seemed alive. The weaving circles and flaming sylphs, ciphers and hieroglyphs that marked him appeared to move over his bare skin. Arcus recognized many of the symbols from the temple walls as the boy held the deadly aim at his heart.

Clade moved toward his master but Arcus motioned him to remain steady and nodded to the ferocious boy. Setting the girl free Arcus drew his sword. She ran to take a place between the others. The youth relaxed his hold upon his bow while he studied the strangers with great care and when his eyes fell upon Clade, a strange looked crossed his face. The others grew silent and still, as their leader stared at the red-haired boy.

Finally, he drew a long breath letting the tip of the arrow

drop away from the mark.

"Who are you?" he said to Clade. Clade met his gaze but did not answer.

"Where do you come from?" he pressed him taking a few steps closer ignoring Arcus as if his presence no longer mattered.

"I care for the horses of the Queen." answered Clade.

"The castle." whispered the boy, "Why?" he said louder, "You are not of that line."

Clade shook his head confused by the strange questions but Arcus nodded that he respond and Clade answered by explaining, "The Queen said it should be so after my parents were lost."

"Lost? In what manner were they lost?" demanded the boy taking a step closer to him but Clade did not answer and he cast his eyes away, inciting the boy to focus upon the him even more intently.

"Did they die?" he asked.

Arcus stepped closer to his friend and putting his hand upon Clade's shoulder he placed his body between the two boys. The sound of muffled sobbing stirred the tense moment and the girl they had caught in the cave looked up at the painted boy.

"Go." he spoke motioning toward the entrance and she hurried to the cave returning shortly with two young children. Their faces were streaked with dirt and their tousled red hair was matted against their damp heads. Arcus studied the children as the boy and girl clung to her plain skirt. They were almost identical to look upon but what caught his attention more, was that these children were not just identical to each other but also to his young friend, Clade.

Arcus looked to the gaunt leader. "Why did you come to this place? This valley is within the hold of the Queen."

"We do no harm by being here." he answered. "Take your horses and leave us in peace."

"Why are you here? Where is your kin?"

"Our kin cares not where we bide." he answered and the prince caught a hint of an odd accent. Its cadence was common of the southern farming boroughs of Tessera.

"It is not your concern." the boy continued.

"It is my concern, boy. I am Arcus of the House of Tessera and I need to know how is it that a group of children come to live in this valley alone. Much is amiss if such things occur in the shadow of the tower."

"There is much amiss in the shadow of the tower." answered the boy bitterly his tone revealing he had known he spoke to the Prince all the while.

"Then tell me boy, how did you come here? And from where do you recognize my companion, and who are these little ones who share his face?"

"You ask too much of me, prince." he answered icily, "I am just a poor lad. I hold no status. I possess nothing you might desire. So leave us. Leave your Kingdoms' refuse as it is meant, discarded and forgotten." His blue eyes flared as his tone grew sharp, "while you still have the opportunity."

Arcus ignored the threat. "Why do you keep secrets boy?"

"Secrets are for the trust-worthy and you, Prince, are not one of that company." and the trees trembled as he spoke.

"Who has betrayed you?" pressed Arcus.

"Ask your infirm queen about betrayals. She would know better than any." said the boy

"The Queen?" he responded, "She would not allow children to live in this harsh fashion. It is not her way and it has never been the way of our House."

The boy studied the Prince. His eyes were dangerous as he paused for an moment, almost as if he were considering the words of the gentle Prince but he answered Arcus' question in the grimmest of tones.

"We are the Tahmurath. Do you know the word? In the old language, the name means "unmentioned". Have you heard of us, Prince? The "Unmentioned Ones." He paused then, allowing the sarcasm to ring in the air and a dark temper covered his face as he added. "There are many citizens of your pathetic kingdom who take great interest in us. We have gifts they like to, "acquire." The accent became more evident with each sound and his blue eyes darkened to deep shade of twilight,

"The Kingdom you rule is built upon lies and treachery. But fear not Prince. I have seen many things and I know that you will not be burdened with the pain of its fall." Then the boy mumbled a sound and it moved from him like a wave. His fury passed through the trees and the upper limbs of the elms above them were suddenly filled with the rustling of small creatures. Their sharp eyes were fixed intently on the group of humans below, awaiting a command. What had, but seconds before, radiated from his enraged eyes was now concentrated before him. Arcus felt the force of the boy's anger push through him like a violent shudder. He looked toward his untouchable attacker, wondering at the awesome strength the strange boy possessed. The vibrant heat moved through the tips of his fingers forming a sphere of blue fire. The orb rested a moment and then slowly the sphere began to through the canopy of leaves. The birds responded and left their hiding places to fly in tight circles following the orb as it moved though the air. The sound of the beating wings became deafening as a suffocating pressure expanded through his chest. He was on his knees, gasping for breath as the flight of the birds spun out of control until they had became but dreadful dark shapes moving up in spiraling rush. The adolescent stood amidst the funnel of force, his arms stretching toward the sky until finally he drew a deep breath and shouted out in a thundering voice. Its power sliced the thick, magical air like a blade piercing though a gut. The birds screamed with him. The pattern they had formed exploded across the forest sky. Free once more to do as they pleased they rushed across the afternoon clouds.

A single shape burned in Arcus' mind. The power of the boy's invocation had been released into the heaven and he found himself able to rise to his feet. The sound rattled through him as he struggled to catch his breath Looking up he saw the boys eyes set directly upon him. But no longer did the youth seem angry. Instead he looked pale and drained, almost as if his own magic moved through him as deeply as it had Arcus. The Prince was not sure if beads of sweat or tears streaked down his cheeks.

They watched one another, the tall young man and wiry boy, and the younger seemed distressed. It was a long time before he spoke and when he did his words surprised them all.

"The Word did not kill you. I am surprised. I did not expect you to survive." he said looking gravely into Arcus eyes,

"But alas my Prince, it does not change what I have seen and the price will be high." and with that remark, he bent one knee and rested it upon the ground and what he said surprised all who stood within the glen.

"I am Pelius, Guardian of the Tahmurath. You must know now that it was the Sister Earth who chose not to destroy you. Not I. I would have enjoyed watching you die." and then the grim boy bowed his head. "I am at your mercy."

Arcus was stunned by the words. The sudden change of heart took him aback. This child before him was both fierce and brutal and Arcus knew well the legends of the "unmentioned ones". The Tahmurath was the name the Eratosthenians gave to a certain breed of soul. It was written that those individuals would possess powers enabling them to control the elements. Some among them would be great healers and hold within the powers of harmony. While others would be changelings; adept in all aspects of telepathy. The old writings held that as the Tahmurath walked the land many people would not know them and those who did recognize these "Unmentioned Ones" would be the souls who held within themselves either great evil or great good. Arcus did not hesitate to accept the loyalty of the strange boy.

"Mercy is granted boy. Rise now and do not fear me."

Pelius stood up. "I have no fear, Prince, only far-sight which leaves me able to see the changing times."

"Yes. The signs of it are all around us and those of us who see such things must stay together. Come with us to the castle. There are folk there that will help you."

The boy glanced around at the others. They did not speak. They waited for his word. Arcus felt his heart as he struggled between the two sides of reason and he was surprised as his voice was steady and strong as he spoke.

"The Tahmurath will return with you to Tessera and there we shall seek service before the Queen."

"She will be honored, Pelius." he answered as questions filled his mind. "And there will be time for questions later." he told himself silently. Then looking upon the other children he wondered, "They are so young. Why did they come here?" then he smiled at the ragged band and said aloud, "Know that all of you are welcome among us." and the quiet, bright eyes stared silently back at him.

The falling leaves whispered in the cool air. The "Unmentioned Ones" would now return to city of Tessera as the children gathered their belongings. Pelius remained distant and spoke little as they made ready for their journey. Arcus wondered of the queer state of affairs which had caused his change of heart. He helped the children prepare their simple burdens and he knew that Pelius was still torn by his decision to serve. "Torn he might be to serve in the House of Tessera." thought Arcus, " Nonetheless the castle is the best place for this strange brood. They are still children. They need us." But still he decided to wait and give the boy some time before pressing him for his story.

"We will leave in the morning, if that would be alright with you."

Pelius nodded and taking the young ones by the hand he led them back into the cave.

There was no need to waste their efforts in the capture of the yearlings. The young horses came obediently to the children's whistles. Standing still as pack ponies they allowed the light bundles to be tied around them. The children climbed upon their backs holding lightly to their manes as the yearlings walked with no halter to guide them. Taking their leaders strength as their own, all were obedient to the boy's silent ways. Pelius sat upon the red filly with one of the young twins before him. The child had lost its fear of the strangers. He laughed and laid his head against the horse's neck and waved to his sister. The other twin shared a horse with the girl they had first found hiding in the cave and Clade rode beside this pair. The girl's name was Mileah and she was not yet twelve summers old. Clade looked often to the two children which shared his face. He wished to ask her what she knew of them but he could not find the courage to form the words.

Pelius was subdued. His thoughts wandered into a place where none could follow. Sadness would often cloud the clear blue eyes and it seemed to Arcus something spoke to him and what that voice said was meant for his ears alone.

The Voice spoke on and on to young Pelius that long afternoon. The same Voice that others had called "a Gift." The Voice had instructed him on how to concentrate force and move objects with his mind. It was the sound which resonated through him as he called the beasts and birds. In the stillness of the glade he could hear it call him, always in the distance; just beyond the laughter of the children; beyond the footfalls of the horses; whispering ahead in the sound of the waters, moving through dry leaves, pulling him forward upon the path he swore he would never walk. The Voice called to him and again he was willing to follow. He knew well its sound. It held his destiny and those he loved so dearly had given all to protect this burdensome gift. Scarcely could he believe his road led back to Tessera. But it could not be denied that he had witnessed the will of the Sister Earth as he had sought to destroy the Prince. Her power had intervened with his hasty violence. This man was not his enemy and the revelation had thrown him into confusion. If those of the House of Tessera were not the enemy he no longer knew who to fight. His thoughts ran in circles as they came closer and closer to the city.

It was well after dusk when they moved in single file through the long channel which marked the entrance back into the farms of Tessera. Clade jumped from his horse and opened the gate and the group passed silently by the farm of the milk-maid they had met the previous day. It was through the eyes of the Tahmurath that Arcus now saw the enormous city as it spread under the slopes of the mountain. Sand and mortar dwellings rose from the shoreline to climb up into the steep foothills. Roads from the city led to the farms which dotted those hillsides. Goats grazed freely along the rough terrain of the higher cliffs and upon the lower tiers, community gardens were terraced above the northern entrance. Fruit trees and arbors were carefully placed alongside of the kitchen gardens to shade the tender shrubs. Space was a precious resource and the gardens design were not only for beauty but for utility as well.

The castle marked the boundary of the sea. The dark

silhouette of its spires and turrets were ancient in design and for centuries they had stood soundly against the ocean winds. As the night approached, the steps leading to the castle were lit by hanging lanterns and a few late travelers could be seen hurrying down the wide stairs into the streets below. But it was the Tower of Malthrom which rose precariously above all. Tall against the water's edge the dark tower loomed and beyond its shadow, the masts of the fishing boats stood in the faint moonlight. The evening sky held a scattering of small clouds. Lavender and gray they hung complacently in the advancing night.

Down the pebbled road the entourage went along. The children's mood changed as they walked though the tightly lined streets. Curious eyes peered from behind the curtains and pressed against cracks of closed doors. Pelius dismounted to walk in silence. The children followed him, riding slowly with their heads bowed. Nervously they moved along the lower, less traveled alley ways making their way to the barns. It was great relief to them all as the stable doors were firmly shut behind them.

The children scrabbled down from the horses stretching their sore limbs while Clade lit the lanterns which hung against the walls. Walking down the aisles of the barn they were all curious to meet the other beasts that lived there. The horses stretched their necks to greet them as they passed by, flapping their lips in hopes of a bit of carrot or maybe some sweet thing. The children rubbed their soft noses, admiring each one as Clade introduced them to the many horses in his charge. Arcus watched for a moment and deciding that the children were content, he left them and went to prepare stalls for the new yearlings. The children had so tamed the young beasts that they stood still, allowing themselves to be haltered as they waited in the aisles. Pelius lingered at Phaedrus' stall when Clade went to assist his master. The yearlings had become impatient. Stamping their feet, they looked over their shoulders as Arcus threw down bundles of hay. Clade appeared with buckets of grain and all the children gathered near to measure the scoops for the eager horses. No one noticed as the stable door slid open. No one but Pelius who stood in the shadows of the grey stallion.

He watched her cloth slippers step lightly upon the dirt floor. She looked down the rows following the sounds of the children's voices. Her plain cloak covered a simple gown and her red hair hung long down her slender back. Only by the golden circlet she wore would she be recognized as the Princess. The reflection of the band caught the light of the lantern and Pelius stepped forward to reveal himself. He faltered as he tried to speak for again his "Gift" was upon him. Unbidden, as it always was, the "Voice" whispered and the appearance of her physical form faltered as true sight was upon him. He had grown accustom to its sudden appearance, altering its perceptions and changing his state of mind. The girl before him was now revealed in the form untouched by time. The seeing of her true luminescence told Pelius more of her than a ocean of words could ever render. The stream of information flowed like threads of warmth. He found himself able to perceive the both the past and the future of the presence before him and he watched as history of the kingdom moved into his widened mind. He saw this girl was connected to all that was and would be of the Kingdom which he had so long despised. Her power reached toward him and he became a living part of what had once abandoned him.

In that instant, a larger wave of perception then crashed upon him and he became an observer of his own essence. The points of emotion shifting like a kaleidoscope of weaving colors. Anger and frustration moved as grays and reds, pain twisted in shades of sickening browns, hate glowered in glistening black. He was alarmed for a moment. The hairs upon his arms stood up and his breath came in shallow pants. His thoughts began to reel but the Voice spoke to him gently. Gradually new sensations began to move through him and he found himself washed in pale greens and blues. The colors revealed the source of the burden he carried, the burden of being left alone. Then something lifted this weight from him and he looked up to see her gaze resting upon him. The human form had been restored. He wanted to speak but no words would come for there was more she wanted him to see. Frozen to the spot another page was turned in his mind and he saw himself from a different view. He saw he was not his anger nor his happiness, his pain nor grief, and he was not his sense of relief. All that had just overwhelmed him was just the passing of the moment. The future stood before him open and uncharted. He was free to step forward from his past. The Princess looked into his blue eyes and she smiled.

Arcus appeared from around the corner of the passage. He was surprised when he saw the two, his sister and the strange Pelius, face to face with one another.

Aleryn turned away from Pelius and looked upon her brother to say. "Where did you find our guests?"

"In the Valley of Opherus. They had made camp there." The other children were now beginning to gather around and the Princess looked at them and said. "Welcome. All of you. We are glad you are here. Come and I will show you to your rooms."

Arcus nodded wisely. His sister's powers of foresight did not surprise him but Pelius could only stare. They followed the princess though the garden along the west side of the castle. Stars filled the clear sky as they walked beneath a steep turret and just beyond it stood a low building with a thickly thatched roof. Its windows were small but there were many of them and every one opened out to the sea. They entered the hostel to find their rooms waiting. Bright fires crackled in every hearth and sweet loaves, cheese, and pitchers of cold milk were set out on small tables. Clean bedding and blankets were waiting for them. The young ones, with their handfuls of bread, tumbled into the warmed sheets. The older children sat by the fires and ate slowly, happy to find the chill melting from their hands. They listened to the princess as she showed them their nightclothes and sinks.

Aleryn saw each to their rooms with Arcus and Clade following behind her. The servants were sent to bring more food and to restock the wood for the fires. Pelius walked with the children, offering words of reassurance and good nights to those he knew so well. The red-haired twins begged Clade to stay the evening but he promised instead to return in the morning to share breakfast with them. If they had not been so sleepy they would have fought him harder, but with only a few more complaints they allowed Mileah to tuck them into their beds. Soon they were fast asleep and Clade said his good nights and returned to the stables.

Aleryn led Pelius to the end of the hall and opened the door to his room. It seemed larger than the others for it so sparsely furnished. Its windows faced both west and north. A fire burned at the far end of the room and its stone hearth was framed by two round windows which looked into the inky night. The moon hung low upon the horizon, silhouetting the sharp cliffs where Tristus had passed by just days before. The three of them walked inside and closed the door. Along the wall a desk held a platter of bread and cheese. Arcus went to the board and began to cut thick slices. He poured himself a cup of wine and then he poured milk for Pelius and his sister. Aleryn motioned to the sitting chairs which waited before the hearth. Pelius drew a deep breath and sat nearest to the fire accepting the bread and cheese which Arcus brought him and for a moment they rested, nibbling their food and looking into the flames.

He felt her question in his mind before he turned to look into her face. He glared and answered her without spoken words.

"How could I know?" he returned silently as the familiar rage surged within him. Confusion had taken him for the moment, his mind struggled. He knew too much and he knew to little. His mind fought the intrusion of the girl and frustration exploded from him. Its power flashed as the milk pitcher crashed to the floor.

"You are going to need to control that." she said aloud.

"You need to keep to yourself." he spoke silently.

"Your thoughts run over the room." she answered.

Arcus shook his head, the tacit communication between them was unnerving. Aleryn sighed with vexation and settled back in her chair refusing to look at Pelius again.

Arcus finished his wine searching for words to say. Finally he spoke to the boy. "Pelius, we mean you no harm. We wish to understand what drove you from the city." he explained attempting to bridge the gap between them. "There are many things amiss in Tessera and if you can help us mend them, we are in great need."

Pelius did not answer. He looked ill in the changing light of the flames.

"He is just a boy," Arcus reminded himself and stepping back he allowed Pelius time to collect himself.

Pelius scolded himself, despising his weakness in the presence of the Princess and for a moment he panicked, feeling trapped and afraid. He knew he must stop so drawing a breath he pushed the frustrations away and he chose instead to remember. He moved his attention from the comfortable room and placed it in the memory which gave him his purpose. He saw his brother's face before him. It had been a year since they had parted and Pelius had been alone with the responsibilities of the children. It had not been easy and he suffered dearly from the grim loss. What pushed him forward was the Gift and Pelius forced himself to recall their last conversation.

"I am broken." Tarin had whispered. "Of all the portents I have beheld I did not foresee this." he said choking on the words. "It is by denial I have failed you." His brother struggled to pull another ragged breath. "You must lead them now. They do not understand who they are. It is more than strange oddities they posses. These powers are but an illusion to hide the greater gifts. They must survive Pelius. They need to live and be given the chance to recognize their true natures." A trickle of blood ran from his mouth and Pelius drew him closer to hear him murmur. "You have gifts and you must use those powers now. Protect them. They will need you." Then his breath grew shallow and Pelius looked helplessly at the blood leaking from his torn belly. But after a moment Tarin spoke again. "Pelius, there are dangers greater than any shadow. They speak in countless voices. Beware my little brother. Be aware of the sadness that whispers in your ear. Do not let it cloud what you see with your heart. The greatest peril will come from within."

Pelius watched his brother's blue eyes glaze and the breathing stop. How well he recalled the moment. It was an instant frozen in time. He stirred from the memory to find himself back in the castle. Aleryn and Arcus were standing before the fire waiting for him to speak. He knew this was the point that his brother had spoken of. The moment when he could not allow anger, nor despair, to cloud the way. In those dying words Pelius had found new meaning. He would tell them the truth they asked to hear and he would leave nothing out.

CHAPTER EIGHT
THE TAHMURATH

Through the window a pale moon waned and he allowed himself to stretch along its soft light as he began to remember. "Where was the beginning? Had there ever been one? No." he decided. It seemed that the Gift had always been. Its ancient tongue was woven into every fiber of his body. Closer than his own voice the Gift spoke to him. Nearer to his mind than his own thoughts, it was aware of his desires before they held any substance of their own.

Searching his memories he could find few that his brother was not a part of. Alike as a set of twins, they both bore the same dark hair and clear blue eyes. Scarcely four seasons lie between them and hardly an inch or two set them apart in height. Their mysterious abilities had drawn them close as they found themselves able to do what few others could even imagine. In the solitude of dusty mangers they perfected their magical games. They were lucky, as the children of the Tessera go, having room to run and good air to breath. Their father farmed a narrow strip in the southern boroughs. Their small cottage was just an hour's walk from the walls of the city that they shared the house with their mother and father, sister and grandmother.

But the fields their family tilled were not easy plots. It took great skill to coax the seedlings from the stony land. They learned to waste little and were careful to return to the earth that which they took. Waterfalls tumbled from the black cliffs and often he and Tarin would play in cold pools that overlooked the fields. He remembered the times they had helped their father alter the path of the mountain stream to flood the crops in the dry months of late summer. Their burden of hard work was not borne with bitterness but with honor and necessity.
Nonetheless, times grew difficult and the years when the greater part of the land would lie fallow, the family would seek their living by other means. They kept a small herd of goats which they used for milk and cheese and what they did not need they sold in the market place. Along the ridge, beyond the upper fields, the brothers would go each day to graze the beasts. They would spend their hours among the trees practicing the silence

needed to join with the thoughts of the other. He recalled how simple it became and how the communication was much more complete than the ill tempo of noisy conversation. The gift grew and soon other powers began to develop. The ability to move objects was the next to come. In the beginning, it would happen without their full control. Objects would rise, oddly disconnected from the forces which normally held such things to the earth, to slowly follow behind them until, for no reason they could be sure of, the thing would crash to the ground. But time passed and control increased and soon they learned to bring the things through the air to rest obediently beside them. They would spend joyous days experimenting with their new powers and competing as brothers will. Which one could lift the object highest into the air? Which one could throw it the farthest? But what they found was when they lifted the object together they could lift more than ten times the burden either could carry alone. The trials went on and soon they found, not only ability to read each others thoughts increasing, but the thoughts of others formed in their minds as well.

Year by year, times grew more difficult for the family and it was not the cold, nor hard work, or harsh land that caused it. It was the Haarshaim. The Guildsmen sought to control the prices of the wheat and corn and as the larger landowners wished to remove all competition from the marketplace the Haarshaim would find ways to buy the crops for much less that they were worth. Pelius' small family held little land and though they saved their seeds from year to year neither frugality nor toil was enough. Finally there came a time when their father would take work in the fishing boats and, for at least that evening, the table would be laid. Their mother also returned to the city where she would sit long hours in the dim factories of weaver's guilds. The Haarshaim played a heavy hand in the operations of all Guilds. Sharp-faced overseers reproached the women, threatening them with punishments while inciting the weak-minded to do twisted favors in turn for small partialities. Their mother would return home each evening, tired and disheartened, from what she had seen each day. She was not alone in her distress, for most of the city folk felt the harsh weight of the Haarshiam influence. Some days it became necessary for the brothers accompany their mother to the city. They would spend their time in the storerooms, playing among the barrels of dye and skeins of raw wool as they waited for her to finish her work. Their telepathic abilities became frightening in such places, for the words that were spoken by those around them did not often mirror the thoughts they held within. It was a childish instinct which kept them from showing the unusual abilities they possessed and they were careful to watch through the cracks, careful so no one would know. Games such as theirs were not meant for the prying eyes.

But all this changed when tragedy had shattered their home. Pelius shuddered as he recalled the horrid day from years before. Though Tarin was the elder of the two brothers, the true firstborn of their family had been a daughter. Lovely as an elf-child and strange as thunderstorm upon a sunny day, the beautiful babe had been born a mute. It had been the first day of her fifteenth year when she had walked to a neighbor's cottage never to be seen again. A disturbing mystery had surrounded that ill-fated afternoon as rumors of black shadows spread through their small borough. The search for the girl went on for months. People combed the hills and streams, the beaches and city streets, but his sister was never found. Grief consumed their mother and, though she had two lovely sons, her broken heart would not mend. It was during this time of sorrow that the boy's grandmother came to help the family. Her name was Nadinia and though the old woman mourned the loss of the child her wise hands had handled more of life's pain than most. Through the long years of her life, Nadinia had been a mid-wife and a healer. She knew well of troubles that lie inside the days and had often glimpsed the freedom which came through the release of death.

The brothers were now left with her company when their parents were called to other work. They thought themselves clever in hiding their ability to hide powers but Nadinia's eyes were sharp and she was well aware of what they were up to. In the mornings the boys would take the goats to the mountainside to graze. They would lie upon their backs and watch the clouds take shape in the skies and sometimes, quite unexpectedly, the wind would come to meet them. Placing their wills upon that breath and the wild force could be set into motion and when this was done the birds would respond as well. The flocks would fly over them in glorious formations and from her garden, the old woman saw these designs form in the sky. Intuition said it was her grandsons who guided the motion of the restless, winged creatures but she held her tongue and secretly observed their progress. The day came when the boys realized they could command the waters as well. They would lift the stream from its narrow bed and the water would rise to form any shape they desired. Liquid herds of rushing horses crashed down the mountain sides, writhing serpents twisted their way upon the craggy rocks and fluid mountain lions charged through churning waters. They perfected their abilities upon the along that upper ridge and the old woman witnessed all from her garden below.

She kept their secrets as she worked. Her hands were never idle for there was always much to do. A great portion of her day was spent milking the nannies and preparing cheese for the market. It was whispered among the fishwives that the old healer looked to contain a bit of blood from the tiny folk who, at least in legend, once populated the hills leading to Tessera. When they would ask her age the old woman would smile and cleverly steer the conversation away from herself, telling them instead stories of the ancient days when giants and fairy folk held the lands outside the city and reminding them of the time when Tessera was a small fishing village and life was far simpler.

Through the years she had spent many cold nights gazing upon the stars, for the stars will tell fantastic tales if one knows how to listen. It was from these whispers Nadinia became aware that a new breed of babe was passing through her hands. Never before had so many come forth covered by the white web that presaged the second-sight. When she freed those babes from that bondage a blue flame would burn bright upon their brow diminishing as the babe drew its first breath from the cold air of the earth. The names of those infants she wrote in a book which she kept hid in her chambers. Though Pelius' mother had not borne the white web all the grand-babes which passed through her had that sign and there were others born with Tessera who held the gift as well. Diverse in physical characteristics the children grew seemingly unnoticed in the realms of Tessera. Nadinia had kept a record of their names and placement of their stars as the children entered the door of the world. Diligently, she searched for the meaning of the signs and eventually the importance of their presence was revealed to her. Under the full of the moon, the stars whispered clues as to the true purposes of the new breed coming forth into the world;

> *Under the cover of a blinding storm*
> *Far suns will kiss the raging day.*
> *In beams unseen the tide to shift,*
> *Within the turning of the way.*
> *Upon the face a flame burns strong*
> *For within the eye a bridge is born*
> *And through the hands the way is set*
> *To bind the buntings of time's breathe.*
> *It is the heart of the elder ones*
> *That turn the hand within the storm*
> *And as seas are still as sheets of glass*
> *The fire burns to light the path.*
> *And tides will rush about their feet*
> *To stand unmoving where the lines do meet.*
> *Revealed once more they will become,*
> *The Tahmurath, the Unmentioned Ones.*

Nadinia continued to listen to night and she found the stars held more secrets than just that of the Tahmurath.   It was though the milky haze that she saw the evil eye growing restless in the night.   Dull and ugly, it sensed the strength of the hybrids and it wandered through the streets seeking ways to satisfy its dark urges. The shadow found its strength in each course deed and gleaned its power from every violent act. Nadinia sensed the danger rising as days passed and she worried for her grandsons.

Pelius remembered the day he realized the old woman watched them. Tarin went to feed the chickens while had gone to fetch the goats but instead of carrying the bucket as an ordinary boy would have done, Tarin had lifted the bucket with the power of his thought. The corn bucket floated obediently behind him and the kernels, compliant to his command, scattered themselves behind him. Pelius stood at the fence waiting for his brother and laughed at the strange procession walking from the shed. Their mother and father had risen before the sun to go to their work in the city and brothers had thought themselves alone. They did not know that Nadinia was in the garden, standing with a basket of dew covered greens, watching Tarin as the noisy chickens pecked after the hovering grain. When he saw her there Pelius and sent a sharp thought to his brother and immediately the bucket fell to the ground. Nadinia returned the look with a knowing glance. There was no need for words for all was revealed beyond any explanation.

That morning, the three of them took the goats to graze upon the ridge. Amidst the sound of the falls, they spoke freely of the gifts and Nadinia told them the things she had read in the stars. This news was thrilling as the brothers realized they were not alone in the possession of such strange powers. Nadinia explained to them the danger surrounding their gifts but even as she spoke she realized how difficult it would be for the boys to truly understand her warnings. Their perceptions of any dark spirit were innocent. Such cruelty could be easily dismissed by their open minds as if it were no more than an ugly daydream. To them the shadow was a powerless vapor, effortlessly replaced by the sight of a butterfly wing, a bright ray of sun, or the sound of gray, green sea. In this childish view there was little ability to understand how far into to the depths of malice the shadow would sink. Neither could know how such a shadow could, over a lifetime, slowly choke the wonder from a mind leaving it hollow and without imagination. As she spoke in that misty morning, Nadinia became aware that the long awaited conversation was known to the awful force and the threat grew as the day passed.

When evening finally drew the curtain upon the day's work Nadinia took Tarin aside. She showed him the book of names that she had kept hidden in the floorboards of her chamber and spoke to him in the ancient tongue of fairy folk. The elder language relit his memories of the lives that had come before. He understood who he was and he took the book of names from his grandmother and kept it as his own. Looking through the window he sensed them coming over the moonlit field. The faded shadows were creeping slowly toward the small house and their icky malice spread black upon the ground. Nadinia followed his gaze and acknowledged the wraiths. A silent embrace was the last touch they shared and Tarin knew he must run if they were to survive and run he did. He went first to Pelius, startling him from sleep while the goat barn outside his window leapt into flame. Their father rose from his bed, suddenly aware of the danger surrounding them, and their mother followed after him. The animals screamed as the flames took the roof and the fiery splinters fell to the ground. Tarin took Pelius by the hand and they slipped under the floor to the cellar hole. The smell of fresh fire was everywhere as the heavy footsteps echoed above them. The evil was there. Huddling close in the low basement the Gift revealed the way to escape. Together they pressed the bulkhead door and when it burst open they realized no one was watching. The same shadows that had veiled the attackers was now protecting them from notice. They helped each other from the tight space as the flames painted the nightmare world in shards of light and dark. Then they ran. They ran with a speed that can only occur in times of dire need and when they reached the hedgerow they turned to look back at the devastation which lay behind them. What they saw surprised them for the shades that assailed them seemed oddly human under their long robes and hooded masks. Through the smoke and shadow they witnessed as the gray shades pulled the tiny Nadinia from the burning cottage. They watched as they shook her fragile frame and then, with a hard blow to the head, Nadinia crumbled to the ground. Pelius leapt up to fight the hopeless battle but Tarin had held his shoulder. The stars had whispered in his ear that their battle waited for another day. The helplessness raged bright but there was no more that they could do. She had given them their lives. It was a bitter pill. They turned their faces away and ran to the safety of the ridge.

Swiftly their young feet carried them away from the blistering fire. They raced to the mountainside where their goats just that morning had peacefully grazed. In the glare of the terrifying present the brothers lay awake in the cold air and the night passed slowly by. The morning came and the vivid moments of the waking nightmare clung to the new dawn. Pelius crawled to the edge of the path where he vomited the remains of his last meal. Tarin sat near him and wiped his forehead.

"We cannot stay here." he said. "They will come for us."

And so it was, the brothers left their fathers land to find a place to hide the secrets that grew within them. Tarin showed Pelius the names their grandmother had written in the book. He told him of the others who faced the same peril; explaining to his terrified brother that the shadows would seek to destroy them and their families as well. Pelius was filled with horror by the news. The names of the children ran through his mind and he could hear their voices calling out for his help but there was nothing he could do. The hideous strength of the shadow had left him powerless. The grim visions would him no rest and wild images would come upon him by day and night. With his Gift was no longer at his command, Pelius would cry out in his sleep and weep in the light of the sun. Tarin waited for him as he healed. His patience never faltered for he knew Pelius as he truly was and recognized that only time was needed for him reconcile from within. The weeks passed into months until finally Tarin's kindness began to restore his mind and as the storm moved away from his heart Pelius recalled the day of his first smile.

The forest was pale with the green newness of the spring leaves. White was clinging tenaciously by its withered threads to the vines above. They had camped under a crude shelter. It was becoming easier to fill their bellies as the sun warmed the ground. A stolen pot hung above flames steaming with aroma of spring onions and fresh rabbit. Life stirred everywhere as he tended the cooking fire that morning Tarin had gone to the stream as Pelius stirred the broth wishing again for salt. It was a taste he had long ago grown accustomed too but now it was far too dangerous to acquire. Above him a young squirrel chattered noisily and when he looked up to see what was the matter a nut struck him square in the center of his forehead. He stood up then, shocked at the boldness of the small creature and the squirrel raced up and down the narrow branch and aiming another nut, the beast struck Pelius upon the bridge of his nose.

"Ouch" he shouted rubbing his sore face. "What is the matter with you?" The squirrel dug its legs into the branch and hanging upside down it scolded Pelius again. Then it turned suddenly and in a rage it ran down the truck of the tree. Through the creature was small, Pelius felt its fury pass through him and he jumped away and then he saw why the creature had become so enraged. On a patch of hard ground a young squirrel lie still. Pelius looked up and noticed the large nest above him. It seemed that the babe had fallen. The mother now waited at the base of the tree daring the boy to come any closer. He looked at her and said silently, "I shall do you no harm." and the animal stopped her chatter and stared at the boy. After a long moment the creature moved to the first limb of the tree. It seemed her permission for him to approach was granted. Pelius bent over the still body and as he reached out his hand the small eye sprang open. The little beast rose unsteadily to its feet and called out for its mother. She answered him and the trembling baby climbed the tree.

"Steady." said Pelius in his thoughts sending a healing wave through the air and the young squirrel stood swaying alongside his mother on the branch just over him. The creatures rested for another brief moment until finally the squirrels scampered upward to the nest high above.

"Pelius. " Tarin called out to his brother. He had been watching from the glade. Pelius turned and smiled as Tarin ran toward him, "Pelius, you spoke to them." Pelius looked up to where the squirrels had hidden themselves among the branches as he realized he had allowed the Gift to touch him once again. The link with its powerful presence had been sorely missed. He turned to face the sun. The warmth touched his face and he knew he would heal from the bitter stroke the shadows had placed in his heart.

That night, as the stars burned in the sky, the brothers made plans to return to the city. They would seek out those whose names were written within the Nadinia's book. They knew they must protect those who needed them the most. It was after this the scouting missions began and as their gifts guided them to be in the proper places at the proper times they discovered they could watch the ones who watched the Tahmurath. One by one, the brothers salvaged the children from the hands of the shadow which sought to destroy the hybrids. They helped the young ones reconstruct their worlds, understanding all to well the sorrow of leaving a home and family in ruin. The little band grew strong and before many seasons had past all they became ready survivors in the wilderness around the city.

Pelius and Tarin drew closer as their powers continued to develop. They helped each other realize the broad nature of their capabilities. They began to understand their weaknesses as well as their strengths and saw that both were complimentary aspects of their natures. Tarin found how easily he could connect his mind to the movement of stars and through the spattered confusion of the night sky he could see the order and harmony. When he reached his thirteenth year, and began to become a man, his far vision once more increased. His youthful mind was pulled far from the nature of the physical realms and Pelius remembered growing angry at his brother. Tarin's focus seemed perilously detached from the waking world as the boundaries of his reality now lay deep into the spaces of the night sky. It seemed to Pelius it was more difficult for Tarin to balance the exactness needed in the dangerous rescues. Tarin could now reach a place where he could no longer follow and as he traveled in these spheres unknown he would leave Pelius by himself to piece together the duties they had once shared. But even with this new turn the brothers remained close and when Tarin spoke, his words would always ring true. Nonetheless, Pelius was more acutely aware than ever of the physical world. He sensed their tasks had grown more dangerous and the shadow groped through the night airs more desperately than ever to destroy them. Pelius wondered if Tarin considered the dangers at all. It seemed the visions that Tarin now held swallowed up the shadow, making its presence but a minor detail.

He had been troubled the night they watched the dwelling of the red-haired twins. For several weeks they had made their plans for their difficult rescue and the shadows were on the move, appearing again just as the twilight set. Still as stone through the long night the boys remained unnoticed as the shadows waited for the opportunity to steal the two children. Their long gray robes and hoods wavered in dim alleys as they observed the comings and goings of the household. These babes were the last names which Nadinia had had the opportunity to write in her precious book. Pelius was torn with new uncertainties. The bond between his brother and himself was changing into a thing he did not understand. The danger crawled like an insect over his skin.

It was an unusual house, made of pale bricks, and its long windows were filled with thick green glass. The building was one of the oldest structures in Tessera. It had weathered many storms and known many uses. Since their fathers time the old place was used as a travelers Inn, selling rooms and ale. Its narrow porches jutted from the main room that looked over the sea. Upon the highest roof stood a covered lookout point and on that peak appeared the symbol of the circled arms. Over the years, the home had fallen into disrepair. The paint of the casements had long worn away and many of sharp roofs were now covered in a thick green moss and this evening the broken shutters swung precariously in the wind.

The twins lived in this run-down hostel with a distant aunt. Though it was home to them, to the others that lived within its noisy walls, it was a brief stop along the way to some other place. Noise, clatter, and music spilled from its open doors and it was difficult for them to remain still. The brothers were accustomed to the quiet ways of the wood and this tavern house was rarely silent.

Outside, upon the open porches, several fisherman sat smoking pipes and talking of the days work. Inside a fiddle played, while the rich aroma of the late evening meal filled the air. The twins, unnoticed and on their own, jumped from the porch railing into the dusty street below. Laughing happily in the late twilight hours the children did as they pleased for rarely was there anyone to tend them. Their sweaty hair was stuck fast to their heads and the grime was smeared their cheeks.

Pelius ached from the long nights he had spent crouched among the kegs of ale. His head reeled with the stench and his mouth longed for the taste of clean water. He knew tonight would be the one the shadows would choose to act. The moon burned wide in the sky. Its reflected light was touching an ancient cross and it shown like a cold beacon above his head. He was agitated as the night crept slowly on and in the blackest moment, when the moon slipped behind a cloud, and he saw the shades move upon the house. The shadows approached the pale light of the open door. In the meeting room the fiddler still played a slow song and near him a fisherman lay with his head upon the table, a thin pool of ale swimming through his hair. In the corner, a couple sat sleeping in a long chair, intertwined in the flickering darkness of the candlelight. The old aunt was sipping a steaming cup of tea at the bar surveying the room. She sighed aloud for the hour was late and she still had much work to do. A barmaid wiped the long counter. A broken pitcher lay along the blemished floor. An old man sat alone playing a solitary game of cards, his image reflected in the shiny darkness of the window behind him. The fiddler played the song just for himself and the room smelled. She frowned when her eyes finally rested upon the twins. They slept huddled under the stained cloak of the drunken fisherman on a couch facing the wall. She rose to fetch them and carry them to their beds. She wished there was more time; more silver; more quiet; more of herself, to care for them in the ways that would better fitting for such lovely creatures. She climbed the stair, carrying Mora to her bed, and her tired eyes widened when she found Tarin standing before her. With his subtle gift he placed in her mind the image of what lie ahead and she glimpsed the moments soon to be. She realized that this boy had been speaking to her in her dreams and her time for this world was short. Tarin took the little daughter from her arms and whispered a blessing in her ear just as the old aunt saw the shadow passing the windows of the porch. Pelius crept down the stairs and roused her brother, Mikel. The time to move was now. Using the power planted by the shadow itself they disappeared into the cover of the darkness. They knew the point of invisibility within the web and they vanished into the night. In and out of view they appeared, traveling upon the unseen threads they moved swiftly to the third floor of the inn. There they reached window which faced the forest cliffs. Opening the casement, they climbed upon a low roof and saw the flames glow beneath them. The hooded monsters had begun their work. The children's eyes were glazed with fear as their rescuers helped them from the porch roofs to the refuse covered alley. Mora glanced around the unfamiliar streets and Pelius touched her shoulder pointing toward the mountains. The little feet followed him as shouts for help began fill the night air. The fire had spread to the sleeping quarters of the guests. The children raced down the alley, intending to leave an uncertain trail for their deadly pursuers. Their aim was to mislead the shadows, hoping they would think the prey had perished in the flames. The city began to wake to the cries of those trapped by the fire. Mora stumbled upon the rocky street and Tarin bent to help as shadows darkened his way and he looked up to find the pursuers facing him. Three hooded forms stood like giants before them and the boys wavered as a gleam flashed from the folds of their robes. The force of life surged through their veins and they fought the shadows with the fierce grace that can only come when the promise of death stands before you. But even with strength unnatural, the overwhelming size of the men soon began to overcome them. Mikel raised his small arms causing a hanging sign to snap from its chain and strike one of the men upon the head. His hood fell from his face and the man lay still on the ground. Mora moved her hands and as she did a heavy barrel fell over. It turned upon its side and began to spin wildly. It slammed against the hooded shade and brought him to the ground. He was motionless then with his back crushed against a wall. But from the darkness another wraith leapt upon them and with a cruel hand it seized the little girl. Pelius leaped into the air and kicked into the back of the hood. The shadow turned from the child and clutched Pelius by the neck in an iron grasp. The world turned dark as the shadow hand crushed his throat and in his fading sight he saw Tarin leap upon the attacker. Pelius felt the grip loosen and he struggled to his feet. He saw the gleam of the knife just as the shade covered his brother. Picking up the broken leg of the fallen sign, he stuck the robe and the man moved no more. In the next instant, Tarin was beside him and grabbing the little ones they ran. And they did not stop until they reached the safety of the trees.

Under the cover of the forest they found the others

waiting for them. A hush of relief rustled through the orphan band as the rescuers arrived. Pelius let Mikel's hand go as the others gathered round offering sips of cool water. The twins were the last names Nadinia had written in the book and now they could leave the danger of the city to make a new home further into the mountains. Here, they would not have to face the menace of shadow again. These thoughts of relief poured through him as the dawn begin to rise and he turned to face his brother. Tarin had run the miles from the city and all the way he had carried the child, Mora, upon his back. Up the steep mountain path he had matched Pelius' steps one for one but as Pelius turned to smile the smile of relief he longed to share, his hopes crashed to the ground. Tarin face was pale as a fading moon and he dropped to his knees before him, his blood changing the leaves beneath him slick and black. As the life force drained from his brother, the old anger rushed through him, piercing the wounds of his heart with a sharp new sting. He held him in his arms. The shadow knife had found a mark. Tarin's belly was slit, his insides exposed. How he had run up the path at all Pelius could not understand. The others came and stood helplessly around them for even with all the great powers that lie between them, there was nothing any one of them could do.

"Do not let it cloud what you see with your heart, my brother. The greatest peril will lay within." and as those last words faded forever into the forest their tears fell. It was now Pelius who would lead them. He spoke little in the days after Tarin's death, conserving his strength for the times ahead. His mind burned as he walked through his hours and soon he found the means to guide them amidst his sea of quiet desperation. Nonetheless, he led them all to the safety of the hidden valley. It was warm and food was plentiful. The children joined in an intimate bond with the nature around them. They understood the voices of life they shared and they painted their bodies with the images that poured through the earth. They learned to live from the land taking only the lives that they needed to survive. The birds and furry creatures became a part of them and the beasts taught them the lessons of the wild lands which lay high above the city.

Arcus and Aleryn listened to all he said and they learned many things they did not know before. It was painfully clear that the people suffered and those who lived behind the castle walls had been blind to their plight.

CHAPTER NINE
THE PIERCING OF THE MIST

Ten days had passed since Tristus had felt land beneath him and he turned toward shore to seek a place to fill his water skins. Never before had he traveled so far from home and he was anxious to know what sights the northern landscape held. After several hours the rocky tips of the Apennines, looming like titans over the impassable cliffs, came into view. As he drew closer to the beach he noticed a shift in the wind and in moments the air was filled with an unbearable reek. The scent of death settled upon his clothes and he looked ahead hoping to see the source. The stink become stronger as he made his way along and when he rounded a sharp bend along the cliffs he beheld the reason for the stench.

Upon the beach lay the contorted bodies of a large group of whales. Tristus moored his boat close to shore and walked through the cold water covering his face with his cloak. The creatures were bloated and scattered among them were dozen upon dozen of smaller fish. Sand rattled in the heavy air as he walked slowly around their swelling remains. The smooth skin of the giant beasts had begun to twist as it dried in the beating wind. Their mouths hung open and the small eyes were squeezed shut as if the dying had been painful. The largest of the creatures was twenty lengths his own body. Passing his hands gently over the strange rubbery skin he studied the creatures carefully, looking for signs of wounding.

Whales were never harmed by the fisherman of Tessera. They knew them to be intelligent creatures that maintained a social order of their own and the realms of their watery kingdom were respected by all his people.

"What killed has these beasts?" he said aloud as shock gave way to anger and he remembered the many times the creatures had guided him home under twilight skies. His tears fell as he counted the dead.

Thirteen whales lay scattered in rotting heaps. Looking about his feet, Tristus picked up one of the dead fish and found an oozing sore running along its belly. He took his knife and cut deep into the scaly underside. Carefully he pulled back the meat to inspect what lie within the smelly gut. He knelt down and spread the carcass upon a rock and he did not notice the speckled foam reaching around him. He muttered as the dampness soaked through his clothes and he got up and moved further up the beach. His legs began to burn as he walked. Looking down he saw foaming piles of froth hissed upon the sands. He laid the fish upon a stone and walked away from the water until he reached the deep sand. There he removed his boots and scrubbed his legs with the dry grains. It seemed to sooth the burn but where the water had touched him his skin had begun to raise in red welts. He walked along the ridges searching for fresh water and soon he found a spring spilling from a crack over his head. He washed and washed again under the clean trickle and when the sting finally eased he returned to the fish he had left upon the stone. Careful not to touch the carcass he lifted the body on a bed of leaves and he sat down to continue his inspection. Meticulously slicing the underbelly he pulled apart the air bladder to see a shining film stuck to the interior of the fish. He cut the along the stomach tissue and found it filled with crystalline grains. He pressed one of the grains with the tip of his blade.

A poisoning, he considered looking again over the bodies as they lay still in meandering pattern of red foam. The design told him that the tide had brought the stain to the shore. Then his eye caught the dark shape of a fishing vessel moving across the long sky. The implications stunned him. Tristus sat among the dead, his eyes stinging from the smell of decaying bodies and realized a poisoned sea would touch every aspect of the lives of his people. A trolling vessel moved north through the tossing waves and he knew they searched for the very fish that lay dead at his feet.

The seaman of Tessera were a grim folk and the years of harvesting the sea had hardened them. Among the fisherman, there were only a few Captains who would be willing to take their boats this far from home and those who did come this way hoped to fill their nets with uncommon fare that would bring them a higher profit in marketplace. He closed his eyes and brought to mind the familiar picture of the crowded ports. He could see the wagons pressing into the narrow streets heading to the docks and ships of varied shapes and sizes cluttering the bay. White sails filled like billowing clouds would skim across the waters carrying their cargoes out and back from the deep ocean. The sound and smell of the seafarer's life was a part of the fiber of his body and it seemed he heard the distant call of the tower bells in his mind. The sound brought with it the other waking dreams. He opened his eyes and remembered the mood of the kingdom. Such a helpless indifference now plagued his people and he perceived the shadow as stealing their spirit to change their lots. He pushed the thought away, refusing to dwell upon the possibilities such indifference might bring. The people would need proof it they were to realize that dangers lurked so far from home and he began to gather brush from the back of the cove. He dragged sticks and cut green limbs and with bits of wood and cones, dried grass, pieces of saltwood, he prepared to set a fire. When he had finished gathering and setting the fuel under the greater beasts he pulled the smaller fish away from the whales and placed them in a pile further down the beach. All the morning and though the noon meal he worked and the shadows had grown long before he was content with his store. He took out his flint stone and soon had set a blaze upon the shore. He knew that within the body of each whale vast stores of oil were hidden and the fire would burn strong through the night and continue on for days. The oily smoke would be seen for miles and he held hope that the seamen would be turn their ships back toward home as the sun began to set.

"Certainly any prudent Captain would send a craft to investigate the burning shore." he thought and when he was well assured that the flames would not fail he sank to his knees and called to the dead beasts.

> *May your life return to the source of all,*
> *And your form befit the giving ground,*
> *And may you know the face forgotten,*
> *As you hear the thrice loved sound.*
> *In flames reveale,.*
> *In flames destroyed,*
> *Each heart's song to revere.*
> *The radiant one just beyond the door,*
> *For now its touch draws near.*

The blaze leapt higher, taking strength from his words, as far out to the northwest a ship headed swiftly to the south. Slipping from the cove, Tristus set a wish upon the wisps of smoke that seamen would find the bodies. In the lengthening shadows the fire stretched behind him and he walked at a hard pace. Hastily he returned to his boat and he moved the craft to the next cove. He found a minor fissure along the stones and pulled the vessel from view. He would wait through the night, leaving the others to draw their own conclusions from the grisly scene. His mood was gray as the evening obscured his view of the sea. He felt no hunger. His stomach was still tight from the memory of the dead and his hands were raw from the contact with the scummy waters. The thread of smoke rose high above the cliffs in the twilight sky and he began to search for a place to pass the night. He heard the rustle of birds settling in to sleep among the brackish pines. The moon left a silvery trail upon the waters and first stars began to pierce the darkening sky when he finally closed his eyes to sleep.

There was no sun when he woke. The gray dawn clutched his clothing with its damp fingers. Rising stiffly from his sleeping spot, he mechanically prepared his breakfast and he ate without realizing the food had passed over his lips. Splashing a handful of water upon his face, he slung the pack over his shoulder and went to see if his signal fire had done its work. He climbed along the uneven ridge and within a few moments he came to the edge of the cliff. To his relief, he could see a fishing vessel waited close to shore. The ship's flag bore the sign of Black Tower and the Rising Sun and her sailors walked along the beach studying the dead. He sat down and watched the sailors as they worked hoping that other news of this strange malady would help him forewarn the city. He would wait until this ship sailed and then he would turn his own boat around and follow them back to Tessera. The responsibilities of the Kingdom hung heavy over him and he felt he must return to uphold his duties to the realm.

The morning was still young when the fishing boat pulled its anchor and headed to the south. He watched its departure from his secluded vantage point and then returned to his own craft and slowly made preparations to leave. He took his time and packed the hull carefully. He had no need to hurry for he wanted the fishing boat have a fair head-start. Skillfully he maneuvered the vessel in the gray gloom. The sun had ceased to cast a shadow and he rode upon the choppy waves becoming more and more wary of the weather. Many unsettled hours had passed when Tristus first caught sight of a black gull circling above him. The bird would dive repeatedly behind the misty cliffs and return moments later to circle overhead again. Occasionally its harsh screech would reach his ears. The sound troubled him. The bird moved closer in the dismal sky tightening its circles with every passing turn. The gray sky was changing quickly into a dark gloom. A hard wind rushed noisily across the surface of the water and at its heels roared the angry drone of the sea. The wind began to come upon him in vigorous gusts. Fistfuls of icy rain pelted the water and Tristus looked up to see that the sails were freezing as he watched. He went to the ropes, hoping to free them before they became to set, but the storm pulled the lines from his hands. Clinging desperately to the ship he heard the mast snap overhead. Wind and water rose as a single beast and began to crash over him in violent surges. He fought the gale with all strength he had to give. Hour after hour passed but the storm showed no sign of relenting and when the dark night began to consume the day his body began to fail him. Blinded by driving rain yet another massive wave crashed upon the deck and his grip on the rail was lost. His feet were pulled from underneath him and, in an instant, he found himself pressed under the frigid waters. Stunned and disoriented, he did not know which way the surface lie and the moments of his life passed before him.

He came back to himself upon a quiet beach and with a great effort he climbed to his feet struggling to find a place out of the ocean wind. Exhausted, he pulled his heavy boots along the gritty shore. The morning breeze tore through his clothing and his skin burned with cold until the fading dawn was fractured by yellow sun. The new light offered Tristus a promise of warmth and he found the strength to climb from the sand and up unto a low ridge. Hanging his wet cloak upon a low branch, he rested on the warming rock realizing how dreadfully weak he had become and wondering how far had he been pulled off course. The sounds of the surf filled him with desperation. His motives for entering the lonely wilderness now seemed empty and doubt crept into his heart. Confused thoughts spun as exhaustion and pain allowed neither sleep nor awareness. After a time he realized he heard the sound of falling water. He looked around to see that a stream spilled from the cliff several dozen feet away. The falling water had done its work well, as the years had passed by, leaving a series of small pools that dropped down from the jagged edges above. He drank from the fountain for a long time and when he had finished he climbed upon the next ledge just above. On the beach ahead lay the shattered remains of his boat and he scrambled over the rock to reach it.

The little craft was no more than a broken shell, a great hole rent in its belly, and all that was left of the mast was a shattered stump. Tattered bits of sail clung to the splintered wood as climbed aboard, holding hopes that some of his supplies would still be there and, to his great relief, he found them still safe deep within the hull. Tristus changed his wet clothes and put a few other necessities in his pack. Gathering his fishing gear, a sword, and his climbing belt he laid them upon the shore. He started a fire on the beach and, wrapping a blanket around him, he rummaged through his pack. At the bottom he found a sheet of travelers bread and several bits of dried fruit. He sat close to the flames as he ate, arranging his belongings.

He could not be certain what signaled the danger but without hesitation he responded to the inner call. He put out his fire and left the exposed shore to hide in the grassy dunes. Crouching low he crept to the back of the bay and, there he waited, wondering at his sense of apprehension. It was not long before he noticed another stream struggling its way toward the sea and he followed the trickle back to a large, jagged crack. Tristus looked briefly back at the white caps tossing over the water and then he turned away from the sea to enter the small split within the rock. His clothes were soon covered in dust for the crack was tight and he had to use his legs to press against either side of the narrow ravine. Straddling the break, his strong hands held firmly to the ridged cleft and he made his way through the crevice like a spider scrabbling along a petrified web. After a short time his foot scraped against something sharp. Tristus slipped down a bit and strained his neck to examine the thing. An odd metal shape was half buried in a cleft of the grimy soil. The queer piece was stuck fast in the side of the gully. It was a dull gray and rust had begun to crawl upon it and Tristus began to search the ravine for more metal pieces.

Among the scrubby brambles were broken bits of machinery and as he went on the gap soon widened. He scrabbled up the crumbling sides of the gulch, maneuvering his body carefully through the stones and then he noticed a foul smell around him. It was not the smell of rotting flesh but a more metallic scent. The odor burned his eyes and left an unpleasant sensation upon his tongue. Looking down at the shallow water at the bottom of the crevice he saw the stream was now parted by a red vein of foam. The putrid scum was the same as he had seen the day before.

"It's not working and someone will pay the price for it."

Tristus stumbled in surprise as the harsh voice rang out above him. Gripping desperately to the sides of the gulch he pressed himself behind a dry bush. So many days he had spent free from the sound of people and the foreign tone cut through him like a knife. Barely covered by the scrubby branches he huddled beneath the tangled underbrush and listened to the conversation going on above.

"It will have to be taken apart again." said another man, "They are none to happy with these failures." Pieces of heavy metal crashed down the slopes, barely missing Tristus in his hiding place.

"It is less than a fortnight before they want them ready" said the other, "the mines are working day and night. Many men are dying."

"Do not let anyone hear you," said the first voice "You will come to a quick end if they do."

"They do not come here and dirty their hands with this work." said the other uneasily. "It's messy. They prefer to watch as long as their whips are close in hand."

"But their spies." added the other.

"Yes. We must hurry. They will notice us if we stay

away too long."

Another loud crash resounded through the gully and more fragments of machinery bounced past Tristus' hiding place. Their voices faded away as the last piece hit the base of the ditch. Cautiously he looked between the branches to see what direction they had taken. Climbing up the sides of the ravine he was careful to keep himself hid under what sparse cover he could find. When he finally reached the top, he slid upon his belly to the shelter of a fir tree and pushing himself up its branches he found a better view.

He was in a jagged gulch. The lonely fir was the only green thing and it afforded him only minor protection. Its base was littered with many discarded parts of odd metal debris and the dry ground was filled with patches of dead grass. He looked toward the path the men had taken and saw a dusty lane running between two spires of black stone. It appeared that these natural formations marked the way into a larger canyon. The velvet shadow which hung between them stood as a black curtain in the sullen sky. He turned behind him and could see nothing but the barrier wall which separated this fractured landscape from the sea. He climbed down the tree and approached the guardian spires. Straight cliffs surrounded the gulch and bleeding from a stone above red stream flowed. He followed the trickle down the face of the wall until he located a puddle of red ooze trapped between two stones. He reached down to stir the muck with a broken twig. It had a peculiar odor. He let the stick drop from his fingers and he walked into the shadow between the tall stones.

He waited a moment, allowing the darkness to fade, and soon he was able see a canyon cutting away sharply to the north. An uneven stair had been carved into its sides and it rose up into a nearly vertical slope. He listened carefully to the treacherous dark, making sure no others were near. A sheer drop lay at his feet and just beyond the trail, filtered rays of light barely lit the crumbling stairs. Cautiously Tristus followed the path through the deep rift and in moments his view widened into a different scene. A long valley now lay before him, bordered by icy mountains, but what had once been majestic was now defiled. Drear buildings dotted the floor of the bleak landscape and large smokestacks rose from tall warehouses. The stacks were covered with metal caps and rising gas belched into long piping that led away to the river. At the mouth of the channel, a red steam of upset water gushed from the hole. The strange city was alive with motion. Men walked between the buildings attending to their tasks and upon the mountainsides he saw many more pushing carts along the narrow ledges. The steep cliffs were riddled with holes and the mines extended along the whole length of the canyon. Tristus knew instantly what they were.

These were massive atricault mines and the structures along the river bed were the foundries that prepared the amalgam for use. Tristus took a greater chance and climbed higher still. Thin arms of metal spanned the valley and men and material moved back and forth along them. The sides of the mountains were covered level after level of uneven scaffolding. Stream rose from the mouths of massive vats touching the bridges. Tristus knew the mining process well. After the ore was refined the melted sludge would be allowed to combine with other metals to produce the atricault amalgam but even after this blending had taken place the atricault mixture could not be allowed to cool until it was ready to be shaped.

The operation was far larger than anything he had ever seen before. The metal buildings showed signs of weathering and the wooden barracks were gray with age. The years of toil were well marked by the awesome piles of refuse. The great cylindrical vats stood amongst vast heaps of garbage. Men laden with large baskets moved up and down the ladders and ledges. He looked closer. These workers were not the people of Tessera but the island people of the south.

"They are slaves." he muttered, realizing the rumors whispered in the marketplace were true and for the remainder of the day Tristus forgot himself. At the risk of being discovered he crept slowly toward the boundary of the camp. Just as he reached the outskirts of the mining city, he passed an area where tall posts were buried deep into the ground. The posts were smooth excepting a large iron ring embedded near the top of each member. He crouched low making his way cautiously by the barren place until he heard a stirring above him. He looked up to see a man hanging upon the stake. His face was pressed flat against the wood and the dark skin of his back was rent. Welts of shredded skin oozed from under black scabs and his long hair was matted in the bloody scabs. He groaned and he called out in the strange language. Tristus went to him and spoke a greeting in the common tongue. The man was raised up high upon the tall stake with his arms fully extended above him. His hands were tied with thin leather strips and his knees were bloody. Tristus could not reach him to give him water nor could he set him free. In the refuse, he searched and soon found a discarded metal rod. Tristus tore his shirt and tied the rag to its end. He moistened the tip with water and raised it to the man's lips pressing the wet cloth into his mouth. The man tasted the water and he closed his eyes. He did not stir again. Tristus looked out at the field of tall poles realizing they were sentinels of death. There was no voice of justice that echoed over the silent ground and he wondered of the man and his family. Using the thin shadows of the killing stakes he hid himself as best he could and slipped closer to the complex.

Evil thoughts poured into his mind as he passed by the steaming stone cylinders. "Why is the need of this metal so great?" he asked the Airs, looking upon the legions men who toiled along the slopes. But the indifferent blue sky only taunted him as it hung above the ruination and, for the first time in years, he wished to return home.

"I have been a blind man." he thought coldly as he turned and passed back through the death field.

"If I had paid more heed to my people this could not have happened." Dark thoughts raced through him and his stomach lurched as he passed the man now who now hung stiffly from the stake. Despair and anger poured through his gut and its wrath gave him new strength. Entering the blackness of the stone gully he climbed the stairs into the entrance of the cave and he made his way swiftly through the black channel of stone. Passing by the lonely tree, which marked the way to the gulch, he descended the gully and returned to the beach just behind the grassy dunes. In the setting rays of the sun he followed the poison stream which flowed to the sea. Among the dunes, he found more evidence of the rancid muck as it crawled through the marshes. The greasy pools ringed the sand and islands of caustic foam swirled among the waves. He watched the water release and pull as the foam crashed against the shore. Silver flashes caught Tristus' eye as the waves returned to the waiting sea and in their wake tossed the dead bodies of a silvery fish. Tristus now understood the cause of their death. Deep in thought, he walked over the thick dunes to trip over a rotting heron. The creature lie contorted between tufts of sea grasses. Yellow grains of debris sealed the eyes of the dead bird. The shriveled legs stunk and its bloated belly was tight from the heat of the sun. A few steps away, its eggs lay forgotten in a bowl of sand. He walked on, realizing the poison touched, land and sea; man and beast. The light was fading as he searched for a safe place to pass the night knowing somehow he must return home at first light. He would find a way back to Tessera and tell the folk of this awful place where poison poured into their life blood, the precious sea.

He walked slower now as the last shadow of sun slipped under the waves. His anger was ebbing away to leave him exhausted. The night closed around him and he attempted to rekindle the heated wrath that had driven him through the afternoon but another type of clarity was now settling upon him. His fury had failed and a new door opened in his tired mind. He was himself once more, cynical and bereft of all his passion. He struggled against the tasteless reality remembering the final breath of the dying slave, alone and un-championed in a sea of pain; what knowledge could be more devastating than a poison which steals the life from the giving sea; what crime more disheartening than the ruined face of the majestic mountainside. But the voice of the unerring logic blotted these things from his mind. The folk of Tessera would find it far too difficult to heed his words. The ancient nation had grown numb. Dulled by oppression, any change they would not be willing, or unable, to see. The chill of quiet desperation swept around him and he perceived his people as but pawns in greater trials they did not yet understand.

The landscape wilted into sickening night. The day was done and Tristus no longer knew his path. Exhausted, he could walk no further. Disheartened, he could think no more. Alone under the invisible moon, he took no cover but lay exposed upon the sand. He closed his eyes and he drifted into a fitful place where no faith did dwell.

The sun was above him. As is its noble custom it had risen releasing again the burden of night. Tristus stirred from a place more real than waking or sleep. The woman who rode the roan horse had been whispering in his dreams. Her scent lingered on his skin as he rose from his bed of sand. He was washed clean by her memory and he saw things in a new light. Through her eyes had appeared realms far beyond the world he knew and those distant stars had touched faint memories inside him. He felt his mind clear and his emotions steady.

"And what is the answer?" he asked to the waiting sky. The indiscretions of men were not novel affairs. The errors of humanity were as common as blades of grass. The sky gave no answer but still he knew; the answer lay in the freedom to choose it. The wind stirred around him and the shifting light caught his eye.

"Follow me." the wind told him plainly now and he had no doubt as to what he must do. He understood the folk of Tessera were the fortunate ones and, regardless of their faults, they were still a free people, able to make their own choices. Choices they would live by; be they right or wrong. The information he sought did not lie in the realms of courtly ceremony but instead it waited for him at the Wall of Mist. He looked upon the silver thread of sand which separated the land and the sea and turning his face to the north he left his city behind.

He traveled at a hard pace for more than a week. The pounding surf filled his ears as his skin darkened in the low hanging sun. He could see nor hear no sign of man and he no longer found evidence of fish kills. Making his way north, always expecting the chill of winter, he found instead the weather was comfortable and food was plentiful. With each step his heart lightened as the death he witnessed had along the desolate beaches and in the killing fields of the mines faded into the indefinable hope. Deep in private thoughts, he traveled the winding silver ribbon that marked his way.

Wet, gritty, boulders had left no path to walk upon the beach. The tide reached in, forming pools around the stony bones buried in the sands. His sore muscles complained as he jumped and scuffled along the rocky beach. At last he reached the promontory which formed a barrier blocking the next bay. Its sides were sheer as glass and his only choice was to enter the water. The tide crashed fiercely against the barrier wall. He slipped into the green waters and he moved carefully from one slab to the next, blocking himself the best he could as the constant swells as they crashed to shore. He was a strong swimmer but the sea took its toll upon him and he struggled in the surf. Exhausted and weak, he finally rounded the tip to set foot upon the shore again.

The cliffs upon this shore were massive. Their ebony faces gleamed against the fluid sky. His senses seemed sharpened as the wind wrapped itself around him and from far across the waters swells he could see a stand of trees high upon the rising headland ahead. A flash of light broke the stillness. His eyes followed the beam as it streaked across the water, leading his gaze to the towering cliffs. He refocused his eyes and saw her. For an instant it seemed she was directly before him hovering above the sands but he blinked and she was gone. He found her again standing on the high ridge, her robe rippling in the strong breeze. She raised her arms to greet him; beckoning for him to follow. He took out his ropes and hooks and prepared for the climb. His progress was steady but the way was long and much time past before he reached the crest of the summit. When at last he pulled himself over the edge, he looked up expecting to see the woman waiting for him. Searching the cliff's edge his mind reeled with dismay as he realized she was gone. Bewildered and alone in this soaring place he looked down wondering if it were possible to descend the slope he had just now so willingly climbed and the Voice whispered there was no turning back. So he looked ahead to the forest and found he had a long view through the woods. The first gray limbs hung high over him and green, mossy beds were spread evenly between the massive trunks. The soaring trees reached straight to the heavens and their silver-green canopies were woven into the fractured bits of blue sky. His answers must lie within the deep, shadowy arms and so he walked on into the silent glade. The trees grew more wide apart as he moved away from the sea. Pools of cool light dappled the ground around him but no end to the wood did he see. Desperation swept over him and he started to run. He must find her. Moving swiftly he began to race at a speed he never thought possible. His breath came evenly and efficiently as he glided through the trees. He ran for mile after mile and the woodland stretched endlessly on before him. Faster and faster he went until, at times, it seemed that she was close ahead and finally a glimpse of her robe caught his eye. The woman raced ahead of him. Illuminated by a strange light and she moved at an unnatural speed between the trees. Tristus found he could keep her pace but as he followed behind her she moved still faster. He let his climbing belt drop and soundlessly it fell to the forest floor. He increased his pace again and still she remained far ahead. His terrific gait seemed insignificant for she always remained just out of reach. His pack slipped from his shoulders to be lost somewhere in the endless forest and his sword soon followed; to lie forgotten on the ground. Winding his way among the trees the forest moved behind him and he realized he was ascending yet another massive slope. The trees blurred as he flowed past them and his feet did not touch the ground.

Then she turned. So sudden was her movement, Tristus stumbled and found himself close enough to touch her robe. He reached out and as he did, she vanished. He looked around hardly believing she was gone once more. The scent of the sacred flower hung in the air. He could taste it as he breathed the clear wind. He saw that she had led him to another summit. A vast valley spread before him marked by stiff peaks and rocky crests. Vibrant with the slow breathing of living stone, the mountains loomed miles high ahead of him and beyond those impassable slopes stood the greatest of all barriers. Tristus was before the Wall of Mist. The place of legends, the impenetrable veil which held apart the earth and heaven, now hung like a curtain through the stone and sky. The silver mist reached across the horizon as far as his eye could see. How could he have reached this place so suddenly? How could he have run so far? Where was the woman he sought? But he could not dwell upon these questions, reality had become too fluid. His heart raced and he gasped for breathe, feeling the ground meet his knees as the Mist covered his eyes.

He could not know how long he lay blinded by the fog
as a deep rumbling began to shake the ground. Tristus forced
himself forward. Crawling to the lip of the canyon, the mist
began to clear and he could see a jagged gap that slashed the
earth. Like a wound that could never heal, the earth writhed and
as he watched the motion of the ground intensified. He pulled
himself to his feet, grasping a tree branch he attempted to hold
himself steady as the shaking of the earth increased. Shards of
stone broke away from the mountain faces and dust clouds
churned in the belly of the canyon. The quaking of the world
overwhelmed the land as the deep cries Sister Earth pierced his
head. Mechanically he covered his ears as the valley beneath
him began to churn and groan. The land below became an
undulating pulse. Great clouds of debris rose up, its smoky
fingers climbed from the deep crack and a thundering roar began
to shake the airs around him. He could no longer keep his
footing so he lay down with his face upon the ground. The
thundering cry had changed. It had become a human sound and
it cut the airs like a whip. The land around him was tossing like
water and the groan of the new world shook his body. The noise
of the shuddering ground had been replaced by a curdling
scream. Unnerving and horrible, the sound rattled through his
skin as great walls of earth began to rise from the gorge and the
scream moved through the valley. Blood trickled from his ears
and he lifted his face to behold the source. Through the
ascending haze she appeared; a massive form; a colossal
giantess; a horrible monster; her presence, both hideous and
deafening. More alive than the fire of the molten mountains she
rose from the cracked earth to her full height. Tristus shook in
awe as the face of the Vulcane loomed before him. Her eyes
were filled with the heat and her skin burned a brilliant red. Her
hair moved with fiery sylphs about her shoulders. Radiant with
the heat of living flame, her name rumbled in the bottomless
valley. The strong arms beckoned him though the heated air and
then the woman spoke. The words blazed in the sky and her fire
passed through the boy entering his flesh. The sound had
pierced his breast and the rent became an open door.   In her
hand she carried a sword and lifting the fiery blade above her

head, she struck him where he stood. From the center of the flame, its heat leaped forward into the hollow his breast. She had given the command. His heart was spread wide apart, leaving a mortal wound and he watched as points of light expanded from his body. Concentrated above his head a multi-layered reality formed and starlight poured upon the top of his skull. He found himself connected to something much greater than himself. Rapt with fire, her salamanders lifted him and carried him to her. He stood at her feet in the midst of the flaming river. She was the presence that lived at the foot of the mountain and all around her was the purifying flame. The molten stream was the heat which pours from the nucleus of the earth and as she whispered over his brow and his sense of calm was complete. The Vulcane breathed slowly upon the river of flame and flaming vessel formed around him. The strange boat floated above the searing heat and yet it remained unburned and cool to the touch. Tristus stood upon its bow witnessing the moving picture without thoughts or dreams. He was healed from the wound of her sword and left with but a single riddle to hold too. Its essence was symbol instead of sound and its intention passed through his skin.

"To know purpose; dare not seek land." the voice had whispered, "To know will; remember me." And with that final impression the prince was carried back towards the Kingdom of Tessera.

CHAPTER TEN
THE BIFROST

Tristus opened his eyes and the weathered faces of the sailors slowly appeared before him. They called him by his given name. He tried to answer them but no sound would come. He gazed about for a moment noting the neatness of the ship. The dark wood of the cabin was polished to a bright shine and the green ocean rose and fell gently outside the small, round windows. A cup of water was on his lips. It was cool and he closed his eyes slipping again into a dreamless world.

The Captain stood near the door watching as his men tended their unexpected guest and questions poured into his ordered mind. There was much amiss in his world. It seemed strange happenings were spread about in all directions. They had spotted Tristus, just that morning, slowly drifting in the first rays of the rising sun. His craft glowed silver through the pale violet haze and when he sent his men to investigate, the mystical vessel had moved toward them as if guided by an unseen hands. The men tied the curious boat to their own but such a thing was not necessary for the magical craft followed them on its own accord and when they lifted the boy from the radiant bed the boat broke free of the rope and sank beneath the waves.

The birth marks were unmistakable. The five stars of Tessera were burned black along his brow.

"The boy-Prince of the prophecies." he thought turning the notion over in his mind. "How did this strange youth come to be in these far northern seas, so far from the protection of his castle walls." and as he pondered it the unmistakable impression of magic hung in the air. The atmosphere gave him no peace. He had no place for such musings so he shrugged his shoulders considering prophecies and magical things much better suited for the minds of women. He sighed as he turned to leave. This boy did not match the things he had heard in the marketplace. He did not seem a foolish lad. He seemed instead more gentle and somber. The thin body was badly seared from wind and sun yet the youth was not close to death. The captain looked down at him as he slept wondering what destiny the fates had woven for this unusual traveler. He ordered a light meal and a bottle of wine brought to the young man's bedside. Then the Captain pushed the troublesome reflections away. He had work to do for there was more strange cargo he carried within his hulls so slipping unnoticed through the door he left the prince in the care of his men.

He walked upon the deck. His solid legs were accustomed to the pitch of the sea and the biting air that clung to his beard. Icy spumes rose up to spray the boards beneath him and he grasped the railing and glanced down at his hands. They were in need of a wash. The dark skin upon them was yellowed and cracked. They looked old as they held the balustrade. He raised his eyes to see yet another sun descending under the waters, its bright finger playing upon the choppy waves. He had lost count of his sunsets through the years of working the tough nets and pulling the glistening fish from the sea. He could not say how many evenings had lain themselves down under the ocean as he watched from this familiar deck.   Since he was a young boy he had brought his catch home to the people of the city.   But their numbers had grown high and their demands upon the sea were forever increasing. Tessera was too crowded for his quiet nature and he had responded to the petulant demands of its citizens by taking his vessel far out into the sea; much farther out than most dared to travel. There he would stay for weeks at a time. His crew was ever-changing for most did not wish to go the distances he sought to explore. It seemed his restlessness had grown with the each passing year, and as it did, his treks extended further up the hostile coastline. He would justify his treks as economic to his changing crew but his true reasons were his own. An ache lay inside him as he would watch the churning sea and he would dream of the Wall of Mist. He could demand a high price for his delicacies in the marketplace but he had no need for gold. He needed little more than his ship and the Sister Sea for his journeys were but an excuse for the questions that turned in his mind. He spent his days traveling, successfully avoiding the city. Its scent choked him. The hand of the Haarshaim was everywhere attempting to control each enterprise with threats and payments. The Queen appeared helpless against them. Tessera had become an unwholesome place for an honest man. The crown was only pretense. The people had grown numb with want and now it seemed the sea was tainted as well.

It had been seven days since the Captain had observed the red foam swirling in the waves and he had called for the Bifrost to turn about. When they arrived an acrid smell hung upon the wind. The strange substance clung to the ropes as they made anchor. When the men drew a sample from the water he had reached his arm into the bucket as it raised over the railing. In seconds, the red foam had set his hand afire. Quickly he had cleaned and dressed the welts but the strange burns had left him wondering. He ordered the sample stored in a sealed container until they returned to the city. Later on that day, as the first catch was pulled to the deck, all saw the nets were filled with sick fish. Barely living, the ailing creatures lie languid in the tangled netting. Concern rippled through the men as they studied the catch. The Captain had ordered some of the fish opened and found when its flesh was exposed the same unpleasant odor was released. The men separated the living from the dead as he debated what to do. The cook suggested they feed the remains of the tainted fish to the rats the kitchen staff would catch with their traps. At first the hungry creatures avoided the meal but they waited and watched. It was two days later before the need of food surpassed their caution and that meal proved to be their last, for within the hour, the rats lie dead in their cages.

Among the lobster and squid, the Bifrost now held a store of infected fish. The Captain would return each evening to study the bloody sores that continued to grow upon the bodies of the dead. Shark, tuna, or cod, were all affected by the strange disorder and each day more infected creatures were pulled from the sea. As the days passed most of the catch proved unfit and though the stores were not filled he ordered the ship turned round. Now the Bifrost sailed toward home with its peculiar cargo. Then he remembered the new passenger upon his boat.

He returned to the Prince's cabin feeling the need to check on the boy once more before taking his evening meal. He found Tristus awake sitting upon a stool and looking out the window.

"Good evening Lord." he said with a courteous bow.

"Good evening, Captain." said Tristus slipping from the seat and bowing to his host. "Thank you for your hospitality. It is most appreciated."

"It is freely given. Is there anything you require?"

"No sir, I am at ease."

The captain studied his face. The swath of dark hair covered the five stars and his black eyes reflected the lantern's glow.

"I suppose you wonder how I came to be so far out in this part of the world?" Tristus said softly.

"It is unusual to find any soul adrift in this far north, particularly one of such lineage." answered the Captain.

Tristus nodded, the stars upon his head seemed to crawl upon his sore skin. He felt the weight of his crown.

"I have sought answers Sir, and what I have found is I have only more questions." he replied. " But even as that may be, I have seen things that call for resolution. It is time I return home. "

"That order has been given. Our course is set to Tessera." answered the Captain, "and may the swift wings of the Airs be with us."

Tristus knit his brow and turned to look out the window. Both were quiet as their minds turned over the menacing news that they would bring home."

"Lord," spoke the Captain, "when you are able, I ask you come with me to the stores. I would like you to see the catch we bring back to the city."

Tristus sensed the trouble in his mind and knew instantly what he carried within his hold. "So you have seen the red death that rides on the waves." he replied gravely.

"Yes, we have seen it. It destroys the flesh of the living and the dead." The captain said, a bit surprised that the boy had known his thoughts. "You have seen this as well?"

"There are many strange things I have seen of late." answered Tristus. "And the flesh eating foam is not the least of it."

"This voyage is uncommon in many ways." answered the Captain, looking again to the mark upon Tristus' face. "And while it is true I have never before seen such a bane that I carry now in the ballast, what I find stranger still is the circumstances of your arrival. Granted, it is a bold question sir, but what I saw this morning was like no thing I have ever witnessed before. A magical craft bore you too us. It is only a supernatural hand that could hold death away from any soul drifting through these dangerous waters. And again sir, I shall take great liberties with my questions, but I would like to know why you travel alone, so far from Tessera?"

Tristus was struck sharply by the question. There was much about his odd journey he had not answered for himself and now he was faced with the difficult task of explaining it to someone else. His agitation vexed him.

The Captain perceived his uncertainty, "Sire, do not let my questioning distress you. Eat and drink now. We will talk again later. You are not yet whole from your journey. When you are fit enough to walk I shall show you my ship. And if you chose to do so, you may answer my questions then."

Tristus looked to his host and nodded. "I shall explain sir, when my mind has cleared a bit. I hope you shall find my answers adequate but for now I fear they are not."

"We shall reach the home-port in ten days time. That will give you some opportunity to rest and recuperate. But frankly Prince, I do not understand how you are not in danger of death. Truly it must be the Mark that protects you." he replied with a slight bow, " Call me if there is anything you require." and the Captain left him with his thoughts.

Tristus found that he could neither sleep nor eat. His moments of insight were now brutally contrasted by confusion. Soon he would return to his family where he must tell his story. He knew the knowledge he held would provoke the Guilds and he was certain that their recourse would be ruthless. "But this is not new", he reminded himself, "balance between the Haarshiam and the House of Tessera had always been a struggle." He felt the boat pitch and the motion matched his own waves of distress. The Haarshaim would find it simple to color his words with lies. His voice would be a bland sound in the murk of their deceits and treacheries.

Isolation swept down around him. He would be ridiculed; just as he had always been and the tone of that mocking was a sound he had come to hate. He could say nothing the people of Tessera would want to hear. Just under their sense of awe, he knew well of their fears and loathings. He would worsen this situation; not improve it.

"The strangeling." he muttered to himself, their whispers stinging his thoughts as the ship pitched upon the restless sea. He whispered to the Airs for guidance and the image of the tower flooded into his mind. The dark sentinel of Malthrom stood high above the city, bringing with it the memory the chimers who tread along its narrow steps in the early dawn and dusk. He found his thoughts growing steady and the face of the Vulcane came to his mind leaving him with a new impression of the ancient ritual. The sound of the bells told him the Priestesses did indeed feed the flame of a fading city, keeping the fire alive between land and sky. The echo of ridicule lost its terror as his perspective shifted. He rose from the floor and left his room. He went to find the Captain, unaware that his call had been answered.

The night had stolen the color from the skies as the restless sea carried the vessel forward. Her full sails, ripe as storm clouds, pressed the ship toward home. Small lanterns lit the helm and he saw the Captain standing upon its deck. His steady hands were resting upon the wheel. Tristus went to stand with him. The man acknowledged his presence with a simple nod of his head and they watched the night close deep around them. The Captain called for a larger light to be placed upon the helm of the Bifrost. Its beam sent a strong bright ray over the waters and they traveled swiftly, never slackening their pace. The Captain guided the Bifrost though the night with the Prince of Tessera at his side.

The sun rose and as the darkness was once more banished in its light Tristus felt no need for rest. The Captain led him to the storerooms of the ships hull where, together, they examined the bodies of the dead fish. The bitter smell filled the room permeating the walls with sickness as they studied the bloody sores.

"These blemishes grow even though the fish perished days ago." said the Captain, "It breeds still; slowly consuming its lifeless host."

Tristus' eyes widened. The bloody masses had thickened into calloused welts. The sickness was climbing upon itself to dissolve the dead flesh. Pools of infected liquid seeped through the barrels to stand upon the floor.

"We can take these fish to the healing houses." said Tristus careful of the slippery boards. "Maybe they will understand the nature of the disease. Maybe they know of its cure."

"I have heard tales of this before, sire. Old sailors have spoken of it to my father and I long ago." then he chuckled softly, "But through the years of sailing the seas, I also come to know that what old sailors say must be taken with a grain of salt. They called the blight, *Pyrrohmarin* and they speak of it as if it is a living thing. From what I remember, most all the legends have centered nearer to the warmer parts of the sea. The sailors say a red tide will spread upon the shores when the earth spits fire and the rains are unusually heavy." then the Captain shook his head, "But from what I have been told cold waters do not seem a likely place for the scourge to breed.

Tristus considered his words carefully before he spoke.

"Captain, all places are not cold within the Northern Apennines. There are strange pockets of warmth existing behind the cliffs." then his voice dropped to a whisper, "and I believe that I have seen the blights origin. Far to the north there is a valley and from that riverbed, the red tide makes its way to the ocean."

Turning the fish in his hand, the virulent liquid touched his skin. The place where it touched began to sting. Tristus put the animal back in the vat and watched as the mark swelled to a thin blister.

The Captain shook his head as he gave him a clean, soaked cloth. "Why has it not been seen before?"

"I think the place is intended to be kept hid. Far up the northern cliffs a vast mining camp is concealed behind the mountains. It is a home to many men and I believe many are there against their will."   Tristus answered wiping his hands.

The Captain looked on him with surprise, "I have never, in all my travels through these northern seas, seen any sign of other folk dwelling in these icy waters. Can you be sure? Do you know where this camp is located?"

"I am not certain. A storm carried my boat to the place. I was cast away and I happened upon it by chance. The entrance is hid within a most ordinary shoreline but behind those cliffs are hid the barracks and foundries. The mines within that valley are enormous. Atricault is refined there. It is the vats that constantly heat the amalgam that send the red tide into the waters."

"What is the need of such quantities?" the Captain wondered aloud.

"I do not know this either, Captain. But I do know that my mother has never given leave for such an operation to exist, nor would she ever see fit to do so."

The Captain pondered his words as he ordered the barrels sealed and moved away from the stores of good fish. They left the hull together to walk upon the deck of the ship. The morning was calm and the light wind left a bright chill in the air. Tristus wrapped his cloak around him as he stood looking over the vast sea wondering how much more of his story he should reveal to this good man. The hills and valleys of the ocean floor moved swiftly under the shadow of the Bifrost. Schools of fish passed in shades of light and dark playing over the scene beneath. Then a sudden flash of light caught his eye. He followed the dazzling light and noticed quickly that something moved with them. Keeping pace, the reflection faded in and out of the shifting waters. The Captain was at his elbow and Tristus knew the man had seen the reflection before.

"It is a Thalassisan. He has followed us for days." said the Captain softly. "The deep water is where they bide. It is most unusual to see them in the shallows."

Tristus looked closer to see. It was indeed a man-like creature that followed beneath the waves. The strong upper body was human but his lower self was the form of a fish.

"How effortlessly he moves." thought Tristus leaning slightly over the railing and watching his trident flash in the fleeting bits of sun.

"I had thought they only existed in the tales of old fishwives."

"They are real Lord and have dwelled in the deep waters

for centuries. The one we see beneath us will outlive you and your children's grandchildren. Nonetheless, a glimpse is rare."

"Is he following us?" said Tristus.

"Yes. The scout has been with us for most of a week. Their curiosity concerns me. They do not care for us Prince nor for any creature which walks upon land. They see us as thieves and spoilers who steal from their Sister." answered the Captain. "And if the disease we carry is spreading into their realms,"

"They too may know the death it brings." he finished the thought.

The Captain nodded. Tristus looked again to the mer-man who traveled beneath the ship. Grim and powerful, he kept his pace with the swift vessel and Tristus wondered if there were others of his kind nearby.

"I would like to speak with him." he said.

"He would care not to speak with you, Prince. The time of discourse with the Thalassisans is long past. It was two thousand years ago, when the oceans were stained with blood and not blight that the Thalassisans lost faith in us. The mer-folk moved their underwater cities far from our shores to make their homes where men fear most. They left our realms to dwell closer to the Misty Wall." The Captain paused, staring under the water waiting for another glimpse of the mer-man. The glint of his trident flashed under a beam of sun. "He is leagues from his kingdom now and yet he follows us relentlessly. It is not love that brings him here for they are long-lived and forget little. It seems to me they are concerned."

Tristus' eyes widened. "And if they harken back to the time of the first war, it will be my folk who will be held responsible for this taint."

"Yes Lord, this I fear as well. The Thalassisans are not a gentle folk. "

Tristus shook his head. "What is worse sir, is this assumption is likely founded in truth."

The Captain paused before he spoke. He needed to understand the problems that now pressed into his world so he cast aside his courtly manners and questioned the boy once more.

"I have told you what I know of these strange days" he

said quietly "and finding you, drifting alone upon the coldest waters, is certainly not the least of them. Why are you so far from home, my Lord?"

Tristus looked into the sun-scorched face of the fisherman and knew his grey eyes would recognize truth even if it were hid behind a cloud of lies. In that instant, he chose to trust the man and as he did, he realized he did not know his name. To Tristus' surprise the Captain responded to the silent question,

"My name is Jason, Lord." he answered with a slight bow, "Jason, the only son of Beron and it is Beron's vessel upon which we travel. The <u>Bifrost</u> is her given name. I have cared for this ship and she for me since I was a young boy. She is both a mother and a friend. Five years have passed since Beron went to his rest beyond the Wall of Mist. And now I travel where I chose with such a crew as I can find. I do not have need for much and I have no one to answer too. My mother died in the birthing bed when I came into the world, and my elder sister did not meet her third birthday. But Prince, do not think me a lonely man, for the sea and my ship provide me with greater riches than the most finely dressed Haarshaim who cast their shadows under the Tower of Malthrom.

Tristus saw clearly that this man was not bound by the influence of the Guilds and did not need what they offered to survive. Truly, he was a freeman and Tristus knew he could trust to him the burdens he carried.

"It has been said these stars upon my face mark me as a prophet, but that is not nor has it ever been true. These marks hold a livingness of their own. They bring thoughts into my mind which are not of my own making. Rarely have I known a time when confusion has not shared my world" he told him nervously worrying with the stinging hurt along his hand.

"The brand is more a burden than a gift. It brings me an unsettling clarity and I see all to well how my city filled with hurtful, loathsome things. Since my father's disappearance the pressure they set upon me has only increased. My heart speaks true when it shows me how the House of Tessera has failed her people. The Guildsman are ever so willing to take all matters into their hands. They pilfer and lie and I do not have the stomach for it. The only comfort I have known since is when the voice has spoken of the Mist that ends the world. Three years ago, my mother saw that no good would come by forcing me to my courtly duties and she set me free from the responsibilities of the crown. Since that time I have sought to understand the riddles whispered by the stars upon my face."

Tristus hesitated, watching the ocean move in all directions and he said more softly,

"It was not until recently that the first glimmer of truth appeared to me but alas, I can not hold to it. I am left with impression that it is the very substance of the world which keeps us captive. Like all other living things, I am trapped in a place where the good and the evil stand side by side." and he looked to the Captain to see if he had understood the words.

Jason did not answer and for a time they rested from the effort of speech but as the hours passed Tristus told the Captain of his journey to the Wall of Mist. He described the forest and the woman that led him to the edge of the world. With words, he painted a vision of the Misty Wall and finally he shared his recall of the fiery giantess who stood guard over that place. He explained to the man the events which had carried him to that edge of the world, telling him of the mines and the horrors endured by those who were enslaved there. During the course of the day, Jason listened attentively to each word.

Tristus was relieved to speak of these things. But as he did he realized all events were not meant to be spoken of, so as he retold his adventures to the resolute Captain he left out a single thing. The wielding of the sword of fire was not something he could share. The sword which pierced him into two parts was a knowledge only meant for his mind and memory. The truth intended for the ears of this good man was not diminished by this omission.

"Come Lord." Jason's gentle voice stirred the air. "Time has played tricks upon us. We have stood though the long night and now the long day wanes. We must go beneath and take refreshment."

Tristus looked at the settling sun and realized that they had been standing at the bow of the ship for hours. He was stiff as they walked along the deck passing first mate standing at the mast. The sailor acknowledged them while he worked the lines and Tristus noticed that the forefinger of his left hand was missing.

They went below to warm themselves by the cooking fires. Tristus found ship's cook was a jolly man who soon began to tell him stories from the Dock Houses near the fishing piers. Tears trickled down his red cheeks as he delighted in the wide-eyed uncertainty of the boy. A bright colored bird sat upon the cooks shoulder and it chuckled along with him.

"What are you laughing at?" spoke the Captain to the macaw and the bird responded with a rhyme rather unfit for the ears of the young King.

"I am afraid many of my men, and their pets," Jason added glancing at the bird, "have spent much time looking at the world from behind a bottle."

"Aye." grunted Tristus, at a loss of how to respond.

"Take no mind of him." said the Captain, "He means no harm but he has no talent for knowing when he has said to much." and he gestured to the cook.

The cook smiled widely and gestured back, "My good Captain has failed to introduce us properly, Sire." said the fat man. "I am Edward Owyn Tarvos Hanann Dwu of the House of Seafarthing. I am pleased to know you, Tristus, royal prince and twenty-fourth heir to the House of Tessera. But your name, as well as my own, seems to much a mouthful so if I might call you Tristus, all on this boat call me Cook and you may rest assured that the meal I prepare is worth the wait," then he laughed again, "but it seems my Redhead has not yet finished his song, so you must allow me to finish up what has been left unsung." and with that, and a slight bow, the jolly man continued the rhyme where his bird had left off.

It was a long limerick with many verses and the bird screeched with him as Edward worked happily over his hot kettles and steaming pans. Chortling with glee he finished up the song with a particularly scandalous phase as he lay down a plate of fish, onions and fried yellow bread before them. Tristus realized how hungry he was. He sipped the Captains good wine and while its savor washed away his tiredness, it was the laughter in the warm kitchen which truly set him right again.

After bidding Edward a friendly goodnight, Tristus went to his hammock and Jason walked with him to the small chamber.

"It will be seven days before we arrive home. We will send a messenger immediately to the castle to let them know that you are safely on board." he said.

"I do not know if I am ready. There is much that I must try to set back right." said Tristus looking to the Captain.

"There no simple answers." responded the Captain as they reached the door, "Events such as these do not come to us suddenly. They have their roots in years long passed by."

"Aye. It is a long road that has led us to this place and as surely as that is true what we do now will set the stage for what will come next," agreed Tristus, then he turned to face the elder man and said, "Will you come to the castle to meet my family? I would like you to tell them of your travels and share the things you have seen."

"As you wish, Lord. I will tell them what I know."

"My concerns have grown as I have watched the mer-folk follow us home." he said, fretfully brushing his tangled hair away from his eyes. "I am worried by how they have been affected by this red disease. I think it is vital to find a way to speak with them."

"That could prove difficult. They are not a gentle people." replied the Captain, "They hold a high regard for the sea and would view her spoiling as an act of war."

Tristus frowned as the weight of his birth pressed down upon him "Indeed, I am glad you will be coming with me Jason." he answered finally. "And I am also glad that I have found a friend. Perhaps I might even sleep easier because of it." he said looking over the unsettling waters, and then bowing politely, the young prince of Tessera said his goodnights.

"Good night, my Lord." answered Jason and closing the door behind him and he went to bridge and looked forward toward his home.

It was cold when Tristus woke. His night had been dreamless and he was rested and hungry. When he arrived in the kitchen he found his breakfast already prepared. As it warmed on the stove the cook shared a few more verses from the song of the night before. Over the next few days Tristus spent much time in the happy kitchen. He was not burdened by the labors given to him but was glad to be included in the smooth workings of the ship.

The Bifrost held her heading and they traveled south with the brisk current. Soon they passed the place where Tristus had set fire to the bodies of the whales. Leaning over the rail he watched the beach slip past them and he found the memories still sickened him. The waves seemed sharp against the sky. The jagged rows of threatening shadows were scattered over the twilight sea and as he glanced beneath the surface he saw the mer-man still followed under the belly of the Bifrost.

When the day of their arrival finally dawned Tristus rose early and ate quickly; wishing to find the Captain before the hour grew late. It did not prove to be a difficult thing for Jason stood at the ship's wheel. He was looking out to the sea, apparently lost in thought, as he stared at the familiar coastline. The black cliffs gleamed in the rising light and the reflection of Bifrost passed by in fragmented frames against the mirrored surface. Tristus went to the far rail and looked beneath the waves.

"I have not seen the scout this morning." said the Captain, "He seems to have turned back during the night. We are very close to the city."

Other ships passed by them now, heading swiftly out into the deeper waters as they made ready for another day of fishing. The time went quickly for the route was familiar and soon every man was at the oar, maneuvering the ship skillfully toward the piers. When they docked the hulls were opened and the men hustled to unload the stores. The captain sent the cabin boy on to the castle with the message that the Prince was on board as the crew worked steadily carrying the barrels to the dock. Tristus did not join in these labors but waited upon the deck watching the bustling activity of the streets that rose from the piers. The alleys of Tessera twisted their way from the wharves. Narrow buildings, standing four and five stories high, were pressed tightly against each other. The thick window glass mirrored a brilliant green as it reflected off the water. Steadily the dwellings climbed over the ascending hills. Rows of thin houses wound round the busy paths and rising above the gables of every one was a covered balcony that faced the sea. All about him stirred the aromas of fish and bread, oils and spices, rot and waste, hanging like dissonance in the airs. Great lobster traps were piled upon the piers and heavy damp fishing nets, in need of repair were spread across the wide boards. Young boys climbed upon them, cleaning away the bits of tangled bracken as they repaired the ties and knots. When the nets were made whole once more other laborers worked to stow them upon their ships. Along these ancient streets lived the Greenseas and the Fishfarthers, the Pearls and Blackstones. He recalled most of the names from his history books for born within all the families were both heroes and scoundrels.

The sound of his name broke in upon his wandering thoughts. He looked down to see Arcus smiling as he sat upon his own black stead and quiet at his side was Tristus' gray stallion, Phaedras. Arcus sprang lightly for his saddle and before Tristus could speak he had grabbed him in a strong embrace. The blue eyes danced as he spoke.

"Where is your boat, Tristus? What tales do you bring home to us?"

"It is good to see you too, Arcus." he laughed, "But I fear that my stories are best told in front of a fire with a full table close at hand."

"I am ready to hear them all, my brother. I am glad you are back."

"How are the others? Mother and Aleryn?"

"There are tales both of us must share, and soon enough Tristus." he answered placing a concerned hand upon his shoulder. "Aleryn is making all the preparations and,"

Then the voice of the ships mate called down from the helm. "Lord Tristus. The Captain wishes to speak with you before you leave sir. He is coming now from the hulls."

"I will wait!" Tristus shouted back as they walked down to their horses. He stood next to his brother and gestured to the noisy city beyond. "I am glad to be home Arcus though indeed, strange times draw near." and with that he looked back to the ships deck to see the Captain standing at the railing.

"We shall meet again Jason, son of Beron." he shouted up to him "Tonight we shall each attend to our homecoming but in the early morning, I shall send a sealed wagon to carry that cargo you keep in your stores. Tomorrow we will speak again at length."

The Captain nodded in agreement and then turned away to continue his duties. The brothers began to move among the crowd. The people cleared the streets as they passed. It had been years since the two princes been seen traveling together in the streets of Tessera. Children ran beside them through the alleys between the shops and houses. The young women peered from the windows at the young princes. The dogs barked in the excitement. Simple and joyous, the beasts held no concern with why the procession moved along the alley for their thrill was in the delight of the march. The brothers could not speak freely as they traveled toward the castle. They nodded and waved as they sought to avoid stepping upon the people that pressed so close to them. By the time they had reached the castle gates, several hundred folk walked with them, shouting and calling for them by name.

Turning to the crowd the brothers waved a farewell and the gates closed behind them. Aleryn was waiting upon the stair and a strange boy stood with her.

"This is Pelius." said Aleryn before he could speak his thought. The boy nodded, his gaze peering straight into Tristus' face.

"I am Tristus." answered the prince.

"That is known to me." he answered with his usual haughtiness but catching his tone he continued more politely, "I am glad you have returned safely, Lord."

His accent was strange and Tristus wanted him to speak again, but at that moment he realized that someone was missing from the group.

"Where is mother?" said Tristus looking around the courtyard.

"She is ill Tristus."

"What ails her, sister?" he asked growing concerned.

"We are not yet sure." Aleryn answered reading her brother's moods. "Come now, we must let you refresh yourself. You have been away for more than two fortnights. Much has happened since then."

Tristus looked down at his travel stained cloak and worn boots.

"Can I see her?" he said.

"She is sleeping. It is what she needs most. I will explain as we go."

Arcus took his cloak and they began to walk toward the hall.

"How long has she been ill?" he asked.

"The disease came upon her soon after your departure. It began with wicked dreams and then a slow weakness began to possess her arms and legs." Aleryn hesitated, "I must know Tristus, what happened to the amber stone?" she questioned. "How long ago did you lose it?"

Tristus took a moment to recall. "It was early on. A flock of blackbirds attacked me when I was just a few days out to sea. I have never been certain if they stole the stone or if the tide took it for its own."

"I thought as much." Aleryn nodded. "We were aware when the link was lost. That was when I believe her failing began and I have wondered often if the two things were not connected. A fortnight ago her condition worsened once more. She has not been able to keep food and has held a steady fever. She has not risen at all from her bed for several days now. We are doing all we can to make her comfortable."

Tristus felt the eyes of the young Pelius probing the back of his skull while he and Aleryn talked.

"I would like to look in on her." he said, "I will not wake her if she still rests."

Aleryn agreed as they entered the hall. Tristus noticed nurses and maids scurrying busily about and he wondered why so many were needed in the sleeping chambers.

"She is not the only one who is ill." spoke the unfamiliar voice.

Tristus turned to look at the thin, muscular boy. He had removed his cloak and Tristus could now see that his skin was covered in symbols. His pale eyes burned from his tanned face. Tristus knew the boy had perceived his silent thought.

"So you intrude upon the thoughts of others child." replied Tristus in a princely tone.

"I did not do so intentionally sir. I. . . I. . .I am sorry. It can be difficult to know if a word has been spoken aloud or kept silent. I did not mean to offend." said Pelius, unnerved.

"It is all right. I take no serious offence. Who are you? Are you a servant of a priestess?"

"I do not attend any priestess of the Dark Tower. I am a sworn servant of the House of Tessera. I am a friend of your sister and she, a friend to me and my people."

"Your people?" said Tristus, raising a brow, "and who might those folk be?"

"I am the Guardian of the Tahmurath. We have been given sanctuary behind these castle walls."

"The Tahmurath." he answered surprised by the ancient name. He looked to Arcus and Aleryn and they nodded in agreement. "So they too exist." he mused silently as he looked over another living prophecy as it stood before him. "Indeed we live in a time when myth becomes reality." he answered the boy graciously, "You, and your people, shall certainly have sanctuary within these walls."

Pelius lowered his brow before the Prince as Arcus touched Tristus lightly upon the arm for they had arrived at the door of the Queens chamber.

CHAPTER 11
THE REUNION

The Queen lie still under the coverlets and when Tristus saw that she did indeed rest comfortably he quietly closed the door and left her to sleep. Holding his thoughts to himself he listened as Aleryn told him of the others that also lie ill in their beds. The news of this ailing distressed him but his sister seemed anxious that all wait to be explained at once. They decided to meet again at the noon hour and Tristus agreed to go below to the baths. They bid one another a brief good bye and Aleryn and Pelius walked together down the dim corridor while Arcus and Tristus went to underground pools.

The stone caverns were thick with steam for a warm mist continually rose from the heated waters. Plants hung from the low ceilings. Their twisting stems were wrapped thickly around the arched openings. Mirrors sat in the corners of the honeycombed rooms. Their angles were bent to bring the outside light into the bathing chambers. Dozens of scented candles burned upon the deep alcoves giving the rooms a cloudy glow. Arcus sent a young maid to fetch his brother fresh clothing. Tristus undressed and slipped into a deep stone pool. The hot water seeped into his sore muscles and he stilled his thoughts allowing the tiredness to drift from body. He washed his matted hair pulling the tangles apart with his fingers and then he scrubbed his nails noticing the thick calluses along his palms. Gently he rubbed his sore skin with the mild soap of honey and oil allowing the steaming water to calm its fiery sting. He closed his eyes and breathed in the healing steam.

"You are changed." saidArcus, idly adjusting the candles which surrounded the pool. "You look at us though different eyes. What have you seen, my brother? he asked turning to face him. "This illness does appear to surprise you."

"No, it does not." he answered opening his eyes. "But what I have seen in my travels is only a part of what needs to be put together. I fear there will be much trouble in future days but let us not speak of that now. Please Arcus, tell me more of mother."

Arcus looked concerned and lowered his head in

frustration, "It is an sickness of the mind as well as the body. Some days she can not seem to remember who we are and other days she is so weak she can not raise her own cup to her mouth." then glancing down the hall he lowered his voice, "but no others, excepting those who dwell within the castle, have been afflicted by it. What would you make of that?"

"No others?" said Tristus, somewhat surprised.

"No," continued Arcus, "I have sent Clade to the market each day to listen but have there has been no news of this illness spreading through the kingdom."

Then the sound of soft slippers echoed through the hall as the maid returned with Tristus' clean clothing. She spread them carefully on the stone bench at the near end of the pool. Arcus excused her and she took her leave with a polite bow. When he was sure she had past from hearing distance, he continued softly. "We have kept the Queens condition secret but it is my fear that she is being poisoned."

Tristus measured Arcus' words as he rose from the water. He dried himself with bulky cloths that waited at the end of the basin and pulled on the soft, brown breeches and clean blouse. Then he and his brother walked to the main chamber of the cavernous baths. A fresh wind passed though the open windows high above their heads and Tristus sat down upon the edge of a large fountain. The marble fountainhead rose elegantly from the tiled floor. Its deep base was filled with water lilies and bright fish swam among their roots. They clustered tightly together, rolling their bulging eyes and flapping their long mouths, as they looked to Tristus expecting food. The carved statues of four winged presences stood in the center of the flowing fountain. Each face looked toward one of the four directions and each carried a large pitcher which poured unceasingly into the wide circular base. Tiered above them, winged children danced with arms intertwined, dressed in vines and carrying flowers and fruit, their eyes looked expectantly toward the heavens. Above their shoulders, water spouted from the mouths of three great fish. The three were joined at the apex by their powerful tails to form a perfect triangle. The large spume of water pushed from the center of this triangle to almost to touch the domed ceiling but the water fell back gently and bathed the floor in a fine spray. In each new breath of wind which passed though watery mist Tristus felt his heated skin began to calm. He strung the laces though the eyes of his boots and tied them tightly.

"Who are the others who lay ill?" said Tristus finally.

"We shall meet them. They are most unusual." said Arcus.

"The children of the prophecies?"

"Yes. I find it encouraging that there are others who carry the old magic during these troubled times."

The unanticipated words surprised him and he looked upon his brother with wide eyes. "They too bear gifts?" he asked.

"Indeed, and those talents burn strong." Arcus smiled feeling his brother's relief. "We are not alone."

"When can I meet them?" he said and Arcus smiled and led him to the hall where the ill children rested where they found Aleryn and Pelius standing close to a narrow bedside. The huddled figure seemed buried in the blankets and when they came nearer Tristus could see it was a tiny dark skinned girl who rested under the coverlets. She was coughing and Aleryn was holding a cup of steaming liquid to her lips. The girl drank as she could between the harsh spasms.

"I really am feeling better." she complained between the choking sips of tea and she tried to rise from her tangled sheets.

"Mileah, you must stay to bed." said Aleryn gently holding the child's shoulders back.

"I want to see them. They are afraid. I can feel them though the walls. They cry out for me. Please Pelius! I can not bear this prison. They can not bear it either. Take us away. We do not belong here. We are not beasts. We can not be caged, no matter how lovely a cage it may seem. Oh please, Pelius." she pleaded. "You must understand."

"Mileah. It is not wrong that we stay among friends. Please calm down. The twins, they are fare better than you do."

Mileah began to cry and Pelius laid his hand upon her brow.

"I have never lied to you." he said taking the cup from Aleryn and setting it upon a small table next to the bed.

Her face was flushed as she lay back. Tristus and Arcus stirred and Aleryn turned to see them standing near the open door.

"Mileah, this is my brother. Come Tristus. Come and meet Mileah." said Aleryn holding out her hand as Tristus walked forward to grasp it. "He has been away for some time now. He has just returned, only this morning."

Mileah cast her eyes downward, her childish shyness overcoming her.

"Do not fear me little one. You are welcome here and know that I understand all too well how these castle walls seem made to cage one within them."

Mileah glanced up at the prince. Her brown eyes were liquid as a wild does. He felt her appraising his words and then he heard her gasp when she glimpsed the stars which reached across his face.

"He shall help you, Mileah." said Pelius. "You and the twins as well."

"Yes, he will help us." whispered the fevered child and drawing a labored breath she closed her eyes to sleep.

Tristus looked down upon the girl. "How long has she been ill?"

"Two weeks now," said Pelius. "and the twins showed signs of the disease a few days after."

"The first obvious thing was this." said Aleryn gently pulling the covers away from Mileah's arm. Tristus looked down at the bloody lesion that oozed upon the smooth skin and though he had expected to see the sore, he found himself sickened.

"How many of these?" he asked.

"Less than half of a dozen," spoke Arcus, "but they worsen each day."

"Mother has thrice this number. They consume one another as they grow. We have found no way to keep them from spreading." Aleryn added.

"Agitation causes the sores to spread. It is important they lie still. We have herbs to make them more comfortable but this is all we have been able to do." said Arcus, glancing down at the sleeping child. "but the time goes late now and mother may be awake."

Pelius kissed Mileah's forehead and they left her in the care of Tristus' own nurse. Closing the door softly behind them, Tristus followed the others down the hall to the Queen's bed chamber.

She was sitting up on pillows when they entered, smiling and holding a cup in her lap.

"My son!" she cried, "Each day I have called to the Wizard in hopes he would bring you back to us, safe and whole. Truly my calls have been answered!"

"And I am home, safe and whole, mother and I am glad to be home again mother."

"What have you seen, my son? What mystery lies beyond us in the dark, cold, sea?"

"Many mysteries I dare say. So many things I have yet to understand. I have succeeded in my quest. I have traveled past the Wall of Mist that divides the world into parts. But what hand of grace that did guide there, I dare not say for sure. I know only that I was drawn by a power far beyond my own making and though I bring back much news of this world; I hold within me only a briefest glimpse of what might lie within the next." and then he went to the bedside and embraced her.

Speaking in a whisper he continued. "Beyond the Misty Wall which waits at end of the earth there dwells a fiery life. It was upon her breath mother, upon the breath of the Fire Goddess, that I was returned to my home."

The matron pulled up a bit straighter upon the pillows color climbing into her cheeks for his words carried healing.

"Tell me what have you seen my son. Tell me of everything." she said faintly in his ear. "Tell of the good? And what, tell me Tristus; And what of evil?"

"Good and evil, mother?" he answered more quietly still. "All I know of those things is that we each bear both within us."

The Queen brushed the hair away from the brand of stars and her chilled hand trembled as she spoke, "We are all lesser creatures and, what simple virtues do we hold within, ebb and swell like a restless tide." She sighed as if the weight of the world pressed in upon her, "but of late I have dreamed of more than just the simple failings of men, Tristus. I have seen an evil that stands within a red sun and it feasts upon the faults of all folk. Eating away at everything they hold dear. I have seen it growing in my mind. I have seen it creeping like a rot over the streets of Tessera."

Her eyes dimmed as she spoke and Tristus knew from his own visions what had touched her dreams. The memory of the red sun sent a troubled wave through his heart.

"What have you seen Tristus?" Arcus asked him gravely, "The time is short where we all must know the truth."

Tristus lowered his black eyes and peered into the fire. "I have seen many things not of this world and I too have dreamed of a Wraith that stands before a red sun. It is a wicked dream, a dream which lives within our streets, twisting the very fabric of our lives to its own ends. I fear it is not of this world and I believe, we have only begun to glimpse what we must fight."

He felt Aleryn tremble, struggling with her doubts, as she stood next to him. Pelius was close at her side

"Do not let hope fail you;" he spoke to them in a soundless thought, carrying on the two conversions at once, he continued aloud, speaking in an measured voice.

"There are countless lives that are not of this world and the thread that binds us together reaches far beyond what we see." he explained, "Indeed, it seems to me now, that all realms are layered one within the other. The notion I am left with is the image of an interwoven web that reaches from the Airs to the Earth. And what happens in one place shall impact upon another; be it for good or ill"

"But what of the shadow, Tristus." asked his sister probing silently into his thoughts, "Tell us how does it touch us? How may we know what to fight?"

Again he acknowledged her concerns with a gentle touch of will but he continued to explain to the Queen aloud.

"Along my way to the Mists, I was caught up by a great storm and it was more than happenchance that left me upon that deserted beach. A greater fate had called me there and when I rose to my feet I stumbled into an isolated valley where I saw what I could scarcely believe. Concealed within the vales of the far Apennines a mining camp exists. It is larger than anything I have ever seen before and it operates by day and by night." and as he spoke he recalled the ruin of mountains and men. "I watched as hundreds were forced to peck metals from the bony earth against their will. I saw their lot when hope or strength breaks down."

"So the rumors of the slave trade are true." said Arcus quietly.

"They are true." he answered.

The Queen looked helplessly upon her hands and did not reply

"How could we not have known of it before?" Arcus asked himself struggling with news.

"These mines are carefully hid, buried deep behind the walls of the northern Apennines."

"What do they seek?" asked Pelius

"Gold and silver I am sure, but mostly it seems that Atricault is refined in this place. The amalgam boils in enormous vats and belches a red fume into the riverbed."

"I thought the northern Apennines to be impassable." replied the Queen, a distant wariness creeping through her tone.

"So it has been said." he answered gravely, looking to his mother, "Nonetheless they are there."

"Do you believe the Guilds of Tessera responsible?" asked Arcus frankly.

"We are the only power capable of such a undertaking." murmured Aleryn softly. "And it is only the Haarshiam that would seek to settle in such barren lands for the love of ballots."

"The Haarshiam use deception as a way to means." Tristus answered, his voice holding a hint of anger, recalling how often the thin voices of the Guildsmen had surrounded his mother with their cold reason. "We have refused to grant their desires for the expansion of the mines and as they plead for a change in the laws they have been allowed to move freely through our sovereign walls. Hiding behind soft-tongued consuls, I believe they have now taken all law into their own hands. "

"You have seen this with your own eyes, my son?" asked the Queen.

"I have mother and as one evil begets yet another, I will

say once more new connections are born."

"Connections? What connections Tristus?"

"I believe the disease, which affects you now, is spawned from the very refuse of those northern mines.

"From the sea?" questioned Aleryn

"Yes, the refineries spread their filth into the water and in this waste a red tide is spawned and that, in turn, runs into the sea."

"The illness is along the water? How can that be?"

"A waste is formed as the metal is refined and as it flows unchecked into the river valley the red tide is bred. The blight carried on then by the tides. It will bring death to all it touches. But of late I have heard it called by another name. The south island folk refer to the blight as *Pyrrohmarin*."

"And so the water will pass the infection into the food we bring from the sea?" said Aleryn bleaching pale as she put the implications together.

"Yes, sister, and when left alone the disease will continue to grow in the flesh of the dead."

"You believe it is the waste of these far-away mines which causes these lesions to grow upon their skin." said Arcus.

"I have followed its path of destruction from the cold sea through my own doorway. Yes. It is what I believe." Tristus nodded as all his family stood near, their dinner growing cold behind them and he felt the mind of the boy, Pelius, watching him intently. He turned to look upon him and did see no fear within his grim face.

"Indeed young sir." he spoke sternly, "Indeed I do bring grave news to the door. The infection spreads swiftly through the waters of the far north bringing death to all it touches be it fish, or fowl, or mighty whale, and I am not the only one who has seen its devastation. The Captain of the ship which bore me home witnessed a living swarm of this *Pyrrohmarin*. In his hull, he carries many stricken fish but it is not that which concerns me most."

"Then what thing does concern you more?" asked Arcus in disbelief.

"It is not only the eyes of men that have seen the death the red tide brings." he answered gazing out the window to the watery sea. "The Thalassisans have seen it as well."

"The Thalassisans!" cried Arcus, casting an eye to Pelius, "What myth now is not alive!"

"They are no myth," Tristus assured him, "and they are as fierce and proud as the stories tell. A scout followed our ship. Day and night, he stayed with us as we made our way home and the soldier did not turn back until we were but a day's journey from port. I fear he tracked us for the Thalassisans believe we are responsible for the red tide and that belief may not be far from truth if indeed it is the Haarshiam who spoil the waters."

"None of the mer-folk have been seen for two thousand years. But if those old legends bear truth at all it is said that we did not part on good terms." said Arcus.

"What is the fear, my son?" asked the Queen.

"They bide close to the source of the blight. I do not know what damage has been done to them." said Tristus. "But I do know that they share no love for us and they watch now as we come and go. I believe it is necessary we speak with them and we must speak soon, before misconceptions have an opportunity to grow."

Aleryn moved closer too the window and poured a cup of tea. She sipped the brew as she looked over the bay. Tristus watched as she turned the truth in her mind and he spoke to her,

"I have told you many things. But all of it; greed, slavery, and thoughts of war, are easily bred in the world of men. Now I must know what news you have for me. Tell me of the Tahmurath."

Pelius shifted on his feet keeping his gaze aligned with upon the stars of Tristus' brow.

"Truly strange times breed strange times." said Aleryn, still looking out to sea.

"We found the children dwelling in the Valley of Orpheus." explained Arcus, "In secret, they had camped there for many seasons," and then he hesitated for a moment thinking back upon Tristus' auguries. "They were driven from their homes and their kin was destroyed. Pelius has told us much of the cruel wraiths who have sought them in secret. They strike in the form of Shadows and, though we can not know how many lives have been lost, these are the few who were rescued by Pelius and his brother. Twelve of them dwell with us and among them lay many gifts. But even as we speak, I fear their safety is compromised. Secrets in these castle walls are not easily kept and in a place where they should have no fear, it is necessary to be afraid." and he paused again, his face growing gray, "In my reckoning, we deal with a ancient power. It is a force which is able to use ordinary men as its hands and common folk, as its ears."

"I believe those hands and ears may take on other forms as well." answered Tristus recalling the birds that assailed him upon the beach, and a new thought rose in his mind. Touched by the realization and he looked to Arcus, "A traveling belt came with me from the ship. What has become of it?"

"Clade saw to your things. They were carried to your chambers."

"Then I shall be back in a moment." said Tristus and he left them standing in the room. When he opened his door he saw his few belongings laying upon a chair by the fireplace. He pushed the cloak aside and opened the leather pocket that lie hidden within it. The flask he sought lay on the bottom of the coat. He took it and returned quickly to the Queen's chamber.

"Mother, where does a sore lie upon you?"

The Queen winced as she pulled the sheet from her chest. At the base of her throat, consuming skin and bone, a wide lesion leaked a thin, bloody fluid. Tristus soaked a swab in the sharp smelling water. He touched the lesion lightly, allowing the fluid to drip into the oozing sore. When the liquid touched the wound, a cleansing foam raised from the hole. It hissed and complained each time Tristus dropped more of the healing beads upon it. He continued until no response came from the sore. Then he washed the wounds with clear water and soap. He leaned over to inspect the gash. Its redness and heat seemed diminished and he gave the Queen a mouthful of the bitter drink.

"I stumbled upon these springs in the first days of my journey. The yellow bite carries curing powers." he explained, "The birds attack had been fierce and I had been stabbed dozens of times. When I soaked in these waters their poison was pulled from me and within a day there was no open mark left."

Aleryn came to inspect the wound, noting the edges had already grown less angry. "There are many other sores upon her. May I be left to attend to them brother."

Aleryn pulled the thin curtains which hung around the bed while the others left the main chamber to rest in the large bay window. The table within it held their forgotten meal. Over their shoulders, Aleryn worked quickly, applying the yellow fluid to the spreading infections. They looked at the food which lay before them with a sense of distress. Pelius probed a bit of fish with his fork, turning it over slowly.

"I will be difficult to eat at all today." He said to the others.

Tristus agreed as he poured the wine. They settled back with their chairs looking to the bay that stretched beneath them and watching the white sails which dotted its surface. Pelius contented himself with a cup of water. They ate sparingly of bread and cheese as they waited for their sister to finish. As they sat, Pelius explained his first meeting with Arcus and Clade. Tristus was silent as the boy told the tale of his upbringing and the loss of his family.

"Has life always been filled with such treacheries." Tristus wondered to himself. "How is it that such evil can be laid out by one man to another?" He probed the thought, over and over again as Pelius told him the story of his grandmother's murder. "What is this force which grows in the bodies of the Tahmurath and why is it such a threat to the shadow?" Tristus mused silently.

"It is more than the Tahmurath the Shadows see as a threat, Prince." said Pelius.

Tristus raised his brows and said. "I did not speak aloud, Pelius."

"Oh, I am sorry." Pelius answered with a sigh.

"I suppose I must grow accustom to intrusion. Truth is known to those with ears to hear and the unspokenness of a thought is not enough to hide it." Tristus replied gently. "You must become more aware of your power, Pelius. It is dangerous for others to know of it. Many will not understand and what they do not understand, they will hate.

Aleryn appeared at the table. "Her sores have been

attended too. We must treat the children as well. Please come with me Pelius. They will trust this remedy more if you are with me."

"You have not eaten, Aleryn." said Arcus.

"I do not hunger." she said with a slight wave of her hand and she hurried from the room with Pelius was quick at her heels.

"Leave her to her work. She is tireless and will not rest until it is done." spoke the Queen from her bed. "I have come to know my daughter well as I have lay upon this bed. She has changed; as we all have Tristus. Ever since that day we found the castle gate broken all things have been altered. Time does not turn to face the past."

"Indeed it seems that change has left us with some interesting charges," answered Tristus looking after the sound of their footsteps, "and it appears that they have established a bond."

"I trust this boy, in a time when few can be trusted." said Arcus. "Since mother and the others have become ill Aleryn has all but forgotten herself entirely. The two of them spend all day together. She has tended the sick with Pelius at her side. There is no need for words between them. They are much alike."

"He reads thoughts with great ease." said Tristus. "And he speaks of these Shadows as a something he knows well. Has he ever spoken of the Haarshiam?"

"He knows of them but they are not his concern. The Haarshiam are but dull and greedy men in his eyes. The boy does not focus in that world, instead he seems to search the wind for answers." then Arcus smiled, "But you may rest assured my brother, I do keep my eye upon their doings."

"What have you seen?"

"I have seen them cluttering the castle stairs, just as they always have, seeking audience with mother, finding every opportunity to whisper flattery and lies. They attend their meeting houses and temples with great regularity. Their influence is felt in all places and their strength increases each day."

"You have caught them in no wrongdoing?"

"They are clever and they know well the laws. They

skirt the edges of what is right and what is wrong. But now it is the Winter Festival that worries me. They are making much ado of it. The Haarshiam say they are to unveil a great marvel. They have told me that many different Guilds have worked in tandem to create this "miracle" and the fanfare about this mystery increases each day. It is their plan to expose this "wonder" at the Festival."

"Wonder?" Tristus felt uneasiness pass through him.

"But I think the Haarshiam will find it difficult to deceive the people in the presence of true seers." said Arcus thinking of the children.

"Maybe we should speak to the Guilds. I would to know what news they have of the far north mountains." answered Tristus, thinking of the mines.

"My dear sons, indeed there is much trouble upon us. But, Tristus, your remedy has had some effect. I believe I could take a bit of food."

Tristus hastily prepared a plate with small portions of fruit, bread, and dried meat; carefully avoiding the fish. Pouring a small glass of wine he carried the dish to his mother bedside. She took it from him and was able to feed herself. When she had finished he reached out to take the plate.

"I do not wish for more, my son. It is a relief to taste food. It has been many days since I have been able. I will take another bite later."

They finished the wine at her bedside allowing its warmth to fill their veins and when Pelius and the princess came back they seemed more relaxed as well. The potion had transformed the lesions of the children more rapidly than it had those of the Queen. Aleryn was pleased when she heard that the Queen had taken a meal. They all took the opportunity to eat and Tristus told them more of his story. Magic permeated the room when he spoke of the vessel crafted of a wood that could not burn. He revealed the tale of how it carried him from the Valley of the Vulcane outward into the open sea. He told them of Jason, Captain of the Bifrost, explaining how the man knew much of the ways of the Thalassisans as well as the nature of the *Pyrrohmarin* and he spoke to them of the arrangements to meet the Captain on the next day.

"This malady that affects the children, and you mother, I believe it has its source in the food. I do not know if the hands that bring you your meals are aware of the taint it may carry but I would refrain from taking in the fare of the sea until we understand more." said Tristus.

"Yes, my son. That is good advice and we will see to it shortly," said the Queen a bit too quickly, unwilling to have the conversation linger upon her condition, and she pressed him. "But I must ask you now, if it be true that magic and prophecies are alive at every turn, then that is a rare and precious thing." she sighed wistfully, "But the faults that exist amongst men; well my son, those things are not rare at all. My mother, and the many grandmothers before her; have long been aware of the failings of people. The lesser qualities of common folk and the greed of Guildsmen are part of the life we are honor born to protect. Could we consider this trouble that is spread across the kingdom more liken to dung as it is spread upon a fallow field and it is false hope that calls out for a miracle."

Aleryn turned from the window to answer. "It is the stars which lay down the greater cycles of circumstance. We are a free folk mother."

"Aye that we are and it is difficult to be wise with such a gift." answered Tristus, "But how our troubles will be resolved are things I can not see,"

Aleryn touched his arm softly, "I know there is something else we must do, Tristus and through she does not wish to speak of it, the need is great." she whispered so only he could hear, "Already I have used more than half of the potion in the care of the children and there is scare more than a single application for each left in your flask. The wounds should be washed out once more before the night falls and again at the break of day. Is it possible to have more of this remedy, brother?"

The Queen's ears were sharp and she cried out, "Not so soon Aleryn! He has only but arrived. I can not bear to see you leave again so quickly."

"There is necessity in this mother. I assure you these lesions you bear will bring death with them." he replied, "We must fetch more of the yellow water for I worry we have only seen the beginning of this scourge. We can reach the place easily by boat. It is but a day and a half journey if we take no sleep. I dare not allow it to pass in idleness."

"I will stay with them," said Aleryn, glancing up at the Tower standing tall against the sea. "We have learned much from one another and there is but little time to consider all that has been said."

"Tomorrow then; please send for the fisherman, Jason. He is the one who brought me back from the northern sea. He shall tell you the things that he has seen and he will show you the bodies of the tainted fish. He is a man that can be trusted. You will be well informed when I return."

"I will see to the outfitting of our boat." said Arcus rising to leave. "But who shall we take upon this errand?"

"The three of us should suffice." said Tristus glancing over his shoulder to look at Pelius. "This place hides in the face of the mountains and a time may come when each of us should each know how to reach it."

"Then look for my return within the hour." said Arcus, kissing his mother upon the brow.

"Do you need my help?"

"No, it is not necessary, Pelius. The boats are always stocked and it is but a few extras that I wish to see brought on board. Prepare yourself to come with us. Aleryn knows where you shall find traveling gear."

"We shall gather some clothing for you and see to the kitchens" replied the princess.

"Thank you, Aleryn," he smiled and then turning to Arcus he replied. "I will be ready when you return."

"We shall meet back here when our tasks are complete." said Tristus.

Pelius, though aware of the urgency, was delighted to be included in the errand as he went with Aleryn to the castle stores. Arcus went to prepare the other details and in a moment it was only Tristus who was left to linger at his mother's bedside.

"Tell me of this place, my son." the Queen whispered as the door closed and Tristus smiled.

"It is extraordinary mother." he smiled, happy to share the beauty of the strange world. "The trees are very old and stand higher than our castle turrets. The sky barely shows from the forest floor as vines and bowers fill the spaces between earth and air. The place is home to birds of every color and there are times the walls explode with sound. This wood has never known snow, nor frost. The creatures that dwell there are very different from other beasts I have seen and they are everywhere."

"Should we not send our larger ships to investigate?" asked the Queen.

"It is a fragile place, mother. I would be concerned of spoiling it. There are those who would wreck this land for the love of the ballot."

"Indeed, the love of the ballot has ruined the hopes of many" she sighed tiredly.

"Do no lose hope, mother. We are able to handle the needs of the hour. We shall be back before the Winter Festival begins. It is not helpful to fret."

"The joy of seeing you again is not dimmed by the news you bring to us. I have not lost hope. Trust in that."

It seemed all too soon when Arcus returned. Promising to be back by the dawn of the third day they spoke their difficult goodbyes.

"All is ready, Tristus. The boat waits upon the dock. We can depart before the next hour strikes." said Arcus.

"Make haste now. We need you back quickly." said Aleryn and Tristus kissed her cheek just before they slipped through the door. She watched from the window imagining them descending the long stairs to the dock and after a time she thought she spotted their little boat heading out to sea. "May the Watchers guide your path." she said under her breath.

Tristus waved his arms towards the castle windows but already they had grown small and difficult to see. The wind pressed the little boat swiftly along and it raced up the shoreline as if it had grown wings. Arcus was excellent with the sails and together, the brothers worked as one. Pelius had spent most of his life, under the shady cover of leaves, and he was not accustomed to this wild open place in the bold light of the afternoon sun. But he learned quickly and he helped where he could. The brothers found him almost uncanny in his ability to be at the place where he was needed, at a time when his hands could be most helpful. Together they worked, grabbing all the speed they could from their fleet little ship. They raced across the water and as the day changed into night their course remained true. Taking turns, in pairs, they continued the work of the sails throughout the night and in the moments before the dawn they looked to the paling skies. The morning stars shimmered in the heavens above and for a few moments they rested under the diminishing night.

"It seems you have worked the sails for years, Pelius." said Arcus. "It is hard to believe you have spent your life tending goats and tilling fields. You are a born seaman."

"You are generous." Pelius smiled. "It is a fine thing being here upon the waters. I can see why it is you like it."

They lay upon the deck watching the light rise over the open sea. The pastel shades of morning stretched through the soft sky until the burning face of the yellow sun finally appeared. Around their boat, a deep mirror now gleamed and in that perfect reflection, sun and clouds swirled upon the surface of the waters.

"How far before we reach this place, Tristus?" asked Arcus.

"It is hours yet. I reckon it shall be the late of the afternoon before we come to it. The landmark is a long headland of rocky bridges and the cliffs, just beyond, are streaked by shade of light colored stone. There is a short space of beach and as I recall, there is a stand of mangroves. It was here I lost the amber stone. I do not know if it were the birds or the sea that took it in the fray but I recall it was growing dark as I made my way. Somewhere along that beach a narrow cut breaks through the cliffs and leads to a wood below. The split is hidden by brambles but just beyond it a jagged stair runs down to the forest floor. The pools we seek are near the center of the gulch."

They traveled without incident under the glorious autumn skies and as the sun was dropping low they saw the stone bridges stretching their spidery fingers into the breaking waves and soon after they entered the shallow bay. Tristus signaled to slow the boat down and bring her closer into the beach and he recognized the shore where the birds attacked him. He recalled the small group of desperate evergreens which clung to the sharp-face of stone. Guiding the boat close to the sands they made their way among the mangrove trees. Tristus jumped out to steer them as the water grew shallow.

"Are you sure this is correct. I see no place here." said Pelius grabbing a large batch of empty skins from the hull before jumping to the sand.

"Yes, it is there." Tristus answered gesturing toward the sloping wall. They followed him through the sea grass and soon came upon the place where the briars barred the way.

"Come this way." he shouted over the wind, disappearing into an opening just out of sight. Pelius pulled the thorns away and Tristus called out for them to follow as they scrambled after him down an uneven stone stair.

The rocky steps were damp and Pelius clung to the odd vines that climbed over the canyon walls. The sounds of a thousand birds swelled up and in an instant the forest was filled with vibrant colors.

"Remarkable." Pelius whispered as he jumped to the ground staring up at the trees that blotted out the sky. "And such peculiar roots" he wondered, running his fingers along a huge, knotted mass. The immense root ball stood higher than his head so he climbed over it to follow the others. All around him, climbing flowers clung to the stretching limbs desperately hoping for a glimpse of the sun. A stream of water cascaded down the cliffs. Laughing, brown skinned water nymphs sang as they splashed upon stone. Their long black hair was filled with wisps of lily and reedy vines clung to their thin bodies. Their long arms moved gracefully as they danced among the falling water. They smiled down at the travelers and the song they sang changed when looked upon him. He felt them searching his mind with persistent questions. They knew him and they called out his name. Pelius looked to Tristus and Arcus and pointed to the watery dancers. But before he spoke he hesitated, realizing he was the only one of the group who could see the magical creatures. Confusion seized him.

"How could he see what this marked Prince of Prophets could not?" he wondered.

He followed the brothers through the trees keeping his thoughts to himself. The floor of the wood was filled with ferns and strange noises from strange animals echoed through the air.

Pelius walked in this new world with his mind wide open. His grandmother had taught them the names of all the plants and trees which grew beyond the fields of the southern boroughs but in this place he did not know the names of any of the growing things. The abundance and variety was astounding and he looked all around trying to take in every new thing that he saw. Tristus and Arcus were still moving quickly through the trees and were soon they far ahead of him. In the bushes near him Pelius heard a stirring. Almost hidden by the fronds of a massive fern alongside his path there sat a little man squatting upon the ground. His skin was a yellowed brown and his eyes were bright, black beads. He chuckled as Pelius paused before him with his mouth gaping open.

Gasping Pelius called out in surprise. Tristus turned, "What is wrong?"

"They will not see me." rasped the little man. "I am for your eyes alone." and his black eyes danced with delight.

"There is something in the bushes," said Pelius and Arcus turned back to meet him while Pelius waited at the paths edge staring at the little man.

"Where?" said Arcus.

The little man raised up and walked up to the Prince, barely reaching his shoulder he looked him square into his face, grinning widely.

"You see boy. They can not notice me. I have been waiting for you. You do not think that you have come to my garden by chance, do you?" and his grin widened until Pelius thought his face might split.

"What did you see, Pelius?" spoke Arcus.

"I do not know, maybe it is just the light or. . . well, there are many animals in this place, maybe. . . ," Just then a strange screech filled the air and a masked beast, with long arms and short legs, was dangling just ahead of them. It had a great bearded chin and along the sides of its shoulders hung a thick growth of long white hair. Its back shone a glossy black and its strong tail clung to the tree above them like a long plume of white. The beast scolded them and gnashed its yellow teeth.

Arcus stared at the strange animal. "Such creatures in this wood. No one shall believe us." he said shaking his head

Pelius could only nod in agreement as the beast aimed a fruit at his head. He ducked just in time to miss the shot.

"Do you like my pets?" the brown man chuckled.

Pelius glanced back at him, not knowing how to respond. Arcus stood close at his shoulder, still unaware of their invisible companion.

"Go on now." he continued in his thick voice. Its sound was like water mixed with wind, "Go and gather what you came for. It will heal them but make haste. There are many waiting for you." and with those odd words the little man disappeared.

"Come, Pelius." interrupted Arcus, "You must have seen this irritable beast that throws his supper." and he frowned at the screeching animal.

"Yes, I suppose." responded the boy unthinkingly glancing around for the man.

Tristus had moved far ahead. The under-layer of trees swayed as he passed it by and they hurried to catch him. They found him waiting at the stand of cedars. He motioned for them to follow and then he pushed through the evergreen that encircled the spring. Hot wisps of stained vapor moved through the air and along the edge the bubbling waters a yellow crust lie upon clay. Their minds cleared as they breathed the mist but the light was growing dim and Tristus set a touch burning as they went quickly to their work. Whispers moved in the shadows around them and the night swelled with the sound. Just beyond the light of the torches, unseen inhabitants moved. They returned to the boat with their skins stowing them securely within the hull, only to turn back again to complete the task they came to do. All along the way Pelius thought he could hear voices calling out his name. Unnerved, he moved faster seeking to stay near Tristus and his brother. They knelt once more at the yellow spring to fill the last of the skins and Tristus held the torch above them. The circle of light it cast illumined the eyes of creatures that watched them from the edge. When they departed, weighted with their final load, darkness was complete.

The nights ceiling was painted bright with stars. The pale moon reflected its shimmering path upon the water as they cast off into the churning sea. The brothers had no difficulty charting their course from the brilliant guides hanging as steady beacons in the darkness. Above them was the constellation of stars traced by the mark of Tristus' brow. The names of the stars had been translated by the Eratosthenians, long, long, ago in a time before Malthrom. Their distant light watched them as they sailed toward home. The brilliant pattern of their design burned in the East. The travelers knew their names and they cast up their eyes from the dark sea and sent their sweetest wishes into the peaceful sky.

It is written that each invocation is met with its answer but it is also known, by those who call, that the time of the heavens is not the time of the man. But this night brought comfort for the answer did come directly and they were washed in the forceful presence of the starry light. The power of their names rang through the sky; Madios; the bringer of hope, Sammael; the bearer of the burden at the end of days, Thamael; the messenger, Baraborat; the translator of truth, and Amabiel; who faces away from the sea and is concerned with souls not yet born. In the combination of those five great lives were many possibilities and each of the three travelers found themselves touched in a different way.

The sea carried them toward home under the protection of the guiding stars and watching sun waned once again before they returned to the city. Gently docking their boat, servants rushed to greet them for they had waited all the long night for their return. Quickly the skins were unloaded and carried to the castle. The boys followed behind them walking slowly up the stone stairs. Aleryn stood in the lit threshold, light spilling around her. She embraced them all in turn, holding each one close for a brief moment but as she reached out to Pelius, an image of the jaundiced dwarf appeared in her mind. She heard the little man laugh and to her surprise the image spoke her name and it said,

"Queen Aleryn. Look to the one who carries the gift of earth and may his true origins be revealed." The Princess stepped back, confused by the words he spoke, staring at Pelius for an explanation the odd voice still echoed in her thoughts.

Pelius sighed and shook his head. "We must go." was all he could think, "These waters still hold warmth. Now the healing will be most potent."

So it was, that late in the night they returned to rooms of the sick waking them gently to cleanse the bloody sores that climbed over their flesh. Each was given a drink of the bitter waters and each was left with a whispered blessing and when these labors were finished they went to their chambers to rest in the few hours left before the dawn.

CHAPTER 12
THE FESTIVAL

The flames burned low in the belly of the hearth when the clear light spilled into his bed-chamber. Tristus opened his eyes. He felt surprisingly refreshed. After tossing a bit of wood upon the fire he pulled on his clothes and went down the hall to see if Arcus was awake. He knocked softly and his brother's voice answered. Tristus opened the door to find Arcus kneeling at the fire. He had dressed hastily and his light hair was matted against his face.

"Did you sleep well?" asked Tristus.

"Better than in weeks." came the reply. "The springs seem to have more than one healing property."

"Yes, they do indeed. My appetite is back. Why don't we go find breakfast."

They went down the stairs to the castle kitchens and there they found all they could ever wish to eat. The Winter Festival was only two days away and the cooks had been busy with all the preparations. Sweet breads, kettles of soup, wheels of cheese, and great cakes stuffed the heavy pantry shelves.

They stole in as quietly as they could but, as they entered, every eye stared in their direction. It was not long before heavy platters had been prepared for them. They took the plates and steaming mugs and left the busy kitchens to breakfast in the sunny room which lie off the dining hall. They sat together at a small table looking over the kitchen gardens. The fragile herbs were lightly spun with frost and the cold breathed through the glass.

"The Festival," said Tristus looking down at his filled plate. "I had forgotten it. There have been so many other things on my mind."

"Be assured the Guildsmen have not forgotten it. Each time I hear of the "marvel" they are to unveil a black chill runs through me. I do not trust it, but what is new in that, I have never trusted the Haarshaim."

"Even so we have trusted to much." said Tristus, looking over his shoulder. "They watch us even here."

"It has been difficult to keep up appearances under these

circumstances, particularly since mother has been ill."

"I wonder how she passed the night?"

"It is early yet, but I would bet Aleryn is up." said Arcus finishing his last bite of bread.

So they took the last sips of tea and left the room. When they arrived at their mother's door they found Aleryn was in her chamber. She was dressed in her long nightgown and her red hair fell loosely abut her shoulders but she wore a smile upon her face. Behind her the Queen was sitting up in her bed, a plate of food upon her lap. Her color and strength had returned during the night.

"The others show even more improvement." Aleryn announced. "Mileah is well enough to leave her bed. She is with the twins. The water has done its work. Healthy skin has already sealed their wounds. Mikel and Mora, have only faint remains of their sores and they are eating and arguing. It is a great relief."

"I feel like walking this morning, Aleryn. The tide is rising and I would like to watch the ships leave the bay. Who knows, I may even have the strength to serve as Queen once more." she smiled.

And it was true. Her eyes were no longer listless and her skin had healthy glow. She walked alone to the window and looked to the East. The great city sprawled beneath the castle walls and to the West the ocean waved in green-gray swells. The pale moon clung still to the flat horizon as the morning sun climbed into the sky. A flock of black gulls scattered themselves noisily above the houses and shops. Screeching shrilly; spreading their bad tempers over the dimly glowing streets. Young lamp-wrights moved along the alleys turning down, one by one, the pale orbs which lined the way. Already the city was filled with travelers and the young morning bristled with activity. The Festival brought together many people from foreign lands. The merchants and vendors had been preparing for days and their tension filled the marketplace.

They watched the sun burst over the walls and suddenly the streets overflowed with sounds. Stirring as a single wave, the people crowded into the markets and Tristus became aware of the single mind that caused them to think, to speak, and to act.

The Queen sighed looking to the streets beneath her feet, "We have so many now, so many to consider."

A servant knocked gently upon the door announcing that the fisherman, Jason, had arrived. Tristus and Arcus went ahead to meet him and found him upon the balcony, its doors standing open behind him. The scents and sounds of the city filled the room.

They greeted one another warmly and soon had exchanged all the news of the past days. Tristus watched the conversation that took place between Jason and Arcus recognizing how similar in countenance they were. As the conversation continued, he saw how they moved, gestured, and spoke in a like manner and he reckoned to himself this was the reason he had trusted the man so quickly. It was not long before the Queen came to meet them in the library. She was dressed comfortably in a light robe and she walked graciously with Aleryn close at her side. Her streaked hair was braided loosely and hung long to her waist. The pale green of her skirt flowed softly against the dark wood of the floor. Her sleeves touched the edge of fingertips for the lesions were still raw upon. Nonetheless, she moved as herself again with her health regained and her mind restored.

"Good morning, Captain. It is good to see you again."

Jason bowed to the Queen in the formal fashion.

"It is my pleasure, Lady. I am happy to see you so much improved. The cure your sons have brought back has certainly done its work."

The Queen smiled.

"I am glad you had the opportunity to meet with my mother while I was away." spoke Tristus. "Thank you, my friend."

"Jason told me of your miraculous return and I have seen for myself the affects of the *Pyrrohmarin* has upon the creatures of the sea. It was not a pleasant sight." she said thoughtfully, "and since our meeting, I have thought often of our words shared. Though most of our conversation was of a grave nature, a portion of your tale brought me piercing joy. I am grateful beyond words to you, Jason, for bringing my son back to me. I hope to compensate you for this deed." said the Queen.

"No reward do I require my Queen. I have all the possessions I could ever need. Know only that I am ready to assist with any task you may require." said Jason gently.

"Now that I have seen the effects of the scourge, it is the news of the Thalassisans distresses me most."

Tristus agreed. "I believe we must seek them out, whether they wish to parley or no, it is necessary we know how they are affected."

"Do you think they are aware of the source of the disease?" asked Aleryn.

"I would suppose that they have ways of finding what they need answer too."

"Maybe they hold a solution for us? Perhaps they have seen the *Pyrrohmarin* before." said Arcus.

"Aye, it could be that they have, but it seems to me that such knowledge might hurt us more than help us. If the starting place of the trouble should truly lay with the activities of our own people and such knowledge could be enough to set off war."

"I have known of the Thalassisan's existence for many years." replied Jason. "and since I travel frequently outside the boundaries of the fishing fleets and the mer-folk are familiar with my ship. They have seen her often in the Northern Sea and, though they share no love for us, I do not believe they would do the Bifrost any harm." replied Jason.

"And this may be our only protection." said Tristus.

The Queen listened and after a time she spoke her thoughts, "The Festival takes place during the full of the Moon. We have just two days before it begins and another three before its end. Already the castle is filling with guests and the city is overwhelmed with the preparations for the games and the bidding. Your presence would be sorely missed if you should choose to leave before that time. If it is the lust for metal which stirs poison into the waters, I must remind you that this same lust was the fall of Tessera before. I do not find it difficult to see that the stage could be set for history to repeat itself. If a greedy few are seeking to realize their own schemes, feigned concern for the greater good will fly most quickly from the lips of those with the most to gain. Indeed, though our problems may lie at our own doorstep, we must remember the Guildsmen hold a certain prominence among us and the people will find it difficult to pick the truth from half-lies."

"But if the Guildsmen are involved in the slave trading, wealth can not shield them from law." said Arcus.

"There will be foreign folk attending the Festival and many will come from the southern islands. If the slave trade comes from that region we may learn something of this situation." said Aleryn. "If we know the right questions to ask."

Pelius then spoke out for the first time. "It would do us well to consider these things another way. What lies behind these shadows is more than just a physical force but a magical force as well. These wraiths are no longer as ordinary men. Whoever they were, or whatever they had been, has been changed. They are controlled by an intent more cruel, and more potent, than the most awful of your Guildsmen." he said as his eyes grew fierce, "And you must remember, this force can move between the worlds and this makes it is more dangerous than any man."

"It is true." agreed Tristus, "We must understand what we fight and what we know best is that this force is capable of dreadful harm."

"It is not just the folk of Tessera who have been affected it." Arcus said grimly, "The south islanders may have paid a price more dear than our own. I have dealt with them often and I can tell you that we share much more than just a fondness for horses and I would expect the legends of those lands are also filled with the threads of the old magic. When they come to buy and barter they might be able to shed some insights into the true nature of these strange days."

Aleryn listened and then kissing Arcus upon his forehead she walked to the window and spoke to the air.

"To release the night, the sun comes forth.
A center point enraged.
In time and moments, the vessel fills
With tranquil seas and rings of flame
Left to shine in narrow rooms,
Unmentioned shades upon its rim
Moving out till no surround remains
The center knows itself again."

And as the plea moved across the housetops, it was decided that the voyage to the Mer-people was better off delayed. The Festival heralded the rise of the Full Winter Moon and the time point of the year when all the days would begin grow longer. The low hanging sun stirred the unseen excitement within the sleeping seeds. The cold chill spread through the air and the first flakes of snow fell over the folk of Tessera. The crisp briskness added to the anticipation as each Inn was filled and every stall occupied. The city overflowed with people.

While the others went about the business of preparing for the Festival, Tristus spent much time with the Tahmurath. He watched as the children tossed objects in the air with the power of their minds. He heard their speech uttered in his own thoughts as they sent their words from mind to mind. Since their communications did not require the common use of sound he soon noticed the silent contacts were spread to all other creatures of the castle. Cats, dogs, or kitchen mice would follow the children obediently through the castle halls. Pelius knew each of the children well and explained to him their talents. Most could speak in some fashion, the varied languages of beast and birds, while others had the natural ability to manipulate the elements. The wind, the earth, or the water, were often biddable to their wills and still there were other gifts. Mileah had the ability to speak to the growing things. The dark-eyed child would entice the green shoots to stretch their leaves in the direction of her voice. Tristus had looked on in the kitchens gardens as Mileah invoked the fairies who lived unseen within the plants. For a brief moments, the lovely creatures would hover soundlessly in the air, blinking at the tiny girl in wonder and disbelief. Centuries had passed since they had been called from their finer realms of sun and rain and they too became aware that a great change was coming. Tristus was amazed by the Tahmurath for their powers seemed to surpass any he held himself. Aleryn was the only one among his own household that held any indication of such abilities. The children healed rapidly, gaining focus and strength as the moon came round and full, reflecting the light of the sun.

The night before the Festival they gathered for the

evening meal. Arcus and Clade had been busy all day in the stables with visitors coming to look upon the Queen's horses and throughout the city, every stall and room was filled. The Queen had been receiving guests from the far-east and south. Princes and Queens, Noblemen and Ladies had been invited to lodge in the castle. All travelers had come to purchase the scores of goods offered by the Guilds. Horses, lights, or flying machines, powered by the atricault amalgam, were in great demand and throughout night and day the coming and going of messengers and courtiers did never cease. The constant whirr of machinery continued to unsettle the air and the lights, glassware, metal-crafts, gliders, cloth, tools, and jewels, all lined the crowded walkways of the market place. The kitchens flooded the streets with vivid aromas by day and night. Exotic foods were prepared for the many different peoples met in Tessera at this time every year. The great dining hall of the castle was set several times a day with long tables of strange, succulent delicacies. The Queen had been busy. Her illness, apparently overcome, left her able to see to the visitors with her usual grace and hospitality. The preparations for the games had been taken on by Arcus and Clade. The races and competitions had been set up in the larger of the city squares as well as along the shores of the bay. Boats lined the docks and while some of them were meant for competition most were up for sale or barter. The Haarshaim courted the visitors with fine wines and spiced meat, hosting various feasts to entertain the prospective buyers during the course of the event. The heat of buying and selling filled the city as the morning of the Festival found the family settling down to a quiet breakfast.

"How many horses will you bring to auction this year?" said Tristus breathing in the steam of his coffee.

"More than a dozen yearlings," answered Arcus, "But that is only because tradition dictates that I do it. This group is a special one and I am finding it hard to part with any of them. But even if we choose to keep a yearling or two, there will be no lack of horses in this year. All the stables in the city are packed. Herders from the Western Isles have come with their ponies and the Highlanders have brought working beasts. The island folk have sent four boats and each is filled with war horses. I must say Tristus they are fine beasts. Clade has been helping me with them as the dealers have come into the city. We have been setting up races and shows, and contests of strength. It shall be a fantastic event. I have never seen a Festival when there has been so much ado for so many.

"Have the Guilds responded to our requests for a meeting? I would like to see what they have to say about the northern mines."

"They have avoided our requests for a council." said Arcus his smiling fading away. "The unveiling of their mysterious surprise is their reason for being to busy to meet with us just yet. They say a new day will dawn after this new creation is revealed but I think otherwise. It is the first time you have sought them out in many years and I believe the request has unnerved them. This morning a diktat was sent to the Head Chancellor. It will leave him no choice. We are set to meet at noon the day the moon turns full."

"I have asked that there be a representative from the mines, mills, farms, and fleets in attendance." the Queen replied. "The Guilds are being unusually secretive."

"I find it strange that they have avoided audience with us." said Arcus, "What they are keeping hid worries me."

Tristus frowned into his empty cup, "And what we are keeping hid worries me. Do you think they are aware that it is the Tahmurath that dwell in the castle? My concern for their safety grows each day."

"I have passed the word the children are from the western provinces of our father's kin and that they are here to be educated. But I too am concerned. I worry that unfriendly eyes have witnessed the unusual things they do. It is difficult to convince the children to conceal their powers." said Aleryn.

A soft knock from outside the room interrupted them and Pelius swung open the heavy wooden door to find the young servant boy standing in the hall.

"The Head Priestess seeks audience with the Queen." he announced in a polished voice.

"She is free to enter." responded the Queen.

At the word the Head Priestess flowed into the room; her silvery blue robes tracing a scented path along the floor. She took a place in the center of the group and her blue eyes reflected the flames of the hearth fire.

"My Queen I have come to you in morbid haste," she said bowing low. "for this night a portent was revealed to me. I ask that you take the time to hear it."

"We shall hear your foretelling." the Queen answered gravely and the Priestess' eyes gleamed as she raised her head to speak.

"Without sleeping I have dreamed of a creature; terrifying and powerful. I sat in revelation as the beast watched me from its realm, seeing me as I saw it. It is the son of a serpent and a daughter of earth. It is hideous to look upon, for it is a beast with three heads and three minds. One head is that of a lion that can not be satisfied and another is the head of a goat that can not be pure. The last of the faces is like the Wind that pulls the light from the body. Its power pours from the fires of the earth's core and its strength flows like a sea storm. It mocked me as I witnessed it and then the creature leaned toward me. The stank of its breath blinded me and it revealed to me the destruction of our people. Dripping from its cruel jaws, bits of men cried for mercy before their dismembered parts fell into the streets. All around me the wails of children filled the air. Thunder rolled and the wind lamented and the ground shook and I saw the Tower of Malthrom crumbling apart. I watched, unable to utter a sound, as its black stones were swallowed by the angry sea until a lightless shadow blotted out the day. Then I heard the creature speaking to me; telling me its name."

Her eyes gleamed and Aleryn gasped aloud. She could see the priestess' error before it was to happen. To utter the name of a Demon is to call it into the world. She tried speak out and stop her from this thing but it came too late. The deed was done. When she uttered the Demon name and the Word shook the room. The Priestess had, though the power of her speech, had served its purpose and invoked the shadow into the chamber. The hall rocked with terror. The Priestess stood before the curved glass of the bay window and her body wavered in the destroying force. The demon had been called into the world and it was too late to turn it away. It leapt towards them like a hot flame; filling each with the power of its evil and pulling from them all hope and strength. Pelius fell against the door and wretched. Tristus felt the blood draining from his face. Lightheaded and reeling he grasped the bedstead as Arcus stumbled toward him. The blue robed priestess shook like a fragile leaf. From the corner of his eye he saw Aleryn crumble to the floor, her frail body fading like a vapor into the airs. She struggled to speak, but no sound could she utter for the princess was no longer a solid form. Tristus reached to help his sister and his hand passed through her as if it were water. The Queen stared in horror as her daughter faded like a wraith into an unseen realm. Her heart shuddered. She could not allow it to take her. She drew up straight and found a new strength welling up within her. Somehow she knew the monster that stood in front of her and she shouted out a single word, the word that is held secret in the heart of every Queen. Standing still as death, the creature coldly measured her with the black holes that served as its eyes. Then, as suddenly as it had come, the phantom was gone and when the darkness began to dissipate they found the room was damp with cold.

Aleryn lay still, Arcus and the Queen knelt by her and raised her head. Pelius touched her face and when her form began to grow solid before their eyes, she was able to speak their names. Tristus turned to face the Priestess. A strange glint in her eyes caught his attention and he glimpsed the presence that lingered within her. The spirit flickered for just an instant and then the woman was alone before him. She trembled when she felt the touch of his mind and he perceived her fear as real and not imagined. He went toward her, intending to comfort her but when he touched her arm, she recoiled in pain.

Bowing her head she murmured a choked apology to the Prince. Shuddering, with her eyes cast downward, the Priestess waited to be given leave to depart. Tristus nodded his consent and stood aside as she moved with painful difficulty through the door. Aleryn rose to her feet and leaned against her brother.

The Queen was icy pale when she looked up to her first born son,

"This contest before us is indeed more than physical." and she took a deep breath as she sank down in the sunlight of the balcony.

"It has returned to its master." said Aleryn in a trembling voice as she glanced down the hallway. "This beast has been watching us. It knew our hearts and it knows our names."

"This ghost." Pelius said bleakly. "It is the same creature that killed my brother."

"I know it too. It has been with me always." whispered Tristus, looking toward the door, still noticing the scent of the Priestess within in the room. "It has whispered in my ear through the years of my life. It is what chills us with boubt and stirs alive our fears."

"It is the thread of dark touches all. It is bound into the course of every life." murmured Aleryn in quiet desperation, putting her hand to her face. " It is made into the very fabric of our world. How can we fight such a thing?"

"There is just one way." Tristus answered in a voice so low it seemed he only spoke to himself. "We must hold no shadow within ourselves."

"That is not possible." thought Pelius.

Tristus shook his head but did not answer the unspoken thought.

Pelius' gut churned and troubled questions filled his mind. He looked to Aleryn as she struggled with despair. He was drawn to her, but nonetheless he found her the most difficult to understand. The royal family misjudged this evil as it did its work through the shadows of the city. They had grown too insulated, barricaded behind years of traditions and fortress walls of the castle made it impossible to grasp the certain reality that loomed beneath them. This battle would not be won in a transparent inner world they seemed so familiar with. The phantom that pursued them held the ability to wield solid force in the planes of earth and as Aleryn cried silently in her brother's arms, Pelius found himself filled with an absolute hopelessness.

The Festival began at noon and the Queen and her children went to preside over the opening ceremonies. Trumpeters heralded their approach and guards walked ahead holding bright banners. The burnished hooves of their horses clattered over the cobbled streets. The Flag Bearers held the placard of the House of Tessera. Its symbol was a single tree with five stars blazing against a field of deep blue. Slowly they made their way through the throng. The Knights of the Tower walked just ahead of them, clearing a way through the swarm as the people shouted out and crowded close together in the narrow streets. The Queen rode upon her white mare. Tristus was at her side, stern and calm, astride the gray stallion, Phadraus and Aleryn, small as she was, sat deftly upon her restless red yearling. All were adorned in the conventional dress. Warm tunics colored in shades of white hung loosely from their shoulders, the silk edging lightly touched with bits of soft blue and pale orange.

Arcus was at the elbow of his sister smiling at the crowd. As they walked a mist spread before his eyes and he found, for a moment, he had the ability to see within the form. The people looked to be elongated spheres of light as they pressed close upon them. Faulty and desperate, he sensed the mindless longing that drove them to reach out and touch their garments as they passed by. Blind hope flew from them and he saw the ease in which they could be manipulated. The mob was lost in the pounding of a singular mind. The rising pulse of the throng clouded the airs and soon its strength had become alarming. He felt their mood pervade his senses. The rooting pressure of their desires grew more terrible and he reeled in discomfort. He closed his eyes and focused upon his beating heart, waiting for the steady calm to grow within, as he realized the people were not aware of their dilemma.

The sun was dazzling through the brightly colored tents and banners when they reached the center square. Rivulets of melting frost ran over the stone streets and the rich aroma of breads, beer, and meats filled the air. The people cheered as the family left their horses and made their way to the chairs waiting for them upon the dais. Standing upon the platform they waved to the audience before taking their seats. The voices of singers and the pure notes of the harpists filled the air as the musicians breathed magic into the crowd. Winding from the fingers of the players, the sound grew steadily. Dancers emerged from behind the colored pavilions and the motion of their bodies fascinated the onlookers. The music spun its rhythms as the dancer's spinning scarves trailed the path of melodies. The song rose to meet the clouds above and the tune flowed though the white vapor and blue skies. The notes drew each other along their way until finally only its whispered memory remained.

The day passed and its hours were filled with contests, feasts, and commerce. Children, minstrels, travelers, and thieves wandered freely in the street. The evening found the city ablaze with lanterns and song under the clear winter sky. The Tahmurath enjoyed some freedoms as they went with the nurses to the celebration. Surprisingly at ease, they moved in and out of the masses of people with skillful grace. Tristus kept watch as closely as he could from the confinement of his public appearances until Pelius finally gathered them together. The hour was late when the children returned to the castle.

Tristus slept poorly and found himself standing at the window, wrapped in his coverlets, waiting for the sun to rise. The second day of the festival was the one he had always liked best. It was the day the boat races were held in the bay. Along the wharfs, a stage had been built where they could watch the contests. Wage earners and ticket men crowded the piers. Burly men held the people back from entering the docks while the boats were made ready to race. Tristus had a good view of the activities and he wished he was with them while they worked. In that crowd, he saw Jason talking with some of the contestants as they prepared their ships. Under the disapproving gaze of the nobles, and their ladies, he took leave of his seat and went to speak with him.

"How is it with you, my friend?" he said when he reached where Jason stood upon the pier.

"I have been all too occupied with this Festival business." smiled Jason.

"As have I." answered Tristus, moving his head slightly toward the obvious empty seat in the stands.

"It seems to me you are missed, Prince."

"Aye. I suppose that is what they call it," answered Tristus, shrugging his shoulders. "I do not fret over courtly jabber and I can be assured that they will not think any less of me than they did at breakfast. Anyway, I have wanted to speak with you. Tomorrow we are meeting with the Head Chancellor and several of the Guild Masters. We will talk to them about the northern mines. With any luck maybe we can learn something."

"Luck, and truth, may be in short supply." Jason said looking over the watery horizon. "I feel danger swelling in her currents."

Then suddenly the crowd let out a great cheer. The first event had begun. The sails of racers stood white and tense with the chill wind. The sleek vessels, each with a crew of three, sped toward the first marker as the winter sun dazzled the sea. The contest was one of speed. Boats carrying judges followed the contestants outside the set course and from shore other arbiters watched the racers through long telescopes. The wind blew across Tristus face, tousling his unmanageable hair. He stood upon the pier, watching the race, longing again for the freedom that waited outside the walls of his city.

Before he returned to his seat among the Lords and Noblemen he made arrangements to meet Jason once more. The journey to the Thalassisans should not be delayed any longer. They would leave as soon as the Festival Auction was over. The people parted to let him pass as he made his way back to his mother's side. Sitting quietly he watched the races throughout the afternoon but his mind was faraway and filled with troubled thoughts. When the last boat returned to the docks, it was Arcus who presented the cups to the winners of the day. Damp and exhausted, the crews waved at the roaring crowd and soon after the people began to disperse. The kitchens of the Public Houses were busy and their tables overflowed with food. Long lines formed outside the doors of the crowded inns while venders pressed along the streets, selling food from carts to those who did not choose to wait. Tristus was relieved when they turned toward home. He walked with the Lords and Ladies, nodding politely at their conversations and almost feeling a tinge of shame as he attempted to appear interested at the trivialities that consumed their lives.

The dinner was a formal affair, another obligation he was required to endure. He stared in the looking glass he laid the silver swath, which symbolized the authority of the House of Tessera, across his breast. His crown was a thin circlet of atricault. The luminous metal glowed faintly under his dark curls. Arcus appeared in his doorway, looking as much a Prince as his brother. He was wearing royal suit of arms. Being second born, tradition held that he would wear the uniform of a first officer for his birthright dictated that he would uphold the honor of the first-born child.

"Shall we sit near one another?" asked Tristus hopefully. "I believe the Lady of Celphia wishes to continue her account of her eldest daughters' coming of age celebration. I fear the young lady, being now ripe for marrying, shall be present at my table. I may require your protection."

Arcus laughed, "I shall keep you safe, brother. You can trust that no maiden's soft hands shall stray to caress your coal colored locks when I am near. I am duly sworn to uphold your honor." and he bowed so low his head touched the soft carpet. "Fear not, I shall keep her eye turned in another direction."

"Hmm, I suppose I feel I better now." said Tristus, raising an eyebrow.

Dinner seemed an endless affair and as Tristus had expected, the young Princess of Celphia was presented to him as he took his seat at the banquet table. Politely, he suffered the conversation of the mother as her eye roved greedily over the fine furnishings of the banquet hall. Arcus championed the better part of his discomfort with the graceful art of conversation. With delicate diplomacy he drew the banter away from any plans Tristus had of marrying and settling down to the business of running a kingdom. Instead he discussed the food and music that filled the warm hall. Grateful for his brother's gift of charm, Tristus was left with many opportunities to look about the room and soon his eye landed upon Pelius. The boy sat at the other end of the long table with Aleryn at his side. It was apparent that he was even more ill at ease than Tristus himself. Tristus caught his eye and winked at the young boy from over the sea of food. Pelius smiled back weakly but as his clairvoyant senses caught a breath of the social nature of Tristus' dilemma, his eyes brightened and he picked up his napkin to stifle a laugh.

The younger children did not attend the affair for no open displays of their magical talents could be risked. Pelius had seen them safely tucked into their beds before the late dinner began. He watched with silent interest the interactions of the people, perceiving the oval fields of force that surrounded each body. Their moods were not unlike wisps of smoke he thought observing their lusts and jealousies float about the tables. How different it was from the clear dealings which occurred between sun and tree or prey and predators. These human beasts groped mindlessly amid themselves, filling their mouths with food and drink as their motives ran together in a muddy stream.

Eating slowing, he considered these things until he felt a sudden cold wind brush by his face. The garden door was opened and a new presence had entered the hall. She stood with her hand draped over the arm of a well-dressed Guildsman. Around her brow she held no murky thoughts of desire; but instead there lie the clarity of one who understands the need of these things. She walked between the tables collecting the unused force spewed forth from the lot of the drunken guests and Pelius watched as their light floated towards her in packets of luminance. She smiled, seemingly innocent of the experience but Pelius could see the lie behind her smile and he leaned over to touch Aleryn by the arm. This woman understood the power she wielded and she used it to steal the light from those less aware. Intentionally, she chose to pull their light to her and they responded, unthinkingly like moths drawn to flame. Looking over the crowd and her eyes lighted upon Tristus and a smile twisted ever so slightly over her lips. She nodded at her escort guiding him closer to the table of the Prince.

Pelius sent a blast of thought toward him as Tristus choked on his sip of wine. Tristus glanced up but immediately his gaze was pulled toward the woman as she neared the table. She was moving toward him with focused grace and his mind was filled with confusion as her presence pervaded him. He trembled as she smiled upon him. He was standing; though he did not recall getting up. He was taking her by the hand and placing it to his lips. He was saying words he did not understand. She was smiling back, liquid in her pleasure, saturating him with weakness and desire. Pelius saw as she sent her escort away with a light brush of her will. The man moved from her side blending into the shadows as if his body stuff were but a deception of the mind. She was left alone to focus upon the Prince. Tristus moved another chair in towards his table and he motioned for the lady to sit down as poured her a glass of wine.

Aleryn could not recall ever having seen the women before. Worriedly she watched how the ebony eyes held her brothers attentions at the exclusion of all others. She exchanged a look of concern with Pelius but at that moment the dancers appeared in the ball room. This was the Dance of the New Year. Ancient in its origins, it was performed annually to symbolize the coming of the longer days and the release of darkness. Men, wrapped in loose linen cloths, and women, covered by fragile gowns, moved upon the tiles between the long tables acting out a saga of courtship and consummation. Revealing as they danced the turning cycles of creation, they rendered the moment of birth into life, and life into tragedy, and tragedy into hope, only again to change and move forward again unto yet the another doorway. The doorway the mortal mind calls death. The story of each life was portrayed moving from one form to another until the bits of the smaller stories were shown to fit together into the larger kingdom. The magical rhythms moved in ever widening circles. The lights were lowered gradually and as they dimmed, colored shades were placed over the lanterns. The dancers now moved along the walls, appearing now as terrible shapes flowing across the room and each guest saw their own life played out upon the moving screens around them. The reflection of every hope and desire was alive in the room.

In their motion, the dancers reenacted the experiences of life, the pain of being, the lust of living, the tragedy of fulfillment, the passing of the form from its dusty sheath, and onward through the threshold of a new beginning. As the dance ended all the remaining lights in the great domed hall converged to the center point in the ceiling above. The motion beneath faded with the extinguishing of the candle flames until finally only one light did remain in the room. The faint beam hung from the highest point of the vast ceiling. Far above, the guests and the dancers, the single light shone. All eyes rested upon it in moment of silent reverence and as they watched the small light suddenly leaped forth filling the room with a great brightness and the dancers shouted out. For an instant no shadow remained within the hall. Blindingly, it illuminated the center hall as the dazzling light released the dark. Then, just a suddenly as it had come, the brilliance was reduced back to the lesser light. When the sightlessness passed from the eyes of the people, they saw a soft glow had appeared at their feet and there, in that new light, lay the babe. Newborn just that day, the child cried out and a promise of change was carried on its breath.

The lights rose in the room, revealing once more the guests, the dancers, and the newborn child. All rose to their feet in joyful response to the birth as the dance symbolized the fulfillment of The Promise. Arcus had watched the full flow of the ancient ritual and he was happy for the remembrance of the vow always brought him a measure of comfort. He turned then to look toward his brother and saw that he, and the lady, were no where to be seen. Aleryn and Pelius, at that same moment realized the same thing and in an instant they were at his side.

"I can find them." Pelius whispered, "She leaves a scent." and he hurried from the banquet hall. He needed no light. The imprint of the woman's intentions left traces that were easy for him to sense. He felt as if he were with Tarin once more; following his intuitions as they rescued the Tahmurath. He was familiar with the path that the evil would leave as it cut through the air. The danger spread before him and part of his mind rebelled unwilling to recall its violence. But he breathed in the clear night airs and silenced the despair. He would not allow this specter to steal the hope that once more murmured in his heart. Moving swiftly though the shadow of night he did not lose a step as he followed the phantom. Allowing his inner voice to guide him he moved with an intuitional force and in a space of time, that did not allow for such quickness, he found himself upon the high cliff behind the castle which overlooked the sea. He could see the garden and beyond its destroyed gate lay the beginning of the long stairway which reached to the beach far below.

A twist of malice lightly brushed him. They were there. The woman rested above the prince and he saw that their lips touched. But it was not a kiss like that of lovers, it was instead more a puncturing, like that of an insect as it steals the life force from its victim. Pelius shouted out. Startled, the shadow lifted her head from the wilting body of the Prince. A ripping agony flashed through her and she released her grip. Pelius called to the clouds and a flash of light broke through the sky. In that instant she was gone but where she had stood, a crack remained, hanging like a dark slash above Tristus' motionless frame. Its blackness sucked the light from under the dome of the heavens and Tristus lay dangerously vulnerable under the gaping wound. A vile stench escaped from the unworldly cut and Pelius flew to his side pulling him away from the crack. The woman had escaped through the hole which hung in the night. The doorway remained for but an instant more and then it faded, leaving the castle grounds to look oddly normal once again.

He grabbed Tristus by the shoulders and shook him. White as a sheet, he opened his eyes and returned to himself. Freed from the spell, Tristus looked away from his young rescuer and wretched into the bushes.

The next morning Tristus remained in his room. His frailty tormented him. His connection was broken. With a mortal weakness revealed, the point of higher contact was no longer available to him. For the first time, he saw himself as an ordinary man, able to be consumed by the passions of the lower nature. He looked at his reflection and was disgusted by what he saw.

Pelius worried about him though the night. Though the woman had caused no physical wound, he had seen her effort to rob him of the vital force. Pelius understood the potency of the power she wielded. The source of her cravings spewed from a well of shadows and, though the intentions of the sorceress had not been satisfied, she had touched him. Pelius could not be sure how deeply her touch had reached and when Tristus did not come to breakfast his concerns increased. He followed Aleryn and Arcus to his bed chamber, and there they found him, staring out the window. The glass looked over the pale mist rising from the ocean. Tristus was not yet dressed for the day. They discussed the events of the night before but soon became aware that there was little he was willing to share. The Prince's mood was black and he could not be moved from it. Aleryn was troubled when she kissed his forehead. Arcus stood with his hand resting upon the bent shoulder of his taciturn brother. Pelius could not understand why he punished himself. They closed the door and left Tristus alone with his thoughts.

The meeting with the Haarshiam was held at the noon hour. It was the final day of Festival. The expensive silks of their long robes rustled as they entered the meeting room. The Queen sat in the middle of a long table. The Head Chancellor and the rest of the Guildsman filed into the chairs which had been set up before the rostrum of the Queen and her children and they waited, unconcernedly, to be questioned.

As was expected, those present denied all charges, stating ardently that they were not aware of any illegal mines nor did they have knowledge concerning the gathering of slaves. Throughout the inquiry the Queen found them cleverly ambiguous but their words were not what she watched. She questioned the Haarshiam to perceive the reality behind the words they spoke and, oddly enough, it appeared that no single person present, seemed wholly responsible. As planned, Tristus demanded records of operations but his voice echoed with a hollow tone. Weakened from his contact with the woman the night before his tone was stripped of any intention. The Haarshaim immediately noticed this shortcoming and fed upon his failing. The Princes' tone of voice carried no power. The Chancellor offered a dry explanation of their record keeping practices assuring him that the books were in order. He told the Prince that the records would be available for examination. Their practices were above reproach and always ready for the scrutiny of the Queen. There would be nothing that they would find out of order in those accountings. He reminded all that their operations were lucrative and many people of the Kingdom were beholden to the commercial practices of the Haarshaim. He spoke to Tristus as if he were but a silly boy unable to fully understand the complex inter-workings of business and economy. The Chancellor smiled as the group left the room. He took special care to ask if the Prince felt well and if was there anything that he could do to be of assistance. His politeness was sticky.

CHAPTER 13
THE MOUNTAIN

MALTHROM WATCHED HIS DESPAIR from the tower windows. Perceiving his waves of distress the wizard considered the possibility of revealing to his form to the boy. He measured the advantages of showing the Prince the true nature of these moments of acute sting. He read his frame of mind, understanding the sickness that crept under the skin. He knew Tristus sought to forget, as well as to remember, the devastating touch of the shade. Malthrom watched the plight of the Prince and considered his options. He had the authority to decide what action would have the greatest benefit to all. All possibilities under the blanket of the heavens were at his disposal. There was but one law to which he must remain loyal. He studied the Prince from the Dark Tower, seeing the Princess as she moved with kindness, and reading the great heart of his brother as he called to him in quiet desperation. He witnessed these things take place within Tristus' chambers and weighed them within the balance of his wisdom. Malthrom chose to remain silent. The life's journey of this Prince of Prophets was not ready for another obvious intervention by the numinous.

The soft sound of the chimers slippers echoed through the Tower. The morning ritual of descent was drawing to a close. Ten thousand spiraling steps the Priestesses had walked once more. Along either side of the corresponding walls the identical stairways complimented each other in form and function. The cold stone stairwells were an integral part of the organization that held the massive structure together. They showed no trace of wear, even as the centuries of spiraling ascension and return had passed. The lamp bearers walked in unison carrying the light of the morning away from the heavens and Malthrom waited until the last footstep faded and the sound of the locking door reached the upper room.

Tessera was awakening. The movement of men and beasts pushed the hushed sounds of the other lives deeper into the backdrop of the city. Unnoticed, the others lives remained hidden and they fed in one way or another upon the light of the sun. Crawling along the garden walls and spreading between the bricks each living thing was consumed by what was common to its nature. From these varying perspectives all creatures were aware of the odd activities of the people. Avoiding their clattering presence when possible, the insects and scavenger, molds and moss, continued their unremitting quest for food, shelter, and mates. They too were woven into the mosaic of the city, as they flew through the air or scuttled through the alleys for one life was inextricably dependent upon the refuse of another.

The Eratosthenians had held the understanding of force which shaped the form the life. They knew the ancient hand had once worked in different ways. When the Mist, that separated heaven and earth was finally prepared, it became necessary to shield the infant from that knowledge. The promise was concealed within itself and since that time, it remained obscured, lest the hidden gift be destroyed. Time past and changes occurred but still the seed slept within the body of the people. The old books but faintly echoed the original intentions. The knowledge of the Eratosthenians now served other purposes and people could no longer separate truth from lies.

To most, the body of Malthrom was imperceptible for his form lay in the ethers which exist just outside the physical realms. They did not see the Wizard as he moved among the mists. More alive than ever before, he was profoundly misunderstood and though it was well within his power to be seen, he rarely found it helpful to those he was bound to serve.

Often he heard the people call his name. Day upon day, they pleaded for small favors, cursing him as their days of trial plodded on. The decisions they made, the actions they took, the resentments they harbored, all served to bury deeper the secret which lie within. It was the place they never considered searching.

Malthrom had seen the future, "An unfortunate ability under the present certain circumstances," he thought once again. The options converged in his mind. He stood at the window of the tower, feeling the moments, and tasting the breeze that came off the water. So intent was he upon sensing the rhythm of the people that day he was nearly solid enough to be seen by the untrained eye. But there was not one who walked beneath him who took that moment to raise their eyes and perceive his presence. He was alone and unaided looking down into the hustle of city. Again, he must piece together the threads of action which had brought the people to this juncture of time.

A vision stirred before him and he saw a red sky smoldering over a burnt field of ash. The steady darkness rose and fell over the uneven ground as the shadow swiftly moved over the land and the sea. The shade spread across the world finally reaching the place where it could go no further. Impatient and ugly, it waited but Wall of Mist kept it from going further in. Malthrom watched still from the tower and when his eyes pierced the fog, the ever-present mountain appeared. Its great head rose over the clouds and the airs above it were fine and clear. For many years the paths at its base had lain obscured from the vision of the people. But on this day, the Wizard sensed the beat of stirring heart. Strong and humble, the seeker approached the door and a bright light illuminated the clearing. Underbrush and brambles released their thorny grip upon the gate and as their stiff fingers pulled away from the threshold of the door, the seeker was allowed to enter. The clothes of the traveler were stained and soiled with the dust. The journey had been demanding but as light filled the entrance, its warmth touched the pilgrim. The wanderer's garments were made clean and all the weariness was washed away. The seeker moved toward the door but again the view became obstructed. A mirror blocked the way. Questions rained upon the traveler; was this way sought in vanity, but another illusion fueled by the futility of a common life.

"No," the wanderer reminded itself, "No, it could not be." and in the fleeting moment the pilgrim gave the last of its illusions and blinding mirror vanished into a light. A new path appeared and the traveler glimpsed the deeps that led through the circles of stars. The valley moved. The earth cracked. A wisp of warmth brushed the frozen soil and the people of Tessera felt a stirring of hope. Malthrom watched as Tristus' kin left his chamber and he steadied himself for the storm.

CHAPTER 14
THE UNVEILING

The festival was alive with light beneath the full winter moon. The Haarshaim hurried through the throng breathless in the anticipation of their long awaited moment. Their prize had been slow in preparing and the time for its unveiling was almost upon them. Attentive to the mood of the crowd, they noticed each time their costly robes were admired, or a glance was stolen of the rare stones in their rings. The eyes around them deferred to their social position. Pelius found these unspoken acts disturbing and sensed their smiles as crawling upon his skin. He was not accustomed to the nature of interactions which passed between the people. He walked with Clade though the tight crowds, grateful that there was no place for him in the stands where the royal family must assemble. The freedom of anonymity was far superior. The people advanced, as would a herd of hungry beasts, moving toward the center square. A large ring was set up where the horses would be led before the crowd and all about its edges small lanterns glowed. Banners waved in the night wind but their whispering sounds were lost in the bustle of the crowd. All day the people had walked among the stalls and paddocks, admiring the beasts. At the far end of the midway a platform had been raised where Tristus, Arcus, the Princess and the Queen would watch the activities from that balustrade. The trumpeters put their instruments to their lips heralding the beginning of the event. A loud shout came from the people as the Royal Family came forward to take their seats.

One by one, the horses and ponies filed into the center ring and the voice of the Caller carried over the heads of the people as the bidding began. Children, propped upon the shoulders of the adults, stretched their necks for a better view. The working beasts were the first to be auctioned and farmers came to the fore to stand near. The creatures looked suspiciously into the crowd but they moved obediently under the hands of their trainers. Long plumes of white hair covered their brightly polished hooves and the rich coats gleamed. Thick with muscles, their sturdy legs rippled as they stepped up to the ring. The auctioneers read from their pedigrees and gave a brief description of the height and weight before the fierce bidding began. One by one, the horses were lead off by their new owners where their legs and coats, muscles and teeth, were examined and admired but none stayed away to long, quickly returning to the center square, hoping that nothing had been missed.

When the working animals had been traded, the carriage and pleasure horses were led before crowd. Among them were the young and untrained as well as the old and gentle and the beasts came in every size and every color. The sorts of folk who bid upon the creatures were as varied as the animals themselves. Many of the travelers had come with the express purpose of finding the ideal horse for their precise need. The castle guests took their seats at the fore, Lords and Ladies, Barons and Danes, pushed the crowd aside as they made their selections before the rest of the common folk. Spirits ran high in the brisk bidding. The cold night air was eased by the many people and warm lights. Peddlers walked along the edge of the crowd carrying food on flat trays which hung from around their necks. Children gathered around them with their pennies to purchase sweets, excited by the late hour and noisy crowd.

The war horses of the southern islands followed next. They arched their proud necks. Their wide nostrils flared with excitement as they were led to the stage. Impatiently they pawed the ground, whinnying and tossing their powerful heads. The crowd pressed closer. Only the horses of the Queen's stables were more striking than these beasts. The handlers were from the Southern Isles. Their bright garments glowed with vivid yellows, scarlets, and blues and in the lantern light their golden skin glistened. Long black hair was pulled tightly back from the proud, hawk-like faces. In each hand was a long whip. The thin tip was quick to sing out commands and the great horses quickly obeyed. Their accents were thick as they commanded the horses in a brusque common tongue. Skillfully, they guided the horses though their paces and the beasts showed themselves to truly be the servants of men.

Barons and knights of foreign lands fiercely competed for the purchase of these stallions and mares for they knew that these creatures would bring forth superior foals. In this fierce exchange the Haarshaim were oddly silent. Normally, the most aggressive of all bidders, tonight they lingered behind the throng, unexpectedly restrained. Standing in small groups, not one among them chose to participate in the usual barter. Tristus watched intently as a small group of Guildsmen stood near him. They spoke softly with their heads close together, keenly aware of the tone of the trading. He realized the Head Chancellor stood with the group and as he looked closer, he recognized others as well. He had seen them in the stables just before his journey. It was Berdias and his crippled servant, Hyand. They stood shoulder to shoulder with the Head Chancellor. He nudged Arcus and nodded slightly in their direction. Arcus turned and recognized them as well. A sick nervousness exchanged between them. There was no action to take and the night crawled on. Tristus took a deep breath to settle his uneasiness.

Finally, came the time for the horses of the House of Tessera to take the stage. Arcus had chosen two dozen to be auctioned. Roars of approval filled the night as each horse was brought forward to be formally presented. All folk, the rich and poor, the ignorant and educated, the content and mournful, now pressed closely against one another in hopes of getting a bit nearer to the stage. The men of the Southern Isles acquired several of the group, including one of the young stallions that Arcus and the others had brought back from the canyon just a few weeks before. Arcus watched the handlers study his flawless form. He knew this one would be well treated, though many demands would he soon come to know. A black mare and her new foal caused great excitement among the Baroness' and Ladies. The women set their jaws and prodded their husbands onward in the tense bidding until finally only two remained in private competition, a Baron of Bugess and a Lord of Luzon. They carried on and the stakes were raised higher and higher. The Baron eventually yielded as the Lord and his Lady offered up an exorbitant price for the two creatures. The Lady, flushed with feverish determination, smiled thinly at the Baroness, watching her expression sour as she failed to face down the triumphant glare. Arcus raised his brow slightly at the exchange.

At last the bidding drew to a close. The horses had

brought a fine price. Tristus and his mother rose from their seats to stand before the people holding the heavy pouch of gold. As was the custom, this gold was bequeathed to one of the cities charitable organizations. This year the Queen called upon the stage a representative from the orphanage. A young woman stepped forward and graciously accepted the donation. A cheer rose from the crowd as they bowed and the Queen and her son stepped aside allowing the Haarshiam the moment they had long waited for.

The Head Chancellor, with two others at his side, strode unto the platform bowing to the Queen and the Prince before turning to face the crowd.

"Ladies and Lords, Princes and Princesses, Knights and Noblewomen, Queens and Kings, and let us not forget all other fair folk of this fine city, we are honored to be here." A great cheer rose up once more.

"Tonight we welcome you to witness a glorious wonder the likes of which the world has never seen before!" The Chancellor stood back and waited for another roar to rise from the street and as the sound died away he continued.

"This special evening you shall bear witness to what a few men have dared to dreamed. And though it is the dream of a few it will benefit the lives of many." and with that remark he began to thank the Guildsman "whose unceasing dedication had at last paid off in what would change the known world." The man went on and on to say that it was the accomplishments of a dedicated few that would be forever remembered as all the folk of Tessera would step forth into a new era of change, and opportunities, and though the hour was late the speech droned on. The people became restless, waiting for the talk to cease. Tristus shifted in his seat. He was uncomfortable. He set his jaw and wished the endless stream of noise would stop. The memory of the unsuccessful afternoon's meeting compounded his discomfort. He had found out nothing and worse than this, he had revealed himself as weak. He felt exposed. His temples throbbed as he waited.

Finally the long oration ended and the High Chancellor raised his arms to direct the gaze of the audience upward to the full yellow moon. There, against the backdrop of its butter-colored light, a strange silhouette appeared. The black form was difficult to accept as real for what had materialized in the skies above them they had never been seen before. Its shape was that of a massive horse and from its shoulders spread the wings of a monstrous bird. The people gasped as they watched the creature move across the clouds. A low humming filled the air and as the creature spiraled slowly downward and the sound grew steadily louder. The acute hum grated the air as the beast touched the ground to meet its keeper. Before them the long-awaited promise of the Haarshaim, was revealed for all to see. Reflecting unnaturally in the lantern light, the creature paused moving its head to peer into the crowd. Some of the people strained for a closer look while others backed away from the stage. The beast was constructed of a living metal. Its blood colored eyes flashed as it absorbed the scene around it. Its skin was unyielding and when the High Chancellor touched the rippling membrane the beast moved its lips in response. Its mouth clattered as it opened and shut. Its sharp ears pulled forward and the wings twisted in a peculiar motion.

"It flies and can not die!" he shouted. "It lives and yet it is not wholly alive!" the Chancellor paused, feeling the rush of force coming from the folk below him.

"His name is Cyzicus. The creation of both the Man and the Ancient One. Behold his glory!"

Pelius felt the monstrous force of the creature on the stage. With his Gift full upon him he peered into the mind of the creation. Impassive, it perceived everything in its vacant red eyes. Upon its brow something gleamed and Pelius looked closer to see a facetted crystal of atricault deeply embedded into its metallic skin. The dim glow intensified with the Chancellors touch and as the stones power increased, the Chancellors inner light diminished. Pelius observed that the creature was fully aware of the exchange and it moved his lips. Somewhere in his being the Chancellor shuddered. The knowledge of his stolen force had spoiled his potency and his words were lost in the agitation of the crowd.

Arcus studied the creature from his place in the stands, noticing though its motions were quick, it did not move as a normal beast. He watched the tail flip and as the hooves pawed the boards he noted the creatures feet were not those of a horse but instead it hooves were cloven like those of a deer. Its wings were un-feathered. A translucent membrane spanned the sinuous cartilage and the thin material allowed the light to pass through. A web of vessels, networking through the gray skin, carried the salty waters of life, through the creature's wings. He reached out to touch the creature's mind, hoping to receive a better understanding of the animal's true nature but what he touched jolted him. Colder than frozen metal was the black muscle that beat the heart. The beast was disconnected fragments of what had been stolen from the bodies of others. Arcus could hear their hollowed voices crying from inside. Trapped bones and the pitiful calls smarted like the sting of a thousand bees. Arcus had glimpsed the inner mind and saw the monster was a prison house for the creatures it had been made from. Knowing no heart of its own, this creature was unaware of the connectedness that even the lowest of all organisms possess. Next to him, Arcus felt his brother tremble.

Tristus stared at the living distortion and wondered if it been ignorance or arrogance that had driven its creation. Entombed within a crust of metal, this beast was indeed vitalized by the blood of the living but it held no union to the whole. It slavered upon the stage and the flood of a future swept over him. Its rushing tides carried him to the brink of thundering waters and forced him under a churning sea. He was not alone as he slipped under the waves as the wails of others filled his ears. They cried out as they too were pushed down by the violent swells. Choking in the unbidden dream he saw himself as drowning in the thick air. In the midst of the tempest he became aware of Aleryn. She was calling his name as a challenge flashed into his mind. He looked up to see that the creature upon the stage had turned to face him and it stared directly into the point behind his right eye.

The next day the streets were filled with refuse. Groups of young boys gathered before the dawn to clear the roads of the waste with brooms and pails. Tristus and the others had left the bidding circle before the crowds had dispersed. But not one of them had found their beds that night. The unveiling of the hideous beast had caught them unawares. Pelius had paced the halls of the west wing to wait out the hours that remained before daybreak. Tristus stood at his window looking out to the black cliffs as they stretched away from the city. Arcus was in the stable. This was the place where he could rest his mind. He made sure that Clade was warmly covered as he slept in his little room. He spoke gently to the horses and fed the kittens. Then he walked outside to sit just beyond the door where he passed the night away looking over the fading stars.

Aleryn stared into the fire and the flaming salamanders danced joyously before her. Her burden did not touch their fiery lives. She quieted her thoughts and in this state of meditation she waited for the dawn.

The Queen was alone in her chamber. She rested at the table which looked to the sea and laid her head upon her hands. She had let the Haarshiam do as they wished too long. She had not watched closely enough and now she could not see clearly truth nor lie. She felt clammy and the inside of her head burned in a sick fever. A soft knock came at the door. The Priestess was there, holding a single candle in one hand and in the other she carried a cup.

"I felt your worry, my Queen. Please take this tea. It will be bring you comfort," She said. "And aid in sleep as well."

"Thank you, Priestess. Your kindness is appreciated."

"This evenings unveiling was a truly awesome sight. The powers of men continue to grow. It is my hope that much good shall come of this creature."

"Good? Its creation did not stir within me a sense of goodness. This beast, it does not seem right."

"Change is a fearsome thing. Be it bad or good, it always has an uncomfortable quality. That is the motion you sense my good Queen. The motion of change, you have always been so sensitive to the Kingdom. Here now, drink your tea. Things will not seem so grave in the morning."

The Queen took the cup of tea and returned to her table. Soon her thoughts grew muddy. She was very tired when she lay down upon her bed. In some dark place she dreamed of shadowed things that she would not remember in the light of day.

The tower bells signaled the rise of the sun. Its sound

found each alone with their thoughts. Whether they were pulled by the responsibilities designated by a burden of birth, or by the inner obligation that draws souls to the certainty of a private death each was aware of themselves as participants upon the battlefield. From his window, Tristus watched the boys as they cleaned the trash from the narrow streets.

The bells stirred the city from its own fitful dreams. They were drawn to the sparkling world offered by the powerful men. The glamour of the strange creation would change them. It was easy to remain blind as they left the cost of their actions un-tallied.

Tristus felt their burdens in each pulse of his heart. What words of caution could they hear? What truth could they understand when did not wish to hear the truth at all? He looked toward the cliffs recalling the Vulcane as she had stood before him, surrounded by the backdrop of the icy peaks. The Fiery Goddess was untouched by the flames of the eternally burning valley and he now recalled once more the words she had burned within him, "To know purpose, dare not seek land." and Tristus turned his eyes from the narrow band that separated the earth from the sea and he looked out over the gray ocean mist.

CHAPTER 15
THE THALASSIANS

Tristus looked to those left standing upon the piers, his warm breath hanging in the salty air. Aleryn waved farewell to her brothers as they pushed away from the dock and Clade was repeating over to himself his promise to serve the Queen in Arcus' absence. Pelius was apart from the others. The chill wind burned his eyes. Grim and troubled, his misgivings churned as he watched them take their leave of the city.

Since the Festival, troublesome delays had sprung before them. The Guilds were hosting private affairs with many of the wealthier visitors and to their dismay the Khimerah was paraded daily through the streets but more worrisome to all was the festering sores had begun to emerge upon the youngest and eldest of Tessera and the wise women were doing their best to minister to them. The healers believed that some of the rare foods served at the Festival had carried the infection into the city but Tristus had greater concerns and images of war filled his dreams. If his own folk were now stricken with the *Pyrrohmarin* he was sure the Thalassisan would be feeling the affects as well. The trip to the mer-folk could be put off no longer for Tessera was not able to face open battle from such an army. The brothers had left Pelius with a secret duty. The bond between the Tahmurath and the elementals could serve them now. Pelius would travel to the hidden forest if the time came that the yellow waters were needed for the healing of their people.

Tristus must leave the Haarshiam and their creation to his mother for now. The House of Tessera still held some oblique powers. There were official delays she could utilize to keep the Guildsmen occupied. In any case, he did not believe his presence would help the city and silently, he hoped a solution lie hidden in the mysterious words the Vulcane had burned in his heart.

Arwyn stood between her mother and Clade. The early morning sun gleamed upon the red curls. Slight for her years, she still looked a child but a new power now coursed through her veins. She had spoken little since the Festival spending her time with the gentle women of the city and as hands had brought comfort to the sick a new purpose began to possess her.

The Bifrost went swiftly from the bay as an unyielding current pulled them out to sea. Once more, Tristus raised his arm in farewell. The voice of destiny was clear to his mind and yet doubt twisted like thorn over his strained heart. The weight of recent days had fractured his focus. His contact with the shadow had left him shaken and more clearly able than ever before he perceived the weaknesses that lurked within him. Looking over the waters to those he loved he realized the shadow moved within them as well. Like flames in a rising blaze, hope and despair flickered like twin fires. He drew in deep breath and through the cold morning mists he felt the shadowy wraith creeping through the streets of Tessera.

The Bifrost was a fast boat and Jason kept the oars manned both day and night. Watching the ocean pass under her belly, Tristus soon began to remember the familiar sense of attunement. The endless days he had spent alone on the ancient sea had served him well but times had changed. Tristus traveled now with both friend and kin and for the first time in years he had time to speak with his brother. There was much to be said between them and so each evening they would look upon the stars and talk of things to come.

"When do you think we will find them?" asked Arcus.

"I do not think it will be so long. We are traveling fast and Jason believes he knows where the Thalassisans are apt to be."

"As a child I often dreamed of mer-folk." he said looking over the swaying deck. "We will meet under disturbing circumstance, nonetheless, it is good to know that they are more than myth." he smiled.

"What strange times we live in Arcus, where the oldest legends share our days. Surely there must be hope in this, and if we can find them," then he paused and looked down at his hands. "and if our conversations go well. They might be able to help us to grasp the nature of these times. They are an ancient line and would remember more of stars and histories than our records have ever held. It seems to me that the Thalassisans could shed light upon these changes that sweep us. They may even be able to understand what dark force haunts our streets, and may be. Well may be, they might understand how to fight it."

"That they might." Arcus answered softly but it seemed to Tristus that his brother's thoughts had suddenly drifted far away.

The lookouts kept a close watch by day and night but no sign of the Thalassisans did they see and after a time Jason began to grow worried. A heavy air of oppression began to pervade the waters. He knew their scouts must be near and their secrecy concerned him. After several weeks the Captain decided to turn the boat from the open sea and the Bifrost set her course closer to the shoreline. The moon was dark when they reached the place where the warmth of the fire mountains began to mingle in the hard crush of winter. The airs grew thin as they began to near the Wall of Mist. Still the crew held fast to their northward heading and Tristus noted the quality of his thoughts had changed once again. The presence of the mysterious woman began to drift in and out of his senses. He knew she lingered near but she remained silent and invisible and would not whisper a word to his thirsty ears. He felt as if she was waiting for an action on his part, but he did not know what to do.

Then the night came when he woke suddenly. His clothing was soaked in a sickening sweat. The scent of the White Blossom filled the room. He rose from his hammock and dressed in fresh clothing, leaving his small chamber to walk along the deck. Specks of light pierced the black sky. Their weightless faces reflected sharply in the dark waters. He struggled with his doubts, under the quiet light attempting to pace away the tension that crawled through his skin. Looking up he noticed that the night-watcher was sleeping unawares in the high loft of the crow's nest. He slipped past the man and then, with no formed thoughts, Tristus loosened the small boat that hung alongside the fore of the ship. Letting go of the rope he allowed it to drop to the restless sea and he climbed down to the vessel beneath. When his feet touched the tossing deck, he set the boat free from the mother ship. Lifting the mast he fastened the canvas sail to its brackets. Unseen, he stole away from the Bifrost as the dark closed around him.

He traveled under the deepening night and soon found

himself surrounded by wisps of fog. Listening to the sea gently lapping against the sides of his borrowed vessel he pushed himself forward with all the speed he could pull from the sails. The hours went along and he gave no thought to what he was looking for. He had become seamless in his motion and was lost the sound of the sea. Then, without warning, an object collided against the boat and his vessel pushed away in sudden response. Awaking from his flawless dream, Tristus bent down over the water attempting to grasp the thing that floated there. It was large object and it drifted again just beyond his reach. Pushing himself closer he lightly touched the thing he sought. The night hissed and the hostile murmur brought with it the weight of another reality. The connection he had followed had been tersely broken. Wondering at the sudden change, he strained to see in the misty night. Tristus whispered his doubt aloud and for an instant, the mist cleared and he saw the form drifting in the inky waters. Wrapping a rope round his belly he dived from the vessel. He struggled through the choppy waves until he hooked his arm around the thing and realized it was a corpse that floated in the dark sea. He pulled the still body to the side of his waiting vessel. Releasing another rope he threw it gently around the lifeless form and pulling himself safely aboard he wrenched the corpse upward into the floor of the small vessel.

The dead face gazed upward with unseeing eyes. No longer would this boy draw a nourishing breath. His smooth skin and fine features to be forever still. He was slender and well-muscled and it seemed horribly wrong that that which was so young had lost the spark that brings life into a form. A tangled mass of hair and seaweed hung down his slender back and at the point just beneath the navel no lower limbs grew. He was a man-child of the Mer-folk and where legs would have been there was instead a powerful tail.

"So it was not these salty seas that stole your life." whispered Tristus as he pulled closed the boy's clear eyes. A glint in the pale hair caught his attention and he touched the circlet of gold that graced the dead boy's brow. This son was a Prince of the Sea, just as Tristus was a Prince of Land. The pitiless call of the woman was now clear to his mind as his shudder of realization shattered the night air. Beneath the golden ring, a wide lesion gaped. It was the *Pyrrohmarin* that had taken the life of this young prince.

He looked to the heavens just as a host of stars blazed across the sky to fall soundlessly into the black sea. It was as if the light paid homage to the Boy-Prince. Isolation set in upon him. The dead youth lay cold in the belly of the boat as Tristus realized the faint glow of the morning was beginning to lighten the night sky. There was no other thing left to do so he turned the vessel around and set his heading to return to the Bifrost.

The watchman called out when he saw the small boat pierce the fogs. The others hurried to the railing. Jason shouted for the ropes to be dropped and Tristus and his vessel was quickly pulled up to the main deck. Gathering around him the crew saw the body that lay in the bottom of the narrow boat. Arcus lifted the dead Thalassisan from the damp floor. His green and golden hair fell back and the mortal sore was exposed for all to witness. The Captain's men took a step backward. A slight man with ruddy skin pushed his way into the group. Tristus recognized him as the same man whom had been assigned to watch the seas the night before. In his haste to put distance between himself and the dead boy, he dropped the small anchor hard upon the deck. He winced and his hands trembled but Jason ignored his cowardice and stepped passed him.

"So this was your errand," he said softly, "I had hoped you would have brought us a less ominous sign." The Captain took the boy from Arcus' arms and said to those upon the deck. "They will be here soon." and he carried the lifeless prince down the stairs to his own bed chamber.

Tristus sat with his brother in the galley. He took some food and he sipped wine. Arcus rose often from his chair to look from the round windows which surrounded the dining table. Anticipation layered the heavy airs until, from the west, he caught sight of a long line of rolling white foam. Quietly he watched as the gray swells reached unnaturally high along the distant horizon and finally he said.

"They are near brother. I can see them."

They left straight away to speak with the Captain. They found him in his chamber carefully wrapping the body of the boy in a fine, white linen. Solemnly he worked alone and as they approached they heard him whispering in soft rhythmical tones over the body. He turned to look over his shoulder when he heard them at the door. Their eyes told him all he need know. He gestured quickly and Tristus saw the blessing he left hanging in the air.

By the time they reached the deck the sky had darkened. Heavy watery arms slapped the sides of the ship and the Bifrost reeled and pitched with every strike and then the rains began. The crew labored under the pelting skies to steady the sails but the boat turned like a toy in the crashing swirl of foam. The tempest screamed around them and the sky changed from gray to black. Watery spumes rose up in a twisting wind and the sea began to spiral downward. The funneling force now sucked the sea from the pitching waves and they felt the Bifrost began to slip toward the center. A terrible wave crested over the helm and as the vast wall of water began to splinter apart a great man rose from the rent. In his massive hand he held a trident and its tips burst furiously into flame as they touched the air. His eyes were the color of the sea and riverlets of brine ran down his broad chest. He was thrice the bulk of a human man and the mass of his arms bulged as he moved above the water. A golden band about his brow told them he was the Thalassisan King. Jason looked like a child as he stood before him. The Thalassisan raised his arms and massive waves mounted up around him and began to batter the helm. Like an army of war horses they rose and fell at his command. The crew struggled to keep their feet as the Bifrost pitched helplessly. The angry sea seemed set to consume them and the King rose still higher above the fray of foam. In the mist behind him they could see his warriors, five hundred strong and mounted upon the strange horses, the King's soldiers moved as he moved, their forbidding faces awaiting his word.

The command came and dread, like a black void, moved through every heart. A fierce cry bellowed through the storm and the clouds converged into a black fog and, in an instant, all the light of the sun was shut away. Another great wave swept over the deck. The brothers grasped the rail, holding for their lives as Jason clung to the wheel. The Bifrost pitched and her flag was torn from the masthead. The ship rocked and the water crashed.

and Arcus was knocked loose. He slid over the pitching deck and somehow managed to rise to his feet. Moving his arms upward, toward the unseen sun, he shouted out to the horde. The decree moved out over the angry waves as he called to men and beasts alike. Like a great flame the command passed over the legion. Its warmth touched them and the motion of war ceased. Like the escape of breath after a hard blow to the belly, the hostility was cut suddenly short and the white rag tossed helplessly upon the waters. The King paused. He lowered his trident and the army stood suspended behind him. Standing in the still eye of the storm Arcus held the gaze of the Thalassisan. The merman to his right moved to retrieve the drenched flag from the water and Jason stepped forward. He waited and as the voice of the wind died away he said.

"Hail Lord of the Waves." but, at the sound of Arcus' voice, the trident flashed and the King's eyes burned from gold to blue.

"We bear a dreadful onus, Lord." he continued, attune to the flickering wrath of the Thalassisan King.

And in the same tones which initiated the first life, the Mer-King spoke to the men. "I am quite aware what you bear." he said in a voice like rushing maelstrom. "The falling sky told us of his last breath."

Jason paused, the King's fury crawled over his skin and in measured response he said. "Aye my Lord, we too witnessed the sign of that dark hour."

The King's eyes blazed, his anger and grief barely contained. "The bright stars of heaven mourn his loss as bitterly as I." he answered grimly. "We have come for him." The sound of his wrath filled the sky and his voice shook the waters. "Your ignorant hands have fouled him, as they foul all that they touch."

The vessel lurched and all on board fell to the rail. The force of calm that Arcus had summoned was fading with every instant.

"We have cared for him as we would our own." answered Jason evenly, intensely aware of the treacherous ground upon which they ventured.

"The words of Land Walkers are empty shells, swaddling naught but their own unclean desires." came the ferocious response.

The ship rocked again and the men found themselves with their faces pressed flat against the drenched decking. Tristus picked himself up and stepping forward he faced the King knowing clearly his peril.

"Your perceptions are keen, Lord. There is much amiss in the world of men, and I shall not bear to you a false witness. I only hope that the truth of my words will ring in your heart." he said sternly. "In the darkness of the evening past, a guiding hand led me across the waters to your faultless son. There was no life in him when I pulled him from the waves and as his face shown under the heavens I too did witness the perfection therein. I fear Lord that I am not without blame for his passing for I recognize the scourge that took him. The deadly bane is a red venom that belches from the mountains in these northern seas." He stood straight and looked into the face of the Thalassisan King and said. "I stand prepared for your judgment. I am Tristus, the first born of the House of Tessera and heir to her throne. If it is the actions of my people that has caused you this hurt, then I am the one to bear its ultimate responsibility."

Arcus bowed his head and Jason stepped aside. They understood no argument was allowed on his behalf, for the duties of a true King reach beyond the realm of earthy affections. The Thalassisan's smothering wrath filled the dull skies and the silence surrounding seemed far more deadly than the sounds of war just moments before. The ocean became still as a glassy mirror and no man dared breathe.

Tristus was quiet as the King set his jaw and considered this brave Son of Earth. The courage of the boy had touched him. This youth had not the years to truly know of the virtues of manhood and yet he was ready to die for those less worthy that he was born to serve. The unselfish act steadied the grief pounding through his heart and the King recognized the greater part of himself in the Prince of Tessera. He lowered his trident and as the skies began to settle, he released them from his deadly gaze.

So it was that in the quiet of the clearing storm, Jason and Arcus carried Thalassisan Prince up from the chamber below and they placed him aboard the same boat that had borne him to the Bifrost that very morning. Tristus was alone as he ferried the small vessel under the overshadowing form of the waiting father. The King looked down upon the body of his dead son and then lifting the boy from that resting place he held the still form up to the heavens. The sounds he uttered were coupled to the motion of the sea. Tristus felt the perfect tone form in the heart of a father. It moved through the sky, passing though the curtain of time until it touched the son that waited beyond the mists. Tristus cast his eyes down as eternity passed and the liquid voice spoke again.

"The nations of men are spoilers but as are all things they too are comprised of the wisdom of the elements." then he paused and stared into the heart of the boy. "Your race has not yet conquered their natures but it seems the gift to do so may be at hand. See to your people, Prince of Land Walkers."

There was no tone of forgiveness in his voice just the gracious gift of a bit more time. Moving upon an unseen signal the warriors behind him disappeared under the waves. Tristus bowed low to the Thalassisan King knowing that war still lingered at his threshold.

CHAPTER 16
RETURN TO THE FOREST

Pelius stood upon the shore and studied the cliffs. The stone bridges were now behind him and he knew the entrance to the hidden forest was close at hand. Scooping up a pile of water skins, he pushed aside the brambles and headed to the opening. Clade, Louie, and Mileah, carrying skins of their own, followed close after him. Bits of snow stung his cheek as the prickly fingers tore at his clothing. The briars were brown and dry from cold. Gently he lifted the thorns away from his coat and moved inside the stone walls. The path reached sharply downward along the face of the black cliff. The small band descended over the fragmented ledge and down the steep stair to soon reach the forest floor. Warmth overwhelmed them as birds heralded their intrusion. Deafening screeches and scoldings filled the hollow as they lifted from the branches of the towering trees. Moving in sheets though the forest, vast flocks of vibrant yellows, reds, and blues scattered in the terracing branches. Winter did not touch this place. The twisting leaves still fingered their way upon the shaggy bark and the thick cords of thier bending vines dripped with sweet scent. The heat of the inner pools and the high walls of black rock kept the warmth near. Pelius pulled of his jacket and left it at the foot of the ragged stairs.

The trees were far taller than any which grew in the mountain glens beyond the city. The woody beings towered over them, spreading their thick canopies into the moist air leaving the ground dimly spotted with traces of dancing light. Nowhere did they see the same plant, shrub, or tree and few of what they did see could they name. Peering eyes watched the children. A long, enormous cat walked effortlessly upon the top of a broad limb. Mileah gently touched Pelius upon the sleeve and pointed to where it waited. Its sleek fur was mottled like bits of sun and shade allowing the creature to blend into the living motion of the forest. The green eyes turned to look back at them. Then it moved its mouth and the sharp teeth barred into a loud snarl. Taking cautious steps backward, they kept their eyes set to the beast.

"Her speech, does it frightens you?" came the sound of

odd pitched voice.

Pelius' heart leaped as a light touch brushed his shoulder. He thought he might collapse under its suffocating pressure. Laughter filled the air. The voice seemed amused at his distress. He wrenched himself around searching for the presence that had crept into the glen but no one was near. Micah and Louis exchanged uneasy glances. They had heard the voice as well. The great cat rested calmly upon the branch, her tail twitching slightly above them.

"Where are you?" he whispered to the air.

"Closer than your breath. Have you forgotten?"

Terrified, Pelius felt his temperature rise unnaturally. A sickening sensation passed though him. He could not breath nor speak. A cloudy vapor condensed just outside him and then a wrinkled face appeared just inches from his eyes. Pelius choked down a mouthful of air and sat down hard upon the ground. The tiny man was standing above him. His brown hands rested upon his hips and his eyes danced in wicked delight. He was wiry. His knotty muscles stretched tautly over bone. He wore only a cape and cloth. The fabric was made from the threads of wooly vines and they wrapped around him loosely, leaving a shoulder exposed. His long feet were bare. Black hair hung loose about his shoulders and it was filled with crumbs of the forest. Insects moved across his head as he laughed out loud and he jumped to the branch above them. The motion seemed effortless.

"So you have returned to me Little King. What do you want?" he said, looking down at them from the branch. "Kings always want something." The cat seemed to smile at the little man then it turned to bare its teeth at the children.

"Who are you?" gasped Pelius.

"A question for a question?"

"How do you know me?"

"And what if I give you an answer? More questions, I suppose," the little man sighed and scratched the big cat between the ears. "I will tell this. You have so many questions only because you do not know how to listen."

"I am not a King." said Pelius.

The little man laughed and then vanished from the branch. The cat stood up and lowered its shoulders, readying itself to pounce.

Clade grabbed Pelius by the arm. "We must go. This beast is not to be reckoned with."

Pelius shook himself in frustration as the group continued on through the woods. Thousands of brilliant birds called out above their heads. Life crept all around them and a rich cascade of sound filled their ears. Everywhere beasts climbed though the trees and slithered upon the ground. Grunts and snorts, screeches and hisses, echoed through the green woods and behind all these sounds was the echo of falling waters. Crystalline streams called out as they poured from the sheer black cliffs. The thin cascades jumped and splashed to the deep pools far below. Silver fish flashed in the clear basins and near the edges giant insects hovered over the reeds and muck. A warm misty rain fell and the air was thick with the aroma of the White Blossom. The sacred flowers hung in great clusters as they climbed down the sides of the canyon.

Pelius moved quickly toward the bitter springs. He wanted to collect the yellow waters and leave this place as soon as he could. Glancing over his shoulder he saw the others following closely behind and he sighed with relief. They had seen curious man, but Tristus, nor Arcus, seemed able do it. This thing still puzzled him.

"Could it be that Kings and Princes did not hold all the powers of the Tahmurath? No, that did not make sense. It must be a magical trick, a spell of sorts, placed upon them all by this emaciated dwarf."

He scolded himself for not asking his name directly for he knew the creature would have been bound to tell it, if only he had remembered to ask. Pushing a branch back from his face he saw gurgling spring steaming before him. He knelt down and motioned for the others to do the same.

Upon the other side of the bubbling pool he heard a stifled giggle. He looked up to see the little man squatting close to the ground. His brown, bony knees were protruding from the folds of a thin cloth wrapped about his middle.

"You have come for the yellow waters." he said casually. "Hmm, are the people in your realms ill?" he mused as his brows feigned a false concern. Pelius found the familiar sensation of anger welling inside him.

"I demand to know your name!" said Pelius.

Pelius' irritation delighted him. He stood up to dance along the crusty edges of the spring and as he splashed, the scent of the rotting eggs filled the air. Pelius' eyes began to leak. Clade and Louie covered their faces with their sleeves.

"I am Puthon." he said finally and with a gracious bow he waved his hand across his face. "Eternally at your service."

But as his hands moved through the air something peculiar began to happen. The forest blurred and the trees behind the little man rippled like waves in water. Shadows of hands chasing hands appeared before Pelius'eyes. Then the man laughed and the world stood still and solid, once again.

"What do you want from me?" said Pelius, unnerved by the ripple in reality that had passed through the wood.

"I am a humble servant of the gracious earth. I have no desires." he answered sweetly, "It is you who desires of me."

"What need have I of a dirty little man?" Pelius answered, shocked at the thought.

Puthon convulsed with laughter. Wiggling his feet and slapping his knees his glee spread through the glade. Behind him, Pelius heard the others giggling as well.

"What are you laughing at?" he said turning sharply to face them.

They shook themselves, quickly planting grave looks across their faces.

"You are here to help me?" he said to them feeling somewhat shaken.

Chuckling happily, Puthon scratched himself as he danced along the edge of the spring. Finally the dwarf regained possession of his manners. Splashing water upon his face and said loudly, "Ah, that is better." his somber tone marred by the smirk on his face.

"Fill your skins." he commanded motioning to them with his fingers. They obeyed pressing the skins under the water. The children bent over to watch the thick bubbles flow from their narrow mouths.

"Do not look too closely and you shall see."

"See what?" quipped Pelius, still angry.

"Shhhh. Your words blind you."

"My words!"

"Yes indeed, King of Chatter."

Pelius looked down at the gurgling skins, squinting he tried not too look to closely but all he saw the blur of the water.

"Healing is of value to the living." stated Puthon, a thoughtful tone ringing in his voice.

"Oh, course it is." said Pelius impatiently, still trying not to focus upon the stream of bubbles.

"Ah, finally we agree upon a thing." he said happily, watching Pelius stare down at the water. "You are trying to hard. Let me help you."

Puthon jumped up and struck Pelius with a hard smack at a point just between his shoulder blades. Pelius fell forward into the spring and his chin hit a jutting rock. He felt the skin split open and warm blood trickle down his throat. Raising his head and cursing he shook the bitter water from his burning eyes. Sharp pain passed through the base of skull through his spine. He struggled to focus and found he could not. Suddenly everything around him was freakish. Vague shapes came upon him from all directions. They pressed upon his body moving chaotically both with, and without, rhythm. Finally, among the haze and the light a pattern began to form. He realized he was on his knees and it seemed he was vomiting. He looked up to see a shrill, sharp, world had appeared around him. Just ahead of him a woman was standing before a mirror of green glass. She was old and frail and in her wrinkled hands she held a rope of white cotton. Her dark eyes gleamed from her brittle skin and he noticed that her feet did not touch the ground. She floating in the air, several feet above him and did not appear to notice that he lay near. She called the rope by a name he did not know and the line rose from her open palms. Bending and twisting, it climbed into a upward until the sight of the end was lost in the thrashing shadow. All above him moved in a nauseating, discordant rhythm and what had been darkness now became a clear black void. He noticed his mouth was dry. He tried to moisten his lips with his tongue but found he had no lips and he had no tongue only his ears remained keen and a song began to form around him, and to that song was drawn a harmony, and to that harmony, solid forms began to appear. Before him now danced a green leaf trembling in the light of a golden sun. The veins within it pulsed and changed to become a human hand but within that hand the structure of those veins remained the same. The image remained for but an instant before they too twisted into change. Pelius' mind crawled with discomfort. He could not find his body and the perceptions which swirled before him were as wrenching as a stormy sea.

Starved for solidity, his mind no longer his own, Pelius was thrown into the clear dark void. Submerged and helpless, he drifted in this place for an endless time. Hazy thoughts flowed before brilliant lights and after an eternity his vision finally clarified. He found himself between the writhing bodies of two enormous snakes. The intertwining serpents held him encased between them and without words they begin to speak.

"There is no reason to be so excitable." One of the two explained to him calmly. "You are just a human thing. There is only so much you can do."

This had never occurred to Pelius. The serpents behaved as if his human existence held as little consequence as the flight of a mindless gnat on a summer day. He felt bottomless.

"It is all fine." said the snake. "It is the same as it ever was. It has not changed."

As this remark seemed to be some sort of slight consolation, Pelius attempted to form a clear thought. He wished to converse with the powerful vibrating serpents but as he tried he experienced himself to be nothing more than a pitiful and lonely creature. None of his words would stick in his mind. What he had once considered solid reality had become only a thin memory. His identity rested sluggishly in flat world.

"Humans are quite limited." said the one snake to the other snake.

"Please forgive us. We do not intend any discourtesy." replied the second serpent glancing sadly upon Pelius.

He was still pressed tightly between them but since they seemed to hold no expectations of him he found he could rest. The bodies of the great snakes held him intact and soon a sweet music began to play once again. A delicate thread of what he called himself moved to a place where he could not follow.

He was lying on his back. The others had pulled him from the edge of the spring into a spongy bed of moss. His mood matched the soreness of his chin. Above him a great vine twisted through the forest canopy. Its peculiar shape gave the impression one could walk upon its countless turns until they touched the heavens. It vaguely reminded Pelius of the snakes that had held him through his delirium.

"The Liana spoke to you." said Puthon. "Did it tell you what you needed to know?"

Pelius shook his head, "I did not have any questions."

"Oh." answered Puthon, seemingly disgusted. "Then up with you. There is work to attend too." and he poked him in the side with his brown toes.

Pelius rose to his feet, trying to shake away the dizziness. Puthon winked and grabbed an empty skin from the pile by the spring. He bent down and helped the children fill their bags. He told them the proper way the waters could be administered to the ailing and when they were finally ready to leave, one hundred skins lay at their feet. The children focused their thoughts and lifted them effortlessly and Clade watched in awe as the skins followed obediently. As they walked, Puthon gathered leaves and roots along the paths and shared with them the healing secrets they held. Mileah followed close at his side intensely interested in all he had to say. They filled their packs with roots and leaves as the little man instructed.

"How did you come to know these things?" questioned Mileah. "Are there times when you fall ill?"

"No, I do not fall ill." laughed Puthon, "I am the keeper of this forest and the lives within the walls speak to me. They tell me of the ways they provide for one another. It is my place to listen."

They stood at the base of the jagged stair and before they turned to leave Pelius went to Puthon's side and asked the question that was fretting his mind, "Why do you call me King?"

"Have you learned nothing this afternoon?"

Pelius thought a moment and said. "I do not believe that I deserve any title."

"Still it is the title that you have taken for yourself." said

Puthon. "It was not I that named you."

"Then who did name me?" pressed Pelius.

"You did. Who else would have so?"

Pelius shook his head in frustration. "Can a question be simply answered by your riddling tongue?"

Puthon shrugged his shoulders. The airs had thickened and a warm rain began to fall. Its droplets moved downward though the layers of leaves. When the first beads of water touched the forest floor Puthon vanished into the mist.

On the other side of the cliff the sky was heavy with gray clouds. A blanket of silent snow had fallen over the sands. Quickly the children shoveled the cold powder from their boat. Wrapping their cloaks well around them, they pushed out into the icy sea turning the craft toward the ailing city as they tirelessly guided their vessel home.

CHAPTER 17
THE BOOK OF WINGS

Arcus was at the rail staring into the green waters. In the sky above, black gulls circled and dived to scoop their breakfast from the waves. The men were pulling up the nets and soon the pitching bodies of silver fish covered the deck. Jason walked among the catch, studying their scales for any sign of illness. Carefully he observed fish after fish and when he was satisfied he returned the creatures to the floor of the ship. All seemed well. This harvest could return to Tessera to be sold as food. His men worked steady to stow the catch in barrels and carry the wooden drums to the holds beneath the kitchens.

A brisk wind burned Tristus' cheeks as he climbed the stair to the upper deck. The Bifrost swayed from side to side moving south over the choppy waves. Winter's breath filled her clean sails and the clouds moved with them forming shapes in blue airs above. The water mirrored the changing sky and the airy mists cast shadows over the shifting seas. Tristus saw his brother leaning upon the railing lost in thought. Tristus followed the twisting threads of his attention to the place further on. Beyond the playful motion of the clouds and the hungry cries of the gulls, moved the thoughts of his brother. In fragmented images he witnessed the flight of his vision. From a void, flecked with the stars, he saw his brother's farsight in his own mind and he knew Arcus watched the burning of far-away suns. Peacefulness was upon him. Tristus touched his shoulder and his brother turned to face him. The stars of that far place were still reflected in his eyes and Tristus watched as those points of light fell from the sky.

"You have been far from this world?" said Tristus.

"Aye, but you know that place. Do you not travel in your mind as well, Tristus?" Arcus smiled.

"I do." he nodded. "And I wondered often which is more real."

"I believe they both are real places. Though one is more bitter and one is more sweet."

Tristus laughed sadly, "And what sweetness lies in this world in which we walk?"

"Sweetness? Is it not sweet that we walk in the world together. It seems to me that loveliness lies in the eye of the viewer. The harmony of life is everywhere we choose to look."

"I suppose that is true, if your eyes are stuck to that direction. But it seems to me dear brother that most of what lies in this world works only to disturb us. It lurks in shadows, always preparing to assert its onerous nature. Though we stand here together, content in this moment, another moment lies hungry at our back. I brace for a strike. I fear we return home the bearers of the worst news."

"There are good folk in the city. I believe that there are those strong enough to withstand what is real. Truth founded the House of Tessera and truth built the Tower of Malthrom. It has found its way through the moments of our histories. The people have the capacity to understand the right and the wrong of the world."

Tristus sighed, "You have great heart, Arcus. You see more honor within them than do I."

"You slight yourself. You give your days away to understand the nature of these times. Truly you put your duty before any comforts."

"Duty? Is that what you think presses me on? Well I can tell you brother, you are most wrong. Indeed, it is some other thing that whispers in my mind. There have been times I have believed that that voice was the better part of my reason but then there are the times that its whisper leaves me empty and dark. Comfort, well you are right in that. Comfort is something I have known little of. To often bitter things have appeared to my mind's eye. Bitter loss, bitter ignorance, bitter greed, that is the Kingdom I have seen. The people of Tessera are free folk and yet they do not understand the choices set before them." he sighed looking toward the guardian crags that separated the sea from the mountains, "We shall arrive home in this evenings twilight hour, if I have reckoned correctly."

A fishing boat then passed between them, it looked small against the black shoulders of the sea cliffs.

"We are near. This part of the shoreline is familiar to me," said Arcus. "And I have seen other ships pass that bear our flag."

"We shall reach port soon enough, but until then we stand and we wait. I have not the patience for it. It does not seem to me we have the time for so much waiting." said Tristus.

"Well Tristus, I have not eaten this morning. It seems time has made room for that." said Arcus.

"Time has concern for our breakfast?" answered Tristus, slightly amused at the notion.

Arcus shrugged his shoulders and grinned as he headed for the galley.

"Ahhh, if you say it does" said Tristus, shaking his head and laughing he followed his brother to the kitchen.

They opened the door to find a large kettle steaming upon the stove top. Cook stood over the pot with a spoon in his hand and a spoon in his mouth. His belly danced as he stirred the stew and a bit of melody rippled in his rolls of fat.

"What is for breakfast Cook?" asked Arcus.

The cook turned to see the two brothers standing at the open door.

"Oh, well that would be a feast of incomparable tastiness," he announced, "for any time is a perfect time for tardy sailors to arrive at my table."

"Do not scold us, Cook. We are sorry we missed breakfast. We were talking and we lost track of the time. May we wash some of those dirty pots to redeem ourselves. It is too much a burden be out of your favor." said Arcus.

"My favor, indeed. Ummm, washing pots. Yes, I believe that could be arranged." and he waved his hand to the corner of the cluttered room where a large pile of dirty pans and dishes waited upon the stained kitchen board.

"What have you gotten us into?" whispered Tristus, careful to be loud enough so Cook could hear him.

Cook raised his eyebrows and sighed pitifully. "I need a barrel of water brought from below. My knees are griping me terribly and there are so many steps between us. It waits with the other water barrels in the furthest storeroom to the front of the hull. You, Sir Tristus." he said, very nearly batting his thin eyelashes. "Would you be so gracious as to fetch it for me."

"Of course, Cook, of course. I will return in a moment."

He left the room to the sound of their combined laughter.

Chuckling to himself as he turned the corner he stumbled over a man huddling close by the door.

"What are doing there?" He said, startled. "I could have brained you, crouching there like that."

The man scrabbled to his feet and Tristus recognized him at once. It was the cowardly fellow who had shoved behind the crew on the day they had met the Thalassisans. His pale eyes glowered and he wrung his hands together.

"I dropped something, Lord. I was bent over to look for it."

"What was this thing, then? I shall help you find it." said Tristus.

"No sir, no. I shall find it myself. It is of no real consequence, just a trinket. Do not worry yourself about my petty bauble, Cook needs his water."

The man had given himself away and Tristus knew that he had listened to each word that had passed between them.

"What is your name, man?" he asked.

"I am Belgic, Lord." he answered

"Then to your work, Belgic. And I advise you not lurk in shadows, it does not make a good impression upon your fellows." said Tristus, sharply.

"Yes, Lord." He said. "I am to my duties now." He bent his wiry body into a stiff bow and he hurried to the deck above.

Tristus went on to the forward hull and hoisted the barrel of water upon his strong shoulders. Though he was glad to return to the warm kitchen with the fat cook and his laughing brother the sense of distrust would not leave him. Cook had been teaching Arcus a song. It was an old one they both knew from their childhood but Cook had made new words for it. The naughty rhymes brought an impish glee into the room. The fat man's fat tears ran down his cheeks as Arcus sang out in a fine loud voice. Heaping their plates high with bread and thick stew he added a bold harmony to the chorus.

Tristus' concerns lingered though he joined into the conversation and song. They washed the pile of dishes and pans and soon the galley shone with pristine cleanliness.

"A man's kitchen is his castle, young Lords." quipped

Cook looking about at the shining kettles and neatly hanging pans, "It is sad you will not know such pleasures in your tedious rulings of a Kingdom."

"Aye, it must true." said Tristus removing a damp cloth from the table and hanging it to dry upon the door to the stove. "We should find the Captain. We will make port this day. He too may have work for us to do."

"An idle Prince is an evil thing and if the Captain has no errand for you, come back to see me for I can certainly find something for your pretty hands to do."

They promised to return as Cook began to pull the freshly cleaned pots from their places for there was yet another meal to begin. When they arrived upon deck, they saw that the weather had turned. The sky was growing dark and bits of ice flew in the wind. The low clouds had turned flat shade of gray and a hard wind pressed from the north. They glanced to the steering wheel of the ship, looking for the Captain but he was not there. His first mate steered the Bifrost in his stead. The man saw them as they walked upon the pitching deck and waved pointing to the sails above his head. Jason was up the mast adjusting the rigging. His large body seeming surprisingly nimble as he skirted about on the long poles, tying knots and pulling sails. They watched him from below for some minutes and when he noticed them there he jumped down with a light thump upon the deck.

"It looks as if we might have a bit of weather." said Jason glancing back toward the sails. "It has come upon us quickly. Icy winds make icy sails."

The three stood together in the freezing wind watching the foreboding sky and they were not aware that another looked on. Belgic hid in the shadow of the ships hull studying them as the strange squall gathered and in his hand he held a glowing stone. The golden light it cast engrossed him. No longer did he feel the sense of uselessness which had left him weak all the years of his life. The stone had the power to change him. Its fascinating glow traded his impotence for a sensation of rancorous power. Hatred burned like a fever through his veins.

The stone was the one piece of luck he had been given in his days of hapless wanderings. He had known it was a precious thing the moment he had glimpsed it laying in the mud alongside the reedy stream. He recalled how pretty it glowed when he washed it clean in the flowing water. He had camped on the banks of the clear run that night, clutching the stone as he slept. He was on his way to Tessera to attend the Festival. Every year he traveled to the city for there were always odd jobs to take on and abundant food to pinch and this finding was certainly a boon. Quickly he had seen that the stone's setting bore the seal of the Royal House but he had no wish to return crystal to its owner. He remembered well the moment that he tucked it within the inner pocket of his shabby vest. Patting it fondly he kept it there, checking the pocket often to see if he had lost it. Its secret presence made him special and as they walked together he found that the stone had a voice. It sang to him of his unusual prominence among men and it lured him on with magnificent possibilities. The stone had been the thing which had guided him to the Bifrost. When the Festival ended, he had found himself again in want of money. Though he had few real needs, just a handful of silver to keep his mug full and the occasional woman to lie at his side, he decided to try the docks to seek his next pay. Fingering the gem within his pocket he spoke with this fool of a Captain about his dim-witted mission. The stone altered his vile manners just enough him to pass undetected under the watchful eye of the fisherman. But the amber jewel possessed powers greater than the ability to cast a flimsy illusion and Belgic knew, as he stood holding the shining thing, that it was the force which drew the storm to the Bifrost. He could hear it pulling the wind and waters into a foaming rage. It had the power to change many things and he was a part of the rising storm it shaped. The evil force which stirred the gales outside him worked its spell within his heart, changing the weakling into a murderer. He was strong now. The power of the stone coursed through him in ways it had never done before. Never again would he return to the pathetic beast he once had been. The intoxicating sensation grew as he realized this new Belgic would live on forever. There was just one thing was he required do in trade. The stone made the promise quite clear. A blood sacrifice would seal his destiny and he would never again cower before another man. A bit of drool dripped from the edge of his mouth and his eyes gleamed. Pulling the hatchet from his vest he ran his finger along its blade, smiling at the way Cook kept his tools so well primed for their work. Belgic pressed deeper into the shadow as the unnatural blackness surrounded the Bifrost.

"Could this be the work of the Thalassisans?" gasped Arcus falling again against the side of the vessel.

"I do not know." cried Tristus as they struggled to belay the ropes to the pins of the ships rail. A fierce wave rose to sweep the deck and Tristus saw the first mate clinging desperately to the Captain's wheel. Jason struggled though the icy rains to help him. It would take both of them to guide the ship upward along the violent swells of the tempestuous water. A watery crash swept over his head and he was carried down the deck. Swallowing a great mouthful of water, Tristus choked to catch his breath. Just then a loud crack pierced though the sounds of the howling storm and he looked up to see the mast post had broken in two. Barely held by splintered threads of wood the long beam twisted in the screaming wind just as another wave swept over the ship. The surge of water rushed over the Bifrost and the timber broke free in the crying gale, with Tristus directly in its path. For a strange moment he was curiously aware of the beam as moved towards him. Time seemed staggered as he watched it come and then suddenly his limbs were possessed of a strength they had not know before. Jumping to the side, the broken timber lurched past him to break through the rail, missing its mark by mere inches. Grasping the life boat which hung to the side of the galley head Tristus realized he was safe but what he did not know was that Belgic waited behind him with the sharp hatchet in his hand.

Belgic was startled by the precision in which the power of the stone had delivered Tristus into his grasp. He was an arms length before him. Stunned and still choking for air with the back of his skull conveniently facing him.

"Such an easy mark." Belgic blinked, hearing the voices in the wind plead for the strike to penetrate the brain. "How exposed you are." mused the foul man.

The flawlessness of the circumstances flooded his corrupted brain.

"In this storm no one would see." he realized. He

could capture the life essence and hold it within the stone. The Princes' body would be swept off the pitching deck and Belgic would walk free among men. With his promise kept and the stone as his companion, how natural it would be to approach the castle. The Queen would be vulnerable, drained with grief at the tragic loss of this heir and he would become irresistible to her. How effortless it would be for he, Belgic the Bold, to become the new King?

His thoughts were delicious as he pictured himself in fine clothing carrying the golden staff of the House of the Tessera. He would be a deity. The strength of his authority would be certain to surpass any gentle force held by the Queen. He would enjoy the fruits of husbandry for a time but when he grew bored he would arrange to become singular in his rule. There would be many opportunities to dispose of a woman while sharing her bed. Then he would hold the reins of power all to himself. In an instant, the twinkling of these future possibilities passed before his eyes until the vision drew him back to the moment and he looked once again to his victim.

"Oh how this pathetic boy longs for death." he thought maliciously. "I do a great service to my people by ridding them of him." and he raised his arm to strike the deadly blow.

Tristus saw Arcus struggling toward him. He could see that his lips moved but the words he spoke were carried away by the violent wrenching of the wind. He wondered why his face was filled with panic as he fought to reach his side. Tristus rose to leave his resting place raising his arm in a gesture meant to let him know that all was well.

"I am fine," were the words he intended to say but the boat pitched suddenly and a sharp pain pulsed though his head. He felt the whole of his body weight landing hard upon his knees. Something warm ran along his face and he saw a dark drop explode upon his hand as his consciousness faded into another realm.

He found himself in a quiet place. He stood in an endless hall filled with massive columns. The posts were a man's length apart and evenly staggered along the walls. Between the columns were set tall long windows. The glass was curved at the apex and they reached up the high ceiling like dark mirrors, reflecting little and holding no view. Embedded in deep sills their glass appeared seamless as Tristus walked down the wide hall. The roof curved gracefully above him to form wide arches and inset between the massive rafters were strange shapes surrounded by thin silver cords.

"Where is my brother?" he thought. "What is this dream?"

Far ahead, he perceived a faint glow and he ventured toward the dim light that lay in the center of the great hall. As he came closer he could see the source of the radiance was a large book resting upon a three-legged table. He reached the table and looked upon the book. Its cover was closed and the leather that bound it was simply adorned. Burned deep in burnished gold, three symbols rested one within the other. Tristus did not know what they meant. He moved his hand toward the book and a sharp ringing began to pierce his head. Gently he opened the cover and the pages murmured in response. Tristus drew back in surprise when he realized that the sheets moved of their own accord. Rushing forward, faster and faster, the pages began to turn themselves in a wild fury. The sound filled the corridor echoing between the alabaster columns and bouncing from the seamless glass. Still more swiftly the ivory sheets moved with no hand to guide them until long hall was bursting with the rapid sound. Its hum began to burn his ears and the waves of noise pounded against his body. Suddenly a violent wind burst forth from the book and a exploding light poured from the rushing pages. The old tome groaned as a whirl of white wings appeared. Fragile and palpitating they spiraled toward the arched ceiling. Tristus reached out his hands to touch them. Before him the images of fleeting faces appeared and then were gone. Voices called out to him and some them he knew. The motion was familiar. The beating sound of the delicate wings echoed in the hall. He wanted to follow.

Then a pain in his head woke him. He looked about and realized a shadow stood near. It spoke his name and as the sound faded an old man appeared. Tristus knew the face. It was the Wizard Malthrom. The Mage came closer touching the birthmarks upon his brow and Tristus felt a wind rush through him.

"Where am I?" Tristus asked the Wizard.

"We are in a middle place." answered Malthrom, "We can speak here for a moment; if you are willing?"

"I am." he said.

"Then listen well, though be aware that it is my greater wish that your intuitions will explain true meanings behind this consul." The Wizard paused looking to the mark burned by the five stars as they darkening upon the brow and Tristus nodded to the man.

"Great change sweeps the people of Tessera, my son. And as change begets change variations increase without limit."

Tristus did not understand the idea he was trying to convey. Malthrom understood his confusion and paused to explain.

"Time holds a cyclic quality. Upon the end of one cycle and at the fore of the next, all things move toward a state of upheaval. We live in such a moment. In these junctures, time rushes forth to join the matter of earth, and all forms must respond to the change. Now, as a new cycle comes upon us, the pace of this motion is exceedingly rapid. The bursts of change are so swift that the amounts increase upon themselves only to increase upon themselves again.

Tristus stared at him. He was not entirely certain if the wizard's explanation had left him with a greater or lesser degree of confusion. Malthrom waited for a moment, allowing him time to measure his words before deciding to continue.

"The combined thoughts of the people precede the outward circumstances of the world. It is the quality of this force that bring the events, cast in time, into play. It is these gossamer energies which weave the days of a life. Surely this is not that difficult for you to realize?

Tristus supposed he perceived a faint glimmer of understanding so he nodded his head in agreement and Malthrom continued.

"The dust of earth and the cycles of time do not exist without one another. As they collide," and he paused to study the Prince's face, "as they collide, the doors which normally divide the two are pried wide apart. These times will provide a period of increased coming and going between the two states.

This is done in the hope of transition. If the two realms join, a bridge will form upon the field of battle." His black eyes flashed like a lighting strike. "In this act, all will change."

Tristus listened but Malthrom just looked at him and sighed. "Forms are folded into time; the appearance of a thing can not be the only judgment made. There are doors that exist between worlds, between lives, even between moments. There is nothing as solid as it seems." Malthrom looked again into the Prince's face and Tristus saw that great tears welled in his black eyes. "I shall be near. Try to remember this." and with those words Tristus watched the wizard vanish from sight.

"Wait! Please wait. I did not understand."

"Not understand a wizard's riddles?" came the close response and Tristus looked up to see Arcus standing before him. He was smiling and wearing clothing Tristus did not recognize. Though he was relieved to see him as he looked closer, he realized that this was not the face to he was accustomed too. This Arcus was young as well as old and as he looked deep into his eyes the image of the fluttering wings spiraled upward in his mind. He reached out and touched his brother's solid hand.

"Here use this." came a jolting sound. Tristus opened his eyes to see Jason dampening a soft cloth. He handed it to him and Tristus wiped his face and pushed his dark hair aside. Jason caught sight of the birthmark.

"The marks bleed," he thought to himself.

Tristus sat up, his head throbbing. He felt tired and battered. "Where was Arcus? What has happened?" His head ached as he tried to remember"

"Tristus" said Jason softly. "A great evil has taken place. I could not reach him in time. I am sorry, my son. I am sorry. Tristus, your brother lies dead at your feet. "

"What do you mean? I just saw him. I touched his hand." he answered disbelieving the words of his friend.

"My son, his body lies here but I advise you not to bear witness to it."

And whether it was that he did not hear the words of caution or whether it was that he chose not heed them, Tristus looked upon the body of his brother and its horror took his breath away. Before him the claylike corpse lay prone. Its skull had been cleaved and blood poured in all directions, drenching the boards beneath them in a mordant stain. He did not know if grief or confusion was greater within him. The world splintered in shards and Jason's voice reached out to him through the black.

"Look away, son. This is not as you should remember him." he said. "Look away, now. You are injured yourself. Cook is here. He will take you to your chamber."

"Tristus, come with me. I will see that all is taken care of." said a familiar voice and Edward gently knelt beside him upon the bloody deck.

Tristus blinked at him but again turned his eyes back to the still form of his brother.

"Jason, what caused this?" he choked.

"An assassin, Tristus."

"But who would seek to kill my brother? All love him, why would." then another drop of blood fell upon his hand and his mind began to reel.

Sinking into the spinning blackness, he realized that Arcus had given his life to save his own. He sat upon the bloody boards finding his life suspended a motionless state of horror. His sense was slipping away. Grief crushed him leaving him empty and wide apart. Then a cold wind whispered in his inner ear and another memory emerged lying just before the nightmares of the mortal world. He caught a glimpse of the seamless corridor. "This is where my brother had gone." he thought in a flash of pain as again the path of the palpitating wings came to his mind's eye. The fragile sound of the beating wings echoed around him and he realized there was work to do to set his brother free.

Pulling himself to his feet he said to Captain. "I can not leave him in such a state."

Jason looked upon his stricken face. It was not his place to determine what a man should, nor should not do. Edward gently lifted Arcus' body up and carried him to his chamber.

The sun now streamed through the round window for the storm had withdrawn as quickly as it had come. They cleaned the blood from his matted hair and wrapped his head with strong silken cloth to cover the mortal rent. The tears fell freely as they pulled away the soiled clothing. They washed him and dressed him and then left him to lie upon clean sheets.   It was Jason who tied his boots to his feet.

Glancing wearily over his shoulder Tristus gently closed the door behind him and followed the Captain down to the kitchen. Cook quickly set for them a platter of bland bread and gave them both warmed drinks. There Jason told Tristus the things he had seen that morning.

"The morning skies had cheered me when I was first up. I believed that our progress home would be swift. So I went beneath to check the stores of fish and to make certain that all was well secured, knowing there would be no time for such errands as we reached the city. I had seen Belgic lurking in the passage near the storerooms. He was searching in the crevices that lie between the barrels for something and he had a look about him I had not recognized before. It gave me reason to approach and I asked what he was doing there and why he was not at his post. He told me he had lost something precious that had been endowed to him by his mother. It had fallen he said, as he fetched a barrel of fresh water for Cook. He seemed so pathetic that against my better judgment I allowed him to stay and seek his lost treasure. I saw him later and asked if he had found what he had sought. He smiled and answered, 'Indeed he had." Then Jason paused and rubbed his forehead recalling Belgic's haughty confidence as the man had strode away.

"That moment I made the decision his service would not be required again upon my ship. But soon those thoughts had left me, for in the distance, I saw a black mist racing across the water. The cloud was converging upon us with great speed. I called out to my mate and climbed up upon the mast head to check the sails. The sky was close around us and my vision was short as the storm encircled us, snow and ice rode upon the air. That is when I saw that you and Arcus had come up from below but we were so busy battling the waves I did not see that Belgic lurked near the galley head. I was at the wheel when the mast broke free and I saw you jump from its path. It was only then that I caught a glimpse of Belgic among the shadows behind you. Even from where I stood I could feel his hate and I watched Arcus as he went to warn you."

Tristus listened painfully as Jason told the tale. Easily

he could picture Belgic rising from the shadows with the sharpened ax raised to strike.   Jason explained that it was the blunt end of that hatchet that had struck him from behind, for Arcus had thrown a broken shard of wood to cheat the deadly aim but when Belgic realized what had happened a blood wrath welled up in him and it filled him with new strength. Grasping the axe with both hands he leaped forward with lethal speed and the weapon found a new target. In one blow Arcus lay dead.

Jason's voice shook as he continued. "But in that moment I too had reached you. I lifted up the wretch and threw him upon the deck and as I did a great wave swept us. It purged the floor picking up the evil Belgic with its icy hand and spirited him away with a mighty force. I watched him scrambling wildly in waves, screaming in fright when he realized that death was coming for him. Then suddenly a hideous cry echoed over us and the sound of it froze me in my steps. A black gull appeared in the midst of the howling winds. It swooped down to hover inches just before Belgic's terrified face. For a moment it seemed the man thought the bird had come to save him. His greedy fingers grabbed at the shining feathers but the bird held other desires. Its' black eye seemed to enjoy watching the man toss in the violent sea and just before the waves pushed him beneath the angry foam the bird plucked an amber stone that was hidden near his breast. The jewel shed an eerie light. The golden stone jutted from the yellow mouth and the bird turned on its wing to carry the prize back though the storm"

Edward filled their cups with hot tea. Tristus' hands shuddered as he watched the wisps of warmth drift above the goblet.   He listened silently as Jason told him the things which taken place upon the upper deck painfully recalling the day the gulls had descended and attacked him. He had lost an amber stone during that battle and now it seemed oddly possible that the stone that Belgic carried could have once been his own.

When Jason finished his account Tristus mentioned these thoughts to him but he found he was not able to debate the possibilities. Jason told him gently there would be a better time to discuss such things and soon, they would be home. Tristus glanced up from the table and saw that the sun rode low along the sea. Its yellow face was bursting through fields of white clouds rimmed with gray. The strong rays sent wide glorious beams into the settling sky. On another day he might have marveled at its beauty but this evening its glory only served to mock him. They had been at the table for hours. He felt weak when he stood but he followed Jason to the deck above and they watched the bright sun sink below the waves.

The air grew cold. The black silhouette of the castle stood against the gray light. At its side the tower of Malthrom pointed its long finger to the sky and the lights from its spiraling windows flickered in the twilight. It seemed to Tristus that he could faintly hear its bells ringing in the distance. The broken ship rounded the turn and entered into the bay of Tessera. A small ferryboat waited to guide the crippled vessel into the docks. The main mast of the Bifrost was snapped. The ship had returned home pulled forward by its two lesser sails. As they drew closer the crew saw that lanterns flamed along the pier. Tristus' family was waiting there and he touched the mind of his little sister. They were already aware of Arcus' passing. The group stood in the chill night air, wrapped in robes of ivory, waiting to receive the body. As Tristus and Jason stepped down the plank they were comforted in their warm and living arms. They all looked up to the sky, watching as five bright stars split the night and in a twinkling of an eye their tails of white flame where lost forever under the black waves.

CHAPTER 18
THE BATTLEFIELD

Bright flames leapt from the pyre. The shifting light
flickered softly across their faces as the smoke carried over the
sea. Tristus stood with his family upon the garden cliff and
thousands pressed behind them carrying banners and lights.
Minstrels played softly upon the harp and the chanters. The
wisps of melodies wound their way into the hearts of all. The
cycle of tears had become endless; only ceasing for the brief
moments as he became too numb to weep any longer. Sleeping
had not been possible and he had walked away the nights and
days with Pelius at his side. Aleryn and his mother had stayed
close by the hearthside. The children of the Tahmurath always
near to comfort them while the Priestesses of the Tower had
made ready the funeral bed.

Whispers of gossip had already begun to stir in the
crowd for even the sharp blow of a sudden death can soon
replaced by more common instincts. Tristus stood numb, with
his sister and mother at his side, as their hurtful words reached
him. He heard their minds and he knew they wished he had been
the one to pass. The burden of too many thoughts crushed into
him but he squared his shoulders and hoped that no one did see
how deeply his heart failed him.

He spoke no word while breezes did their work and
waited until the flames died away. Eventually all returned home
to their waiting beds and Tristus found himself in his chamber
watching the glow of his fire. He kept himself company with a
bottle of strong wine and he pulled the window open so the cold
wind would touch his face. He was alone for the first time in
two days. The wine had the power to quiet the waves of grief
and for a moment, he felt almost like himself remembering the
door through which his brother parted. The movement of the
wings passed by his ear and he recalled the touch of Arcus' solid
hand. Pain pulsed through his shoulders as the wizard's words
whispered in his thoughts and he understood none of it. It
seemed the old man had left him with many questions and few
answers.

"But what words could comfort me?" he thought

helplessly, remembering the sounds of the people praying as they knelt against the stairs of the Tower of Malthrom, their damp eyes and clammy hands ever pleading to the Wizard for favors. Its hum rang in his mind as the wine did its work. He rested his head in his hands, finally finding sleep upon the hard table board.

Morning broke through the cloudy sky and Tristus opened his eyes. He had sat in his funeral clothing beneath the frigid window though out the long, cold night. His arms were stiff as he put the fire right and he left his room to go to the baths in the castle vaults. The steam cleared his head as he stripped down to enter the basin. He rested for a long time, hoping the tepid waters would ease the weariness that ached in his bones. Washing his hair and scrubbing his skin he tried to rid himself of the weakness which permeated his body. Finally, he wrapped himself in a drying towel and wiped the water from his hair and limbs. When he finished he dressed in fresh clothing and pulled his fingers through his damp hair. He left the warm baths to find Aleryn.

She was in the garden. The bleak air was gray and large snowflakes fell around her. Soft drifts of the frozen dust rested along the sleeping garden walls. She was watching them as they fell, one after the other, to fill the cloister. A pale blue cloak covered her. Its tint, the only color that existed in the altering shades of white and gray. Snow spun about the rim of her garment as she listened to the quiet. For a long moment he watched her through the thick glass of the corridor windows recognizing all too well the aloneness that sweep around her. Finally he opened the glass door that stood between them and as he walked, he left deep footprints the fallen snow and he noted that her small steps had been covered long before. She smiled when she saw him.

"How long have you stood here, sister?" He asked, his voice muffled by the soft gloom.

"I am afraid I have kept no track of the time." She answered.

"Your robe is white with frost." He said pointing down the edge of her cloak. "You must be chilled. Come in now, and warm yourself by the fires."

"Yes, I know but I hardly feel it." she answered softly.

"It is beautiful," he said looking upon the naked branches and shrubby brambles resting under the blanket of white. His breath left a warm cloud in the air. "But it is cold here, sister, very cold. Please, let us both go inside."

"Just a moment more." she whispered to him and he could not bear to disagree so they stood in the garden and watched the silent snow fall. Patterns of the crystal frost stretched over the casements and climbed upon the glass of the windows. He drew the coldness in through his chest, the crisp cleanness of the air felt alive. They were the warm and living in a world of noiseless white. It grew around them with no sound at all. The cold soon felt its way through the robes and after a time their feet burned. He touched her hair and realized it had become a frozen ringlet against the robe of blue. She understood and nodded reluctantly in agreement. He took her hand as they left the garden. They returned to hearth were the Queen waited and there they found Pelius and the other children. A warm soup simmered in the kettle. Breads and flavored butters lay upon the wooden boards in the warming bins above the fire. Nut meats with bits of dried apple and plum filled crockery bowls. Olives and cheeses, wine and coffee, tea pots and beers sat upon a traveling handcart. A harpist played softly in a candlelit alcove just beside a row of windows which looked out to the sea. In this quiet reverie the House of Sapentheis gave comfort to each other. So it was the custom that for seven days and seven nights all would rest and remember the one that had parted. But after this time it was expected that those of the living world carry on and leave the soul free to travel onward through the new realms of being.

Tristus used those days of mourning to think and spent many of the lighted hours in the stables caring for the horses and talking with Clade. Each evening the wind blew fierce and more snow fell until by weeks end, great drifts lay alongside every door. The narrow paths between the buildings were piled high in frozen mounds. The world around him was a white and frigid wasteland. While the cold fingers of winter slept in chill corners; he would sit in his chambers, feeding bits of wood to his fire considering the things that had past.

He been the true mark of the assassin's blow and he found it a brutal thing to bear. He knew the pathetic Belgic had been an unwitting lout that a greater mind found easy to manipulate for now the presence of that unseen evil spread throughout the hours of his day. Since the Festival the disease of the *Pyrrohmarin* had crept steadily into the food supply and over those weeks, there had been several deaths and the numbers of those who fell sick grew daily. The images of the ruined valley plagued him. Tristus knew well enough that the love of metals could drive men to horrible ends and without doubt it was the Haarshiam that loved the metals best. The Guilds controlled the flow of goods through the city and the folk of Tessera had much to lose if they chose to see the truth instead of the lies behind their rhetoric. Still the Haarshiam denied any knowledge of the northern mines asserting the ruined valley lay inaccessible to all their devices. And sometimes even he wondered if the Guildsman spoke the truth

Frustration would then take him and Tristus would rise to pace along the short walls of his chamber. The Thalassisans had given him only a little time. He was painfully aware that the threat of war waited silently at this threshold. He would pause at his window and look toward the north. Feeling the cold sea empty its wind upon the city he perceived himself as separate from those beneath him. He had seen little of helpful good from the citizens of the city, and with Arcus gone, who would be there tell him otherwise.

When these circular thoughts had exhausted him, his mind would have moments of quiet and he would sense his brother near to him. In this stillness he knew the door that appeared to exist between them would not be closed forever. This silent crossroads was the passage from death to birth to death again. But the glimpse would bring him few answers to the problems he faced at home. Here on this battlefield he was alone. The moments of communication balanced themselves with periods of suffocating despair; leaving him barren and his ability to think impaired. The hours passed slowly and he tossed upon the wretched waves of uncertainty.

The week of the mourning ended with a change in the weather. The sun broke though the gray snow clouds and the people opened their shutters to begin the work of clearing the streets. Ponies pulling heavy loads of filthy ice toiled through the lanes. They plodded slowly straining against the weight of their carts they dumped their frigid burdens in the angry sea. Then the handlers would drive them back to fetch yet another load. Watching this work from the edge of the western tower he heard a large group of black gulls cry out as they flew among the tall houses.

"Their numbers grow," he thought nervously. Looking over the gliding black wings and he saw the Khimerah appear amongst the flock. The beast rose above the birds awkwardly making its way over the walls and rooftops. Its eyes glowed from between the folds its metallic skin and the featherless wings made a rasping sound as they moved. In the light of the sun, Tristus found the creature more alarming than he had before. It followed the black gulls though the city as they screeched and jeered at the people beneath. Swooping and diving, it kept an easy pace with the smaller birds. The people looked up from their work. They pointed to the creature and called out its name,

"Cyzicus! Cyzicus!" they shouted and the wind carried the sound to the tower where he stood.

"Why did the Guildsmen give the beast this name?" he wondered remembering the word from his studies. It was a name of ancient city. It was a mythical place which far to the north and it was said the Cyzicus had been pushed from its moorings and plunged to the bottom of the sea. To Tristus, Cyzicus was a word that held inside it its own ominous force and despair gripped him.

"How did such a beast come to be in the world?" he questioned the airs as he watched it move over the streets of Tessera.

The flock turned from the city and moved over the southern fields with the creature close beside them until soon their numbers appeared as an oily shadow staining the white mountainside. An unease spread throughout the city and he shuddered involuntarily as images of violence, sickness, and death filled his minds eye. Tristus felt the dull suffering of the people pass through the airs like a rising tide.

The works of man had altered the life of the world and

with all his inner powers of fore-telling he sensed the creation of Khimerah heralded a fearsome change which would soon pour over the days. The mark upon his face burned. There was no turning back what was now upon the people. Destiny would have her way. The brand of stars pulled sharply and their sting brought with it a strange thought. For the first time, in all the recollections of his life, he considered the possibility that it was not he who stood at the center of the Kingdom. The peculiar moment held the notion that he was not the nucleus of Tessera, anymore than was he was the creator of the Mark, or the designer of the Sun. In this twinkling of understanding, Tristus became acutely aware that he did not rest at the hub of the world.

The thought left him stunned. The stars upon him were the symbol of larger cycles. He did not stand in the center. Its was the folk of Tessera who whirl at the core. His vanity struck him like a hard blow. Insignificance flooded him. He saw himself as a grain of sand in a rising storm but his mind was not solid enough to hold on to the notion. He had become too fluid. Steadying himself against the wall, he drew in a deep cold breath as his identity spread into bits.

Allowing the sweeping epiphany to settle starkly upon him he glimpsed another shadow of himself. In a perplexing counterpoint to his vanity, a deep fear emerged next to him and the festering terror lie like a gaping hole within his mind. The horror he had never named now came to the fore of his awareness. It was the dread of the fall of Tessera that had always tortured his under-mind. The possibility that he would be the one responsible of the doom of his Kingdom had always haunted him. Fiercely now he understood how the blood stained stars had served to separate him from the others leaving him hungry and isolated. He had beaten these thoughts from his consciousness with a clever viciousness. Never before had he allow them to take form. He was the death knell, the hammer, and the apocalyptic sign. He was the ruin which waited at the end of the world and since the beginning he was filled to his head with terror. Bitterly, he realized the stupendous lengths had he taken to avoid the glimpse of his authentic self. He sat in the center of his private universe, fearful and conceited, with the words of the Promise spinning in his mind.

The promise waits,
As the keeper doth search blindly . . .

Standing upon at the parapet under the looming black tower he felt the coldness of its long shadow stretching black over his skin. With disgust he saw clearly how cleverly the self-hate and self-love nourished one another and how each could remain hid by the shadow cast by the other. What he said he hated most was really the thing that he loved best. Choking upon his self-deceit he saw that he was the greatest of all pretenders.

And as the light of clarity continued to press him, he was left with no reason to struggle and he was willing to look at what other terrors his shadow held. Forcing himself to the point of calm and what he saw did, and did not, surprise him. Just out of his human reach a tear appeared in the airs. The tattered edges were sharply contrasted with the fabric of the physical world and he had the sense of looking in a mirror. A bright presence burned beyond the rent and a communication was transferred to him. A vast multitude appeared before him and he could see the streams of light which connected the throng into in a vibrant web. Everything was in motion all was being swept into a immense whirlpool. He looked down and realized that the ground beneath his feet grew solid. He bent over the turbulent water and he reached out to the wildly grasping hands. They tried to touch them and break free of the swirling vortex. A glittering darkness roared beneath and blinding dust rose up in spiraling waves. He steadied himself as the other hands grasped his arms and pulled themselves from the eddying currents. He felt a familiar presence and he turned just at the moment his brother touched his shoulder. Arcus smiled but did not speak. Instead he pointed to the path that rose up just behind him and Tristus saw that many others walked along the way. Their vast numbers lead up a high mountain and a brilliant web of light connected all flowed from the above to the below. Looking more closely at the interlacing streams of energy, he perceived a transfer of force moving upon these radiant threads. The threads formed a spiraling ladder and a song was . .

"Tristus."

He startled and turned to see Pelius at his shoulder.

With his mortal eyes Tristus looked upon the boy next to him. He was clad in a brown cloak and breeches. The thick locks of his black hair were messily scattered under its hood, but with his single eye, Tristus perceived more than this. Before him was a luminous egg and within this oval shape were three other distinct energies. These fields of force moved fluidly in shades of changing color. Upon the boys head, a soft light glowed graced him like a radiant crown. Over the heart, soft yellows and reds blended gracefully into gentler hues of blues and greens. Hovering outside the physical body, Tristus noticed that certain points within the elliptical form spun with every breath he drew and the glowing filaments networked into the upper and lower limbs. The shining between Pelius' brows glowed with a particular intensity. A strong gold flared upon his forehead and within this golden light ran living streaks of white-orange heat. These liquid colors pulsed into a design of iridescent indigo. The motion reminded Tristus of a unsettled flames and he knew that Pelius was troubled. He blinked and the world faded back to a degree of normalcy.

"What is it, my friend?" he asked the boy.

Pelius pointed to the market square far beneath them.

"Tristus, there is news in the city which disturbs me. The Haarshaim have created more of the beast they call, Cyzicus. They stand now with a dozen of these creatures in the market square. Many people have gathered to look upon them and some few have made arrangements for their purchase." His young face was stern and the light upon his brow pulsed brightly as he continued.

"The beasts lack basic qualities common to the other creatures of the earth. The Khimerah is a living dissonance, then he turned looked to Tristus, his blue eyes burning.

"When I touch its mind I perceive another presence hovering about its form. I can feel it. It is coming for us."

"What is the source, Pelius?"

"That I still do not know." he sighed.

Tristus looked toward the flock of gulls. They were moving south with the Khimerah looking a small dark blemish among them.

"It is hard to understand how the living may be

combined with what does not appear to live." he said as he watched. "For seven days I have mourned my brothers passing and that is not nearly long enough. But the time of the world passes by and indeed there is a change in the airs. I fear my young friend I cannot say if what will come is for better or for worse."

They waited together upon the battlement until the flock faded from sight and then they walked though the castle halls listening to the sounds of life within it. The maids and pages moved through the dim-lit corridors nodding politely as the Prince and Pelius passed by. In the large wing where the Tahmurath had their bed chambers they heard the noise of children. They opened the door to find them content in play. but watching the Tahmurath at play was not the same as watching ordinary group of children. The eldest, Louie and Micah, were in the corner of the room standing over a large basin of water. Gesturing, ever so slightly with their fingers, as liquid forms of birds rose from the bowl and floated above them and while one gave the birds their form the other gave them their color and sound. For a moment the translucent creatures would flutter above them and shimmer in the air. Then the birds condensed back into the watery vapors and returned to the basin. It seemed to all that each creation was more lovely than the one before it and the children watched happily as the shapes began to fly across the long chamber.

"How can such miracles be found amongst such trial and despair?" Tristus considered as he watched the magical shapes. A childish squeal filled the air as one of the twins lifted several pillows off the bed and spun them with the power of her mind. A heavy cushion moved though the air to fly directly into the face her brother. A pitcher and basin crashed to the floor as the second twin returned the pillow to his attacker.

"Stop this." said Pelius. "You are not here to bring the walls down with this nonsense." The twins stopped and looked sullen.

"We're sorry." They said together. "I shall fix it." said one. "No, I shall." said the other. The vase leaped from the floor and began to spin about in broken bits; forming and reforming, before their eyes as each twin struggled to repair the ruined porcelain before the other could finish.

Pelius went to them and held them by the shoulders. "Stop this argument." he said. "You shall work to repair it together." The twins glared for a moment at one another and then reluctantly clasped hands. The shattered vase lay between them. They focused upon it and in a twinkling the pieces pulled together, sealing perfectly and leaving no blemish, nor crack. Tristus nodded in amazement at their powers. Pelius raised a warning finger to the shamefaced children and they closed the door.

They smiled at each other as they left the room. The children brought a happiness into the castle that its halls had not heard for years. Entering the corridor, they realized they shared each others thoughts once again. They both wished to speak to Aleryn and they knew the first place to look. Walking briskly, they descended the long staircase and followed the long hall of the west wing until they reached the windows which overlooked the garden. She was there, seeming so alone and isolated in the icy garden, listening to the cold airs around her and they waited for a moment, wondering if they should disturb her solitude.

"She listens to the hearts of her people." said Pelius, noticing how pale she had become.

And she turned and smiled as he opened the door. Tristus embraced her and kissed her forehead seeing a single tear as it ran down her cheek.

"The time draws near, my brother, something approaches the city and it will not be long in coming." she whispered. "I fear when it touches us it will swallow up all that it can call is its own."

"Do not despair for the folk of Tessara." Pelius answered softly, "Close at hand a bell waits to be sounded and as its voice rings over the realm the Tahmurath will know it." and then he stepped closer, his eyes burning like a lamp. "It is that note which will stir the flame. It is the voice that will ignite the heart."

She trembled at the words and blinked back her tears. "Then who shall strike the hammer to the chord Pelius? Who can awaken that which sleeps so deeply?"

Tristus felt stars burn upon him. The crimson stains to

pulled tightly across his face and with this shift of awareness, his eyes once more perceived the bright light which shown upon the forehead of the boy.

"How it comes I do not see," he continued. "but the battle lies ahead. It waits in the hearts of those beneath us. Truly they are the sleeping babe the shadow seeks to smother in the hours just before dawn."

Tristus listened as the boy explained and he knew what sound Pelius spoke of. He had heard it just moments before. He knew what he must do.

He kissed his sister's cheek and nodding to Pelius he left her in his company. He went to speak to his mother.

He found her in the study and at her side was the High Priestess. The stone runes of foretelling lay upon the table and the scent of the sacred flower hung heavy in the room. Tristus saw the Priestess wince when she looked up from her fortune telling, realizing it was he who had entered the room. Of late, it seemed that more and more often her advice was tainted by less than spiritual concerns.

"Tristus, it is good that you have come. There are things that I need to speak with you about." said the Queen.

"And I to you as well, mother."

The Priestess bowed slightly and said, "I shall reflect more upon the messages received in the reading. I will await your call in the temple, my Lady." she left the room pulling the door sharply closed behind her.

The Queen sat upon her cushioned chair. Her eyes appeared dim and lost and her hands lay weakly at her side.

"What is it mother?" he said realizing her disturbed condition. "What has the Priestess told you?"

"The casting of the runes held much ill news. It appears that this festering disease will not improve but worsen and death will come to call at every door in my Kingdom

"And what does she suggest?" he asked tersely.

"The disease is spawning in the deep ocean, filtering through the lives that feed one upon the other. Soon all life will share its infection and the death." she said pausing to study his face, "and Tristus, already food runs short in the Kingdom. Our farmers do not have enough land to grow wheat and corn. You know too well we must depend upon the ocean to feed our people. We hold the largest fleet of ships in the known world. It is what we glean from the northern sea which provides our main source of trade to inlanders of the south and with only corrupted merchandise to barter we shall soon find ourselves to starve."

"Yes mother, I am aware of the predicament. It is this that drives me to seek out the root of the problem." He answered.

The Queen sighed as she continued. "And you know as well the other economic strength of the city lies in the trade of metals. The gold and silver we mine, along with the amalgam Atricault, can provide us with all the resources we need to run Tessera. Soon there will be no food to trade my son and the economic balance must turn. We must give way to the request of the Haarshiam for expansion of the mines.

"What you are considering is dangerous." said Tristus, surprised at her change of heart. "The Haarshaim take all and give back little to the people. How can this serve their good in the long run?"

"It is the only means that will have a certain effect. I am the Queen of these folk and I must act. You must know Tristus, I will do what is required to save the Kingdom." she said in a distant tone.

"The Khimerah, Cyzicus, as they call it, can also become a source of trade. Many of the guests at the festival expressed a desire to purchase one of these strange creatures. I believe there could be a profitable trade. Indeed, it could become a beneficial source of takings with the other countries, particularly those who are not dependent upon the sea for their survival."

"Mother, have you lost all sense?" he replied, staring at her in disbelief. "Remember, just days ago, you too found yourself sickened the night it was unveiled to people. There is something wrong in this thing. I do not think these beasts can be controlled." then he remembered the strange look upon the Priestess' face and he spoke a bit more softly, "Did the Priestess mention these things as she told you the signs?"

"I find myself more sickened by the red plague, my son." she answered sharply, "You would not have the children starve, would you Tristus?"

His eyes flashed with anger. "Are these the words she said to bend your mind to her will? I shall tell you that there is more to this than meets the eye at first glance. The intentions of the Haarshaim have never been so noble. They are working as they always have, with smoke and mirrors, fooling the people as they line their pockets with gold. And I think they fooled you as well, mother or is this slippery tongued priestess cast a spell upon you? I do not trust her words, nor her portents to me she tells you what she wants you to see!"

"Tristus your cynicisms will not serve when it comes time that you rule the Kingdom of Tessera. There are compromises that must be made to keep the city flourishing."

"Only but a few flourish in this city, mother. Suffering is everywhere one chooses to look. To give the remainder of your control to the avatars of greed is the death knell to the common folk indeed. You recall I believe that it is the Haarshaim that are responsible for the taint of the sea to begin with."

"I have worked with the Guilds for many long years and they are not the evil you would have them seem. It is necessary we must work with them for now. They are the only hope of the city."

"They are not the hope, mother. They are not the hope at all." he exclaimed, shocked at her words. "Mother, a war lurks at the doorstep? What of the Thalassisians? They have given us but a little time to stop the flow of poison."

"The Khimerahs can be used in war as well." she answered him grimly. "I have spoken to the Guilds, for the common good this decision is a necessary evil. Even as we speak they are working upon a new design. It will be a beast to bear the burden of war. Tristus, you are aware that we are people of peace. This creation will protect the city from harm."

Tristus reeled at the madness of her logic. "Who has filled your mind with such backwards notions, Mother? War sits at our threshold. The people must know the truth."

"What is the truth Tristus? And even if you did know it and held perfect proof, no doubt are you not aware that common folk have no stomach for veracity."

"They are a free people. They are free to make their own decisions, mother and they must be informed of all the bits of information at hand. They must be told of the Thalassisans and we must explain their point of view. If mer-folk believe it is the Haarshaim who are responsible for the poisoning of the sea. The people of Tessera must be aware that war, as well as sickness and famine, may await them. They can not be held in ignorance any longer."

"But there is no proof that the Guilds are responsible for the *Pyrrohmarin.* Recall Tristus, there is no route to the Northern realms, save by sea and the black cliffs block all movement of goods from that direction. I fear you must be mistaken, my son. You drew to near to the edge of the world. It is well known that delusions are common in those who come to close to the Misty Wall. It seems that your judgment has become forfeit. You will make enemies with these public accusations."

"I have enemies now, mother. I always have had them. The truth is my only shield."

"Truth is unclear and its pieces too bitter. It can not be helped Tristus. It seems you are still too young to understand. We have lost much and we must move to protect ourselves. I am clear in my decision. I will act now as I see fit. " she answered. "I am Queen, Tristus. My judgment will stand."

"How can you leave the fate of the people in the very hands of those who are certain to destroy them?" he replied taken aback by her words.

"I am sorry that we see things so differently, my son." she answered flatly, "But we shall speak of it no more. The decision is final. The act is done."

And with those words she closed her mind upon him.

CHAPTER 19
THE EYES OF THE WIZARD

Circular rings formed as he waited for the image to appear. In the midst of the remembering ethers, a scene formed in the surface of the mirror and Malthrom knew that he found what he had been seeking. Soundlessly a picture appeared in the smooth surface of the water. He saw the nine rise. They were gathered in a cavern-like room. The dim chamber had no windows and the hooded group was surrounded by bare walls of smooth stone. In the center of the cave stood a long altar and the workers formed a semi-circle it as, one by one, the alternating members lit the candles that waited there. When each flame burned bright the group began to chant and their repeating phase pulsed through the chamber. Malthrom recognized the Head Priestess as she emerged from the concealed opening from within the cave. Her head was uncovered as she took her place among them and she began preparing the tools of the ceremony. The others gathered closer around her forming a circle with their bodies around the table. The Priestess shaped symbols with her long knife and when she had finished their red glow hung like a stain in the air.

The group focused themselves and the chant began to rise in intensity leaving Malthrom able to hear the words they spoke. The tone was harsh and the gathering force they called downward moved like a funnel into the circle they shared. The spiraling intensity swelled as they continued to repeat the words of power. The priestess stood in the center of the vortex and the motion of her lips spoke an incantation counter-point to the intonations of the others. With her body she guided the force to the center of the circle until, in the ceiling above, a door opened and from the arced roof of the cave descended a large, bird-like cage. It was filled with prisoners. A crippled man lay twisted against the cold bars and pressed tightly upon him was a woman. Fear was transfixed within her wide eyes and her painted mouth bled. She held a child in her arms. The babe was clothed in filthy rags and it cried out flinging its tiny arms in fury. But it was not only the old or forgotten captured within the cold prison bars. A dog had slipped upon the bars and its leg passed through the spaces to hang unnaturally between the iron slats. It growled and bit the man next to him as it fought to be free. Along the other side of the dog a goat and a lamb were pressed tight against them. They trembled in the crowded cage braying in pitiful tones as they struggled to balance themselves and blood trickled to the floor. The cage descended to hang just above the long table. From four corners of the group, four of the seven drew from their robes pointed javelins and the three who remained cast aside their capes to reveal straight swords. Their hoods fell back from their faces as those in the cage saw their fate. They cried out in panic and their fear of dying heightened the force within the room.

The chanting grew louder and as its pace increased a fresh power was raised. The shadows within the room began to condense and soon the invoked force became solid. Standing now in the apex of the magic ring the presence absorbed all light into it. Voracious eyes now pulsated with the power of sight and the group felt its dark waves move through them. The Priestess, quaked under the its evil spell mechanically moving the tools upon the alter. Malthrom sensed its hunger. The shadow held its hate in fierce control. It would not destroy those who served it. It needed them. Their hands and eyes were the earthy parts of its sinister will. The willing parties trembled in awe as the force touched them infusing the seven simultaneously. Their hearts raced to a death rhythm and with non-human speed the death strikes were delivered. The blood of both human and beast poured onto the table. The warm liquid steamed downward to fill the chalice that waited beneath and the excess was left to fall to the floor.

Watching from within the black stone tower Malthrom was careful to be still of all emotion. He was acutely aware of his every thought, knowing this force had the power to find him through the web. He did not intend to disturb the ritual nor have his voyeurism revealed for he knew the thing that waited there. Every fiber of his being remembered the foul spirit. Two thousand years had past since he battled this same evil upon his own warring fields. It was the day the tower had formed and though he had stifled its victory in those years long past by, his every action had not been without flaw and he wondered if the shadow had returned to claim the debt.

Pity filled him as he watched those who performed the ceremony and he wondered their foolery. How rudely ignorant they must be of the bargain that they were making. They did not see how quickly the lustfulness of earthly power would pale in the face of this enduring darkness. The shadow was waiting to consume them and they were blind to the depths of its malice.

The Priestess was within the swirling vortex. A senseless frenzy consuming her as the force gathered the blood of the sacrificed unto itself. Its passionate hunger leeched the life from the dying but its offering was not enough. The hunger was monstrous. It would take all and leave little, even for its servants. It bent its will upon the Priestess. Focusing voraciously upon her the force sucked her life essence through the skin of her body. But she was all-willing to give this to her master. It was part of the bargain they had struck between them. Just before the point of death the demon let her go and she collapsed over the altar gasping for breath. When she finally raised her head from the table her eyes glowed with the red-black and the others rushed forward in mindless zeal. Their grasping hands groped and pulled at her skin. The shadow of her bloodless body was now able to sustain them and the Priestess fed them with the darkness that flowed through her. Croaking in an ugly rasp and she pledged to the evil that formed itself inside the world.

Ban Zuge
That which you seek is yours to have.
My hands serve you
And your will is my own.
That which has been promised is now forthcoming
It is yours to devour at the moment of its birth
Shall it sustain you and keep you
As the sky falls and the sun burns into a cinder
For now and into the ever
I am your will of darkness.

And when the words rang out from her loathsome throat the blackness of the shadows deepened. The stench of it filled the room and the dark swelled. When the shade reached the confines of the cold walls, its hideous laughter sounded out. The noise shook the room. The candles failed as the table cracked under its force. The robed workers fell to the floor, their black blood running from their eyes and ears mingling with the blood of the sacrifice.

The light in the mirror faded and Malthrom shook his head. He knew that those that lay senseless upon the floor were not dead. They would rise once more to be the hands of the evil. The demon still required them. The people of city faced their greatest challenge. He would help them; where help was allowed. He would even be so willing to call the creature's name, if it came to that. But even this act of self-sacrifice would not suffice. His battle was long past and now he must wait. There were other servants waiting to be to forefront of the destiny.

Malthrom spoke out to those presences in the Airs above him affirming his desire to restore perfection to what had been born flawed. He sensed the evil, filled and satiated, resting upon the floor of the cave knowing well it would hunger again.

Walking to the windows, he gazed upon the city beneath him waiting for the answer to come. The people blindly pressed towards their destinations. They moved in a sea of ever-changing emotion, unaware they were absorbed in a mist of their own mental creations. He witnessed their thoughts as they left their bodies to hover in the airs around them. Some images would glitter for an instant then fade, while others would solidify to form shades of varying grades of force. That fine substance moved through the ethers, gaining strength and drawing to itself a life of its own. The creator became the pawn of its creation and it spun with a power unknown to itself.

How well he knew this error. Through the building of history and the creations of culture, the people built their lives from the forces misunderstood. The same mistakes had been made again and again. Ignorance fed their fears and that shadowed source was left unseen within them.

The despair of the folk of Tessera touched his mind. It did not move him and he allowed a vision to fill his thoughts. Against the blue sky stood a massive tree holding all the earth tightly in its roots. The form was perfect in balance and symmetry. Its branches extended far into the cloudless sky and its limbs' twisted in every direction. A legion of men could not put their arms about its berth. He watched as Shadows clamber upon the under roots seeking a form to forever rule. The wraiths desired something that would not change and something would not die. Malthrom knew the folly of the thought; for clay begets only clay, and could not enter the mind of that which created it. He saw the multitude approach and gasped aloud as the tree was separated from them by a great line of fire.

"Oh people." he whispered softly. "Remember yourselves."

CHAPTER 20
THE WAY IS TRAVELED ALONE

Tristus' brief moments of understanding were overwhelmed by the long hours of his faithless days. Grief consumed him and time after time he allowed himself to be lost in its shadowy warmth. He spoke little, and cared little, for the condition of the people as his mother sought her advice from the Priestess and the Guildsman. He found himself now drawn to the old libraries under the castle and each morning he descended into the dusty catacombs to spend his time wandering the dim halls. In that solitude, he educated himself anew with the old wisdom of the Eratosthenians.

In the streets above him the people battled the plague and the Pyrrohmarin ran rampant in the sea. The numbers of the black gulls increased each day and food grew scarce. Acts of violence grew commonplace and soon it was no longer safe to travel. Children lay huddled in the streets with none to care for them and, more and more, the whispers hissed that many left their homes never to return. Sorrow and loss had dulled the minds of the people above.

As dark smoke belched into the air of the city, rumors now flew that the Thalassisans were responsible for the taint of the sea and the evil words grew like a disease. The Haarshaim continued to increase the manufacture of the Khimerahs. The profits of war attracted the Cartels into joint ventures of speculative wealth and one by one the factories closed as the Guildsmen banded together to increase the manufacture of the unnatural beasts.

The argument between Tristus and his mother continued as the situation in the streets worsened. The people struggled as food is rationed and, as the sick died, piles of poisoned corpses were left in the streets to be dealt with. The Queen was lost in the complexities which surrounded her but even so no means of reconciliation appeared to exist between mother and son.

Jason and Pelius spent their days upon the sea journeying to the hidden canyon in an attempt to keep up with the increasing need for medicines. The sick lined the castle stairs while Aleryn and the other healers treated their eruptions and handed out food. The Haarshaim denied with increasing fury, any association with the plague of the *Pyrrohmarin*. They spoke out in public forums about the possibilities of war and it was the Thalassisans who bore the brunt of blame in their wrathful speeches. Pictures of the missing filled the streets as families searched for their loved ones. A dark gloom consumed all who lived under the shadow of the tower.

In the early hours before the dawn, Pelius stirred from his sleep. Looking into the soft light of the newborn moon he felt the edge of an early spring and remembered the Canyon of Orpheus. A faint ache passed through him for it seemed as if years had past since that fateful day. He prepared himself to go once more with Jason. Wasting no faggot of wood upon the fire he dressed quickly in the dim light of the cold room. He packed a light travel bag as the morning stars began to fade in the skies. Closing the door softly, he was careful to wake no other as he crept along the hall. He followed the shortest path to down the stables and in doing so he passed through the kitchen gardens. The heads of new shoots were pushing above the soil hoping to greet the warming sun. Whispering a good morning to the fresh green life he hurried to meet the Bifrost.

Jason was waiting for him at the piers. Her small crew was once more prepared to fetch another cargo from the Forest. The Queen's decree stated the healing waters would be profitless venture and the law stated that all in the city will have access to their healing properties irregardless of their financial station. But there are many among the Guilds that considered this charity a nonsense, saying that those benefiting from this order were unworthy of such generosity.

"If there is a need, there is a profit." was the common talk among the stalls of the market place.

"Eyes are on us, Jason." said Pelius when he reached the deck of the Bifrost.

"Aye." Jason replied, looking out over the harbor. "There has been much interest of late in our destination."

"I fear harm may come to the forest if we are not discrete in our coming and going." said Pelius.

"I have already set a new course, Master Pelius."

"Good." he answered, worry still heavy in his tone. "The yellow springs are generous but only as our hand is gentle. The forest is a fragile creature."

The Bifrost made a long circle though the sea to mislead any who would try to follow. It was under the cover of night, they anchored their boat and sent forth a small group to gather the thing they required. Leaving them to their work, the Bifrost left no hint that she had briefly touched the shore.

The night was a thick soup under the dense canopies of the trees. No moonlight reached the floor of the wood. The lamps they carried were met with curious stares from many strange eyes and insects rained upon them as they walked. Pelius moved through the forest with an agile grace. Though none of the others could see, it is really Puthon who lead the way. They filled their skins in the yellow pools and turned back to the ship. Along the path, Puthon advised Pelius of the other healing plants that lie in the wood. The little man whispered their preparations into Pelius' ear and as they worked together hope grew in him. The ability to fight the scourge seemed possible for the remedies offered by the shaman were proved to be potent. In the wood, Pelius understood the many voices of those lives in sheltered hold. Their melodies and harmonies became one song and the one song soon became greater than its parts. The song moved through him as Puthon guided them back once more to the entrance to the sea and, without a word, he vanished in the air.

The Bifrost was waiting under the cover of night to fetch her crew and their cargo. Over the dark waves they returned to Tessera carrying their precious fluid. As always Aleryn was always there to meet them. During these days Pelius spent much of his time in her company and their abilities to communicate seemed too increase with every dawn. Under the pressures and pain of death he wondered often at her ability to persevere.

When he would ask the Princess of her mother and her brother she would only answer him saying,

"Both of them do as they deem best. I am not Queen nor am I heir to this throne. There are patterns to things I do not understand. I will do what I am compelled to do and I will be

where I am needed most. There is no more or no less than this."
Then she would smile and touch his hand and he would be glad
that he was at her side no matter what they must endure.

The Queen spent much of her time in the temple. Alone,
she prayed to the Malthrom for guidance. The people were
hungry and sick and that burden of the streets below gnawed her.
Her sense of failure was heavy. She did not understand what
had made things go so wrong. Often she thought back upon the
choices she had made, wondering which one could have been
different and which of these many choices might have changed
the events which now suffocated her. In the evenings, the
Priestess kept her company. The woman would cast the runes
upon the table and interpret their meanings for the Queen.
Listening to her words the Queen would find herself increasingly
lost and the filtering weakness gradually broke into her sense of
being leaving her unable to find the clear place in her mind. She
would often lapse into forgetfulness and the Priestess would to
remind her of their conversations. But even as those the days
went by she would think often of Tristus and wish that things
were different between them. She knew he did not understand
her burdens, and he was not able to see the fundamental
responsibilities which were hers only to bear. His view was
from another place.

"Maybe it is the better view?" she thought as she laid
herself down to sleep at the end of another disheartening day.

Tristus thought of the Queen as well. He wondered why
she made the decisions that she did but that way of thinking was
closed to him and he did not understand it. To find relief he
buried himself in the books and though he did not know
precisely what he sought, the sense that he would find it buried
among the volumes pulled him onward. He journeyed deep
under the city searching the winding halls and he realized his
grief had begun to change him. He found if he did not allow his
sorrow to take him, his sanity would remain keen and no
emotion could sway him from his centered mind. So in that
state he journeyed deep into the realms of the Eratosthenians.
Corridors and cavelets were cut through the solid rock. He
would bring lights and other things he needed to explore the
miles of caverns. Storing his supplies along the way he began to

methodically investigate the narrow halls. Measuring his steps he calculated carefully the distances between one place and another until he began to understand that the halls lead under the mountains as well as the sea. Along the way, he would find rooms filled with handwritten books lining the dusty hallways. He noticed that of these chambers most were dedicated to the understanding of a single discipline and he found himself looking back into the past of ages of humankind. The ancient Arts and Philosophy of Tessera being a living map as to the moods and values of the people.

Nonetheless, the halls of the archaic vaults held a disconcerting edge. Walking through the corridors he often thought he would catch glimpses of something moving though the hall. He would try to catch up to the elusive shadows but they always would remain just ahead. The paths beneath the mountain seemed endless and after several weeks he came upon a corridor different from all the others. He was stowing supplies in an alcove and found a tall archway hidden beyond the blind corner. The arch was covered in old glyphs and as he read the letters found them difficult to translate. His curiosity pulled him on and eventually the hall widened out with long alcoves spreading out from each side. He was in the first hall, the history of sea travel. Fascinated he read volume upon volume finding every characteristic and mechanic of boat building carefully recorded in minute detail. He saw how the craft was methodically improved upon through out the years and he saw how the history of Tessera was woven into every change.

Traveling deeper in, he came across works made for the eyes of healers. The books recorded the workings of the human body and, within their pages, perfect drawings pictured the placement of the inner organs as well as the network of subtle connections which hold the body in accord. As he continued deeper into the caverns and soon he soon found halls that contained drawings of thousands and thousands of creatures. Meticulously classified, he came across many he had never before seen. Page after page, he found filled with both the delicate and the gruesome, until finally he turned to an odd creature of monstrous proportions. It lived under the sea and it had a great, drooping, head which hung from a short, flaccid, neck and attached to that hung a series of long tentacles. The mottled legs were smooth along the top but upon the bottom, round cups ran along each side of the appendages. It was these suction disks which enabled the creature to grasp a hold on its prey. The picture revealed the hideous creature wrapped around a spherical vessel. The beast's ugly eye had rolled back into a loose socket and though he wondered at the horrible monster, the bizarre vessel stirred his curiosity even more. Rapt by the drawings and underwater scenery, he wiled away the hours in front of the text paying no attention to the torch that lit his study room. It was only when the light began to fade that he realized his error and made a quick check of the room where he sat. The chamber was long but narrow and the table where he studied was embedded into an alcove of stone. Its front faced a smooth black surface. The picture books were inset into shelves cut through the rock and symbols were carved above the notched pantries. The opening to the main hallway would be a long walk in the dark and just how far the hall extended in the opposite direction he had yet to find out. Carefully he placed the book back in its spot annoyed with his laxity. He had other lights stored along the main hall but would likely have to grope his way through the dark until he could find the place where he had put them. All around him turned to black as the single light sputtered and failed. Cursing softly, he moved toward the main hall and in his frustration he stumbled over his chair. He lurched forward losing his balance and his head struck hard.

When he opened his eyes everything was pitch dark. His head throbbed and his hair was sticky. Alone in the complete darkness he remembered his predicament but the unwelcome sleep had left him confused. Carefully feeling the stone tiles, he crawled along the floor counting each one as he passed trying to retrace his steps. Soon he began to anticipate the threshold that marked the entrance to the main corridor but when his count reached over a hundred he began to think he had chosen the wrong direction. Slowing his pace even more he prepared to turn back but just then he came upon a cold piece of metal embedded into the tiles. He allowed his fingers to follow the pattern inlaid in the floor and he perceived the shape of a letter branded into the bottom base of the tiles. Moving his hand along, his fingers knew that it was more than a letter but an entire word was written upon the cold floor. His curiosity kept him in the dark space for a moment longer. He would come back to this place once he retrieved a torch. Reaching his arm up, he began to pull himself to his feet and he touched another piece of cold metal buried along the wall. He let his fingers root inside the niche. Pressing against the finger hold and a soft sound tapped through the room. The upper edge of the ceiling flashed and then became warm with amber light. Pleased with the discovery he ran his hand across the catch. He experimented with the mechanism several times, watching the lights come off and on, before continuing along his way. The hall was not straight at all. Instead the walls were built to provide a blind view from the main corridor. He worked the switch several times more and then he continued down the passage.

Making his way through the hidden twists of the hall he found the lights soon dimmed back to black. He searched the walls for another mechanism and he found it. The catch was hidden in the same fashion as the one before and, as the light released the dark, an ornate door gleamed at the end of the hall. When he pushed it open and a dank smell surrounded him. The room seemed colder than the rest. Quickly he found the switch and a great, cavernous chamber was filled with warm light. The thin glowing cylinders of atricault ran along the curves of the arched walls to meet in the center above his head. Raised designs were cut into the polished stone and he instantly realized he looked upon a map. Before him the entire length and breath of the city was clear and he saw for the first time the network of caves that existed not only beneath the land but also beneath the sea. The scale of the massive system extended further into the northern realms than he believed was possible. Following the pictures along the wall, it appeared the labyrinth crawled under northern mountains and along the bottom of sea to finally touch the Wall of Mists. The implications crawled in his gut. It was likely he was not the first to have discovered these hidden paths. The underground paths connected the city far up the coast to the uncharted mountains. The direct route from Tessera to the devastated valley stared at him from the wall.

"So this is how they reached the mines." he told himself

aloud.

He began to look around him and study the other things within the chamber. Toward the back of the room there sat a great black table. It was peculiarly arced like two spoons that set within each other, against the round shape of the room. As he got closer he saw that a form of a hand was embedded in the innermost curve of the bend. Tristus thought it odd that that such a large structure was turned to face an empty wall as he placed his hand within the indentation. A faint whirr echoed in the empty room and he stepped back to watch the table shift forward, gliding smoothly into the blank wall before him. Tristus heard a faint clink when the two parts connected and then a seam appeared along the center of the wall. The perfect crack ran from the ceiling to the floor and slowly the two parts faultlessly separated to reveal a wide view of ocean deeps. Gazing up though the window that looked through the sea, the sun shown high above in the airy world as its play of light cast cool shadows on the craggy rocks beneath the surface. A school of dish-shaped fish moved across the thick glass. A sharp jawed sterlet raced behind them. Its shovel-shaped nose was swiftly proficient in snagging a fresh meal from the group.

He moved closer to the massive window and realized that a series of lighted buttons had appeared upon the black table. Reaching out he gingerly touched the closest one with his palm and the watery underworld that lie just beyond the glass was suddenly illuminated. The light spread in all directions as thousands of glowing lamps ignited beneath the waves. He sat down at the table and stared into the beautiful realm before him. The fish were attracted to the glowing lights and began to dart around them. Other sea creatures came to explore the brightly lit ocean and soon there were sea snakes and sharks swimming above him. A school of stick-shaped fish flowed around the boulders upon the sandy bottom. Their thin, brown bodies, floating in and out of sight, as they blended with the shadows cast through the waters. Sturgeons, thick with bony scales, flashed in the glow of the articault lamps. A giant clam opened and closed its shelly jaws, hoping to catch a bite as it filtered the ocean waters. Large stands of brown algae, holding by a single foot, clung to the stones that grew near the surface. Waving their long blades in the shifting swells the light of the sun fluttered along the floor of the sea. An ugly cuttlefish floated by ejecting a cloud of inky blackness into the scenery. He gazed at the ever-changing scene, drinking in the blues, greens and grays. Eating, living, breeding, and dying in world of water instead of air, these creatures held the same connection to each other as those of land. In the distance a group of whales came to explore the lighted ocean floor. Their large silhouettes dived to nudge the lamps that had been fixed there. A young whale raced along the path of light, following the lanterns to the window glass. Blinking his clear eyelid the long mouth seemed to smile and he studied Tristus who watched from the other side. But after a moment he dashed off to find his father and mother.

"What perfect things." Tristus thought as the family faded from view. The contrariness of circumstance sent a sharp pressure through his head. The gift of time the Thalassisan had given would not last much longer. The spiral of plague, famine, and war-mongering, seemed to have but one downward direction and, with his mother against him, he did not know how to begin to set things right.

Sighed as he gently touched the delicate switches and again the faint sound of machinery whined. The wall, nearest to the glass window, had begun to move apart and the soft play of waves against stone echoed in the room. The gliding walls spread apart to reveal yet another room and from his corner he could see a vessel floated gently in a pool of ocean water. The craft was almost a perfect sphere and was similar to the one he had seen in the drawings just a few hours. The vessel was made of atricault and all around it were round, thick, windows and one round, thick, door. These openings were sealed with large brass straps embedded with silver bolts. Upon the top was a circular deck and around it short railings gleamed. A ladder extended from the top to the bottom and a small hatch was inset near the top. The room was surrounded by a metal railing and a bridge reached across the water to the round door of the ship. Upon the ocean side, another heavy wall reached under the waters and along the side nearest him was another series of controls. Tristus imagined setting the vessel free to travel under the waters as he walked the narrow bridge which led to the door. Turning the brass wheel, he unfastened the silver hinges and pulled the port open to look inside. To his delight, the interior was filled with many elaborate mechanisms. Dials and switches, gauges and lights, were spread in angled tiers upon a long control panel. Two chairs sat before the collection of devices. The round arced windows provided a clear view of the outside scenery and in the corner, next to an iron rack and thick drain, stood a suit which formed the shape of a man. It was built of a black flexible cloth and a series of tubes ran from its chest and shoulders. A glass dome, big enough for the head of a man hung from a hook on the ceiling. He sat down and studied the instruments. Though they were marked in the old language many of the devices were similar to the widgets commonly used by the more intrepid seafarers. The form and function was peculiarly familiar and he knew what to do. Excited and unnerved, he left the vessel and returned to the desk to compare the glowing keys. By their color and shape, he knew which worked in tandem with one another and he also could see the sun had begun to dim. Looking out into the dark water, he began to see flickers of light and soon atricault lamps blazed a path to keep the ocean floor alive with light. He hurried back to the main chamber to study the relief maps which covered the walls. The underground dock lay near the Inlet of Narcis from here he would have no trouble entering the open sea unnoticed. He needed only a few supplies and if he were quick he could leave within the hour. He touched the controls to turn down the lights and close the doors. Staring another moment upon the map he turned back to the main hall to fill his traveling sack.

Soon he was settled behind the window of the undersea sphere and he stared down at the panel. Sealing the door behind him he sat before the myriad of switches and devices. Pulling the large lever which hung above his head lights appeared in the glass faces of the gauges. He adjusted the components and the ship sputtered to life. Clicks, whirrs, and the tapping sounds of connections coming together filled the orb. When all seemed right within the vessel he moved the rotating handle in front of him and the ship began to sink beneath the water. Pushing another control the wall of stone before him began to move aside and when it moved away he could see that beyond was another room which held deeper water and so it was that he passed methodically through several such gates until he finally emerged into the open sea. The night had settled completely but upon the boat was fixed a great lamp and he had no trouble in seeing into the places along the ocean floor. Checking his maps often he soon realized the ship moved at an incredible speed and by the dawn he had passed beyond the point where he had burned the bodies of the whales. Slowing his vessel he rested at his control panel and he took a bite to eat. He needed a moment to consider his next step. Lowering the ship to the ocean floor he waited for the sun to climb into the sky. The light began to filter into water and for a time he released his concerns, merging into shifting life. He moved with the forming currents and perceived himself surrounded by large groups of fish. The mind of the relentless shark pressed into him and he was the instant of fear at the moment of death and the sun shone like a beacon above the water.

In the distance he felt a new presence. The Thalassisan King knew he was there and Tristus returned the telepathic call through the waters. Soon shadows and light began to dance within the thick sea. Holding steady within the stream of contact, Tristus knew the King would find him where he waited. Darkness soon filled the distance and he watched as the forms came closer to the place he sat. The Thalassisan King had brought with him a legion of soldiers and Tristus understood his peril. The soldiers swiftly surrounded his vessel and their grim faces pressed close against the glass. Ornate silver armor covered their broad chests and their sharp weapons flashed in the random glints of sun but he did not allow their forbidding faces to disturb him. He waited for the Mer-King to come and, after a time, the swarm of bodies stirred and the degree of light around him grew. The soldiers began to move away to leave a path through the waters. It was then when he finally saw the Thalassisan King.

He was terrible and beautiful as he paused ominously before the bowed glass pane.

"Prince of Land Walkers, it is your people who break the Laws of the Sisters." he said without speaking.

The force passed through Tristus' belly.

"It is so." he answered. "My people destroy in ways they do not understand."

"Do they seek understanding?"

"They do not seek it." he said grimly,

The King did not respond, waiting for more of an answer.

"They are not able." Tristus finally replied.

"Then be it by ignorance or by arrogance, we will defend that which we steward."

"The hour is darker than you may know."

"I am come to listen as well as speak." he answered.

So Tristus told King of Merfolk of his own household. He explained how events had come upon them. The Thalassisan listened intently when the news of his brother's passing was told and the state of his household. He painted a grim picture, sharing the lies the Haarshiam had decried to the people leading them to believe that it was the Mer-folk who poisoned the sea and how these very creatures would be used against them. When he had finished his tale, the burden weighed heavily in his mind.

"It is the Guilds who hold the true power. And the people, including my mother, are deluded by their reason. They will use the Khimerah against you to keep what they want. They hold regard for no other thing."

"They are fools." replied the King gravely.

"Fools indeed, but they carry great influence. It is easy for the small voice of wisdom to be drowned."

The Mer-King met Tristus' gaze and silently he asked him if he would like to leave the city that has deserted him and travel freely into the northern realms.

Tristus shook his head. "No. I am bound to them, be it right or wrong. I must remain in Tessera even in the greatest of all errors. "

The Mer-king nodded for he understood the burden the boy bore and when he finally spoke he offered him a blessing.

"May the light come to your people, Prince of the Land Walkers, and may it reveal the path to Wisdom before their time runs out."

The King then turned away and his legion settled in behind him, resolutely following him through the deep waters.

Tristus knew they went to prepare for the fight ahead. He gazed over the undersea realm as they faded away. The morning sun still played with the shapes and shadows of the deep but as he watched he noticed the light above him darkening. He glanced up to see a dense film passing upon the surface. It flowed like a thick cloud of syrup, moving in the direction of the currents. He knew it was the *Pyrrohmarin* which spread over the waters. His eyes followed the path. It appeared the source belched from the upland north and Tristus turned his vessel about and went to find the point of entry.

CHAPTER 21
THE BATTLE BEGINS

Pelius' voice carried through the hall, its tone sending a start of alarm through him. Tristus sat down his traveling sack and hurried to Aleryn's chamber to see what trouble had come while he had been away. Opening the door he found the boy violently pacing the length of the room. The hearth flames rose up and died away with every agitated wave of his arm. Tristus ducked his shoulders as a chair flew through the air crashing into the wall behind him. The room was in chaos as everything that was not fastened down was being overturned and thrown about. The window overlooking the sea held a spidery crack running through its green glass. Aleryn could do nothing to calm him. His blue eyes flashed with heat as he cursed the adversary he could not reach to destroy. Aleryn rushed to her brother's side, tears were running down her face.

"Tristus!" She cried. "The Khimerah has broken free. They have murdered and we can not to stop them."

"Aleryn. What have you heard? What has happened?"

"The world is unraveled! There is nothing left to do!" roared Pelius as the cracked window behind him shattered entirely and fell in bits unto the floor.

"The soldiers, they are horrible creatures, Tristus!" said Aleryn. "Things have not gone as the Haarshiam had anticipated. It was the day before last when they entered the city."

"They had been about the business of ruin long before that day, Aleryn." said Pelius, as the bed-frame collapsed to the floor.

"Stop. Please, both of you. Tell me so I can understand." said Tristus.

Aleryn wiped tears away with the sleeve of her robe.

"It was the morning of two days ago when the Haarshaim sent their message. They were set to reveal their new solders to all of Tessera and they were going to begin their march at the noon hour. We took our places in the Main Square to await their arrival. We first heard the grating sound of wings filling the air. Then we could smell their reek and when finally we saw them they were monstrous to look upon."

She shook as she explained their hideous form and the image of their skin, metallic and flexible, grew in his mind. No hair lay upon their heads and black slits served as eyes.

"There is no voice of soul within them. Such a thing I have never sensed in the presence of another life. And Tristus, these soldiers are not separate creatures as I had imagined they would be, but instead each are melded into a steed that matches them. They have been designed together and they are a fierce and horrible sight. They stood along the streets, three thousand strong, and the people cheered them." and then she hesitated and shuddered. "It was the Chancellors' man, Berdias, who stood with them introducing them as the new soldiers of Tessera. Their long wings crackled. The horse-part pawed the ground and the man-part flared its nostrils as it took in the scent of the crowd. Long swords hung by their sides and morning stars were belted around their waists. They stood together, hip to hip and shoulder to shoulder, and everyone of them carried bow and sling. The smell was stinging to the eyes. Dread grew quickly as they leered at us and soon children began to cry. Their mothers began to move away from the center square."

"The beasts were aware of their fear. The horse-parts began to kick and the man-part showed their dreadful teeth. Exchanging sounds between them, they stared us and dull glow pulsed from their eyes." she answered, her eyes filled with horror.

Pelius continued the tale. "Berdias moved toward them in an effort to keep the calm, but as he came too near, the closest creature took up his sword and with a single strike, lopped off his head. The thing rolled upon the floor with the eyes still open and blood spurted from the hole. The horse-parts screamed and then bent their necks to drink from the soaked boards. The people began to run but the beasts rose into the air and went after them. Our folk were not armed and it seemed the creatures took great thrill in the chase. They slaughtered the women and babes as maliciously as they destroyed the grown men."

"Nothing like this have ever happened before." shuddered Aleryn.

Pelius hissed as door rattled upon its remaining hinges. "And that is not all that has been fouled."

"What other thing?" said Tristus laying his hand upon it to steady the frame.

"The forest that lays upland, upon the northern cliffs, it too has been ruined."

"Ruined? How do you mean this?"

"I mean the healing springs are no more and the lives within those walls have fled. The opening that was hid has been laid to waste and snow now covers what has never before known the chill of winter. Indeed a hateful hand has caused this thing. It has set fire to the valley. The path to yellow springs is marred by the blackened stalks of what were once the tallest of trees."

"Do you know who, who could have done this?" he asked coldly the shock settling upon him.

"Only the Khimerah could have dealt such a blow."

"Where are they now? Do they still run free?"

"Some have been called back and it is said that they are confined to their barracks.   But I know that many are still scattered among the sea cliffs and some others lurk in the northern woods but the."

"Who has control of these creatures?" interrupted Tristus.

"The Haashiam give claim too but it is a lie! I believe their numbers are greater than have been told." answered Peluis, "And Tristus folk are disappearing from the city."

"And Jason, where is he?" asked Tristus, shaking his head as he realized his friend was not there.

"We are left with no antidote to fight the plague. As soon as we returned Jason took the crew to the Southern Isles." He holds hope of a remedy there and may be."

"And may be, what?" he asked impatiently

"Thr Tahmurath have had visions of the Earth and Sea. They preparing to cleanse this filth from their bodies." said Pelius pulling his knotted hair away from his eyes.   "In the southern isles there are folk who live by simpler rules; returning to the Sisters what it is they take. They may know of a way to help us balance this wretched state."

"Though we may destroy ourselves before any help may come." spoke Aleryn.

"Indeed." said Tristus softly and then he added, "Aleryn,

where is our mother?"

"She is ill again, Tristus." said his sister "It has been so for some time but she hid her condition from us. The day of the massacre, I found her upon her bed. She was burning with a fever and she did not know me."

"I must see her." he said.

"Come then." answered Aleryn and she took him by the hand.

The smell of infection was thick in the air as they approached the door and when Tristus saw her lying still upon her bed he knew he looked upon one who wavered close to the doorway of death. The memory of the void rushed into his mind. So much had come to pass since the gray-eyed lady had branded him with wheels of fire. Time was running short and its threads drew tight around him.

"I will be in the West Wing, if you need me." said Pelius when they reached and the Queen opened her eyes.

"Tristus, is it you?" she said weakly, pulling herself upright in her bed. "I was dreaming that you were near and may be it is that I only dream now." and she reached out to him to touch his hand. "It is warm." she whispered to herself. "Could it be that you are truly real and you stand at my side once more." she sighed putting his fingers to her face, "If this moment be genuine I must take the chance and speak quickly for there are burdens in my heart that I must tell. It has been my choices Tristus; not your own, that have led Tessera to this breaking point. In ignorance I have set us to the path we now descend."

"Mother, now is not the time to blame yourself for the sorrows of the world. The sorrows of the world were here before you and you are not their keeper." he answered gently, "We do the best that we may."

"You are a good son Tristus, more like your brother than you ever allowed yourself to see." she said as tears ran down her face. Tristus gently wiped them away. "It was my grief that blinded me and all blame is mine to bear. I gave them sanction, knowing true in my heart that answer did lie not in their hands. But now I linger often close to the gate of death and I hear whispers from the other side. I see my madness all too late."

"Then know he stands with us though these dark days."

"Dark they are indeed." she sighed, tiredly. "Disease and famine spreads in all directions. War is upon us, from within our own gates and beyond from those I have yet to meet. Truly, I do not know which enemy is stronger."

Tristus recalled the recent meeting with the Thalassisans but held the thought to himself and said aloud. "It is the enemy within which must be dealt with first."

"You are wise, Tristus." she said, "I have missed our conversations."

"Do not tire yourself," said Aleryn pouring a mouthful of the bitter waters into a small cup. "Please take a few sips."

"Aleryn, you fuss too much. But I shall take a sip or two so that I may have some peace."

"Rest now, mother." said Tristus, "I will go and see to these affairs. We shall talk again soon."

"I am glad you have returned my son," she said closing her eyes. "I will wait for you here."

He kissed her cheek and walked slowly to the door but as he entered the hall, the sound of garments brushing softly against the floor met his ears. He held up his hand and looked to Aleryn. She raised her brows slightly for she had heard the sound as well.

"There are spies near." he whispered.

"Often of late I feel their eyes upon me."

"They seek to harm. It lingers in the air."

Aleryn agreed, "Then delay this errand and let us seek counsel from the Tahmurath. They have other ways of knowing what things lurk about. "

So they went instead to the western wing and when they opened the door of the main chamber they saw that Pelius sat among the children and for the moment it seemed his rage had passed. The twins were on his lap and at their feet there was a family of mice. The tiny creatures were nibbling bits of food the children had brought from their pockets.

Pelius was laughing, "The cooks will not appreciate your generosity."

"But they are hungry, and no one else will feed them." exclaimed the children.

"It seems that these creatures have found some friends."

said Tristus, looking down at the tiny beasts as they held the grains between their pink feet. Their black eyes were calm for they knew no fear in the presence of the children.

"Yes, and they are grateful. It is most difficult for the small to stay alive within these walls."

He bent his knee and knelt down next to the mice. Micah gave him a several grains of wheat and he laid them in his hand. The mice climbed upon his fingers to eat.

"You see Prince, they are grateful to you as well." smiled the other twin.

Tristus smiled, childishly pleased, as he watched the mice enjoy their meal.

"Tristus, Aleryn, I must apologize for my tempers. I regret the damage I cause. It seems I can not walk calmly through the storm that surrounds us."

Aleryn smiled, "Such damage can be undone with small work, Pelius."

"Do not worry. I understand frustration all too well." said Tristus, placing his hand on his shoulder. "You are among friends here. Do not forget it."

"And I am glad of it. Friends!" he exclaimed. "Tristus, I had forgotten. Jason, he has left you a letter. Here, I have it with me." and sitting Mora gently down onto the floor he pulled the letter from his vest.

Tristus opened it and it read.

> *Dear Tristus,*
> *I hope this note finds you well. I have thought of you often over recent weeks as the search for answers is not simple and it is for this reason that I go upon my hurried errand.*
> *The Pyrrohmarin becomes more vehement with every setting sun. Since our last meeting its bitter touch has increased ten-fold since. The Haarshiam have increased the work in the foundries and any fishing ship must now travel deep into the western waters to bring home any reasonable fare. These treks have become fewer and fewer for so many have*

*become too weak to work the nets. Indeed the
ruin of the forest is a dreadful blow leaving us
without relief for sick and dying. It is because
of this that I have headed southward. I believe
the island folk may know a way to battle the
scourge. Long have they lived peacefully with
the earth and sea and maybe their
understandings will serve us as well. I will also
seek news of the slaving trades for it is my
greatest hope that the true connection to the
northern mines may yet found out.*

*But lastly, Tristus I too was witness to
the slaughter and I saw with my own eyes that
the creatures answered not to the Guildsmen
who give claim to them. It appears to my mind
that these beasts know a far more bitter master.
This state of affairs simmers with lies. Be
aware of what walks behind you. I will return
with news as soon as I am able.*

Blessed be, my friend.

Jason

Tristus folded the letter carefully and placing it in his
breast pocket he thought of the sounds he had heard in the
hallway just a little while before.

"Pelius. Again I have heard footsteps creeping behind
the chamber doors and I wish to put a face with the eyes that
watch."

"I have heard it sneaking about as well," Pelius agreed.
"This is not like any shade I have known before. I have smelled
its scent and I do not believe this thing is of our world at all. The
presence disappears at will to leave no trace. It comes and goes
as it pleases, as if it can slip through cracks of time."

"We heard it just moments ago. Perhaps it still lingers in
our halls. Is their one among you who may be able to help us
find out where it hides?"

"Yes, there is one who might be able." he answered,
concern bearing upon his face. "I could call Gwredd to the task
for her gift for sight is greater than of any of the Tahmurath. But

Tristus she is a young child, only six winters old and, when she speaks, her words are often difficult to understand. She is there," he gestured "near the window."

Gwredd was a slight child. Her pallid skin and thin flaxen hair appeared almost translucent in the beams of sun. She sat under the light of the window-glass, quietly staring into the long view of the sea. In her fingers she twirled a bit of golden string. It twisted and curled around her tiny hands as she wove it into itself and set it free time after time again. Tristus had noticed the child often since his return but she had never spoken and seeming so fragile he had never approached her. Pelius softly touched her sleeve and spoke quietly into her ear. She turned to face them and her pale blue eyes met Tristus' own black ones. Their brightness stunned him as the child searched his face.

"Gwredd, this is Tristus, Prince of this city."

"Wi a faire to een ye, Laude Tristes." she said, bowing her head courteously.

"Hello Gwredd, it is fair to meet you as well." Tristus answered. Her skin colored slightly as she smiled back at them.

"We come to ask you for your help Gwredd. Your gift of sight is needed. We seek to understand what spirits lurks among us. Will you use your gift to see for us?" said Pelius.

"For weel I wat ye may?" said the child, looking straight into Tristus' eyes.

"There is something that moves through the castle. It listens at doorways and hurries away when notice is made of it. We seek to know its name, Gwredd. Can you help us?"

The child nodded her head and took Tristus by the hand.

"rember twa a see and I wa sie thee maun answar." she said. Tristus glanced to Pelius for a clarification of her words.

"Remember what it is that you saw and felt. Hold it in your mind, she will search from that point in your own recollections."

Tristus nodded and brought back the memory of the hallway just outside his mother's chamber door. The stirring of robes and the soft sound of padded feet filled his senses. They seemed near enough to the touch and he found he could follow the sound down the hall and, to his surprise, he perceived a subtle mist as it turned the corner. A glint of silver and hint of blue caught his eye and he realized that what he seen was the robe of a Priestess. He felt the pressure of the child's tiny hand in his own, her mind telling him to follow the memory. He did as she asked and saw himself as he turned down the next hall. It was the High Priestess who ran before him. She made no noise her body appearing to fade in and out of view. She glanced behind her and he saw the ugly curl of her lip and the squint of her eye; their spite greatly changing her natural face. He moved after the image following the woman until she reached the kitchen garden. She opened the terrace door and walked out among the sleeping beds of mint. Her body was no longer transparent as it swiftly solidified back into a natural density and as her form regained its fleshy qualities her face took on the grim expression he was more accustom too. Thin streaks of blackness moved from the Priestess's body forming spiraling whorls in airs around her. The living darkness cut through the soft night like a dark smoke. It condensed in the air above the Priestess leaving her struggling for a breath and then the darkness spoke to the woman.

"You are careless!"came a ghastly utterance. "That fool of a prince has been wandering the caverns. He has seen the maps. He knows where they lead. They shall put these pieces together." The sound was like a spit in the air. "It is you, you witless fool! It is you who are to blame!" screamed the unseen voice. Under the force of its repugnant tone, the priestess collapsed as if she had been smitten by a heavy cane. "I will have to alter my plans because of your stupidity," continued the noise. "Bring the others to me at the raising of the moon this night. Make no error or you will die. And know silly Priestess, if I choose to kill, you shall die for all eternity!" A cyclone of dark fog began to whirl around her. The darkness pulled closer and closer until it sucked in upon itself and was gone.

With the airs cleared, he saw that Priestess lying upon the ground, trembling like a beaten dog in the frozen dirt. Tristus cast his eyes anxiously around the garden, trying to see where the other presence had gone. Gwredd squeezed his hand and he opened his eyes.

"Gwredd, did you see?" he asked the child.

"Aye, Laurd Tristas, I wi see the wevil."

"Do you know ow to follow this wevil," he shook his head, "I mean evil, where it dwells?"

Gwredd closed her pale eyes and placed her other hand over his. She sat very still, and her breath came in even draws. After a several moments, her color changed from the pallid white to a faded gray. She opened her eyes and shook her head. She did not seem able to speak and she would only stare back into his face.

"Gwredd, are you all right?" asked Pelius and he took her hands in his.

The child nodded that she was fine. Pelius put his hand to her head and Aleryn handed her a cup of warm tea.

"The thred of time en taen awa." she finally whispered to them. "I nae to fallow." She took a sip of tea and looked to Aleryn.

"Wi you, I taen see een more" she looked to the Princess, her blue eyes fading to a deep shade of white.

"I shall be happy to help you Gwredd. Take my hand child, then we can imagine as one."

Intuition told them all that this action was dangerous. Tristus stood at the Aleryn's shoulder and Pelius sat down next to Gwredd. Together, they formed a sphere of light and placed its circle around them. Pelius and Tristus held their minds steady in that glow as Aleryn and Gwredd pushed deeper into the memory. They held very still until they had balanced the power between them and, as they found the shared recall, they heard the malevolent voice speak once more. Then came the moment when the dark force slipped from view but the child and the Princess had amplified one another strengths, leaving the seers able to follow the shadow as it slipped through the door.

The fog was dense in this between world and it seemed the light they carried in their minds now only served to blind them. They struggled through the murky place, each sensing each other for reassurance and they followed the thread through the mists. Thick fogs and dulled colors moved in the hazy chaos but together they walked through the gloomy web they were able to follow the lightless thread. They caught a glimpse of the darkness as it slithered through the clouds of confusion. The shadow moved with a fine acuity, slipping effortlessly through the shimmering fogs. The children understood their danger was real as they chose to follow.

Stepping beyond the tear, they found a world that was not straight, nor solid, nor did it follow any natural laws. It was a bent reality which folded upon itself. The door led back to an endless starting point where it spread from endless rooms which lie along each side of a long hall. They walked in a place of living dreams. But these dreams were not sweet, nor tender, instead, they were living horrors, incessant cravings which would not be satisfied. Room upon room, they passed and saw that each chamber was filled to overflowing. Disturbed cries echoed all around them. The tones moved through the hall trapping their creations within the ephemeral walls. The shadow continued to move between the shifting realities giving the mayhem surrounding it little heed. Silently, the children followed until a dark door moved into the space before them. It was then that they laid their eyes upon its lair. A massive hollow pitted the floor. Hundreds of glowing candles burned upon narrow ledges which lined crater that sunk deep into the ground. Thousands more of the wax pillars lined the great lengths of the high walls. The sharp wisps of that dark force joined together and a form began to take shape until the fiendish beast rose from a black and sinewy web to stand undisguised in the sinister hall. Around its naked form, there appeared seven heads and one among them was manlike though it held but one large eye protruding from its forehead. Upon the head rested a crown of dull metal adorned with horns and sharp blades and slavering unadorned beneath manish thing was the head of a bull, a lion and an ibis. Other monsters writhed between the four and joined to its thick neck but these creatures the children could not name. The beast had the tail of a falcon and the tail of an alligator and as four arms extended from its body, two of them took on the impression of wings. They held tall lances and about these lances twined the bodies of two snakes. The other two limbs were covered in reptilian scales and these arms held a scepter and a whip. The feet formed the shape of scorpions. The scorpions held in their deadly tails the body of the ouroboros. The demon's single eye, squinted when it saw the children standing at the threshold of its private chamber. A hideous roar formed in its gut and the walls begin to shift toward them. Frozen in the horror, the two found they could not move from the threshold of the doorway and in the castle, Pelius and Tristus felt themselves linking with the deadly force as it seethed through the ethers. Increasing the points of concentration they held within their minds, the light surrounding the protective circle intensified. They called out the names of the girls, in hopes they could hear, as the waves of force emanating from the demon began to fill both spaces.

The room where they waited grew dark and the air writhed with an unworldly stench. Pelius grabbed up Gwredd's tiny body and shook her, reaching into the demon's realm, he called her home. She opened her eyes, and cried out when she realized that Aleryn had been left alone in the presence of the demon. Pelius called out to the others and the children gathered to the circle of light. Moving their hands into its radiant glow, each one touched a bit of the Princess' robe and when they succeeded in joining their powers together as one force, a blinding light leapt forth like a flare. In unison the children called Aleryn's name, keeping their minds clear and still, allowing time for the sound to reach through the web. She heard and remembered herself. Struggling for breath, she opened her eyes to find Tristus at her side but the demon would not let its prize go so easily and it screamed as it followed her from its convoluted lair. The hideous noise crashed into the room and the nightmare memories rushed into every heart. A black split appeared in the airs. The children shouted and, once more, the brilliant light pushed through the bellowing tear. The rent crashed shut and the evil was silenced. Tristus gathered Aleryn into his arms and softly, the children began to hum. The voices soothed the trembling airs and the room slowly began to settle into peace.

"Gwredd," Aleryn gasped. "Is she all right?"

"The child is fine." said Tristus. "It was you the demon wanted."

She covered her eyes and trembled. "I glimpsed into its mind, Tristus. The thing will not rest until it consumes all; all we are and everything we have to give."

"It is true, Tristus. It is the same spirit which hung over you that Festival night." replied Pelius. "Do you remember that moment, my friend? The moment is sought to drain you of your blood's essence. And the moment it slipped back through the rip in time. This is the phantom which has haunted the land for centuries. It is the same phantom that lends its strength to the shadows that prowl through the streets." Pelius shook his head and sighed, still holding Gwredd tightly in his arms, "It is the force which has murdered our kin and yet, whatever it is, it is less than flesh and bone."

"I understand Pelius." nodded Tristus running his hand along the crimson stains. "It is the voice that haunts my darkest hours and more true still, is that I have yet to find the way to rid myself of its presence or its memory."

"It is what lies behind our troubles. I am sure of it now." Pelius replied, thinking hard. "But what sort of being can lay in wait behind the dust of earth?"

"A creature which is not bound to the rule of time;" Tristus mused. "It is a being, which does not bide by the laws of earth; this shadow is able bring its nightmares to life in our world."

"Then what hope have we, brother!" cried Aleryn, shuddering still from her encounter with the daemon. "What chance is there in a realm so illusive and unknowable? How can we fight a force that brings nightmares into our world at will? What we are is poorly able to even understand such things. All that is around us; all that is physical, can not simply slip through time."

Tristus thought a moment and answered slowly. "The force that precedes the physical is first born in realms beyond the rule of time. Just as it is from endless spaces that order of our world is brought to bear." he answered as a strange light began to press upon his reason. "Everything that appears into the physical was once only a vision-dream. A thought is not tangible to the world of flesh, but yet it is the force that guides the building of every form and the intention of that thought is a subjective thing. It is in the realm of thought that every design, good or evil, does begins," he said touching her hand "be it the intent of a man as he lives his life, or the intent of the Earth as she nourishes her creatures, or even the intent of the Ancient as it moves within the circles of heaven. All things are begun in those finer grades of thought. And thought Aleryn," he continued, choosing his words carefully, "thought is a force we all know well. Truly they are strange things. How they linger with us in every moment, reaching out from the past, and probing into the future. Some are as ephemeral as a wisp of wind and yet others are so tormenting they will not give a moment's peace. But consider this little sister, consider how often we have communicated across vast spaces upon those weightless birds. Truly it seems that thoughts do not carry the burden of time."

"Indeed, thoughts are the means by which all things are done, " Pelius agreed thinking back upon his childhood games, "Thoughts are instant by nature, They are weightless and yet they initiate all motion which unfolds around us."

"They penetrate into our world and yet they are not of it." said Tristus. "Their threads are webbed through the layers of space and, by these connections, they are able to press into the realms of clay. It is on these waves of thought the demon travels. It welds its intentions within the same laws that bind matter to itself and, in turn, it is those same laws which matter binds life."

"But the demon seeks to destroy life. I have felt it inside of my own mind. Its intent is an unyielding malice. This is the way its thoughts are bent. It will not rest until it is satisfied. It will consume everything it is able." said Aleryn.

"And here lays our problem." Tristus answered, puzzling the pieces together. "We do not hold the same intentions. This creature hides purposes behind shadow and vice. It lures the weak and the ignorant with shallow lies, ensnaring them to act as its hand and mind. We are not able to fight like with like." Tristus replied. Then he felt a pulling on his sleeve and he looked down to Gwredd's pale eyes staring up at him.

"But the wevil did not rwench us Laude Tristus. We eld it bac. It did not come."

"No, it did not come." said Aleryn slowly, reliving the moment that pulled her home. "It was the sound of the call that held it back." and she looked over the children who were gathered close around her. "The shadow did not penetrate it."

"In that instant our thoughts were united," Tristus replied. "There was no past, nor future. We were perfect in that moment." then he paused and gazed up to the ceiling. "But there was something else as well. Do you remember it?"

"Aye." answered Pelius. "It was a flash of light, and for an instant there was nothing else."

"Yes, I saw it too. And that light sister; that blinding light, flowed to us from the above." said Tristus.

Aleryn nodded and followed the strands of his thoughts upward. "Often, I have used that force to heal the sick," she agreed. "There is a point in the upper airs that connects the higher to the lower. That light marks a door between worlds but Tristus that is a dangerous place to stand between."

"It contained the power to stop it." he said " It is the answer we have been seeking?"

Aleryn studied his face. "The act of drawing the upper light downward there are many risks. Guardians wait at that door and their cures are often testing. Healing will only occur if the body be willing. If all is not in place the patient could perish under the force of that energy. And worse, if error is made, the healer may succeed only in drawing the poison into himself and intensify the very problem the light has been drawn down to cure." she explained shaking her head. "It is a potent place, I agree, but its dangers are clear for both the ailing and the healer."

"But this action may be the hope of all." he pressed. "And I do not mean just those failings of the individual, little sister, but those of the whole as well. I speak of all the failings of Tessera."

Aleryn stared at him in disbelief, "Then what you speak of are mysteries beyond our ken, brother. The wrongs of the Kingdom, Tristus? We are but a handful of souls. We can not succeed against an evil which lies outside of time and worldly circumstance."

"But mysteries are not meant to be kept forever. They are meant to be found out and there are powers, little sister, unspeakable powers which exist just beyond our ken." he answered remembering the touch of the Vulcane's sword.

"Together we are far stronger than we are alone." answered Pelius. "The call united us as we stood together in the higher realms. As we stand as one, our strengths are amplified ten-fold and more. I believe we hold a chance in this. "

"But the shadow knows the powers held in numbers as well. It stands with its own vast minions." Aleryn answered, "Such action is dangerous, Pelius. In every fear there lurks a shadow and within every impurity there lies a battleground. None among us can claim to hold such purity." she continued gravely, "and even if such a chance did lie in this world; there are other dangers. A mind not properly prepared will be lost and a body not able will perish. To invoke the middle force downward holds many risks. To purposefully draw the realities of higher airs into realms of clay will certainly destroy that which is unready."

"Certainty is a comfort we do not keep. It seeks to destroy and what it does not destroy will meet a fate more cruel than any death," said Pelius looking from brother to sister. "but, if we succeed in this act, we may close up the crack where the shadow hides. And fear, nor greed, nor malice would never enter our world again." then he touched Aleryn's hand and said softly. "We know this enemy. We have seen its works and we understand its intentions. If we leave it unchecked, it will breed in every hate and ignorance." he said as he looked out to sea. "We have the power to do this, Aleryn and we are free to use it as we will."

The Princess followed his gaze, listening to the breath of the city as it slept and under it all she felt the dark intent creeping from every corner of her Kingdom as it ate away at every precious dream. For a long time she stared from the window and after a while Tristus thought he heard her whisper to the people beneath. "But are we truly free to will as we might?" he thought he heard her say. "Free enough to chance the ending to our world?"

CHAPTER 22
THE SOUTHERN ISLES

Jason rounded the cape. Many long years had passed since he had last seen the beauty of the island chains. He noted that little had seemed to change during that course of time. The lush green forests and the blue sea glistened in the early morning sun. The rocky beaches were studded with low growing palms. They reached their shaggy necks away from the waters as the constant winds had curved the trees into the natural lookouts. A man sat hidden within the nest of long fronds. He called out a warning to the village the moment the Bifrost entered the lagoon. In moments, men in canoes had filled the waters. Their swift boats soon encircled the Bifrost and the men of the island cast cautious eyes upon its crew. Jason came to the fore to speak to them and tall man with rich golden skin answered him in the Western tongue.

"Ho, Captain. What business have you upon our shores?" His accent was thick as his strong voice carried over the wind. He wore no shirt. A red mantle was slung about his shoulders and around his waist a wide colorful belt swung freely. His dark pants were loosely gathered at the ankle and strapped upon his feet were wide leather thongs. His black hair was pulled tightly back from his sharp-featured face. Upon his right brow, a bit of gold gleamed and Jason could see that a metal bit was pierced through his face. Around his neck he wore the symbol of the knotted circles. It was by this sign, Jason knew he was the leader of band.

"I have come to seek advice from your people." Jason answered.

"And what do you give in return?"

"I fear I have little to give. Our city is besieged by plague. Our people starve and we have no food to trade. I have only the working hands of myself and my crew to offer in return. I am willing to make whatever arrangements necessary."

"And how many men are on board your vessel, Captain?"

"Twenty six in all, sir. Hale and strong as our city can

lend for now our kingdom suffers dearly. I hold hope that you may understand our disease. We suffer from the *Pyrrohmarin*."

"*Pyrrohmarin*. Yes, I am familiar with it." he said looking over the ship. "but your flag tells me that you bide from the North. The *Pyrrohmarin* needs warmer waters to grow."

"Our seas have been changed and the blight flows free in the northern tides."

The tall man turned the words Jason spoke over in his mind. He looked over the crew and in a moment replied. "We have our own problems as well, Captain. But it may be that we can find a way to help one another. I am Lochlan, leader of these people. You are welcome upon our shores."

He raised his hand and several of the canoes returned to the beach.

"Set your anchor Captain and come with me. There are other boats are coming for your men."

So Jason's men lowered the anchor and swiftly made preparations to secure the Bifrost in the lagoon. Jason went aboard the boat with the red caped leader. As the men arrived upon the shore the villagers were waiting for them sharing flowers and words of welcome. Among the crowd were Lochlan's wife and children. His little ones ran along side the crew, touching their clothing, shouting and laughing as they followed along the tree covered path. Soon a village appeared along the protected walls of the mountain slope, its buildings made of sand and clustered stones. The thick walls were cleanly whitewashed and the roofs were thatched with fronds. Shady arbors of woody vines grew thick with flowers and resting upon the porch railings were great white birds with pink plumes. Frightened by the intruders, the creatures screeched as they took wing through the thick trees. Soon they entered open circle and the air about was sweet with spice and flowers. The cascading sound of falling water caught his attention and Jason looked up to find the falls that spilled behind the stucco buildings. It was then he beheld the looming mountain and he watched as a pale stream of smoke rose from its peak. Lochlan followed his glance and shook his head.

"She is unsettled. We have been doing what we can to prepare."

Lochlan showed Jason's men a low building with many long, low windows. An old man opened the door and gestured for them to come inside. The men followed.

"The northern rooms face the open sea. Your men can sleep and smell the surf at the same time. The keeper will provide for their comforts." then he smiled. "We make a potent beer. I am sure they will find it refreshing."

"Thank you for your generosity, Lochlan. It is most appreciated."

"You are welcome here, Captain, and your men are in good company." he said placing his hand upon Jason's shoulder. "Come with me now to my home. There we shall share our stories."

Jason bade his crew a short farewell and left them in the company of their elderly host. He followed Lochlan from the center circle of the village and together they walked up a narrow stair. The air was sweet with spice. The aroma came from a waxy vine growing along its stone sides. Buzzing things hovered among the shining leaves clustering greedily to long strings of butter-colored flowers. At the top of the stair was Lochlan's home. The door was open and two of his children stood giggling at the door. They moved aside to let them pass. It took a moment for Jason's eyes to adjust to the cool, shaded rooms. Alcoves of fat candles and colored glass gave the open spaces a peaceful glow. Lochlan lead him to a covered porch which looked out to sea. A rough table held baskets of fruit and platters of meat. Flat bread lie in baskets and alongside these were bowls of pale juice. Lochlan began to fill a plate.

"Please eat, Captain. We have no lack of food upon our island."

Lochlein handed the filled plate to the Jason, who took it gratefully. Rations had been poor upon the Bifrost. Only the past few days had they been able to glean a fair catch from the sea. Jason picked up a large slice of yellow melon. He bit into its fleshy side and the sticky juice ran freely along his face and fingers. Its taste was not like anything he had had before. Looking around the table he saw clean white clothes lying in saucers of cool water. He wiped his face and hands and placed the empty rind back upon his plate. Lochlein offered him a bowl of the pale juice and as he raised it to his lips he found that the aroma familiar. The spiced tea was sharply citrus and he felt its warmth flow into his chest. Taking a long look around him he saw that Lochlein's home was built upon a broad slope of the mountain. A grayed wooden stair wound its way to the beach beneath them. The waves crested gently in the calm waters and beyond the sand other thin islands stretched far along the field of blue. Wide leaves shaded the balcony from the bright morning glare and from over his head Jason heard a soft rustle as he caught a glimpse of a small brown creature which sat among the branches. The dark eyes watched them from within the shade of weeping limbs as Jason finished his tea. After a time the creature got up enough courage to run along the railing and jump spryly to the table. Snatching a bit of fruit it gnashed its teeth at the men. Lochlan laughed loudly and stood to wave his arms at the beast. It ran from the porch, screaming in a fury.

'Those creatures are quite disagreeable when they do not get they want." he chuckled.

"Then they are much like men." said Jason.

"Yes, they far too much like men." he answered his face growing serious.

"I have seen a creature much like this before. Do you have a name for it?" asked Jason.

'We have many names for it and most of them are not suited for gracious company." answered Lochlan, forgetting his frown. "The common name is *mungki*. They are clever beasts and some of my people choose to keep them as pets. They will mimic and play but their true natures are far more ill-tempered. They steal and bite. They must be watched closely, for meanness will easily overwhelm them. There are many types upon our island and they can be either large or small. The larger ones are gentle if left in peace among their own troops but the smaller *mungkis* are the most intolerable. Where have you seen such a creature before?"

"Well, something much like it. In was a place a little north of my homeland. The cliffs kept the ocean winds separate from a long gorge and, in the center of the rift, there was a chain of steaming pools. Their heat kept the forest filled with warmth. The hot water was bitter but it held the power to heal. It was quite an unusual place, filled with strange and remarkable creatures. For a time we used those bitter waters to fight the plague that torments us."

"You do not use it any longer?"

"No, not long ago we found the forest ruined. The mountain side had been destroyed and the canyon razed. The bubbling springs no longer flowed and the creatures have fled. I am afraid most of the life that once bided there has perished in a cold world."

"What caused such a thing?"

"Men." he said, noticing the *mungki* still lurked in the tree branches near them. "Many of our folk were ill and our Queen decreed the waters be given freely. But the amounts were scarce and some sought profit in the healing of the people. It was not long before small amounts brought high profits behind closed doors." he sighed, "Such is the way of exchange in the city."

"Your customs have always been strange to us. We do not separate ourselves from the land in such a fashion. Goods, and the profits they bring, have little meaning to my people. We do not suffer from the burdens of your rich or your poor. But this is not what brings you here. There is more troubling you Captain. Tell me what is on your mind so I may better understand your plight."

"Yes there is more. I have been told of a huge mining camp operates further to the north and I believe metals are refined there in great quantities."

"Metals. I have seen your metal craft often as my folk take our horses to your realm to trade. Your people have a great love for it, do they not?"

"Aye that they do Lochlan; Some can not seem to get their fill of it and the making of the stuff is a messy business indeed. The smoke and run-off of the foundries pour filth into the airs and into land but that is not all. I fear I have seen stranger things than this. There is a filth that rides upon the far northern waters and there is word of a mining enterprise operating in the mountains there. Its waste streams from the foundry, day and night, and a red blight breeds in that river bed. From here, it flows freely on into the ocean; killing all along its path along the way. I have heard the tide called *Pyrrohmarin* and it is believed that slaves are the labor force in these mines. It seems that thousands are kept in service to the brutal work. And through the bits of information I have gleaned about it all, it has led me to think some of these men are stolen from your shores."

"From these islands?" answered Lochlan and for a long moment he was quiet as he looked over the sea. "There is a legend among my people, Captain." he continued thoughtfully, " Fisherman tell of a beast that rises from the sea. They call it, Chelydrus. It is said that Chelydrus has been part of the earth since the beginning of time. But I must tell you that in recent years we have lost many folk.   They leave the island to fish and are never seen again." Lochlan looked to the smoke which rose from the mountain peak. "And as the years pass more and more signs appear. Portents of change are everywhere. Strange occurrences are commonplace. What is ordinary and what is myth now blend freely."

"And what was once only words of dead prophets now walks freely through the streets." he paused. "What legends walk through your days, Lochlan?"

"Only a few have returned to tell it but all have the same tale to tell. They say is begins with a sudden squall. A torrent comes on without warning from a once still sky and soon the vessel is surrounded by winds and furious seas. When the ship is overwhelmed, the Chelydrus comes. It rises from the water and lays its gigantic mouth around the boat. It can swallow a ship and its cargo whole and, when everything has disappeared into the vacuum of its enormous belly, then the storm will suddenly subside, leaving no trace of the boat or its passengers. But I will tell you Captain these stories are not new ones. I have heard them since I was a child and the same tale has been told since the eldest of the elders of the island were but children."

"And what is it that you believe?" asked Jason.

"I believe the world holds unknowable things. But I have often thought that the loss of so many of our people must have a more obvious explanation. It seems to me if the answers were ever to be found out, the explanations would lie more certainly in the realms of men and not in the realms of myth."

Jason looked over the ocean. The long stretches of white sands gleamed in sun. "Your home is beautiful place Lochlan. As a boy, I traveled with my father to these southern seas. It was around the campfires of your people that I first heard of the *Pyrrohmarin*. I could not believe that such a strange thing could exist but now I have seen its horror. I have hoped you would know a remedy for us."

"Well maybe I can help you with that." he smiled, "The surest cure is to stem the source. It grows where refuse decays and when the waters rise in temperature. Most often it has come upon us at the times when the mountains bleed the fire rock but it would fade when the colder currents flowed from the north. And we have learned ways to bring relief to those who suffer." continued Lochlan. "In the mountains, there are many growing things. I will show you how to prepare the concoctions that heal them. We can collect slips of certain plants as well, for some of these will thrive in any place with light sun and ample moisture."

"We have such places within the castle grounds to grow the plants. It will be a great boon to us. These things that you offer will comfort many."

"It is my honor to help you but there is something that I need to ask in return."

"Then tell me what that is and I shall do it."

"In recent years we have lost many of our men. The old and the young have been left alone to do most of the work of the village and for months now the mountain has stirred. If the skies fill with smoke and the molten stone flows we will have need of new shelters. These buildings must house all the people. It has been slow work to raise the new structures. We build as we are able and we now store necessities upon the southern side of the island. We are preparing places for our horses as well, but there is much labor yet before us. We ask for the aid of your men for a week and a day to help us finish the structures."

"You shall have their hands to help you, my friend."

"Excellent. Indeed it is fortunate that our paths have crossed. It is my hope that we can do much good for one another but we must not stay idle. Let us see too it."

Lochlan took the scraps of food and placed them under the tree where the *mungki* hid. The creature chattered and scampered down the trunk grabbing a bit of orange it sat upon the ground to eat it leisurely. Jason wondered how such an island creature came to be in the cold cliffs so far to the north.

Within the hour they were hiking the trail that led up the mountain. The scent of moist ground crept inside his cloak and the sound of water was everywhere. Lochlan's children ran beside them carrying baskets to fill with plants. Soon they reached a high meadow and running free in a deep green fields were dozens of horses. They turned their sharp ears toward them as the humans entered the clearing and children let their baskets fall to run to them and the proud creatures stood still allowing the little ones to climb upon their backs. Jason was surprised to see that the beasts were as gentle as they were fierce, their noble presence mirroring the essence of the island people. For a bit, the children romped about in the field but soon all returned to the work at hand. The sun was dropping low when they arrived back in the village and Jason went to see to his men before going with Lochlan to his home. He found them all resting comfortably. They had been enjoying the hospitality of the inn. The inn-keeper was an old man and at his side was an old wife. They fussed about, serving drinks and seeing to the comfort of the tired sailors. Already, Jason's men were regaining their humor. One sat in the corner, telling stories as he repaired the rungs of a rickety chair for the old woman. Edward, the cook, was at a stool near the bar. He held a vegetable in one hand and a knife in the other. He was whistling a old tune.

"Feels good to have a firm turnip in my fingers again." he called out as Jason entered the room.

"You have always been a simple one to please, my friend." he chuckled to the fat man.

Jason told them of the plans he had discussed with Lochlan. His crew was good lot and many among them had left their families to fend alone while they sought a cure for the plague. They agreed the arrangement with the islanders was sound and they were ready to begin work the next morning.

The dawn came and the men followed the villagers far upland. They walked through the morning mists and over the sharp ridges to the place where the new buildings had been started. The cove was protected from the smoky tip of the seething volcano. Walls, partially completed, stood clumsily in a thick meadow. Long notched poles, meant to be the framework for steep roofs, lay along the ground and they knew immediately what to do. Jason's men held no fear of heights for they were well accustomed to walking the poles and climbing masts of tall ships and they set to their work with steady precision.

The week passed quickly and by its end the heaviest of the labor was done. As they had shared the hard work true bonds of friendship grew between the crew of the Bifrost and the islanders. The elders had spent the week preparing medicine for the folk of Tessera and Edward had stayed among them to learn the secrets of their concoctions. Many of their recipes were complicated, requiring the parts of one plant to be boiled down slowly over a period of days before it could be joined with the parts of another. It was important for each stage to be properly prepared so it could combine rightly with the leaves and roots of other plants. Salves could be applied directly to the skin or diluted with water to be taken by mouth and decoctions were preserved with bitter wines. The plant slips were carefully cut and made ready for the journey back to Tessera. The Bifrost was almost completely stocked with barrel upon barrel of dried fruit and fish and by the end of the week every nook and alcove was crammed to overflowing. The portly cook could scarcely move in his crowded galley. Lochlan's people had sent all they could to help those they had never met.

"Come back soon, my friend." he told him, grabbing the Captain in a fierce hug. "We will be here waiting. I look forward to your return and the day I might meet your Queen."

"She will honor you, Lochlan for she is a gracious soul. We bid each other farewell upon a strong wind of hope."

"We will meet again, Jason. These things I see in my heart."

They embraced and clasped hands once more before Jason boarded the small boat which ferried back him to his ship. He stood upon the stern and looked at his friends waving goodbye from the shore. The sails fell and the white canvas was filled immediately with a steady wind. The island grew small in their wake as they began their journey back to the city. Jason felt as if a door had opened within him and all the healing of the world could now pour through it. He slept well in his bed that night for his hope burned like a light in the dark.

The morning came and by all counts the weather showed itself to be clear and already they had traveled far enough to feel a change in the airs. Cool gusts of wind began to creep under their capes, its chill presence pressing its way into the stale decks below. The men were in good spirits and sailed for speed, acutely aware of the precious cargo they carried. If all went well they could be in their home port in less than a week. They worked solidly by day and night to put the long leagues behind them. It appeared that the will of the Sister Sea was the same as their own. The waves were gentle and the wind was steady and hope grew in each of them. They felt able to face the burdens which spoiled their home-land. Jason noticed the change in the men and he wondered if it were not the clear, unspoiled air of the island that caused this new vigor to run in their veins. Looking out over the sea he became aware of his steady heartbeat and the image of his father came to mind. His presence seemed extraordinarily close, almost near enough to hear the sound of his voice. A sense of peace spread through him and he knew he was ready for what lie ahead.

Staring the familiar green sea, he noticed a flat line darkening at the edge of the view. A strange mist was growing over the bright day's light as a speck of cloud raced toward them with an alarming speed. In moments, the evil speck had crept out from its distant point covering the light of the sun. Jason watched the storm as it rapidly came upon them and he called out to his men.

It seemed only seconds before the winds hit. Concentrated and dark, the whirling air spun them helplessly about. Blackness covered the blue skies and all aboard could do little more than cling desperately to the pitching vessel. A new sound broke through the screaming gale. Its voice moaned, like a giantess slurping great barrels of gray tide. The sea filled with foam and a billowing wind encircled them. The great swells of water drew the ship toward a spiraling torrent. Closer and closer, in tighter and tighter circles the sea spun, the ocean was fast filling the floor of the boat as they were pulled downward into the waves. The screams of men hung in the air but there was no one to hear for their cries were swallowed up by the wails of the tempest. Helpless, the Bifrost sunk beneath the sea. The gray sky above was fast becoming but a dark speck but to the weary eyes of the sailors a more hideous sight came below them. The glint of metal flashed and an awesome mouth stood gaping amid the rushing waters. The awful maw was pulling them into the belly of its black hole and the sound of the mast, breaking in two, shook the vessel with a horrible splinting shriek of wind they entered the hole. Utter darkness enveloped them and the crew of the Bifrost lie huddled upon the deck of their ship. Alive, they trembled in the center of an unknown womb and a bitter silence spread all around them.

CHAPTER 23
THE PATH

He was cold and nothing about him was comfortable. He stood before him lay a narrow walkway; its path leading through a dark valley. Tristus knelt to the floor of stone and touched the dusty marks branded there. The letters were cut with perfect precision and they stretched long miles both before and behind him. He recognized the story they told for the words they formed revealed to him each and every event of his life. He brushed the fine sand away and followed that tale back though his memories. Walking though each memory, he found the many points where his motion met with the motion of others. Searching his past, he tasted what had come and gone and he saw how that which had been before still lived to create new moments. He walked on and the motion possessed him more completely. Events, frozen in his memories, altered his perceptions. He felt brief passions as they came and went; covering him as a substanceless vapor, coloring his mood as hiding the truth from his mind. He became aware of the fickle nature of his emotions and he watched and felt and recalled alone upon the stony path. After a long time he grew tired of dwelling upon his memories and he looked ahead to see that valley had changed. The path before him was filled a bright light and he moved until he could go no further. The intensity of the beam became violent. He stood within it, perceiving it as an open door.

A fierce cry moved his attention from the light. The dread of the call split through him. Raising his eyes he saw the land now reached out in all directions and at his feet there appeared a body of water. Upon its smooth surface burned bright rings of fire and Tristus strained to see what lie beyond the flames. Beyond the lake, the ground rose sharply and in the distance he could see the summit of a tremendous mountain. Recognizing the peak he knew he stood somewhere beyond the Valley of the Vulcane. He focused his attention at its top of the mountain and this time no clouds obscured his view. He could see the peak of the summit. Looking more closely he soon realized a garden grew there and in its center there stood a great tree. The tremendous limbs and leafy head sparkled in the restless wind. A sorrowful wailing then began to fill the valley and amidst the cries, Tristus heard the thundering sound. A storm was coming. Its black cloud rolled down the valley and soon the ground around him began to dim, but the mountain beyond still sparkled in the light, its peak untouched by the gloom. The pitch of the vapors began to churn in the valley and soon a strangely familiar shape arose from the mist. The Khimerah climbed above the storm clouds and flew to the peak of the mountain. It circled the tree and quickly the sunny place became dull. Just beyond its unnatural silhouette Tristus now perceived a new presence. The cold apex had a guardian and a brilliant seraph appeared before the great tree. The massive being hovered above the mountain pulsating sheets of blue-white and he held before him a sword of white fire. The silver hilt gleamed in his strong hand and from the tip a bolt of light suddenly burst forth. A million crystal poimts exploded from a nether realm and, in that instant, the Khimerah was no more. The beast had vanished before the blow just as would a single mote of dust can be swallowed up by a bright wind. Tristus found himself sitting upright in his bed. The window was open and the cold morning air filled his chamber.

He dressed himself and hurried down the corridors to speak to his mother. When he opened the door he found her lying upon her bed. Her skin was the pale color of ash and one hand lay outside the coverlet, its bandage soaked with bloody ooze. She opened her eyes when she heard him enter.

"Tristus." she spoke softly. "The morning has not yet risen. Is all well?"

"I bring no ill news mother, but a dream has come upon me."

"Tell me of it, my son." she said pulling herself up higher upon her pillows and he sat down upon the edge of her bed and began to explain.

"I was beyond the Misty Wall and I found myself waiting in a valley beneath a great mountain that I had seen before. But this time I was aware that a garden upon the peak. As I continued to stare I realized a massive tree grew in its center and a blue seraphim stood guard at its roots. I continued to wait and shortly a great cloud darkened my view. Black birds flew from the gathering clouds and from within their shadows the Khimerah rose up into the airs. It flew toward the peak of the mountain but the seraph barred its way. The beast circled rolling its tongue but the angel would not allow it to enter the garden. A blast of lighting coursed through the blade and the beast vanished into air.

His mother trembled as he spoke and he could feel her disease. He drew closer and offered her a drink of water. Finally the Queen spoke,

"What is the meaning of this dream, Tristus?"

"I believe it to be a foreshadowing of things to come. I believe it to be a sign of hope."

"My heart holds none of that," she sighed, helplessly. "What hope do we have?"

He smiled gently as he tried to soothe her despair.

"You are the one who has always spoke of hope mother, though I paid it little heed. How many times you have said the old wisdom is hidden in the past and it is not until now that I know it is true. In ages past, the Eratosthenians understood the nature of the world and what they knew far exceeds the knowledge of our own time."

"But what could they know of the problems that face us now? We live in circumstance never before imaged."

"Who can truly say what they did imagine. The knowledge they possessed is beyond our farthest notions."

"But my son, all the knowledge of the world holds no cure for war. Famine consumes the city and the sick perish. I watch my people die and hold myself to blame." she stated blankly seeming not to hear him.

"Do not lose your hope mother, for I do no believe that all is lost. There are books kept in caverns beneath the city and I have seen them with my own eyes. The Eratosthenians wrote volume upon volume of knowable things. Their books are kept in tunnels beneath the castle and beyond the vast libraries there lies a network of tunnels. Those hidden paths extend far past our borders. They lead, not only under the waters but into the unexplored mountain ranges to the north. The Haarshaim must have uncovered these passages long ago. These are the inroads used to build the mining city in northern mountains. This is how their secret has been kept.

She nodded tiredly glancing down at the bloody bandages surrounding her hands. "They have conquered the Kingdom I was meant to steward."

Tristus knit his brow, clearly she was not herself. Her illness burned deep into her core and her mind wandered.

Mother, do not lament. What has been called the "old magic" is in a reality, a practical thing." he spoke gently, wishing there was more he could do to relieve her suffering.

"You are changed, Tristus." she sighed finally looking up at him. "And your words seem nothing but riddles."

"It is true, mother. I am changed and yet, I am the same I have always been. It is the nature of the world which is the riddle."

"And this riddle Tristus, do you understand its meaning?"

"I understand that knowledge was hidden from us long ago."

"Then do you remember what was hidden, my son?"

"Though it is hidden; it is everywhere, at all times."

"And that answer seems but another riddle?"

"Words are not adequate to hold it, it seems. The moments are fleeting and then are changed." and he paused not certain how much more she could bear. "But it is a path which has been walked before. The Eratosthenians knew the way. This is why the built what they did. So we can remember and follow. The corridors through the mountains are wide-ranging, they reach to the mining city in the northern hills; the point that spews the red disease into the sea."

"Then we shall send our soldiers to stem its flow?" she said.

"But Mother recall, we have no army to send." he answered quietly. "The Khimerah beasts have taken their places. The Guards of our House can not control them but neither can the Guilds. The battle we face starts first within our own walls." he said reaching down and taking her hand. "But lose not heart, there is a path which reaches beyond the bitter sorrows of the world. We are tied by the virtue of our birth, and by our death, to another world. I have looked from the place where the Veil is rent. A Fire Goddess waits in her valley, daring us to seek her purposes. It is from beyond her Vale that the Mountain rises. It was of this mountain I dreamed. It is here that the true battle may be won."

"This place you speak of Tristus, sounds no more than a vision-dream? How can such a place be physical when it is nothing more than a thought with wings?"

"What is unseen builds the circumstance of life. The Eratosthenians removed this knowledge from us at the time of the first fall but all the while, beneath the Kingdom, they built a web knowing the need to connect what lies within the world to what lies outside its ken. When they came to point, where it was thought they could go no further, they knew the way to pierce the Wall. The words of the Promise give hint to the narrow way that leads through the Mists and it is those words which call us onward to the mountain."

"The Promise," she shook her head. "its sound has rung over our streets for two thousand years, but those words ring empty to me now."

"Hollow chatter, mindless prayer, greedy intentions, all have swaddled those ancient words in earthy intent and yet nothing has changed, a greater reality still waits all the while we sought out our own purposes." and then he hesitated trying to put the thoughts into form.

"No matter how lovely your riddles sound, I am too weary my son," she said gently, glancing to the brand upon his face. "but Tristus, there is one thing I do understand quite clear. You are telling me you are going way once again."

"Yes mother, again I am pulled from Tessera. It is the mountain which lies beyond the edge of the world that I must go."

"And when you reach this place, my son, what will you do?"

He looked upon her and could think of no word to say and after a long moment the Queen spoke for him. "You are the Star-Bearer, Tristus. Your destiny is not mine to command. There are higher laws than those which tether a Kingdom. It is the nature of change to swallow up one thing as it becomes another. Your destiny calls you. It is to that you are bound."

"I am so bound." he answered bowing his head. "Thank you Mother."

"Blessed be your heart and your hands Tristus, for behold," she said glancing toward the window, "the eyes of a new morning are upon you."

And the gray morning parted and the beam of light spread through the room. And as they turned their eyes to look over the sea as a rainbow appeared across the sky and they knew the time for goodbye had come. Tristus kissed her cheek and left her room. It was time to make ready, but he had yet another farewell left to say.

He sought out his sister knowing he would find her in the western wing with Pelius and the Tahmurath. Opening the door he saw Mikel, sitting in a bit of sun with a harp between his knees. The music fell lightly in the room as he looked over the peaceful scene. Soon the fiddle joined the harp, and soft voices began to drift from across the room. The changing tones blended but in its stream of lovely sounds there was something more. Just beyond the point where the eye would normally perceive he became aware of other presences in the room. Lovely beings of translucent light had been drawn into that place, their forms shifting in every changing tone. He watched them and as he did he found he could see the world through their eyes. He saw the sounds as colors. The tones were vibrantly alive as they released from the fingertips of the children. The seraphs took the sounds and caressed them. As he looked closer he saw, the moving bits of creation were lovingly garnered together and the guardians held each one gently as it went through the air. Binding the fabric of the sound into forms, a blue eyed creature with wings of flaming white gazed upon him and she smiled. Tristus thought his heart would melt in the joy of that moment and he felt a small hand lightly touch his elbow. Aleryn was at his side and she too looked in the face of that unearthly being. The light of the human and the seraphim blended and the room blazed. The radiance faded but the hushed beauty of that union remained.

Finally Aleryn spoke, in voice so soft he could barely hear, "Last night the moon sent a message to my heart, brother.

The darkness and the light converge upon us. The moment will not be long in coming." she said, her face radiant as her words trembled as a soft breeze in a still night. "You have come to say good-bye."

"They are not the words I wish to say, sister."

"A heart's course must be followed. Times come when one must travel alone." then she bent closer to whisper in his ear. "What is real does never diminish," she said gently kissing his stained brow, "Remember my brother, we linger not in the place of eternity. It is to the above that we are ever bound."

CHAPTER 24
THE DARKNESS IS REVEALED

    Malthrom looked down from the tower. He could hear the cries of the people passing though him like a shuddering wave. Many were hungry and many were ill. Their pleas for intercession reached into his mind in entreating swells of pain. Far out to sea he felt the approach of the Thalassisans moving toward the beleaguered city. He knew that the conjunction of the opposing forces burned in the sky and the source of that pre-ordained conflict was veiled by the light of day. He searched the mountain with his powers of telepathy to find the Star Bearer. He found it encouraging that the decision points were now firm in the minds of those whom held the key parts to play. For himself, he realized that his last battle was near and he imagined he heard the Ancient calling his name. Soon he would be going home and the past ran through him in a stream of liquid possibilities.

    It had been a scant five hundred years since the abandon tunnels of the Eratosthenians had been found by the Haarshiam miners. The Guildsman kept their knowledge secret from the House of Tessera as they explored the network of the intricate channels and soon the profit these new routes held became obvious. The Haarshiam expanded these passages in search of precious ores and, in the course of a few years, the valley was discovered. It was richer in metals than any they had ever found before and the determination to rob the hills of every ounce swelled these greedy men with fierce ambitions. Among this elite company there was one more ruthless than all the rest and he saw the new enterprise as an opportunity to gain power over all. He held his head low when he stood among the Guildsmen but his ambitions soared far higher than any of those men dared imagine. He was the first to approach the Head Priestess of that time. He tempted her with flatteries and fine gifts. In time, his finger of enticement lured her from the duties of a Tower and she turned her face from the people of Tessera. At his requests she began to use her influence to shape the thoughts of others and through the force of their combined powers the wicked plans began to take shape. The Priestess' ambitions paralleled the man's lust for power and soon, she realized that her understandings of the laws of nature gave her far more insight than that of her cohort. She saw clearly how lust may blind a man and it became easy for the Priestess to use her skills to mold him. Her advantage included the Art of Ceremony, a precious art endowed by the process of passing of the staff of one Head Priestess to the next, and as her desire for power grew she used her knowledge in ways forbidden by the Ancient. She directed the focus of her single eye upon him, pleasing herself with how cleverly she grasped his needs and how seemingly unaware he was of her manipulations. She took her time and laid her web carefully. Leisurely she drained him of his force and the man went on with his schemes, wondering at the gradual diminishment of his vitality. But both were deceived for neither realized it was the force of opposites that kept them truly at odds; his, the masculine force and hers, the feminine. Though he was weakened by each spell she cast, his span of years reached twice that of the average man for the Priestess needed him to be her face before the Guilds. He was her eyes and her hands. She used gazing stones to view the future of Tessera and watched the people as they moved through the age of Malthrom. It was easy to hold the people mesmerized by the glittering ore. She guided them effortlessly through her whim and strange appetites for her infatuation no longer lie with the shining metals and she craved instead control over the force of life within.

The years passed and the man became decrepit. Eventually she no longer needed him and she knew the time had come to relieve herself of his burdensome presence. She called out his name over the burning coals of her alter. It was a thing she had done many times before but now she intended to undo the man forever. His essence would be lost in the realm of the not-living. His sound would never to be heard again. Sprinkling bits of his body stuff over the coals she did her work. Nails and hair, a bit of food from his plate, a stolen sip left in the bottom of his wine glass; these things carried with them the threads of life she required. Speaking words of power, the components of his material substance had no choice but to obey and the man was drawn to her alter room. The light of the moon flowed through the glass at the peak of the domed ceiling. The smoke of the vile green spiraled toward the lunar light. Her words burned into the airs and the moon changed to a blood red orb. The substance of the lunar glow had responded to her call. The Priestess invoked the barghests and the specters gathered in the moon shadow. Their vaporous bodies took the form of dogs. A contemptuous smile spread across her face as the creatures materialized. Growling from the corners of dark chamber, foam dripped from the mouths of the beasts and their many rows of teeth pushed forward to gleam in the moonlight. The sharp points pressed outward to reveal the gaping throats. They were capable of swallowing a man, whole and alive.

The Priestess had carefully selected the method of sacrifice. The gore of the goblin dogs would excite her. The man had lived for many years under her spell and she looked forward to stealing from him the last bit of his life. He opened the wide black door and barghests glowered from the edges of the circular room. It took only an instant for the shadows to surround him. The creatures barred the door and hissed in excited whispers. The man realized he would not escape the room and he was not surprised. It was the moment he had long dreaded. Though he knew not how nor why, he had been aware through the years he was being destroyed in bits and parts and to this end he was prepared. Looking into her face he saw his doom but it would not be so easy to take him as the woman believed. She was beautiful in the deep violet robe; her red lips outlined in black and her breasts pushed high their tips barely pressing above the top of the sweeping collar line. Her hair was coiled and piled, row upon row, atop her head and the longest of the black locks fell across her shoulders. Within the braids bits of amber, silver and gold flashed in the candle light. Around her eyes painted symbols moved over her face. The paleness of her skin reflected the red heat of the moon and her black eyes were filled with hate as she raised the silver blade. She must be the one to cut the heart from the body if she were to possess the essence of his hollowed soul. But the man was ready for this moment. Throwing back the folds of his cape he pulled from his inner pocket an amulet. In the long course of their silent battles, he had charged the stone with hypnotic chants and the blood of slaves. He held it before him to shield against the power of the

blood hungry woman and she sneered in malicious delight when
she realized that he intended to fight her. This would be a better
kill than she had imagined. But as she gloated, the man shouted
out and the stone he held cracked apart and a sickening light
broke from its center. She gasped for air as the man directed the
beam and its ray pierced her breast. A shattering pain coursed
through her then. Stumbling back, she fell against a great bowl
of embers resting upon the long metal alter and the coals spilled
over the floor. The goblin dogs rushed toward the man and
snapped a piece of muscle from his thigh. Crying out, he saw his
next strike falter and the amulet dropped from his hand. He fell
after it, scrambling wildly to regain his hold upon the stone for
its beam had broken free of the place where her heart should
have been. A bargest laid its moving teeth into his shoulder and
the man bent back with a hideous scream as his precious stone
rolled along the floor just out of reach. The Priestess pulled
herself upright wondering at the painful doubt passing through
her gut. For an instant she was unsure of the power the amulet
had had upon her but then she saw him there, lying vulnerable
before her. The dogs crunched him and ripped his flesh as he lie
writhing upon the floor. The cries of pain delighted her. She
raised the knife to let the blow fall hard upon his breastbone.
The chest split wide apart and as the blood gushed to the floor
she saw the power of life within the surge. The spiraling force
moved upward through the air leaving a transparent fog to flicker
in a deep red glow. She put out her hand and watched as the
pattern rose to the ceiling. Peacefully, the strange mist glided
through the open peak of her ritual chamber while around her
feet spread his life fluid. Kneeling to the floor, she placed her
hand in the spreading pool. She wanted to taste the substance. It
held a fascination as it trickled slowly from his body. She was
pleased when she went to lift the blood to her lips but as she did,
she realized that she was not the same. Her substance had been
altered. Her body was changing into something that was no
longer solid. Her hand had faded into a transparent mist and it
wavered in the air before her disbelieving eyes. Indeed he had
achieved a deadly strike against her and as physical form began
to unravel she recognized that she was no longer bound by the
hard substance of earth. In that moment, she knew that she was

not of the living and she screamed out a blasphemous curse as she rose above what had just been her body. Her hideous oath chilled the winds as a great void began to surround her. A hissing curse moved through the blackness and above the alter table a face began to form. Terror possessed her as she witnessed the One who dwelled from across the void. It was He whom she had called upon to do her biddings. This Evil, which lay beyond the world of clay, would now become her essence. He waited for her as she moved across the doors of time for he would have her as his bride. In speechless horror she was drawn to him and from his grip she could not escape. He possessed her and, when he was spent, he placed her in a prison of ephemeral walls. Within her core now lived the seed of his evil and it tortured her. Every instant it grew and she became more and more like her keeper. The day came when his seed finally overcame her. No longer was she beautiful for his power had altered her form into that of a hideous beast. Tortured by vanity and loss of substance, her hatred grew strong. She must lay another set of plans. Once more she must posses the powers of the world and again she would walk the earth in a body of clay. She vowed to her prison walls that she would again be an Earthly Queen.

The clouds moved apart with the images of Malthrom vision. The force of the phantom vibrated strong into the lower depths of matter. The demon-woman existed in the place that mirrored the reality of the realm of men. She was the voyeur who sent dark birds to cast the twisted shadows upon the ground. They were her eyes and her will as they carried the fragments of her intentions. Her laughter tainted the wind and Malthrom knew she was breaking free. He needed to better understand the moment and he pressed himself further into her memory.

The rushing power of the years gone by flowed into him and he perceived her controlled fury. Watching the comings and goings of the Queens and Kings of Tessera her hatred burned hot as her form become more hideous with time. She found many spies for her vacuous eyes. The light burned her hideous shape and so she learned to move her thoughts through the night for the thralls she required. Some beasts were more inclined to bide by her will than were others. The black gulls, the garbage eaters and the soilers of the gray sand took pleasure in the relationship and she learned much by watching the Kingdom though their eyes.

Nonetheless, these things could never satisfy her as she still remained locked within his power. Confined within his prison, she burned to once again possess the physical form. Pacing the nightmare halls, she looked impotently upon the world of men. The lust for its substance tortured her and, more than this, there were still times He sought to be with her. These visits she deplored but over the centuries she became more willing to bear their pain. He possessed within him a hideous strength and she realized that as a result of their communion her power over the earth grew. This power she kept to use in service of her darker plans and after a time she found the blood of the living could provide her brief moments of physicality. Knowing well the ease in which the ignorant could be deceived she found many clever ways to enjoy the precious substance. She loved the its taste. There was no other thing like it. It held a secret that she did not yet understand. But still the moments would fade and she was once more bound to return the place where He kept her. Years went by and she became a mirror of His awesome power and yet, all the while, her own nature remained intact and her desires grew more and not less. She became insatiable, constantly envisioning the path she would take and finally the day came when she realized that the blood shared properties with the un-living substance as well. She glimpsed the living rope that twisted downward to touch the bowels of the earth. In a flash the concept was revealed and she saw the manner in which the two unrelated things could be combined. The spiraling ladder moved in both directions, even though the many forms of heaven leaving it able to touch the mind of the Ancient. The fusion point lay between the air and water and by this the union of these elemental forces could be further drawn downward into the realms of clay. Understanding finally the ultimate consummation lie within the blood's metal, she knew what to do.

She had no hands to perform the task herself but this did not slow her much, she was quite aware where to find such help. The Haarshaim were of the same nature as they had always been and she would use her skills to press her thoughts into their minds. Drinking from the veins of drunkards and sloths, she often took the form of her old self and tempted those pompous men with promises of gold. It was simple to guide them in her bidding. It was she who revealed to them how to combine the dead and the living to make a new thing. In this fashion she would have once more what He had stolen from her to make for herself a beautiful form. With this thing she would be deathless and would forever hold dominion over the land. She faced the Ancient, knowing well the Old Once would do nothing to still the free will given her. She laughed in black night to taunt the Airs but the silent face did not stir.

The first attempts were repulsive. The monstrous creatures that resulted from the combination of the living and the dead would only briefly survive and the disharmony of their minds matched the deformity of their bodies. They held within them a concentrated viciousness and she lost many servants to their violence as the years of experimentation passed by. There were other problems as well. The need for the metals from both the living and the dead were necessary in large amounts. Gold and silver failed in the task. Its earthly essence was too pure to hold the discordant energies of her creations but she remained unmoved. She forced her will onward and after time, her workers discovered that the atricault amalgam held more promise than the other blends. Again and again, its production was increased and the northern mines grew at a fantastic rate. The new forms required a source of tremendous of energy. The fusion of metal and life continued and its by-product of vile scum spread a putrid waste into the river and onto the sea. This wreckage of the land and sea did not concern her, for her desire was one-pointed. The *Pyrrohmarin* bloomed in cyclic surges of destruction. The darkness of her vision thrilled her. She laughed again in the face of the Ancient for she felt triumph drawing near.

So it was, that the power of her dark influence multiplied in all realms of the lower life. Her hideous creatures could now linger for months and during this time she created all types of anomalies. They were kept cages and held within the tunnels of the northern mines. The laboratories were filled with the large containers holding the disconnected parts of many bodies and between these part was a network of tubing. The organs were kept vital among the whirr of pumps. Headless beasts lay upon tables and beside them rested the separated arms, hooves, and wings. She held the ability to cut and place the parts where she wished. The strength of her shadows grew.

Malthrom watched the past unfold. Reflecting upon the things he saw, he became aware of the great flaw in her logic. So blinded was she by her own hunger, she was left unable to recognize the true source of her rising power. The power of her shadows increased in a direct relationship to the ever-growing light being sent forth by the Ancient. It was the inversion of this higher airs which enabled her shadows to wax strong. She did not realize that as her incongruent forms were being developed, so it was, that the finer forms, were being built in concordance with the higher laws and all things continued on a their forward path.

There were however, some aspects of that greater motion which did become apparent to her. She was bitterly aware that children were being born into the city that possessed abilities long forgotten. They held within them the far sight and this gift could bring a change to the city and these children were able in many ways. They knew the speech of animals and could command the elements but stranger still was their lack of idle fears. These new souls would resolutely gaze into the shadows she so carefully had laid and they held the potential to destroy her spreading web of darkness.

The task of terminating them became an irritating burden for she had other undertakings to attend to; but necessary errands must be completed. First she conquered the High Priestess, knowing better than any the weaknesses inherent of that position. It was prudent to have eyes to spy upon those of the royal house. Soon after, she influenced ignorant men to cover their identities inspiring them to rise in the night and steal the gifted ones from their families. They responded to her desires in a mindless haze, burning homes and killing mothers and fathers as they lay sleeping. She rewarded them in her way and they were loyal to her. Now, with her minions behind her, she stood most arrogantly fixed before the Watchers of the Airs.

"What fools!" she would cry, watching the Kingdom from her chambered walls. "Nothing will stop me." she mused often. "Nothing at all." until the day she witnessed the birth of Tristus. Two thousand years of entrenched custom shifted with the birth of the enigmatic first-born son.

"But what lack of foresight could have caused the Old One to make such an imprudent blunder. Who was this sullen boy marked with the sign of stars?" she thought with contemptuous disdain. It was through the eyes of her avian scouts that she became aware of his pointless journeys. She sneered as she saw him foolishly walking the shoreline searching for nothing. Nonetheless, she did consider it wise to rid herself of the weakling prince. Removing the symbol of his prophetic mark from the eyes of the people would give her a cleaner hold upon them. The House of Tessera was failing and this Queen had further diluted the ancient blood of the Eratosthenians with the blood of a foreigner. After the birth of Arcus she concluded that this second son was powerless as he was gentle. She saw the people of the Kingdom give him their fickle love but these things did not concern her. Arcus held none of the attributes necessary to be a King.

Then finally there was the Princess. Jealousy seethed hot though her monstrous form when, through the eyes of the black gulls, she looked upon delicate child. This was the one she had been waiting for. The girl carried within her the untapped potential of a new race. She understood the substance of her finer-grade body would need time to adjust to the uncommon slowness of the earthen realms but this auspicious detail would give her the time she needed. This child would become the form of her new vessel but she must be cautious and warily draw down her essence bit by bit. The perfect moment would be soon enough in coming so she set to work the trials of combining the living and the non-living parts of earth together. The methods she slowly refined. Holding in her hand, the power of the earth and the influence of stars, her time of conquest was finally drawing nigh.

Still she was vexed. The quiet presence of the Ancient nagged her core and the curious night came when she sensed the other woman. Her descent was marked by the blazing of the red sky and she rode where the sea touched the shore. The demon had caught a glimpse of their meeting upon the sands. The rider carried to the Prince a message from the Watchers and in her rage she bent her mind upon destroying him. It was the seraphs of sound intervened to save him from her hand. She laughed aloud when she watched him leave the safety of the Tower. She would have many opportunities to destroy him along the way to the Wall of Mists. She relaxed, reminding herself that he was whelp and could be no real threat. The Prince was a fool. She could leave his destruction to her pets and so she turned her attention to other matters.

The Khimerah was her foremost concern. These beasts were to become the foundation of her army. The people would marvel at their glory and she found their ignorance delightful as they let down their guards. Still, strangely enough, some of the new-coming souls had escaped her assassins and those bright lamps could not be so easily fooled and, to make matters worse yet, they now held refuge within the Castle walls. The blossoming Princess had touched them with her kindness and their union of minds grew stronger each day and as the situation proved more difficult, she set her evil will upon it.

Malthrom shuddered. He had stood at the windows of the black obelisk throughout the long of the day. The footsteps of the chimers entered the spiraling stairs. The fragrance of the lamps and the scent of the white blossom filled the hall. With a new clarity, he understood the force that opposed him. This ancient evil had survived to breed and would wait no longer. Through that imperfect point, created long ago, the shadows chose the moment to converge. Laying claim to the earth the wraiths of the daemon Priestess entered the west wing. Brutality, like rank sulfur, burned in the air as they passed through their chamber doors. Reaching out their long arms the evil strength subdued the small bodies. Mercilessly they battered them and placed them in black sacks. They banded the children tightly with silver ropes and binding spells before flinging over their backs to carry them to her.

Pelius felt their cries pierce the hollow of his breast. Running toward them, already knowing he would be too late, he flung open the door to see the room shattered into broken bits.

Flecks of blood were spattered upon the sheets and tables. He knew what had taken them. Running out into the night he fell upon his knees. Overcome with helplessness, his fingers clutched the cold, soil and the white light of the moon shone down upon his shoulders.

"Tarin," he cried out as the barren world collapsed. "I have lost them." Looking up into the dark sky he shouted out. "Help me my brother! I do not know what to do."

CHAPTER 25
THE SLAVE HOLDERS

The blackness was chilling. Jason called out to his men and they responded to him, one by one. The sound of their voices was oddly muffled in the stifling air. They could see nothing in this lightless hole but as they listened they heard the sound of waves softly splashing against the sides of the broken ship. The Bifrost lurched sharply as she began to turn herself upright. The men stood up and strained their eyes wondering where they had landed. A young boy ventured beneath the deck to fumble through the darkness and soon returned with a dry torch. When the flame was ignited, shadows played eerily against the sides of the strange prison.

They were trapped, but not in a living thing. This monster had been constructed by the hands of men and the cold smell of damp metals filled the belly of the beast. The Bifrost now rested upright in a pool of sea water. The mainmast lie bent across the whole of the long deck its end buried in the boards of the ravaged deck. The mizzenmast was clipped at the top and pressed against the sides of their massive cage. Their prison gleamed with the faint color of brass, looked smooth in the flickering light. Jason called for more torches to be set. Toward the bow, his eyes could barely make-out a portal; like petals of a flower the entry folded upon itself. This was the hole they had come through and now they were locked inside.

In that strange hull they traveled for days. They had no lack of food nor drink for the ship was well stocked but the smothering darkness played tricks upon their minds. Shadows twisted just outside the glow of the torches and strange sounds echoed through the belly of their prison, bouncing from one curved wall to the other. At times it seemed they could hear the voices of other living things speaking just outside their containment walls. Their harsh tones echoed through the metal cage. The ship did not toss in the shallow well where she balanced. Jason called for the men to take to the oars and row toward the portal but the Bifrost would not budge from where she sat. As the days passed, the air within their enormous cell grew more oppressive. Jason paced the deck in frustration knowing the city needed the cargo they stored and he was powerless to help them.

He could not be sure how much time had past when they finally came to a halt. The water where Bifrost sat became eerily still and the silence surrounding her seemed more threatening than ever. When the portal opened, a bleak red light pulsed through their prison walls and a regiment of armored men entered the hold; their distorted heads and limbs were covered by suits of dull metal. They paid the prisoners no heed as they shuffled along the narrow ledge securing the Bifrost with long buttresses. Slowly the water was lowered in the hull and a plank was set. One by one, the guards herded the men from the ship pushing at them with the points of their sharp spears. The soldiers spoke no language but communicated instead with hisses and growls. If a man hesitated they pierced him promptly and Jason gave the nod for the men to go forth willingly. They followed their captors thought the narrow halls of the great vessel. Through open doors Jason caught brief glimpses of strange machinery but when he stretched his neck to get a better look, he was struck with the flat blade of the spear. Climbing a long flight of metal stairs, a round door finally opened before them and he and his men were escorted out into a dismal twilight scene. The sun was low and newly lit torches lined the dock. Jason cut his eyes about to see the vessel that had carried them prisoner from the southern isles. The ship was a massive orb with a top that stood many lengths over his head. Along the sides concentric series of circular windows spread evenly along the metal globe and across the top a wide band of thick glass encircled the tip. The men had emerged from the belly of the beast and the great size of the ship staggered him. Black water lipped the side of the vessel and a grease like ooze glinted in the reflected light of the torches. They stood upon a long pier which floated upon the surface of a lake. Beyond the water, he saw a road reaching into a massive canyon. The air was bitingly cold and by the scent he knew that the water surrounding them was not salty but fresh. Jason realized they had left the sea and had emerged inland. They were moored in a deep tarn encircled with white tipped mountains. The distorted forms of the guards were even more hideously alarming in the flickering light. Their arms hung low. Their hands were too large and their legs were bowed. The faces of the man-like things were covered by the metal visors they wore and upon the backs of these creatures grew deformities of various shapes. They pointed their spears and the men moved along the floating dock. The slimy water stained their boots as they were prodded toward the shore.

"Ho, Captain!" came a shrill cry.

Jason looked up at the voice that called him and he recognized the man immediately. It was the servant of Berdias, the crippled Hyand. He carried a long staff and upon it was the skull of man-creature. The bony head glowed with the amber light of atricault. Its reptilian eyes were alive and the intelligent skull studied Jason with a grim intensity. It blinked when it saw Jason look upon it and a sickly beam emanated from its evil eye. The light burned his skin. Jason shuddered in his gut but gave no hint of it as he spoke aloud.

"Hyand. What mischief do you reek so far from home?"

"It is not your place to ask questions, Captain." Hyand answered. The pitch of his voice was cutting and its sound was accompanied by the sting of a blade. Sharply it pierced Jason's back and he felt the warmth of his own blood spread against his skin.

"I am in charge here." Hyand shouted. His twisted lip curled and the skull, perched upon the staff glowered with cruel delight. "And I am pleased that you have come to assist me in this great enterprise." he said gesturing toward the mountains behind him and chuckling maliciously. "It seems I never have quite enough men. They keep dying on me." and he paused to look over Jason's men. "What a pity, eh Captain."

A hard blow hit him just beneath the knee and Jason fell to the dock, the filthy water washing over his hands. He heard Hyand's shuffling footsteps as he walked away, cackling. The guards drove the men away from the ship, roughly escorting them to the narrow pass. The night had fallen by the time they reached their destination. Torchlight filled the basin and valley before them was a drear and awesome sight. The river, which split the mountains, flowed sluggishly through a dismal labyrinth of barracks, warehouses, and smokestacks. The sides of the steep cliffs had been rendered smooth from all trees. They were riddled instead with the ladders or metal tracks. Gaping vents beneath their feet spewed a putrid steam and through the eerie mist, Jason could see the hundreds as they labored along the ledges of the pitted mountain.

The company came to a sudden halt and the guards turned them aside and Jason's men found themselves being driven forth into a narrow opening between two sharp clefts of stone. Filth lay at their feet as they walked along the corridor feeling the cold spears pressing upon their backs. The reek was unbearable. The sound of grating metal echoed all around them and soon they found themselves within a cavernous dungeon. High above them hung several oil soaked torches and the foul lights sent forth an acrid smoke. The guards pressed them into the shadowy space. Their fingers twisted the men's exposed skin as they pushed them though the iron portal. The door slammed shut behind them and again Jason and his men were alone.

"Well, this a dandy fix." said Cook rubbing a rising welt on his fat arm.

"Hummph." grunted Jason. "Indeed it is." he answered and he began to explore their prison cell.

The cavern was ringed by a wide ledge. The shelf curved round a kidney shaped depression which filled the center of the stale dungeon. The side furthest from the metal gate sloped sharply downward to form a low overhang and the walls above them were smooth. There was no place to grip and nowhere to climb. A solid roof hung over them. Several lengths over Jason's head burned the dreary torches and he could see small doors behind them. Noticing that the openings were not large enough for a man to enter he reckoned the light were lifted in and out from their notches from the hole. He and Cook walked to edge of the ledge and looked down. The wide hollow looked black but through the shadows cast by the dim torches Jason could see that a steep series of rough steps led downward.

"So you wonder what is down there?" said Cook softly.

"I believe there is water. Can you hear it?"

Listening for moment, Cook nodded his head. "Aye Captain, there is water from down that pit."

"I think there may be something else down there as

well." said the first mate, who had walked up beside them. "I smell the scent of a beast of some type. We should take care if we dare venture any lower."

But Jason had already swung his feet over the lip of hole to enter the darkness and the Cook groaned dramatically as he slipped his bulk over the edge to follow after his Captain. The first mate chuckled as he tagged along after them. The steps were uneven, sometimes several feet apart and they grabbed clefts along the wall as they descended the broken path. They went slowly along the sides of the stony pit. The sound of water became more apparent as the scent of the unknown creature grew with each slippery step.

"Move softly." whispered Jason.

"My feet are as light as they ever were, Captain." grumbled Edward.

"Shhhh." he said tossing up his hand. Straining his eyes he focused in the darkness. The walls had drawn quite close together and he jumped to the opposite side to scambled down a bit further. Touching the black water thatt ran through the terraced channel a sound churned in the distance. Its dull rumble filled the damp gully as the source grew closer with each instant. Suddenly a crash of water was all around them. It rose between the stone walls, its bitter foam splashing from the gully beneath to soak them where they stood.

"Something is coming, Captain!" warned Cook. "Take my hand now. You have to get out of there." he cried, bending down to grasp the Captain's hand. Jason reached for the arm but the monster was upon them. It raised its eyeless head from the stream and waving before them was the awful body of a giant worm. The creature was featureless and nothing but a long pale neck with a gaping hole upon its end. Prong like fangs extended from the cavernous maw and the teeth moved of their own accord. Tentacle-like, they reached their oozing tips toward the prey. The beast could taste with its yawning mouth and the creature shrieked. The sound of the sharp hiss filled the cavern as the monster snapped it head back. The sudden motion intended to provide the beast with the momentum needed to snag its victim. Cook reached down and grabbed him in that dire instant. The great man flung the Captain like he was but a child's toy. The first mate seized Jason's coat helping him to ledge but as he scrambled to safety, another flood of water rushed through the channel. Jason cried out as water filled the rocky gullet, screaming for his friend as Edward was lost from sight just the pale back of the evil worm passed just beneath. He could have touched the creature had he held out his hand. Its long body writhed in the black rush of fetid spume. The stench of its breath filled the shadowy gap surrounding the underground river. They lay upon the thin ridge, panting for air. The rush of water seemed endless. They called out over the din. They strained their eyes hoping for a glimpse of their friend who was now trapped beneath the deluge. It was many minutes before the flood ceased. The men jumped to the lower level and scrambled along the side calling out his name. They followed the black stream, searching frantically. They rounded a sharp bend in the rocks and there they found him. He lay with his face pressed against a stone wall. The bend had trapped his body there as the water had flooded past. They reached him and turned him round. His face was blue. Jason and the first mate understood the art of placing air back into body and they pushed upon his chest and filled his mouth with air. Together they worked and did not give up until finally the big man coughed and a vomit of watery bile spilled out of him. They continued to push the rancid, black water from him until the color gradually changed from blue to pink. He opened his eyes and saw his friends. He choked out his words.

"Not sweet enough for the old worm, I suppose."

"Do not speak, my friend. Your throat is spoiled."

"Ugh, my arm as well." he whispered painfully.

Jason looked down and saw his arm protruding unnaturally from the socket.

"Yes, I see it." he said and Jason stood up and placed his foot against the pit of Cooks arm. With a sharp pull the limb shifted back into position.

"Captain," he groaned. "You surely know how to make a mate feel better."

"I am sorry, Edward. It had to be done."

"Aye, and what a gentle touch you have, sir." he said turning his head to spit more water upon the rocks.

"Can you move?"

"If I do not wish to be that worm's dinner, I can."

"Here, let us help you." Jason said and his mate used their bodies to support the large man as he stood. It was difficult maneuvering along the rocky ledges and broken stairs but all of them had had much experience in the doing of difficult things and soon they saw the light spreading over the lip of the dungeon cavern. The crew was waiting anxiously, their heads bent over the ridge and suddenly many hands present to assist them. In a few minutes Cook was as comfortable as they could make him in the prison cave.

"The guards brought food while you were down there." said a young man who had fetched the torches

"Did they not notice we were missing?" asked Jason

"Aye, they noticed sir. They noticed and I think the sound they made was a laugh."

"Hmm, so the worm does their work for them." said Jason, looking back toward the pit in the center of the cage.

The morning must have come, but no one inside could see if the sun had truly risen to light the sky. The men were awakened with the sharp prod of spears and in moments they found themselves being pressed forth through a labyrinth of dark tunnels. Sounds of hammers and the creaking of wheels echoed through the passageways while the bladed tips of pointed spears stung their backs. Eventually the ground began to rise, forcing the men to climb and climb they did; ladder upon ladder and stair after stair they went. The guards drove them into narrow channels and soon they could not stand but had to crawl upon their bellies in the stifling air. When they could move no further mining tools were passed forward. It was meant that they chipped the stone and pass the bits back to those lay packed behind them. All the day, the men hewed away at the rock within the tight holes. Little water and little food were provided and the suffocating heat and dust confused their minds. The men suffered, and suffered still more, but no relief came. Endless, painful hours passed before they were finally led back to the dungeon. Exhaustion burned through their minds and bodies and most collapsed unto the floor. Urns of thin soup and soiled plates of dry crusts waited along the walls of their chamber. It was their respite meal. They coughed and choked upon the foul debris that remained inside their chests. There was few among them with enough voice to speak above a whisper.

"We will last none too long under these conditions sir." said the first mate.

"No, we will not." said Jason in agreement. "How is Edward?" and he looked over the exhausted bodies of his men. It was not hard to find the cook among them and Jason went to speak with him.

"How are you, my friend?"

"I think I am dead Captain. Except if I were dead I would surely be more comfortable. The belly of that worm seems a better option too me now." smiled Cook.

"Do not say such things. There are those that need us back home. We will find a way out. "

"If there is a man who can think of that way it will be you, sir." said Cook.

Jason smiled at his friend. "Take what sleep you can find. I will be near if you need anything." He sat down next to him and waited until he knew he slept. Quietly he then slipped away to pace the edge of the hole that led to the worm's lair. Soon he noticed another walked near him. It was the first mate.

"These channels beneath likely lead back to sea, Captain." said Dyncin.

"Yes, I believe that they do. I would wager that this place is filled with them and I wonder how many more are trapped in these dungeons?" answered Jason.

"I wonder why it is that they need so much ore." asked the mate.

"I do not know. I do not understand what they are after."

They walked around the edge of the pit. The ceiling sloped at a quick run as they moved away from the door and Jason crawled around the lip and got to his knees for a better look. The ledge cast a dark shadow over the long alcove and he crept back into the failing light until his hand touched a pile of dry debris. He knew immediately by the shape what he had found and he pulled the parched remains of a man from the unholy crypt. Dyncin winced when he saw the bones. It was the fate ahead for them all.

"It looks as if many before us have enjoyed the hospitality of our hosts."

The first mate shuddered as he bent his head to look into the flat pit.

"How many are back there, Captain?"

"An un-godly number it seems."

"Could it be that death is the only escape?" he replied softly.

"Hmm." answered the Captain and he crawled back into the shadows once again. The mate could hear him as he scraped along the low walls. It was packed tight with the bones. "There are hundreds in that pit." and the Captain paused and a few seconds later he sighed. "but mate, I believe I have an idea."

Returning to the others, Jason glanced up at the alcoves which held the torches to assure himself that no one listened from above. Quietly then he explained his idea to his men. They listened and knew that this design held the only hope among them.

"We shall need light." said the Captain.

"I have my kitchen flint, sir." said Edward. He had not been sleeping and he unfastened the cuff of his coat and tucked under the hidden flap was the small fire box.

"But what of oil?" The Captain asked him in surprise.

"I may have a drop or two of that as well." he said and he pulled from his coat a leather wallet filled with oil-soaked cloths. "I thought it might come in handy."

Jason looked to his men and said. "What other tools are among us?"

The men began to empty out hidden pockets. The guards had taken from them their fishing belts and long knives and though the clumsy fingers had robbed most of what lie within easy reach, the dull creatures had not removed all the gear a sailor must carry. Many still had their small penknives for the sharp blades were often used for the delicate repair of nets. Cook chuckled as he watched and pulled from beneath the fatty rolls of his belly several of his better paring knives. They had been wrapped carefully in thin white cloths.

"A few of these I could not see clear to part with." he said with a flat smile.

When Jason told them of his plan, a young sailor asked the simple question, "Is it wrong to carve the bones of the dead?" and all turned their minds to think upon it. After a time, an old man spoke.

"If I had been worked to death in these mines and left to die in a pit of rotting flesh, never did I see my family again or never would I have the chance to say goodbye to the ones I loved. I would willingly offer anything, anything I had, even the bones that made me, to save another soul from facing that same torment that took my life from me."

The men started to work that night. Taking shifts they hid themselves among the dim shadows of the burial grotto and they began to construct the deadly net. There was no hemp for thread so carefully they shaved down the bones of the dead and fitted them, one to another, with hooks and eyes. Whittling with precision they carved out the knobs and pegs that would hold the web together. Their calloused hands were nimble as they were precise and soon the spiky necklace began to take shape. The days ahead were difficult. The air of the mines left the men barely able to draw a decent breath but still they worked on. Some wove the net of bones, while others studied the movements of the worm. Carefully they watched its patterns, marking down the times the monster passed through the channels. It was not long before the men realized that the worm was attracted to the warm smell of a living thing. It seemed to prefer its meals fresh and they learned to tempt it with the bodies of other malformed, animal-like things that shared their prison cell. When the evening rations were brought to them, repulsive creatures crept out from the slits in the walls. They had no natural fur upon their bodies, their skin was tough and snake-like and their snouts were long with strong lower jaws, while their wide mouths were large enough to snap off the hand of a man. The sailors perfected the design of their net upon the vile beasts working in the deadening hours which was meant for sleep and, all too often, they would hear the scream of a man echoing through the underground channels and after this the black waters would rush through the river bed, filling halls with putrid foam.

When the screaming hiss of the worm vibrated through the stone corridor they knew it had found its victim and the man would never see his home again.

The most dangerous moment of their plan would come as they spread the net along the channel. The catches must be well placed if it was to surround the body of the worm and they would have only a few moments to secure their trap. The tips of the bony snare were carved into curved hooks. The skillful tapers were designed to burrow into the soft flesh and, as the creature would twist to free itself, the bones would turn with it and work deeper into the hideous skin. The smaller hooks would in turn pull the larger hooks along with them and the razor edge of the net would twist into the sides of the beast leaving the evil worm pierced from every angle.

Cook spent his evenings trapping the rat-like creatures that hid in the dark corners of the cavern and placing them in the handmade cages of bone.

"Here you are, my little uglies. Rest right in here. Hmmm, you are beginning to look rather tasty." and he would smack his lips so the others could hear. "I have not had a decent meal in weeks." he said looking down sadly at his diminishing belly. "I am beginning to lose my figure and my pants." and he pulled his belt a bit tighter about his waist.

The night finally came when all was ready. The men placed stones under their sleeping places to fool any watchful eyes that might look down from above before they slipped silently into the pit that led to the underground stream. Dyncin carried the living bag of bait upstream and secured himself upon a thin shelf that arched above the water. The others moved in the opposite direction until they had found the place where the walls drew close together and, just beyond that point, a bend in the channel offered them a slight protection from the flood the worm would bring with it. It did not take long before the men heard the sounds of its deadly approach. The water began to churn and the walls resonated with the abysmal hum. He braced himself against his stony perch waiting for the right instant to drop his squealing sack before the monster. As the rushing force filled the channel the man could no longer breathe nor see. Holding tight to the slippery edge he dropped the bag and the worm caught up the bait to find it held within it an awful surprise. The sailors had filled the sack with long spikes of sharpened bone and as it swallowed the bag of vermin the bones stuck in the creature's gullet. The beast vomited a spurge of phlegm and the black mucus floated in rancid heaps. The monster screamed as its slimy body wrenched and writhed. Its tail smacked along the slippery sides of the cavern he lost his grip and fell into the streaming flood.

The others were downstream, listening to the creature's screams with their trap was set and waiting. Pressed tight to the sides of the channel, they heard the screams of their friend as he fell from the ledge. Jolts of fear racked their bellies as the rancid current raced towards them but suddenly, there was another shrieking sound splintering through the mayhem. Looking behind them, black despair filled their hearts for to their horror there stood before them a frightful visage. Its pale skin folded loosely over its featureless face as the gaping red hole of a mouth hung wide apart. The fangs stretched toward them and poison dripped from their tips. The worm had a mate. The torrent rushed violently around the bend and losing their footing in the flood, they clung desperately to pocked sides of the cave. In an instant the monster was upon them and the screams of the hissing beast echoed through the hall, but in that exact moment, the body of the other slammed upon the deadly web of bone. The sounds were deafening within hollow walls as the sharpened spikes did their work, drilling mercilessly into the soft sides of the worm. The beast twisted end over end, working its body into a contorted knot. The shafts of bone protruded from every angle as it exploded from around the bend where the men clung for their lives. Jason glanced up and through the raging spume he saw that it was the body of the worm's mate which now stood before the unstoppable flow of water. In its force, the two beasts were viciously coupled into a swirling mass of flesh and bone, water and blood. The spikes caught the second creature within their deadly hold. The thundering water hurried past them, washing the dying beasts away to their tomb beneath the sea.

The men rose to their feet, looking round to see how many of their comrades still stood with them and with great relief they realized none were lost. Jason hurried around the bend to search for the fallen man. Cook lit a torch and walked slowly behind, searching the hollow nooks and calling out his name as they went.

"We will move downstream. Maybe the water carried him to a safe place ahead."

'I will hope for such a thing."

So they walked on in the dark, shadowed gullies of stone searching for their friend. The ceiling above them raised and a dim light from above softly fell against the stones. Jason looked up and then sent one of his men up to investigate. The young man lithely climbed the stony walls as the others waited quietly beneath. In a few moments he reappeared.

"It is another prison cell, sir. There are men willing to run with us."

"Tell them to come. But hurry," he added. "We must be swift."

Soon two dozen had men climbed from the prison above and they stood in the river channel blinking, adjusting their eyes to the dim light of the single torch. Jason saw surely that these folk were from the Southern Isles. Their skin was golden and their eyes were black. One among them reminded him strongly of his friend, Lochlan and that man walked straight up to him.

"You are the leader of this band?" he said in a thick island accent.

"I am." answered Jason.

"We thank you, sir. Your man told me that the worm is dead. Is it true?" he said glancing quickly up the stream of gentle flowing water.

"I believe it to be. It seems that both of the evil beasts are gone." said Jason.

"Two?"

"Yea, there were two of the monsters."

The islander looked warily around the dank passage and whispered softly. "Then there may be more."

Jason nodded and the two groups joined to follow the riverbed as it ran toward the sea. Jason kept his eye open for his mate as they walked but after several hours had past his hope began to fade. All along the way men were sent up the places that led to the caves above until many more had joined them.

Jason wondered about the time of day as a wide bend stretched before them and when they reached the other side of the curve they found the hideous bodies of the evil worms spread in tattered shards about them. The ooze that swelled from the broken flesh spread over the water and rock. The men picked their way over the carnage both relieved and disgusted by what they saw around them.

"Captain." spoke a familiar voice. "I have been waiting for you."

Jason looked up to see his mate huddled under a ledge. He wore no blouse and his head was stained with blood. Jason ran toward him to look upon his friend and when he arrived he saw his leg was contorted beyond all rescue. It lay pinched and black in its bag of skin. The man had tied a swath of cloth around it. Jason knelt and touched the devastated limb.

"We will not save it, sir. It has gone." said the mate.

He looked into his face. "Your pain must be awful."

"I feel it and it appears I have lost another bit of me as well." Dynsin lifted his right hand to show that his middle finger had been pinched from its center. Jason looked away. The sight sickened him. "Aye now Captain, what was good enough for one hand will surely be good enough for the other." he grinned weakly as Cook knelt next to him and began to wrap his bloody hand.

"I have nothing to ease you, my friend." said Cook.

"Numbness has taken it." he answered calmly, "but I can not rise."

"Well, we shall carry you then. We will save what we can of the leg later."

"Then let me be the first to escort you, mate." said the Cook. "I have sorely missed carrying my own bulk so I am honored to carry yours." and with that he gently lifted the smaller man and held him in his arms. The shattered leg hung from the man like a piece of lifeless meat. Jason bound it lightly to the other and covered him with his cloak. They walked along taking turns carrying the wounded man and speaking softly of normal things. By their conversation one would have thought they strolled upon the beach on a summer day with not a care in the world. They met no other worms along the way and only the occasional sound of the rat-like creatures echoed through the walls. Their number was over three hundred strong when they reached the place where the descending channels finally met beneath the river bed. The sound of the river crashing filled the great cavern and they had to shout to hear one another at all. In this dark and noisy place they found themselves standing under several immense columns of fitted stone. Jason studied the pillars. Along each one there was a tightly sealed door that led inside the structure. He sent a few of the men across the river bed to see what lie there and when they returned they told him that all the other ways were blocked. The series of channels had ended. They could follow underground riverbed or ascend the vats that led to the refinery above them.

"If we venture above, Captain, I believe there are enough of us fight them." said the tall islander.

Jason studied his face for again the man strongly reminded him of Lochlan.

"We have no real weapons to use against them."

"Well Captain, I know that among us that we have a few." the islander replied signaling to his men and every one pulled from his cloak, a stolen knife or hammer or pick. When the others saw this, they emptied their own pockets and soon other strange weapons were laid upon the floor. Jason's men had within their own jackets sharpened picks of bone and as they counted their weapons the decision to fight became real. The ragged band of men stooped down and began to collect smaller stones that lie throughout the channel, stuffing their pockets full. Then carefully they tore from their britches and cloaks, strips of cloth or leather to make crude slings to hurl the stones. When they were ready, Cook knelt down and in a moment had easily picked the lock of a great pilaster. Rising with a grin he genteelly pulled opened the door. Jason stood before the opening holding his torch above his head to see. It was tall, empty, black vat with a metal stair that spiraled upward, a thin rail clinging precariously to its side.

"I will go first." said Jason and he began to ascend the stair.

CHAPTER 26
THE CITY BURNS

The door was a gaping hole. The events of moments just past swept through her consciousness. Aleryn moved through the ravaged chamber feeling the horror that cried from its corners. She knew where he was as she crossed though the bloody room to the courtyard and she spoke his name aloud. Pelius rose from the dirt trembling with anger and frustration.

"Why were there no guards?" he asked.

"Each one of them lies dead, Pelius. They stood no chance."

"I know it, Aleryn." he sighed. "I know. I do not blame them. It is only I who could have stopped this."

"Do not lay the fault on yourself. It does no good."

"Can you tell where they are?" he asked looking up from the ground. "I can see nothing."

Glancing back through the open door she answered, "I will know, but not from here. There is too much distress." and she took his hand and led him through the western wing by way of the outside gate. Numbly Pelius followed the Princess through the clear night to her garden courtyard. Their breath hung in the air as she lit the candles on the altar stone.

"Be at peace Pelius." she whispered, pulling her cloak more closely about her and gently lowering her head.

He steadied his mind and focusing upon the inner waves of agitation he forced the emotions to calm. Commanding himself to rise above his feeling body, he allowed his thoughts to join with the mind of the Princess. Together they searched, following the threads of connection that spread over Tessera. Silently they called the children's names and by fits and starts the answers filtered back through the web.

"They are under the city, Pelius." Aleryn finally whispered. "The wraiths are driving them to their master."

The princess' body had grown pale and she moved like a water in the dim light. In the flicker of the altar flames Pelius was able to see her vision in his mind. The demon-beast was waiting in her dungeon. The eagerness of victory filled the nightmare walls.

"They are in the tunnels beneath the castle but they have not gotten far. We could still overtake them."

"I will go." he said turning to leave her. "I will go now." and then he noticed the candles upon the altar stone were still burning.

"Pelius, you must take care." she said placing her hand upon his shoulder. "This presence knows our minds. She is waiting. We must not rush. We can not afford error."

He stopped himself and waited impatiently while Aleryn quenched the flames and ended the rite.

"There is a place." she said as the wisps of smoke faded into the night, "It lies beyond this world under a Great Mountain. It is there she focuses her will." said Aleryn.

"Then that is where we shall prepare to meet her." he answered grimly.

"She knows we are coming."

"Then she must be a fool not to kill us where we stand." and his remark was answered by a thin cry of wind and a wave of frigid air pushed hard against them.

"Pelius." Aleryn cried. "Listen!"

The rasping sound of metallic wings scraped through the night air as hundreds of Khimerah solders filled the moonlit sky.

"They have come for the city." Aleryn gasped as the shadows blotted out the stars.

The bells of the guard towers began to ring and the people of Tessera scrambled from their beds. Bewildered and confused, they pulled on their robes and britches. Shouts blended with the sounds of the scratching wings as people filled the streets. The Queen's Guard took positions upon the battlement walls. In the torchlight, they put their arrows to their bows but the feeble weapons did little to stop the Khimerah. The hideous creature had been designed to kill and the horse and head behaved as one. Pelius watched as the blows bounced helplessly off of the metallic skin.

"We must get inside." he shouted.

But they had waited too long and from over their shoulders they heard a distorted laugh. A Khimerah hovered in the air just behind them. Slaver dripped from its mouth and its body stench crawled across their faces. Suddenly a clamoring of filled the courtyard and a circle of soldiers moved around them. Raising their swords and pulling back their bows the beast pressed them. The horrible strength of the creature was a match for every ten and the young soldiers were at its mercy. But even as they were struck down by its murderous blows the fight left its mark upon the creature. A mucus ooze flowed from its side and one eye hung loosely from a string of tissue. The lolling ball bounced about its face and the soldiers surrounded the children trying to shuttle the pair through the glass doors but the beast was focused only upon the prey. Its evil eye never left them and, from behind, another Khimerah appeared. Their deformed bulk filled the cloistered garden and their battle cries rattled the heavy windows as the second beast crashed through the glass and the thick panes blasted across the room. The soldiers scattered as the shards flew but the beast was upon them in a single stride. The man-part jerked the Princess up by her head flinging her violently through the air. Pelius watched helplessly as she collapsed across the shoulders of the horse. The man-part grabbed her head in a vicious hold and beast backed from the room and it flew from the garden.

The wounded Khimerah stayed behind to finish the business at hand and those left standing turned to fight it. Its remaining eye was now intent upon Pelius. The soldiers moved before the beast. They pierced the horse in its bony head and a young soldier raised his spear and blotted out the remaining eye. The man-part screamed as its battle axe laid the brave man down. His blood poured over Pelius. The soldier fell and Pelius found himself trapped beneath him.

"The body of the dead to save me." he cried in dismay as he crawled from under the flat weight of the man. Emerging from the gore he saw that all was covered in blood. Pelius then took the sword from the dead man's hand and turned to face the beast. The man-part urged the blinded horse forward. Its wing was loosened from its shoulder but the beast seemed to take no heed of it and barred its squared teeth at the boy. It stood four times the height of the boy and the shadow of its broad wings darkened the bloody floor. Pelius stepped up to meet the beast. He shouted out his command and let the sword fly. The aim fell true and the blade pierced the stone buried in the skull of the man. The head split wide apart and the Khimerah collapsed to the floor. A stained slime oozed over the bodies of the dead. Pelius was alone in the center of the room and he looked through the shattered glass to see the silhouette of the other moving swiftly away from him. Dark against the light of the moon he watched as the Princess was lost. From behind him he heard the Queen cry out for she too had seen as the Khimerah carry the girl across the bitter sky.

"My daughter." she cried, falling to her knees. "The sons of my flesh! Ah by the Watchers! They are gone." and then she looked to Pelius. "The time is upon us." she said, pulling the golden circlet from her head. Her disfigured hand was covered in sickly lesions and it trembled as she extended the coronet to the boy. "Though there be but a fragment of a Kingdom yet to rule Pelius," she said wearily, "you are the only one left to do it."

Gently he took the crown from her hand. "I will bear the weight for now, mother but do not despair, Tristus will return home."

"Tristus is the Star Bearer. He is not bound by this world." she whispered. "There are greater forces at work now. It is death that will play its hand tonight."

He helped her from the floor and found, though her gait was unsteady, her mind was clear. Pelius followed the Queen to the temple alter. Upon the floor lay the body of the Head Priestess. She was sprawled in a pool of her own blood with her own knife jutting from her breast. Pelius bent down to touch the dead face. The warmth of the body still lingered and the newly released soul whispered to him though the ethers.

It was the noisy clamor of the demon that had wrecked her mind. Its nightmare world had filled her and she was lost, the light of her soul blotted out by its raging demands. The demon had become incensed when it realized that Tristus had again slipped away to the Misty Wall and the monster showed its servant no mercy. While whispered fetishes reigned in her mind, the Priestess had willingly poisoned the guards that blocked the way to the Tahmurath and with no hesitation she explained to the Khimerahs where the Princess would be when they came to take the city. In these acts she held no bit of remorse but as she stood, with the knife in her hand, ready to slit the Queen's throat, her hands could not perform the deed. A flickering voice cried out above the waves of hate. She had known the Mother-Queen through all the years of her life. Her living nightmares roared as the small voice within whispered words of escape. The carefully prepared servant did not perform the deed that the demon required and in the moment, just as the bells rang, she fled the chamber. The Priestess did not take the life of her Queen. Instead, the knife she held pierced through her own beating heart and by this act, she thwarted the plans of the evil one. Repugnantly aware of her body beneath her the freshly dead priestess was terrified. Their prayers could not comfort her and her wailing voice filled the castle halls.

The Queen stood at the door watching her fluids creep slowly across the stone as the calls of the ghost chilled the air. Understanding settled upon her, and for the moment, the pain of her own grief was stilled.

"She was the eyes of the evil that lurked within these halls but it seems the dark will has not succeeded in all things." and she drew in a long breath and touched the boy's hand. "Go now to the tower and, if it be that hope still lingers, you will know what to do. Do not judge my people harshly, son of my heart. There is good in them. " and then the Queen knelt down beside the Priestess and pulling the death blade from her breast she said soberly, "I will see to her."

Pelius took his leave. Pushing his grief aside, he made his way to the tower and as he went other soldiers followed after him. A desperate light shone in their eyes as they picked their way though bodies that littered the path. When he reached the battlement, he saw the city was alive with fire. He focused his far-vision and he gazed down into the alleys. The people of Tessera were fighting the Khimerahs and the gruesome scene played out in vivid detail until a rasping sound drew his attention from the streets. A band of the creatures had swept down from the sky. They intended to kill him where he stood. He drew his bow and took aim as a small group of soldiers rallied around him. Combining their force into a single strike, the soldiers simultaneously set free their arrows, pointing the keen shafts at the weak points of the body.

"Strike the stones." Pelius cried as they prepared to set their arrows once again. The archers succeeded and as their arrows fell upon the glowing gem the beasts began to falter. Pelius centered his focus and gesturing with his hands he sent his command over the burning city. His will touched the fire sylphs. He called to the salamanders and they responded. Delighting in the consummation of air they responded to his will and their tongues of flame rose to greet him through the smoke filled sky. The sylphs turned their fierce minds from their work as they listened to his plans. The fires then reached upward and grasped the enemy and they pitched the beasts to the ground in the whirlwinds of flame. Crashing through roofs and belfries, the hideous monsters smoldered in streets. The people finished the work of the sylphs as the Khimerahs lie dazed upon the ground. Pelius stood upon the battlement, commanding the powers of fire and the beasts began to fall from the skies in droves. The city found new vigor as hope flamed around them and the battle raged into the deepening night.

Over the black ocean, the Thalassisan King and his army watched the flames color the sky. He had followed the path of ruin left by the *pyrrohmarin* from the Wall of Mists to the Bay of Tessera. The image of lifeless creatures floating in the red film filled his minds eye. His rage burned deep but still the impulse to move against the city never came and he waited in the darkness.

"What is this doubt?" he wondered watching the first fingers of dawn streak the skies and he sent out his scouts to be his eyes. The birds flew over the ruins of the city observing the devastation and counting the dead. When they returned they told the King of the things that they have seen.

The noble Thalassisan turned to his Captain and said. "It is not those folk that are our enemy." he said studying the grim faces of the soldiers around him. "It is the beast-maker that creates this trouble."

"Aye Lord, I believe that is true," answered the Captain gravely. "and I also believe there is more at stake than just the lives of these Land Walkers."

The Mer-King looked to the smoke as it belched over the waters as a thin beam of sun sparkled in the mists. "My grandfather ruled at the time of the First Fall and he told me of the evil that sought to wrap itself around all life. He said it would come again and it would breed in hatred and oppression. He told to me that one possession would never satisfy it and its hand will move across the whole of the world. It would never to rest until it consumes all of the land and all of the sea." The Mer-King then raised his hand in command. "It is a strange day that breaks over the world." he said to his Captain and the Thalassisan army moved upon the city.

Pelius was at the wall, listening to the war cry that rang clear in the morning light. He looked to the direction of the sound and touched the mind of the King.

"They come not to destroy but to aid." he discovered but even as new hope flashed through him other cries filled his inner hearing. From over the sea, a massive cloud had begun to darken the morning sky. A fresh wave of Khimerah beasts flew from the north. A wretched stench passed across his face and an instant of pain shot through him. He found himself was thrown outside his body. He looked down upon himself as he lay upon the battlement and he heard the voice he loved best. Tarin was standing next to him.

"Rise." said his brother, the bright blue eyes burning like a sun.

"Tarin!" Pelius cried; his senses, disoriented.

A strange split appeared in the spaces before him. He could still see his body as it lay upon the battlement but he found himself standing in a long hall. Around him the faces of all he had ever loved flashed in fragmented images along the wall. His mother and father smiled above his bed and his grandmother bent to kiss his cheek. His sister waved goodbye from the garden path. Puthon balanced upon a branch, holding himself strong with his long brown toes, his laughter welling through the wetness of the green forest and Arcus was there. His eyes glowed as he spoke his name and the weight of Pelius' body pulled him closer. The hall of reflections split into parts and in that instant, he saw Tristus standing high upon a stony peak. His face was turned upward. His arms were raised and the palms of his hands are extended. A brilliant shaft of light poured through him and he is lost from view.

"Get up Pelius!" The plea filled his mind. "Rise or all shall be lost!" and again his brothers face was clear before him.

Pelius fell backward into his form and pain and sight returned. The Khimerah was above him and the death blow was falling. But it was in that instant that another sound formed within his breast and the shout turned outward. An ancient voice ran though his form and the beast burst apart in the airs above. Pulling himself to his feet he realized that he was not alone in his physical self. The Sister Earth now peered through his eyes and by her side, waited mighty hand of the Sister Sea. Pelius knew them well and felt the liquid force of the salty oceans ascending through the air. Covering the clamors of war, her rising waters groaned through the winter sky. Heat began to rise from the ground beneath him and the trembling earth moved like a restless tide. Her cries poured through his every fiber and the clamor of breaking buildings cracked the morning sky.

CHAPTER 27
THE JOURNEY TO THE MOUNTAIN

She was standing in a long meadow. Her thin robe moved gently in the clear wind. She is expecting him. At the edge of the wood is a cottage. Its thick walls are white and the spaces between the timbers are mortared with porcelain clay. The roof is tightly bound in golden twists of rope and the thick rushes hang low to create a broad eave. Under the trembling leaves he walked to her. She takes his hand and it is the first moment that he is sure that she is like himself, made of flesh and blood. He looks into the face of the one who called him far from home but does not speak a word as they follow the path that leads to her door.

Creatures scurry after them as she leads him through the meadow. A bright fire burns inside her house and a broad window, set with many small panes of glass, frames the eastern wall.   Her table is laid with bread and fruit. It stands before the glass window and near the table wait two chairs. They sit down and the woman waves her hands toward the window and he looks into the vista that lies beyond. The colossal mountain looms ahead, wavering in the light like a vision dream. Gleaming in the sun he recognizes the mountain as the one which waits beyond the Wall of Mist. The snowy tip reflects the pastel fragments of light and at the foot of the mountain is a lake. The blue water reflects a massive range of mountains and he reaches out his hand and the window moves as his vision blurs for now each window pane reveals a different scene. Fleeting images appear only to blend back into the waters of the lake. Each view holds a story; and each story tells of another tale and all threads flow together into one single stream, the source of each one driving relentlessly down the mountain.

She is near him holding a cup in her hand.   When she offers it, he drinks from its edge. His heart speaks and her voice re-shapes the words. With both joy and pain, he rises to his feet realizing that yet another journey waits before him. Taking her hand, he kisses it lightly and leaves her good house. It is time to ascend the mountain.

His body is light as he travels toward the lake. All is

silent and alive when he draws nearer to the pool of blue. In the clear water he sees layer upon layer of life. He watches as the worlds spread apart and time starts and he waits as they spread further away and time stops. He could not know if it were days or years which seemed to be passing him by, but a moment arrives when he remembers the mountain and the silence deepens. The way becomes narrow as he climbs and he begins to travel slowly, finally to move at a crawl on hand and knee. Clinging by the tips of his fingers, the wind finds him as he creeps. It surrounds him, compelling him to reach through the clouds and move outward to touch the stars. He follows the airs and soon a perfect sound comes to meet him. Echoing voices enfold around him. Harp and flute, string and drum, pour from the deep spaces. He is thrilled as he listens and after a time he realizes that it is the sound of water which graces the moment. Looking higher up the side of the mountain he sees a fountain and he begins to climb toward it. As he reaches the fall he extends his hand to drink. He allows the flowing stream to wash over his hands. The forms of diminutive undines splash upon the stones and he hears the voices speak his name. The nymphs reveal a passage behind the veil of water. Tristus sees the opening and he enters. The water penetrates into his mind and moves through his skin as he passes through the flowing wall. The cave brims with memories and he turns with the enclosed chamber to view his past. He realized he has lived many lives and though some of those existences were good and decent, others were filled with violence and cruelty. He sees how lessons were lost and gained and how each existence repeats that which had come before. The rapid pace of understanding consumes his body as images tumble and voices echo through the cave. It has been a long path to this place upon the mountain and he turns his face from the past to see the Tower of Malthrom looming dark and solemn under the sky. The voices of the chimers rise up and the sound vibrates through his body. He stands under the shadow of the tower and a silver road waits before him. It is the strip of land that touches the sea and at its end waits a silver gate. His mind races over the path until he finds himself at the edge of the universe. Again he clings to the doorway, looking into the void and all the things he has ever known are torn asunder. Chaos breaks his body and his force is shattered. In the last bit of his conscious mind he witnesses the flames as they consumed the city. Pelius lay dying upon the battlement and he tries to call out but he can not bear the sound. Self-loathing chokes him. Fear buzzes. He is shaking apart. Breaking into bits, he looses his grip. The single thread slips away and he is falling through the edge. Disincarnate he becomes the space beyond the door and as the future pours around him he hears a sound. The voice of his sister is passing through darkness. Her cry is like a living river. A vivid light waits beyond.

CHAPTER 28
THE CHILDREN CALL

Filthy rags choke the children's mouths and ragged strips of rough cloth bind their eyes. They are wrapped cruelly and their arms and legs can not move. Shadows clutch the sacks that hold them. They drag the children mercilessly along the stone floor. The small bodies bleed through the cloths that bind. Barely men, the shadows hiss with violence as their brutality is intended to rob the living of their will to endure.

The children speak to one another without words. Their telepathy is strong. They combine their power of thought and they move beyond the pain they bear, each sending their healing powers to the others. Unseen, the threads of connecting thought move between them. They concentrate their wills and dreadful wounds seal shut. They lie still then, trying to understand the minds of their captors as the shadows haul them through the corridors. Though they are pitiless, death is not their intention and through the cruel night the children are tossed between one and the other of the merciless hands but they pull their minds away from their bodies and endue the torture.

The night of pain creeps slowly on. They know that Pelius is not among them. The unspoken decision is made to seek him out. Together, they join to search for him through the web. They can feel as the city it is filled with flame. The sounds of war spread from the battle below. The smell of fire fills their minds. They find him and they move their wills to assist him but the motion is suddenly stopped. They are pitched to the floor and piled against a wall of stone. The sound of footsteps fade and quiet fills the room. They are alone. Grateful, the children allow the moments of peace to fill them and new strength passes into them. They heal in the calm and when this is done they bring the image of the city back to their minds. Silently they chant and their rhythms pulse through the web. They call to the Sister Earth and to the Sister Sea and those great beings respond to their cry. The sisters know each child by name. They see their deathless bodies gathered in the middle place and watch as they give the signal that all is ready. The sisters move to their aid allowing their legions to pull back the layers of earth and water. Pelius is awaiting her word. A Mist forms over the land and the upper airs pass over the earth. Living and dead now freely mingle and shadows sense the work being done. Through the dim corridors they race back to destroy the threads that bind heaven to earth. In a frenzied rush, they hurry on with their swords held high. They open the door but in that instant, the force rushes through the belly of stone. Darkness is released as light fills the room, its radiance erasing what had been shadow and turning to ash what had been man. The ties that bind the children disintegrate and they rise to their feet. The darkness rules no more. The children gather together and join hands in the greater work. The skies flash lighting and echo with thunder. The wind tears through the city and living clouds converge to cry the cleansing tears. Salty water crashed against the black stone and the earth shakes and her voice began to pull dark cliffs into pieces. The Vulcane hears the command of the Sisters and screaming from the heated core, her river of fire rushes from the valley. Flowing upward it meets the cold hand of the sea and the fire and steam consumes everything in its path. The oceans rise up to embrace the forces of earth and flame. The cleansing has begun.

CHAPTER 29
THE PRINCESS

Icy hands bind the Princess in long strips of ivory cloth. Her eyes are covered but her ears still hear as shadows murmur curses from hidden corners. The chamber reeks of decay. The smell of the Khimerah hangs bitterly in the stale air. Through the long night the beast carried her through the freezing winds but any brief memory is brightly discolored in pain. The table where she lays is cold. The unyielding bonds leave her barely able to pull her breath and the hiss of the pitiless wraiths is unceasing. Waves of fear pass through the darkness and she perceives herself as the prey, waiting the moment of death. Pulling her fear into her mind, she gives a silent command and the fear dissolves into the words. She stretches her perceptions beyond the ties that bind her body. Her thoughts become a cup and she is able to receive the threads of force that hang within the room. The past is alive. Rage and perversion whip though the ethers. The cries of wrongful death call to her for justice. She knows the one who will come for her. The presence of the demon fills the room. Its rasping voice delights in her bondage and her fingers lightly touch the freezing clothes that wrap the girl.

"I have waited, Princess. For centuries, I have waited so patiently." she clucked in wicked pleasure. "I have needed only what you have to give and what you give is perfect." she laughed stroking the prone body. "Your people will be my slaves. Your precious fools, your lovely ignorants, they shall sustain my plans now. How fitting it is that you give me the gift that no other could offer." she mused in a dark humor. "It is your perfect form that I require. With it, I shall build a body nevermore too fade."

The hiss of the shadows began to press more closely around her. Their icy sheets of despair move into Aleryn's body but the princess perceives the intrusion with grave indifference. No threat of harm can disparage her for she holds no shadow within her. Brilliant courage is all that remains and she understands the demon's mind and she knew now why evil force sought out her form. For months she had felt a change coming upon her. Often now she recognized that the all of her did not dwell her body and she recalled the times she passed into light only to fade back into weightier bits of matter. The pair of opposites, the point of meeting which was ever-present within her, was now crystal clear and she knew the place which anchored the push which pulls toward and the power that pulls away from the Kingdom of Clay. From her prison bed she touched the place where the two sides met. It was the bridge between both forces and that connection held a secret. It was the thing the demon desired. The creature believed it could steal the power that touches the Airs and lock it to the realms of Earth, giving her the immortal potential of the Life Everlasting.

The demon raised the silver axe and the Princess' blinded eye does not see that the wicked blade was soiled. It dripped with the seed of her dark master as its edge is rose above the sacrifice. The demon chanted the evil words and the pale force shone through the moonlight. The creature trembled in anticipation, seeing her black hair piled high upon her head and her long curls folded over her breasts. Her white skin was shimmering in the light of the alter fire and her red lips were moist. Carefully she has prepared for this moment and finally all is ready. Everlasting beauty would now remain and she held the image in her mind. At the perfect moment she would allow the death blow to fall. At the time of the turning of the stars, she shall cut free the beating heart and while it still lived she would place it the hollow of her own breast. A thin string of dribble spun from her open mouth and she lingered above the Princess and the moment came.

The forward momentum returns and new alignment of stars reaches through the universe. Its pressure pulses through the web and the demon flows in its white heat. The call sounds. The twisting vine that joins the earth and air trembles with the vibration. The link connecting the source and the seer connects in that singular moment.

Aleryn sees the Kingdom flash before her. She hears the call for she is the perceiver and the perceived just as Tristus becomes the void and steps beyond the mountain. The threads of crystalline color spread through the airs and she presses her will forward into the cycles of stars. She is bridge and through her the greater desire touches the earth. It takes the form of a massive tree allowing the life to merge with the heaven and the earth. Flowing from the tree comes a twisting thread, radiant and ever-glowing, it infuses the lower matter from the above. In that movement everything leapt forth.

"Look up, my brother!" she calls out through the dark. "Look up to what binds us!"

CHAPTER 30
THE SEALING OF THE DOOR

Though the void the white heat explodes and from a place outside, of all that is form and all that was time, the intelligent light moved outward. The eyes of the void press upon him and to the above the source appears. Its eyes burn ebony dark as Tristus finds himself at the breaking crux of the lines. He is now split by the two directions and he spreads himself apart to receive it.

All deeds; dark and light; perfect and imperfect passed before him. Chaos is and he remains; breaking into all and nothing; becoming the within and the without. The wind of time flows until eternity holds its breath. He stands upon a glass sea that is flecked with bits of flame. The lines of force cross his body in two directions and he is both the above and below. The web shatters and from a place far away a pair of twin stars leap from the hidden folds of an ordinary sky. Their heat presses through his body.

A solar fire fills the Princess. The presence descends and flows from every pore of her body. Its voice fills the room and shakes the chamber of nightmares into bits. The wave of sound passes through the heavens and the earth and in that instant, the demon knows its doom. The hollow eyes burst forth from the head of the Evil and explode into the empty spaces. The gaping sockets wag within its head and with its thoughts unfilled there is nothing to replace the foul dreams and the demon fades into bits of dust. The wild spaces surround the cloud and the great wall of brilliant white sun cauterizes the black wound. The Princess sits up and looks about the empty chamber. In the airs above her, the morning sun glows.

Pelius stands upon the battlement, his brother's voice reaching through his skin. The wind howls in a black sky and her massive waves crashing upon the sands. Behind him towers of steam are pouring from the earth. He raises his arms to command the elements to find himself in another place. He is standing arm and arm with a larger group, some of the beings he has known and loved while many of the others he does not know at all. Their shout passes through the world and its living breath moves into his heart. Their joined hands have become a ring of fire. The flash of time come as the blinding and brilliant light explodes.

Tristus is alone atop the cold mountain. The waves of the broad of the ocean stand frozen before him. The flood of time is no more and all things of the world hold no motion. There is no in-breath. There is no out-breath and the outer light fades. There is nothing. Forever comes and all remains constant until the world draws its breath once more. The absolute is shattered into bits and the tides turn and all things shift anew.

With the passing of the brilliant flash the world has appeared. Pelius is on his feet raising his arms and commanding the sea. The waters respond to fall back from the shores of the city as the destruction ebbs in response to his call. He had faced the moment yet still the moment hovers above him.

Its secret now revealed, Tristus looks from the cold mountain to see the two worlds side by side. Within the tear of the fabric he waits between, holding their gossamer threads in each hand. It is his living body that bears the seven strands of conscience force.

"How to bind them?" The question passed through him and he touched the one side to the other and at the touch a light sprang upward and the Earth and Airs touched. He watched the connection as it was made; indifferent and passive; moving and apart, he is filled with its force and the will was moving in a beam of rising sun. The quality was pure and its light poured from mountain, flowing from the slopes and filling the valley like a breath of clear wind. The people stirred as the new day touched them for the dawn had never been so bright. Their gift of freedom shone like a jewel upon their foreheads and the most precious of all desires are met. The motion flowed; uniting all to the living and that life lie all around them. From the above, he watched as the change took place in the people of the valley and clearly he saw, that it was the burden of time which held together the motion of the clay.

CHAPTER 31
THE FALL

Jason counted five hundred steps passing under his worn boots while the others followed cautiously after him. His legs were smarting sharply by the time the low ceiling pressed above his head. He handed his torch to tall islander who climbed behind him. Reaching up, he found the catch and pushed the hatch aside. He heard no others as he climbed through the hole. He found himself in a long tunnel that cut through a wall of stone. Upon the edge of the corridor ran long tubes of glowing atricault. Holding the torch over the portal, the others climbed up to enter the long, low hall. The air was much improved in this place and soon all began to breathe more freely. The dendritic paths led them deep into the bones of the mountain. They met no man, nor guard, only the faint hum of the atricault lamps that blended the soft sound of their footsteps. After a time, the hallways widened out. The men came upon a passage barred by a set of large iron doors. Jason stood aside while his men broke the seal that held them shut. The doors swung apart into a tall cylindrical room. Its curved walls reached high into the air. The sides of the arced chamber were covered with small cells. The narrow compartments were pressed tightly side by side and one atop the other, and every one glowed with the familiar amber light. The walls stretched upward to a dizzying point above them and at its top speck of blue peered into the room. The bit of sky told them that morning was coming. A mass of glass tubing ran along the side of each cell. The clustered veins rose along the walls and, as the levels rose, the individual tubes were connected into larger bundles. These clear cylinders formed a series of bridges delicately suspended above their heads. The vessels met in the center of the chamber creating a larger artery that ran through a great depression in the floor. Hanging over the hole, a central channel flared out and its wide mouth contained within it a peculiar series of golden rings. The shining bands whirled around the center and suspended amid the rotating circles was set an enormous crystalline sphere. The stone glowed as it hovered between the spinning bands. The hum of the vibrating mechanism sent small jolts of electricity over each man's skin.

Jason studied the large crystal. Its mechanism was suspended over a pool of black water and he bent down for a closer look. Within the still waters, a scene appeared. Pelius was upon his hands and knees in the garden of the castle. Images began to flood through the dark water and a confused vision played out before his eyes. He watched as shadows stole the children from their beds. He saw them as they were brutally bound and dragged away in the darkness, understanding now why Pelius cried out to the night sky. The view of the future and the past tumbled together. The men moved through the room gently touching the cells to look inside. Each compartment was large enough to hold a single human form and through the thin mists, they saw the still bodies of women, men, and children.

"Captain." Edward called out. "These cells sir, they are filled with people."

"These spaces," Jason replied looking up. "all of them? All of them are filled with people."

He followed the path of the glass channels that ran through the room and the huge crystal's glow grew strong with strengthening light.

"They are not dead." he thought, looking up in horror at the great number of folk trapped within the cells.

"It stinks of magic." Edward continued interrupting his thoughts and the fat man wrinkled his nose.

"Nothing is right here." said Jason, glancing down into the pool. The scene within had changed once again. Thousands of Khimerahs now darkened the skies above Tessera and the beasts were landing the streets.

"We are needed at home." he said to the Cook as they looked upon the pool. Dread poured through them as they watched the ruin of their homeland. Jason gazed upward at the network of cells lining the walls of the cylinder-room.

"By what means I do not understand, but between here and there," and he gestured to the pool. "there is a connection."

The cells were stacked one atop the other and stretched far over their heads. There were hundreds of prisoners, suspended in a deathless life, reaching all the way to the speck of sky above them. The walls pulsed. Light flashed within the cylinders. The hum of the room crawled inside his head. He felt sick as he forced himself to concentrate.

"This crystal, it matches the stones buried upon their heads." Jason said, watching the Khimerahs pull a child to bits. He could see the crystals within their heavy foreheads pounding as the room flashed with bursts of light. "It is these cells which supply the vigor of the beast." he said in amazement as he realized the life force of the prisoners maintained the crystalline stone.

Cook looked up to the imprisoned people.

"What holds them here?" asked Cook, shaking his head at the quiescent bodies. "Could it be that they still live?"

"Whether in life or in death, they must be made free." answered the Captain and he walked to the cell closest to them and, with the blade of his knife, he pried its seal apart. An emaciated body of a woman fell through the opening. He caught her before she collapsed upon the floor. A narrow shaft was inset within her breast. A network of fine needles were attached into her body and her bones protruded hideously from the thin frame. The fragile skin tore at his gentle touch and the woman drew a painful breath. She opened her eyes.

"Bring water." he called but Cook was already at his elbow pressing a dampened cloth to the woman's mouth.

"My son." she choked.

"Peace sister." said Jason softly. "We will see to it." and he motioned to the others. "Release them."

Carefully the men began to open the cells and one by one, the people trapped within them were taken from their small prisons and laid upon the floor. To their surprise many could stand and some were able to help the men as they freed the others.

"The walls extend up too high, Captain." said Edward pointing to the other cells that could not be reached.

"Sir." said the woman. "It is the walls that move. The motion is always downward." and she pointed with one hand to the center sphere, for the other arm held her young son. "They are controlled from that device in the center. We were filled from the above and are moved downward as at the top is filled with more."

315

Jason looked up to the others still suspended in the glass cells.

"How long have you been here?"

"I can not say sir. May be it is months, may be it is years. I have felt the walls move many times."

Jason walked to the sphere that hummed in the center of the room. The device was taller than himself. Within the spinning wheels of gold, it held itself suspended in the center of the room. There was nothing to see, no controls to touch, no mechanism to manipulate.

"When she comes, she speaks to the stone. It responds her voice." explained the woman.

Jason looked into the scrying pool watching as mother's brave efforts failed and the children of Tessera fell to savage force of the monsters. Thick tongues of flames reached through the gloom and he could feel the ocean roar. In the bay, a group of Khimerahs attacked the Thalassisan King and his army rallied around him. The Mer-folk, with wind and water at their command, funneled those currents through the spears of three points and the murderous creatures were swallowed by the swells. As the beasts were drowned, the skies grew darker still, and the sound of their rasping wings continued to fill the airs. The King took a hard blow and blood drenched his pale blue breast. The room rattled and the glass bridges throbbed with the need for increased energy.

The woman, holding her son tightly to her, cried out. "It is killing them."

Jason looked back and forth between two places. "Destroy this thing."

And with what weapons they held his men moved to destroy the shining rings that kept the massive crystal in place. They struck the metal contraption again and again and as the mechanism began to crumble, horrible sounds began to fill the corridor outside the room. Course voices shouted harsh commands as the pounding of heavy feet echoed in the halls. A host of guards burst through the doors. Hyand was the first among them, his crippled body pulled forward by the strength of his ghastly staff. The bodiless monster that lived upon its tip was calling out the commands to the killing group and in seconds all were fighting for their lives. More and more of the hideous creatures pressed through the door. Sharp axes glimmered in the dim light as blood and ooze splattered the floor. The men struggled desperately as the monsters hacked their way through the room.

The hum of the crystal intensified with every blow spent until its deafening vibration began to jar the room. Jason desperately battled in the midst of the misshaped horde and he did not see as those he cared for also struggled with their last bit of strenght. Tristus looked beyond himself to face the void. Aleryn, in her bondage, penetrated the will of the demon. Pelius rose to call of his brother and the fire of the Vulcane spewed from the center of the earth. In that instant, a bright blast permeated the crystal and from the waters beneath a white beam fills the room. The monsters shrunk back, dropping their swords and spears to the ground. The men turned upon them in their failing moments and with their own weaponry the creatures were slain. Hyand turned heel to scuttle down the hall but the tall islander, grabbed him and tossed him to the ground piercing his heart with the talking staff he carried. The monster head, spat and cursed as the man crushed the bony skull with the hilt of his sword.

Jason removed an axe from the hand of a fallen beast. Raising it above his head he took a mighty swing and the rings of gold burst apart. The crystal dropped from its place but to his surprise, no splash reached his ears for no water was held in that scrying pool. The pool was but a lightless place and as the gemstone fell into long silent abyss and the shadows within the room condensed into a inky mass to follow the orb into the blackness. The Captain heard the sound of a familiar voice. Princess Aleryn was calling to them from the darkness beneath. Her voice spiraled upward like a song and fragile hope began to fill the chamber. She was free.

He went to find her as his men turned to the other work at hand. Climbing the walls they began to release the people trapped within the cells but with the connection broken the prisoners found they were able to free themselves.

Pelius stood before the Khimerah. His arms were

upright and the voice commanding. The beast hesitated. Its cohesive force was lost. The creature burst apart as the ground beneath the city trembled. Over the streets, the strange events began to give rise to an even bloodier nightmare. The army of the Khimerahs had lost the connection to themselves. The link between the incompatible parts was swiftly fading as a result of the destruction of the crystal. The man-part looked upon the beast-part and its hatred flowed. It attacked the horse part but the strength of the blow was hindered by the metallic skin. The horrible mouth screamed and twisting its powerful neck, the teeth flowed forward from its throat and the beast wrenched an arm from the man. Pelius watched the self-mutilations in horror. The power that had focused them was being diminished in gradual waves. It was the force that flowed through the stone which had enabled them to exist together. The ability to fly was first to be lost but that is not enough to stop the killing lust. Wildly, the creatures galloped through the streets waving swords and hewing everything in their path. Dismembered parts were strewn in spreading pools of blood. The horses grew wilder still and began to lap the blood from the cobbled streets and, for a moment, and it seemed as if the life would renew the connection. The amber stone, embedded upon the forehead, glowed dimly. Their teeth were stained with the crimson juices. The human-part demanded the horse-part move forward but still the inner weakness grew as the thirst could not be satiated. Soon their interest faded in the killing of the ordinary folk. The beast was no longer able to relate as a single mind and could see only its rival before them. The loathing within solely focused now upon the body of the other and the two beings battled for the possession of the one body. The sword of the man cut away the head of the horse but the gruesome head refused to die. It fell to the ground, with its eyes still open, trumpeting wildly. Flexing the strong muscles in its neck, it pulled itself forward with its long lips.

Throughout the city, the people watched the hideous drama play itself out as the two parts destroyed themselves. The razor teeth of the horse pulled the arms from its rider. The beastly head shook the limbs fiercely and the bits of flesh splattered back into the unintelligent face. The man-part was left with no arms to hold its sword but the gruesome soldier bent forward to bite the neck of the beast and the horse turned its head to grab the face of the man, pulling with a horrendous force that the man-head was ripped from the shoulders. The horse-part screamed, tossing the grisly prize upon the ground and rushed onward in a mindless rage. As the moments passed the blood of the murdered flowed from the body of the murderer. The life force the two beasts shared poured into the streets. The creatures did not recognize that one could not live without the other and soon the battle was still. Its horror lay in all places. The war was done and ruin was everywhere.

CHAPTER 32
THE CHOICE

The newborn stars appeared in the morning skies and the people walked among their dead. Malthrom looked to the Airs. The battle was over and as its final movement still lingered he wished to go home. His cycle was spent and a new cycle had begun. He longed to touch the face of the Ancient. He had served faithfully between the worlds for two thousand years. Living among the simple people; following the laws laid down by the Watchers and now he waited for the voice of the Old One. He called silently but the voice did not answer. From his high tower he gazed upon the ruin that once was the city of Tessera to see a wretched man as he crawled. The dullard crept among the dead, his fingers pilfering coins from the folds of their robes. Through the awfulness, and blood, and horror, Malthrom watched as the seed of evil planted itself once more in the bones of clay. He wondered at the broken world, not yet purged of its flaw.

"What had he missed?" he pondered and then the greater voice trembled. The hand that reached across the heavens was waiting and realization was there. He turned to face it. The choice burned. The insatiable beast blocked the center of the sun, its spidery legs reaching in all directions. Its wraith was now destroyed and its evil stood alone. Long had the dark intelligence sought him through the waves of space and time and Malthrom watched as its face changed with each instant. It was the ordinary and the horrible. It was birth and death. The connection to the blemished world was held in its soiled hands. It stood facing him and the remaining fragments of impurity took too themselves a life of their own. Their undulating tides were passing through him as the dark bits began to condense back to the source. He heard the upper force speak his dying name and Malthrom cracked from the within. The sound rushed into him splintering his body into a web of light. It was the moment that had never come before.

He was perfect. He was seamless and without flaw. The careful work of eons had culminated and his choice was brilliant. He had only an instant to become it and he did not hesitate. The purity, so long sought, was sacrificed to the world of men and Malthrom let the body of light go. He died once and finally with all the lives that had come before flooding forth in a flowing song. The memory was acute as it spread through all bits of matter and flowed through all fragments of time. The Wizard, Malthrom, was undone and Dark Tower that held sway over Tessera quaked as he faded from the web of the world. The Tower lurched and the spiraling stones that held it together broke apart and it fell in pieces to the ground. In the twinkling of an eye, all fragments of evil were forever frozen within the point of division and sealed behind the closing door. They would never return. And time moved on.

CHAPTER 33
AND THEY LIVED. . .

Tristus approached the city with the gray-eyed woman at his side. The fields along the road were scorched with fire and streaked with ice. Blackened timbers marked the places where homes had once stood. The Tower of Malthrom was no more. No longer did its straight finger point toward the heaven and no longer did its shadow hang over the people. The symbol of its power was broken. The way of life it embodied was at an end. Never again would the chimers walk upon the spiraling stairs and never again would the rhythmical words of the Promise ring over the streets. The city had crumbled. Its roads were destroyed and its buildings lie in ruin upon the ground. The long docks which had once stretched into the bay were gone. The charred remains of the sailing ships lie like dead carcasses upon the water. He looked to the North and saw that the vestiges of the castle still stood. The wide stair that lead to the city's center was broken apart. Great chunks of stone lie fractured at its gate. They walked through the streets and spoke to those they met among the ruins. The work of rebuilding had already begun. Some folk worked to clear rubble from the streets, while others sealed broken doors and windows away from the cold. As they made their way toward the castle, they stopped and helped where they could and the yellow sun moved through the sky.

There was no guard at the gate when they arrived. Its wide arms stood open and the court was filled with people. Stores of food were piled against the walls. Kettles of water steamed and the smell of strong herbs filled the air. Those who could stand helped those who could not. Through the crowd, he saw his sister as she worked among the wounded. Jason was the first to notice the travelers and he called for the others to see. Pelius turned to look and beholding the woman that stood at Tristus' side he cried out in joy. Though many years had passed between them he recognized her immediately. The gray-eyed woman was his sister. Her name was Lilith. Tears fell as they embraced and their happiness filled the courtyard.

Aleryn threw her arms about her brother, her gladness like beam of sun radiating through the courtyard and Jason grabbed his shoulders to pull him close in a rough embrace. The children gathered around them and many smiles and tears passed between the people of Tessera as they watched the happiness of their reunion. Aleryn took his hand and Tristus saw that she was greatly changed. No longer did a child stand near to him but a woman whom had passed through many trials and he thought of the Queen.

"Where is mother?" he asked her softly.

The princess led him through the yard and they entered the main hall. Sweet candles burned in its deep alcoves and scented the great corridor. Among the broad columns lay the many wounded. In the soft light, the healers and their nurses tended to sick. They climbed the stair and Tristus followed his sister to where his mother lay. It was a small room but it was well cleaned and it held a long window that faced the sea. Good air and strong light passed through and she lay in a beam of sun upon a low bed. A fire burned in hearth and he recognized it was his old nurse who tended it. Walking to the bedside he looked upon her frail form. It seemed that she slept but when he touched her hand, she stirred and opened her eyes. They were endless as she whispered his name. He bent to kiss her cheek.

"I have been waiting for you, my son." she said.

"I have come back home, mother."

She smiled at him, "Tristus, have you learned nothing? Tessera is not your true home."

He knit his brow, surprised at her words.

"Aye, yes." he answered, stumbling upon his thoughts. "But to it we are bound."

"Only for the briefest of moments." she answered. "Are you surprised that I see this? It is I who truly prepares to return home."

His eyes widened for the brilliant seraph was now behind her. He knew she spoke of her death.

"The world is forever changed, my son." she said and turned to look into his face. "Just as you have been, Tristus."

Tristus knew the change she spoke of. It had come upon him the instant the light had joined and its light had ignited all that was below.

"A new cycle has turned and it too will have its trials

that come and go." she continued but her eyes did not leave his brow and a brightening light began to fill the room. "Tristus, this change holds within it a new seed. Do you not know what it is?" and he found her words echoing in a far memories other worlds. He had nothing to say.

"The time of Malthrom has passed, Tristus. His tower has crumbled and its dark stones have been returned to the sea. All germs of imperfection are banished, sealed away in a place never to return. He has given the final gift."

Tristus looked upon his sister and Aleryn took his hand. "Use your thoughts, brother. Understand the hearts of the people."

He did as she asked and he bent his mind to perceive the thoughts running through the Kingdom. Though the ruin, he heard no greedy whispers and as he searched the narrow alleys and dark corners, he found the dreaded shadows no longer lurked in those once familiar places. The people worked with a new determination and he opened his eyes and asked.

"How could such a thing come to be? What thing has transformed all of the world."

"We were there, Tristus at the moment of the turning of the tide." Aleryn answered. "The choices came as we faced into ourselves."

"And the best within was released in that single moment." replied his mother.

"There is no fear now. Its darkness no longer rules the day. It is the moment that has never come before." Aleryn answered.

The Queen paused and drew a deep breath. "The final act of the Wizard closed the door. He gave all that there is to give. With the ultimate sacrifice the door is forever sealed. There is no seed of wickedness that remains within the soil of earth and there is no foul taint that flows within the salt of the sea."

Tristus listened and the sound of her voice spread like a healing balm through the streets. The stones were changed and the soil sang beneath them. The trees seemed to stretch taller and leaves seemed more green than ever before as they spread into the clear air. Fresh life stirred deep in the salty waters.

324

Pouring from clear streams and filling the quiet spaces. Everything was different. His mother's voice stirred him once more.

"But Tristus, there is more than this. A new age awaits a new keeper."

He did not answer as yet another change flowed through his willing mind.

"You will bear the burden, Tristus but it is a crown that is not of this world." she paused, her eyes intent upon him. "Have you looked upon yourself in recent days, my son?"

He did not understand and he glanced to the window to see his faint reflection in the glass. To his amazement, the stars that had once stained his brow were not there to face him. Instead of the crimson mark, a faint light hung above his head and he looked back to his mothers face.

"The substance of all is forever altered." she said taking the hands of her children. "It is Aleryn who is the true heir to the House of Tessera." and in the blackness of their void he saw stars falling. Her voice was breaking his heart.

"Tristus, you are the heir to the Wizard Malthrom. The potential of the new stars above has been set upon now. You, my son, you are the Keeper of the Will. " and she paused allowing the words to settle in his mind before she continued. "But think not that you stand alone in this responsibility." she comforted him, "Your sister is beside you. It is Aleryn who bears the Light that shows the way. She heralds the understanding which guides the inner Heart. Together, as brother and sister, you shall keep steady the bridge that reaches past the Misty Wall. It is the living memory of the burdens we have borne which will connect you between and beyond the worlds."

Tristus touched the places the birthmarks had once been.

"You are the Keeper of the Will." she affirmed. "Do you accept the gift freely given?"

Never before had he felt so ordinary but never before had he felt so alive. There was no trace of doubt in when he answered the Queen.

"I will." he answered and bent his knee before her.

Rising from the bed, her frail body lifted up the Sword

that had once been his fathers and the Queen faced the first-born son. Gently, she placed the tip of the sword upon his shoulder and in a word, the transfer was complete.

"So it is." she said and the Word was and it would come to be.

The Queen kissed his forehead and quivering, she lay back upon the couch.

"The promise awaits." she said softly.

The brother and sister stood close to her bed and the old words rang clear in their hearts. He closed her eyes as the soft voices of memory murmured in the airs around them.

The Promise waits,
As the keeper searches blindly,
In stars to seek the signs.
The promise waits,
To illumine the ending,
Of worlds with gift divine.
The promise is,
At the point undivided,
Where it is that all points meet.
The promise was,
In the heart of the Old One,
The children's gift beneath the feet.
And the promise reached on and on
and into the ever,
For it lay beyond all fragments of time.
And the promise reached deeper and deeper into the matter,
In all bits of earth to find.
Through all veils of heaven passed the
Word of Creations mind.
Speaking in tongues of man and beast,
The promise came to bind.
It lies hidden in what can not be broken,
For it is and was forever free.
Unseen, the promise does remain,
In that which comes to be.

The seraph was helping her rise from the bed and the old

body lay motionless upon the cover. She was young once more. Her sores healed and her eyes danced. Hovering in the airs, just outside the windows, a ship appeared. Its sails were spun of glistening silk and its railings were bright with the light of many lanterns. The casements spread apart and the curtains turned outward to caress the gentle wind. The Queen looked toward the waiting vessel. Standing upon its helm was Arcus, smiling and warm he greeted them. He stood alongside him was a tall man and as his black eyes met those of his children. There was no need for words. The King reached out his hand to his Queen and she was suddenly there beside him. Upon the bed, her physical form drew its final breath and, at the open window, they stood together and they turned to face those they would leave behind. The ship slowly moved away from the window. Aleryn and Tristus watched it as it drifted across the sky. It turned to the East and faded into the flat horizon of the sea. They looked upon the empty shell that she had left behind.

"She is free." whispered Aleryn and in that moment, they knew that her death was but another change in the movement of a greater tide. Their grief was comforted as they realized she was there. In the breath and sounds that rang though the city, she was whole and alive.

The brother and the sister returned to the streets of Tessera and joining with the others there, they worked to heal. The twin stars glowed through the night and through the day. No longer did greed rule the people for no fear remained in their hearts. Together they healed and together they worked. The rebuilding progressed and the year passed quickly. The Festival of the Winter Moon was upon them once again.

So it was that upon the Festival Eve that Aleryn and Pelius were joined. The celebration of their union filled the streets with joy. The evening of the Winter Dance brimmed with excitement as the children and their elders celebrated the birth of the year with the archaic wisdom of a newborn soul. The King and Queen were crowned as the music played and the people sang. But, as it is with all things, change did come and when the new morning dawned all knew that good-byes would once more be spoken in the House of Tessera.

"Many seekers shall find their way to your door," said

Aleryn to her brother.

"As the light of our hearts ever remains in your hands." answered her brother.

But even with such words of parting spoken no real sorrow could pass between them and Tristus and the gray-eyed woman prepared to return to the foot of the mountain.

He kissed his sister and embraced his friend, Jason. Edward stood next to him. A tear ran down his cheek as he grabbed him in bear-hug and slapped his back. Clade spoke his farewell steadfastly, assuring him that would be well and Mileah shyly kissed his cheek. Lilith leaned against her brother as the other children had crowded around them. The twins pulled at the hem of Tristus' traveling cloak and he bent down upon his knee so he could hear them better.

"Let us show you the future, Master Tristus." said the boy as his sister nodded her red head in happy agreement.

"Whose future my dears?" he asked them, kindly.

"Oh Master Tristus,' they answered as if they could not believe his question. "Of the Old One that turns the world." And placing their small hands upon his mid-point of his forehead a circle of light formed about them. Its low hum filled his ears as images began to flood into his mind. The fairies returned to the city. The little folk of the stream and field had rejoiced at the change within the people. Again, they helped the folk tend the gardens and fields and never before had the harvest been so plentiful and none among them lacked. The Thalassisans and the folk of Tessera soon resolved their differences and patiently they began to heal the sea. It was not long before the ocean lives began to flourish and balance was once more restored. Lochlan and his lost brother were reunited as all the living slaves were returned to their homelands. Tristus saw the many voyages of the Bifrost and the friendship between island folk and the city dwellers grew strong. It was Pelius who now led the journeys to the Wall of Mists. No longer fearing what lie beyond the form, the people looked upon the Veil with open minds and many wonderful things came to be. Then the far-away mountain appeared in his mind's eye. It loomed before him and he saw himself standing with the gray-eyed Lilith. They dwelled in peace in the still valley and guided the pilgrims as they passed over the path which led beyond the summit. Tristus saw himself as he visited the House of Tessera and he witnessed how wise and lovingly Aleryn and Pelius served the people. The years passed by and finally they received the gift of children. Their first-born babes were identical in every way save one. The boy-child and the girl-child had entered the realm of earth together and upon their brows each did carry the crimson Mark of the Star Bearer. The dark stains ran from beneath their black hair and extended down to pass beyond the ears. The symbol they carried mirrored the presence of the Seven Stars above. The people rejoiced when they saw the heralding sign and a new purpose burned bright in the hearts of all. Freedom was its motion; and it reached into all bits of matter and spiraled through every fragment of time.

www.ingramcontent.com/pod-product-compliance
Lightning Source LLC
Chambersburg PA
CBHW070210260626
47160CB00002B/511